INNER TRADITIONS OF MAGIC

By the same author

SEASONAL OCCULT RITUALS

INNER TRADITIONS
OF MAGIC

by

WILLIAM G. GRAY

THE AQUARIAN PRESS
37/38 Margaret Street, London, W.1

First Published November 1970

© WILLIAM G. GRAY 1970

ISBN 0 85030 061 4

MADE AND PRINTED IN GREAT BRITAIN BY
THE GARDEN CITY PRESS LIMITED
LETCHWORTH, HERTFORDSHIRE

FOREWORD

Had this book been written five hundred years ago, William Gray would have been seized by the Inquisition and burned at the stake. What a bonfire he and the book would have made together! As it stands now, he is destined to be read by a host of readers drawn to the intriguing title in search of dramatic and secret formulae with which they might take the Kingdom of Heaven by storm. Of course they will be disappointed. A few however will find here what they have long searched for—a well-written, well-conceived and highly provocative text that clarifies many 'occult and recondite' themes, to borrow the cliché of the illustrious McGregor Mathers. Gray's treatment and elaboration of Telesmic Images (known in other quarters as Telesmatic Images) alone is worth the effort required to study the book.

A few years ago, William Gray wrote *The Ladder of Lights*, which augured well to become a classic of Qabalistic exegesis. *Inner Traditions of Magic* bodes well to become a worthy successor to his first book.

It has to be stated dogmatically that there are few really good expositors of this subject. In olden times, the hierophant was officially considered 'the Expounder of the Sacred Mysteries'. This should be the author's honorific title, for he has a rare gift for clarifying difficult concepts. The reader will be left feeling, 'Of course! Why didn't I think that before?' Not only so, but his writing is extraordinarily lucid.

As opposed to myself who am now a traditionalist and a conservative—the years of rebellion now loom half-a-century behind me—William Gray is a modern. His rituals are newly formulated and devoid of archaic phrases and formulae. True, he still employs traditional names of Angels and Archangels and he still works the Telesmatic Images of the Old Gods. But his approach is *au courant*.

For this reason, which I applaud, he is likely to appeal

to the ever-increasing number of young people who are turning to Magic for answers to some age-old problems. Originally some were 'turned on' through the agency of drugs, but having discovered the limitations of the psychedelic drugs, they turned to other means to achieve high goals. So Qabalah and Tarot and Magic are enjoying a renaissance such as the world has never previously seen. It is to these youngsters that Gray's book will make its direct appeal, for they need a guide to enable them to cross to more secure areas of consciousness.

Israel Regardie

2 August 1970
Studio City, California.

CONTENTS

INTRODUCTION

There are so many 'books about Occultism' in this world, it scarcely seems possible there might be room for one more, maybe this one in particular. So what is this book doing in print, what justification has it for materializing, and how dare it enter twentieth century life as if it had every right to be here among us?

What follows is unashamedly and perhaps blatantly about something which up till recently has always been called 'Magic'. (Without the 'k' please, Mr Crowley!) Twist, turn, hide, or distort the word into as much modern gobbledegook as anyone likes, Magic is, and always will be, a fundamental mainspring of human aspirational behaviour. We shall not attempt to disguise or apologize for this, but hammer it home with the heaviest blows of which the art itself is capable. And why not? If ever an age of mankind tried to avoid its true reflection in the Magic Mirror of Inner Spiritual realities, that age is with us now. We dither and dissemble in all directions, deceiving ourselves as hard as we can because we are terrified to face up to what we fear within ourselves. Who now KNOWS what to think, DARES to think it, WILLS to do something with it, and has the sense to KEEP SILENT about experiences of Inner Life? Such was demanded of Magical Initiates in olden times, and we have not yet outdated the necessity for those Four Axioms.

We need not look for real Magic so much in ancient and outworn forms of practice, but in the unchanging and vital fundamental principles that underlie the whole structure of human spiritual development and relationship with far finer degrees of entitized Awareness which we may very well term 'Divine' by contrast with our very limited and barely awakened Inner consciousness. Years ago we said and did all sorts of things to establish some kind of working contact with Inner Intelligence which may seem rather peculiar to us now. At least all this started us along our Spiritual Path of Progress, and even brought us to our present point upon it. So what do we use for replacement material in terms that are likely to satisfy souls now looking for Light-Life leads out of the mental and moral muck-heap we encounter everywhere on Earth? That is just what we are trying to find among matters arising in this book. Some means of using ancient and indeed timeless principles of Magical procedures, for growing big enough souls in ourselves to break through the purely artificial barriers which threaten our continued confinement in what has been aptly named the 'Broilerhouse Society'.

Magic is not, and never will be, for the souls content to be docile doormats, so indifferent to their fate beyond their immediate bodily existence that they deserve no future worth waiting for. Nor is Magic for the anarchistic rebels who would aimlessly break what they could never rebuild to the slightest degree. Magic is for none but those with the steady courage to go quietly on in the face of every adversity, surely and carefully constructing a Living Cosmos *within themselves*, which will endure for Eternity—and beyond!

All the Magic of the past is only valuable for providing us with material to use in modern ways so that we can confidently expect a future worth living for, not only on this one pathetic little planet, but AS WE WILL, anywhere in Otherwhere. Magic is for growing up with as Children of Light. Sane, sound, healthy, and happy souls, living naturally and normally on levels of Inner Life where we can be REAL people as contrasted with the poor shadow-selves we project at one another on Earth. Inner Wonder-worlds do not build themselves however—we have to build them. No one will make them for us, however generous Nature may be with raw materials. If Magic supplies us with such materials, then why should we not use them? It has not failed in the past, and it will not fail now if we take the trouble to look where we should, inside us.

Magic is certainly not 'for the masses'. To the contrary, it is particularly for souls who need to evolve away from and beyond the 'mass-mind' level. It is for souls who aim to become Themselves, and No-one else except the One they must Ultimately Unite In. Every Soul its own Star. That is Magic. Not some cold indifferent isolation of selfish sequestration, but a full realization of the responsibilities placed in every evolving entity to become WHAT WE WILL WITHIN US. First we must become fit to associate beneficially with fellow-mortals, then fit for Higher Entities to associate with us. The two injunctions join to form a single Circle. A Magic Circle. What else?

This book therefore, is mainly for those who have the courage to take up the Magical Tradition offered from the past and carry it on towards the future in whatever forms may be appropriate for its continuance throughout its Great Cosmic Circle. The tremendous heritage of this Tradition has incalculable Inner spiritual wealth to offer those brave enough to claim it, and have the Will to work for it. There are no 'hand-outs' to be expected, but only *earnings* to be anticipated as these fall due. Those who treat the art of Magic with spiritual contempt receive exactly what they ask for—and deserve. The true Magi are those who *live* Magic, and not merely tinker with it. Magicians are not made, they make themselves. That is what this book is about.

CHAPTER I

TELESMICS : OR WORKING WITH MAGICAL IMAGES

What exactly are the 'Telesmic Images' we read about in connection with magical arts and practices? A precise definition is not easy. It would be simple to say that a Telesmic Image is an imaginary creation having no existence apart from the consciousness of its creator—a kind of Heavenly hallucination in fact—but this would be very far indeed from the actual truth.

A so-called Telesmic Image (or TI for short) is a perfectly genuine Inner construction of Force and Form, designed for a particular purpose and having as much, if not more, reality in its own dimensions than we have in Outer terms. It is a composite creation, brought into being as a concretion of consciousness inspired by spirit, animated by soul, moulded by mind and based upon body. A TI is in fact made up very much as we are ourselves, except that it objectifies on levels of existence that to us are subjective. Its main function is that of an operative focus between our Inner and Outer states of Being.

We all make TIs of some kind, either individually, collectively, or both. Children make their own 'imaginary friends' for personal reasons, or subscribe to 'Father Christmas' as a kind of Group TI. Later we objectify and personify inner energies in different ways, seeing them as gods, demons, or other entities. The Christ-Figure, or Buddha-Figure are mass TIs. Nor does a TI have to be humanoid in formation. Artificial species of TI are commercially constructed as 'Brand Images' and the like, or made into 'National Figures' and so forth. The principles of construction are similar throughout, but purposes and practices concerned with TIs are very different. We shall deal here with what are specifically called 'Magical Images' or TIs connected with the Occult side of our lives, as distinct from those linked with commerce, religion, politics, or other categories of our continuum.

If we look back and find out why such creations of consciousness were called 'Telesmic' at all, the Greek roots explain quite a lot. 'Telos' signified the fulfilment or accomplishment of anything, its end product, to come about or happen. 'Teleo' had a side significance of an initiation in the Mysteries. The full suggestion of a 'Telesmic' Image, therefore, implied an image which accomplished some end for Initiates of the Mysteries. It is in this sense that it is proposed to approach Telesmic Images at present.

The first thing noticeable about TIs is that they are categorical. Even in the old days there was a Rain-God, a Thunder-God, a Mother-God, a Sun-God, etc. etc. The Images were definitely typified, and indeed still are, because that is how they work. Each Image has its particular type of consciousness which it embodies and expresses. We might equally say that every specialized type of consciousness produces its own particular 'Image' or reaction in perceptual terms to those Life-Entities making use of it, including ourselves.

Link with Inner Existence

No genuine TI in the Mysteries is the outcome of some single human mind inventing images to please itself, and yet all Initiates are responsible for making their own TIs which will link with all others of the same species, and indeed throughout all consciousness along that line. The better job Initiates make of their TIs, the closer contacts they will be able to establish with channels of consciousness beyond the range of average human beings. No human is normally aware of the electro-magnetic energies immediately around themselves, but with the aid of a radio set they can not only become aware of these in objective and specific terms, but also project their own consciousness in the same way. A TI is just as much a scientific construction in its natural state of being as a radio set, which consists of an electro-mechanical contrivance of matter. The TI in its way fulfils all and more of a radio's function in terms of inner existence linking with outer life. A physical radio cannot convey, love, beauty, sympathy, protection, or any of the direct energies that we recognize as more Divine than human. Well-made TIs are capable of dealing with exactly such types of energy on supra-physical levels.

TIs are the objectifications through which we relate ourselves with the realities of inner existence, just as we must relate ourselves with those of Outer Life by means of Images concerned with it such as Images of family, position, status-symbols, or any such creations of consciousness—for that is what they are. We do not usually question the 'reality' of physical individuals and objects with which we have contact in material ways, and the reality of Inner entities is of equal validity in their own state. The object of TIs used in most Mystery workings is to act as a sort of half-way Figure capable of energy transferences between the Worlds. Hence the Archetypal Images of Mother, Father, Teacher, Lover, etc., which have their intrinsic values commonly to both states of Being. If consciousness is real, then we and they are real, but if not, none of us exist.

Although a TI may quite well be a Symbol or any kind of objective representation, we generally think of a Magical Image as being of humanoid type, possessed of specialized faculties far beyond the capabilities of mortals. There would be no point in a Magical Image portraying less potency than that possessed by ordinary humans. Images of such a nature would be valueless except for amusement or annoyance. We make and unmake them all the time. A true Magical Image is the product of many minds and souls over a great period of time, and as such has its own immortality. Generation after generation of humans and a whole continuum of other Entities have combined to produce the Magical Images used both in and out of the Mysteries. When millions of individual minds think in the same patterns for thousands of years, it is a question of whether they produce the patterns, or the patterns produce them. Man was said to have been made in the 'Image of God' because the 'Image of Man' constantly attempts to project the Divine Image out of itself. In the case of a mirror-image, one is a real reflection, and the other a reflected reality, but what reality reflects which?

All human beings build up Images of one kind or another, and indeed 'Image building' is now a very highly paid occupation producing a marketable commodity for those wealthy enough to buy themselves a 'false front' behind which to pursue their particular activities. Such constructions were once a 'homemade' business, but like most private enterprises have now developed into impersonal commercial concerns which offer 'images' for sale just like the idol-sellers in ancient times. There is little difference between ancient and modern image-merchants except in degree, yet idolatry has always been a practice condemned by the very Mysteries using the most technical kinds of imagery themselves. Why? What is the difference between one use of imagination and another?

Ideals not Idols

It is all a question of attitude and intention. If we use images to embody our worst faults and act as screens for our weaknesses and stupidities, that is certainly idolatry of a nasty kind, especially if we allow the image to dominate us into a state of subjection to what it represents. On the other hand, if we employ images for the Figures of forces by which we progress towards ever better and finer conditions of being, then this is imagery of the most helpful sort. The decisive issue is whether we accept an Idol or an Ideal; whether the Image evolves or devolves us. Motive in imagery must always be its mainspring. We and our Images will always reflect each other into states of our respective realities.

The TIs of the Holy Mysteries are not Idols but Ideals which are intended to relate us in the best possible way with the actual Cosmic energies they embody. Unless we have some practical means of relating ourselves with the Forces behind our existence we shall be unable to deal with them or utilize their energies for any purpose. In olden times mankind attempted this necessity for personifying these pure Powers into Gods, then gradually abstracted them into ever remoter Symbols until moderns are approaching the Nil-Concept by an utterly depersonalized Divinity, with Which no means are either afforded or advocated of making personal and individual contact in a direct way. This depersonalization of Divinity is a major mistake of modern pseudo-theology, and probably more disastrous than the inadequate personifications attributed to Divinity in the past.

Divine Energy and Entity

The Mysteries make no secret of the basic belief that Divine Energy and Entity is One in essence. Our problem is precisely how to form relationships with It so as to identify ourselves with

Its uniqueness. Since It obviously makes relationships with us (otherwise we should not exist at all) the issue is a mutual one. If we are objectified by Divinity as materialized behaviours of Its own projected energies (Image of Divinity in Man), then our reciprocal reflection should surely objectify those energies as our Image in Divinity. The Christian Faith attempts this with the Jesus-Christ-Image, but has so muddled (and muddied!) a basic simplicity with a welter of doctrines and dogmas that it has become unserviceable in many respects. God may appreciate Man as an abstraction, but Man needs a concretion through which to appreciate an abstract God.

So the Images of the Immortals came into being. They are by no means merely the products of bewildered human brains making irrational attempts to relate with natural energies, as modern materialism (dialectical or otherwise) would have us suppose. The Divine and other Inner Images are also born of the Creative Consciousness inherent in Existence forming relationships with us. If we are tempted to be critical of these yet evolving relationships, there is only practical thing to do— improve them. They cannot be broken off without breaking ourselves. Nor will it help us if we deny them as impossibilities. To say that what we used to call 'God' is no more than a collection of electro-chemical and other energies presents only a very partial picture. So are we manifestations of these materialized forces in Formations (or Patterns) of consciousness. To admit the existence of consciousness in ourselves and deny it otherwise in the whole of Being is, to say the least, absurd. Perhaps this was best expressed by the saying : 'The fool in his heart has said there is no God.'

It is the old question of horse and cart, and whether we believe that Consciousness produces matter, or Matter produces consciousness. The position in the Mysteries is that Creation emerges from Consciousness as the Primal Cause or 'I AM'. This is the opposite direction to the purely Materialist standpoint that consciousness arises from and returns to physically based phenomena. In fact the whole difference between Mystics and Materialists turns on this precise pivot. Each has a mirror-image of the other's truth. If the two halves were put together, we might perceive the actuality of Energy materializing and spiritualizing via the complete Cycle of Consciousness.

Consciousness cannot be described verbally in other terms than those of ABSOLUTE ENERGY. We are inclined to equate consciousness with thoughts and thinking, but this is not so at all. Our thoughts and thinking are only *effects* of consciousness in terms of human behaviour. Very limited effects too. The after effects of consciousness in fact, according to its medium of manifestation. Everything reacts to consciousness in its own particular way or category, and must ultimately revert to a state of pure consciousness or UNIVERSAL ENERGY. The fundamental basic of our being in existence at all, is that CONSCIOUSNESS CAUSES CREATION. In other words, ABSOLUTE AWARENESS emanates from Itself that which It becomes conscious Of, In, and With. The I brings forth the Not-I. Perhaps we might say to a child : 'God imagines us like you imagine your play-people', and get nearer the truth than with far wordier ways.

Conception is Greater than Thought

Our necessarily limited human minds can only deal with suitably scaled-down Symbols to link with the totality of this Truth. Our senses of Time-Space-Events are inadequate to deal with Concepts beyond their terms of reference. The Consciousness in us has not yet reached anywhere near the peak of Its possibilities. We are not (as Gurdjieff remarked) sufficiently Awake or Aware. We think too much and are not Conscious enough. Over the centuries of our 'civilization', we have exteriorized from ourselves endless productions to be conscious *of* and think *about*, yet how much greater have we grown in Consciousness Itself? Consciousness does not *think*, It *conceives*. We are among Its concepts, and if we would ever exist in Consciousness as we ought to, we must learn to conceive instead of merely thinking.

What is the difference? It is the distinction between Consciousness operating on Divine and human levels. Consciousness *creates*, thought only *adapts* what is created. We think from our minds through our brains, but we are conscious from our spirits through our souls. Our existence commences as Conscious Being, and should complete as Being Consciousness. That is the Ultimate Attainment, and is what the 'Holy Mysteries of Heaven and Earth' try to teach humanity not by Words, but by Ways.

They show that thought must be transcended so that we become fully fertile through our Inner fields of Consciousness and able to conceive with our own creative rights. From creatures, we are being led towards becoming Creators. Such is the Divine Destiny in which true fulfilment is to be found, far though it may be from us in our present condition.

Our original 'Fall' alluded to in Mystery Traditions, is that we were exteriorized in so far as what we term 'Matter', and became involved with a type of conception on lower levels of being than we were first intended for. Matter is unstable Spirit in the process of evolutionary experience, and physical reproductive conception was the working of Consciousness along specific animal chanels, each with a proper purpose according to its order. The 'Garden of Paradise' in fact. Consciousness then conceived Man as an extension of Itself into mundane existence, not to reproduce as a physical species, but to produce on Inner levels a perfected synthesis of what was taking place in material terms. Man was meant to express in 'Heaven' the epitome of experimental existence on 'Earth'.

In a sense, Material Manifestation was and is a 'try-out' and testing of Consciousness in Life. Whatsoever cosmates into a perfected pattern as an Earth-expression, becomes built into the Inner Kingdom of Immortality. The original idea was evidently for Mankind to act as an intermediary energy-exchanger betwen 'Earth' and 'Heaven', transforming the finest developments of 'Earth' into 'Heavenly' actualities. Man was thus intended as the 'Redeemer' of Matter. That which had been 'deemed' or 'doomed' by Divinity into material life-categories, should be 're-deemed' or re-routed by Humanity back to spiritual levels as a finished product, fit for Inner Existence. 'Earth' was therefore to be a sphere where trials and errors took place in the course of Nature. The outcome had only two possibilities. Whatever developed to a state of perfection became too fine for physical manifestation and so 'entered Heaven' or continued in a superior state of Cosmos. That which did not adapt in this direction and proved unsuitable for further physical alterations, became disposed of into Chaos or 'irredeemable' creation for subsequent devolution to a point of undifferentiation where it might be used as fresh material.

Man's over-materialization produces the Fall

An incredibly simple scheme. Only Divinity could conceive it. Required—a state of Perfect Existence. Therefore process every unit of Existence according to this purpose. Three conditions of Being apart from that of Omni-Origin are called for. A 'Workshop' for evolving Existence into Perfection, a state of Being wherein this Perfection fulfils its function, and some kind of a Waste Disposal system for reducing unsatisfactory products back into Universal Energy. What could be simpler than this Cycle of Consciousness? So simple, a child might call it: 'God, Heaven, Earth, Hell', and grasp the idea of it. We can see it working wherever we look in conditions of Nature, though probably in ways not easy to recognize superficially.

So why should not the Plan for Perfection work perfectly? The Plan works all right, but Man does not. Man's first function was to be the intermediary intelligent agent between 'Earth' and 'Heaven', or Outer and Inner Life. The idea was to materialize mankind to a degree of being able to experience and assimilate Outer Life, synthesize these experiences to their point of perfection, then dematerialize into Inner Life and produce the finalized issue as accomplished Ideals. Man was not meant to go through the whole physical animal Life-Death process, and the original human 'bodies' were condensations of consciousness easily assembled or disassembled between the different Dimensions of Being. Man, being Male-Female, 'mated' on 'Earth' by projecting consciousness from one pole to the other, but the 'children of Men' or conceptual outcomes, were supposed to be 'born in Heaven'.

This state of affairs has been mythologized in the much misunderstood *Compte de Gabalis* which ostensibly advocated Initiates not to produce physical children by human women, but create Inner entities by spiritual brides. Had the working principles of such an ideal been properly practised by Archetypal Man, we should never have 'fallen' into our present state. As we know, Man over-materialized (took 'coats of skin') and reproduced his species in animal fashion on Earth, thereby becoming bound to the Wheel of Life and Death until the end of Evolution. Another unfortunate outcome of this 'Fall', was that it altered the position of those consigned to Chaos. Instead of being steadily processed out of existence altogether, they became provided with sufficient 'overflow' energy to not only continue, but even extend their anti-Cosmic form of living. Man had short-circuited powers intended to construct 'Heaven' straight into the domain of 'Hell'. Moreover, the state of Chaos could not be eliminated without abandoning the whole Plan of Perfection, since Chaos is an essential stage in the ecology of Existence, providing it remains in proper proportion.

The 'Fall of Man' necessitated many modifications to the Primal Plan. Mankind now needed 'Redemption', or re-directing towards Perfection, and a further extension of Divine Energy had to be made beyond the originally intended limits. This produced the unbalance symbolized by the lower arm of the Calvary Cross, or the 'Fallen' position of Malkuth on the Tree of Life. It also changed the status of Man as an agent in the Scheme of Things very considerably. Erstwhile assets became liabilities—from a Heavenly viewpoint. Man became too pre-occupied with diverting his conceptual abilities into Earthly channels to provide Heaven with its requirements through human agencies. The once Divinely implemented Inner Vision of Man, able to operate inter-dimensionally, was reduced to the Earth-level of an animal looking for no more than safety and satiety. Yet the faintest traces of far-memory in Humanity remained as a vestigial root connected to other than Earthly Kingdoms. Given a fair chance, Man could still achieve his original mission to even greater effect than proposed. On the other hand, events might result in human extinction as a species. For good or ill, Man's enfranchisement on Earth gave him the casting vote to decide his own destiny.

Creation of an Inner Heaven

Another result of the 'Fall' was that Man lost his value as Telesmic Image of the Divine. Since almost the whole of his consciousness was directed into material objectives concerned with survival and success in purely personal and physical terms, Man had little enough to offer worthy of Heavenly acceptance. If Humanity had nothing better to reproduce in Heaven than its own precarious and unsatisfactory state on Earth, then the Innerworld was that much worse off. The contribution of Man towards the creation of Inner Perfection was certainly needed, and so the Telesmic Images of the 'Gods' came into being, together with a host of other figurative concepts having a similar purpose.

The major function of these TIs was to surround Mankind with a sort of 'filter-network' which would only allow suitable types of conscious energy to pass between Human and Inner-world entities. In other words, to create an Inner Heaven (or any other state of being), make sure no energy enters it except through selected channels compatible with the state under construction. This is a universal rule. Even in modern human terms, if a particular type of existence is intended, the 'Images' are set up around its concept, and whatever enters must do so along those lines. Perhaps the concept is a 'Home', and the 'Images' are those of Pay-Packet, Washing machine, Car, House, and other material structures. The same concept on better levels might have the 'Images' of Father, Mother, Family, affection, and so forth. The principles are still those of cosmating around the nucleus of a central concept by relating it with typified energies through its associated 'Images'. Our Solar System and Zodiac-Images provides us with this Pattern. Early mankind set up Stone Circles in which each Stone stood for some particular Idea-Image. The Gods grew up quite naturally around us, and however indignantly humans deny their Gods, the more they appear in quite unsuspected shapes.

The Gods are therefore Telesmic Images of primal importance to us both in principle and practice. They are collectors of our consciousness into categories of Inner energy which thus become available for re-distribution ('re-demption') on Inner levels having a firmer basis of Existence than the 'matter' we make use of on Earth. Our Gods enable us, while inhabiting very ephemeral earthly bodies in conditions of civilization which could be rapidly destroyed, to construct an Inner Cosmos of Perfection which has an endurance of Eternity. That is what our Gods mean to us, and that is the use of Telesmic Images.

The Great Mother Archetype

There need be no doubt as to the 'reality' of the Gods. They are much more real than our human bodies, since those only live a few years with limited effects, and the Gods continue always in principle, no matter how their formations change. Their 'bodies' are built up from Inner energies supplied by everyone dealing with them, even indirectly. All 'Mother' awareness and feeling of any kind goes towards the making of a Mother-God-Image. Millions of individual experiences over the centuries combining in the Great Mother Archetype. The same applies to every classifiable form of human energy expressed Inwardly. Each to its own God-Aspect or other Concept.

Monotheists who intentionally direct their energies towards a Single Aspect, do so in confidence that they address a Whole Being of infinite parts. Nevertheless, the bulk of humanity is usually quite indifferent about the Inner energies affecting them, making no particular effort at their disposition one way or another. So those Forces find their way wherever Forms claim them.

The Holy Mysteries

The Holy Mysteries in general, as associations of entities concerned with directing consciousness between Divinity and Humanity, are very largely occupied with the use of Telesmics. Initiates (those *inside* the Mystery dealing with Inner Existence) are trained both in the maintenance of existing Images and the production of fresh ones when needed. One might say that the material handled among members of the Mysteries is creative consciousness made up as intentional imagery.

Since most humans use their imagination in all sorts of ways, it is natural to wonder what is so special about Mystery-images. The answer lies partly in their purpose, partly in the manner of their construction, and mainly because they are the result of consciousness combined for such a specific reason from both Inner and Outer Life. The Telesmic Images of the Mysteries are not made from thoughts, fancies, speculations, or any other vague impressions of human minds, but they are *conceived* according to the natural Laws of Life. They have an entire 'apparatus of becoming' like ourselves. Father, Mother, Seed, Egg, Gestation, Birth, all equivalently related with each other Inwardly so that a Concept of Consciousness comes to Being.

This process should be familiar to students of the Hermetic

'Emerald Table'. The elementary stages are described as Fire
(The Sun, Light and Wisdom the Father, shining upon Water
(The Moon, Reflection and Understanding) as Mother. Gestation follows through Air, typified by the wind blowing from
all Quarters of Life so that the Concept may be considered by
everyone concerned, and lastly nourishment is provided by Earth
giving growth and experience. When the Concept becomes an
Entity in its own right, it 'ascends from Earth to Heaven'
(directs energies from Outer to Inner Life) and 'descends from
Heaven to Earth', or impresses spiritual energies upon material
manifestations. What could be clearer than these instructions?

The seed of the Concept must come from the Light within
us, we must reflect this in ourselves by receptive meditation and
understanding, gestate it by considering it all ways among us,
then nourish and grow it by experience and care. Eventually it
will become auto-operative enough to link us effectively between
Inner and Outer states of Existence. Quite a natural and normal
procedure altogether. The Mysteries have evolved a number of
techniques and practices to facilitate this conceptual process
among themselves, and this is their only difference from other
human types of handling consciousness.

An average human does not so much handle consciousness
as let it handle them. Their thoughts are mostly directed towards
objectivity. Everything must be materialized for them to think
at all in most cases. Even their dreamiest dreams are *of* something or other connected with mundane living. Simply to be
conscious for its own sake or in its own state would not occur
to them as a possibility. The Initiate of the Mysteries is only
concerned with materializing Spirit in so far as this assists the
ultimate spiritualization of matter. Telesmic Images in the shape
of Man extended to Divine proportions are the 'equal and opposite' of those in the shape of Divinity reduced to human
dimensions.

Images of the Image

The actual Telesmic Images of the Mysteries do not need
making, since they have already been made a very long time
ago. Their characterizations change with the centuries perhaps,
but not their essential nature. There are only a number of these

Fundamental Concepts in Being, all other Images being variants or combinations of them. Christianity offers the Concepts of the Trinity with a relegated Mother-Concept as the Virgin-Mother Mary. The Qabalah affords ten very practical Images. Pagan Pantheons offer hosts of them, and even the Christian Church admits a very minor pantheon of its 'Saints'. None of these however will be of any use to individuals or groups unless they conceive their own 'images of the Image' with which to work, and such conceptions have to take place through their own Innerworlds. Hence the meditational and ritual procedures adopted by the different branches of the Mysteries.

The actual conception of a Telesmic Image, using the Hermes formula, is not all that difficult. With a minimum of encouragement they breed themselves almost. Were they really able to reproduce their species as we do, they too would 'fall into flesh', and make their appearance in this already overcrowded world. In one sense this is indeed possible in so far as the Telesmic beings are expressed through incarnating human souls, but the degree of identification between humanity and our Telesmics is a very complex and questionable affair. It is obvious that if we relate ourselves with them for Inner purposes, they will necessarily relate themselves with us for Outer ones. The ethics and extent of this relationship are subjects for many unsatisfactory discussions and opinions. The only certainty is that without Telesmics, our Innerworld existence would be like an Outerworld life with no friends or relatives that we were aware of.

On primitive levels, the problem of Telesmics is easy to grasp. Inadequate human beings survey their personal status with dismay. They are not brave enough to fight effectively, clever enough to gain advantages, pleasant enough to make friends easily, and in fact all their difficulties arise from such shortcomings. Supposing, however, they could 'borrow' these needed qualities from those already possessing them? A fraction of each from everyone else would be like collecting a penny from every member of a community to make one poor person rich. If qualities could be borrowed or donated like coins, needy souls might be considerably helped. This assumes of course, that qualities have an objective existence of their own in some Inner state, and might be 'drawn upon' or 'paid out' like bank accounts. Strangely enough, such is a factual possibility by means of Telesmics.

Supposing a whole community of individuals, an entire nation, or even the population of the world decided to combine their various qualities into specific figures which could be re-divisible among them to give an overall figure *per capita*. If say, everyone put their courage together to make up a Defender-God, their knowledge together to form a Teacher-God, their love together into an All-loving-God, and so on. In other words, particular Forces concentrated and contained by appropriate Forms, from which energies might convert into Force again and so continue cyclically. Everybody contributes a fractional amount of kindliness which ultimately builds into a beneficent Mother or Father Figure for instance. Unhappy individuals needing contact with exactly this type of energy, pray to, invoke, or address their focus of consciousness to this Figure and if they succeed in establishing a connection between it and themselves, there will be a flow of compensatory energy from the Figure to the invocant in order to restore the instability of equilibrium. The effect is that the invocant 'feels comforted' or in some way re-balanced. Contact is actually made by the invocant making a minor Telesmic in themselves which connects with the major Telesmic made by a multiplicity of conscious creators, human and otherwise.

The goal of Consciousness

The possibilities of such Telesmics are virtually infinite once practice can be adapted to their principles. They are literally accumulations of typified and combined energies which are available, if not on demand, then on proper application to appropriate contact-points by those seeking them. Granted this may take time and trouble, but surely the outcome will be worth the input. Energy is energy, it cannot be lost, only transformed. Since consciousness is Absolute Energy, the law applies equally. What has happened to all the consciousness expended amongst humanity since we appeared on this planet? To Consciousness eventuating before us? For that matter, what happens to consciousness at all? As Energy it simply converts through its own cycles in the Circle of its own Constant. Its Force flows from one Form to another through the Endlessness of that Circle, the 'perimeter' of which comprises all the differentiations of Existence, and the Centre is the One Point of Everything. Cosmated Consciousness. Such is the Ultimate Power behind Telesmics, though human beings can only deal with it according to their capabilities. To each his own.

Telesmics appear on all levels in various Forms even though the same energies actuate them throughout. As Universal Deities, National heroes, sectarian 'Saints', or Figures of any kind at all, they only form close conscious contact with those who are closely conscious of their Forms. This is precisely what the Mysteries were intended to offer their Initiates : the best means and methods of making most effective contacts with the Telesmics necessary for spiritual development and establishment of the Inner Kingdom. Churches, Temples, and general customs of pagan practice existed to cater for humans *en masse,* but the Mysteries afforded opportunities for individual and Group Telesmics among those souls who, by making efforts, evolved beyond and away from the mean average. It was not that Mystery Initiates had any different Ultimates from the remainder of humanity, but that they made use of approach and dealing methods with those Ultimates which were and are beyond or differ from average human abilities.

The first obvious difference between Mystery customs and others concerning Telesmics is that the Mysteries have their own 'private' sets of Images which only the 'initiated' make use of. The sole reason for this is to ensure that only skilled and dedicated users build them up so that they will act as direct links between the Groups and the Great Ones common to all humanity. Even the 'Names' of those Images are usually kept private (or secret) for that very reason.

These private TIs are really in the nature of 'go-betweens' or shared lines with a limited number of subscribers. The only advantage of them is that of a precision instrument in the hands of a competent user. In other hands they would not only be useless, but also injured probably beyond repair. After perhaps some centuries of successful working among Mystery technicians, many of those once private TIs become 'solid' and 'established' enough to release for wider use among those souls approaching the Mysteries from their own 'Outer Courts'. So the Images, Symbols, Names, etc., become available to whomsoever they inspire with sufficient faith to employ them. A notable example of this is the Qabalah, which in spite of its undoubted antiquity, was unknown to more than a limited number of scholars until last century, and is neither widely known nor practised at present, despite accessible literature.

We shall find this picture repeating itself through history. First the few Initiates formating Inner forces into TIs, then the Group developing them and consolidating their expressions, and eventually a host of good, bad and indifferent people joining in the general System. The whole of this process is analogous to birth and becoming on a huge scale. An original Seed of Consciousness is implanted and conceived, then gestated until able to bear birth among mankind. Of all those ever sown, how many grow to wide physical dimensions? Yet every one fulfils its particular function in the Pattern of All.

Telesmics no guarantee of success

It does not follow that TIs processed by any Mystery School will guarantee spiritual success or perfection among those who work them subsequently on a mass scale. Christianity is an obvious example. People project their own qualities into the Images, and these cannot help communicating such energies to all co-users. An attempt at sorting 'good' from 'evil' was made by building up the Image of the Devil, which was supposed to be a repository for the worst in mankind and doomed to ultimate extinction. All the best in humanity was to be directed into the Christ-God and lesser Figures, while the worst went into the Devil for purgation amid the 'flames of Hell'. We know the failures of this dichotomy too well for any comments to be made. The Qabalah attempts to improve upon this by laying out a Scheme in which evil has no positive existence whatever, and the 'filter-trap' of an Abyss is designed to absorb polluted energies for purification and eventual re-issue.

Whatever System evolves from the Mysteries, TIs remain a necessity among mankind. So many attempts have been made at eliminating them, and rational explanations offered in exchange, phrased in terms of abstract principles or purely ethical values. Take the 'Gods' of humans away from them and what happens? They immediately make far worse Images for themselves. In place of Holy Ones and Pantheons, Saints and Heroes, humanity is producing amorphous concepts of State, 'People', commercial products, 'Pop' images, and all the rest of these unsatisfactory substitutes.

Humans do not want remote abstractions as 'Gods', but solid and substantial ones they can come to terms with on their own objective levels. They cling to their material 'God-forms' in the shape of cars, TV sets, and other Images with the same pathetic desire for comfortable assurance that motivated their remote ancestors to grasp at oddly shaped stones and twisted roots. Humanity needs Gods more than anything else, and should learn how to find Them as Inner Realities expressed through whatever Telesmic Image links their common consciousness together. Voltaire was quite right when he commented: 'If there were no God, it would be necessary to invent one.'

Sincere devotees of particular Systems may say indignantly: 'What! My God and Inner Ones no more than fantastical imaginings? Do I believe in nothing more than my own inventions? Is it all just a trivial fairy story? I cannot and will not accept such a diabolical dictum.' Those inclined to think that way have not begun to realize the nature of the truth surrounding them so closely that they are unable to appreciate its existence.

Human consciousness is restricted to the 'Me and Not-me' outlook. Unless we have something to be conscious of objectively, either Outwardly or Inwardly, we lose touch with consciousness. Divine Consciousness does not need to be aware *of* anything, because It is Conscious *in* everything emanating from Itself. As the Gita says: 'All things exist in Me. "Not-I" in them.' As a rough illustration, we might say that the direction of Force-flow with Divinity is from Out to In, while with Humanity it is In to Out. Divine awareness scaled down to the limits of a single human creature, thus directs Itself Out of that being towards the In of all other beings. Therefore, if we look Out of ourselves In to all else, we shall follow the Line of Inner Light shining through us and find the Real Image reflected everywhere. It is truly said: 'Whoso finds no Divinity in others will not find It in themselves.'

We do not 'invent' Divinities. Not all the humans who ever were, are now, or will be born in mortal bodies could possibly 'invent' the Energies of Existence behind our being. What we can and should 'invent', with the co-operation of those Energies, are suitable Forms for the adaption of our type of consciousness with Theirs. That is what our 'Gods' and TIs amount to, however they appear to us. The more perfectly this may be done, the better for Gods and Men alike, and the closer will be the contact between both. We cannot make, produce, or create any Divine Energy (or Spirit) whatsoever. All we can and should do, is co-construct Forms for that Force. We may call these Images the 'Body of God' whether they have physical representations or not.

Literally everything is the 'Body of God'. It used to be an old practice for a Teacher to tell some importunate pupil in search of 'wonderful secret Wisdom' to pick up any common stone and concentrate upon it until it led them to the Divinity it provided a 'body' for. The stone held no secret, but the concentration of consciousness did. *That* was what really supplied the 'body' or Magical Image. The function of the stone was to be a 'catalyst of consciousness', or provide an objective point for Human and Divine awareness to focus in common. From this focus of Force the containing Form emerges. This is how Magical Images are made.

Possibly the most practical example of this is the Bread-Wine Symbol acting as focus for the Christ-Corpus constructed during the celebration of the Christian Mysteries. The Real Presence is the Divine Spirit dwelling in the Mystical Body built up by the corporate beliefs and concentrations of consciousness coming through the congregation. The Bread-Wine Symbol, with all its wealth of significance, is the catalyst of convenience providing a Time-Space-Event point. It does not change its physical nature, nor have the consecratory words any other power than that of 'cuing in' the consciousness necessary for the construction of the Christ-Corpus as an Inner Reality linked with its Outer Symbolic expression. If the Rite is properly worked, at the Event of consecration—(con-secrare = 'to make Sacred-secret together'), the whole available awareness of participants should conjoin in creating the best possible Christ-Corpus they can build with their Inner Imagery, continuing until they realise their own response to Its objectivity. Few members of Christian churches are given any practical training in this art or have perhaps the slightest knowledge of it above instinctive levels inherited from more ancient sources than Christianity.

Such single consecrations by themselves will not keep a God-Image or any other Telesmic linked indefinitely with Humanity. Energy must be sufficiently supplied to provide the power necessary for their maintenance, and this is derived from the consciousness of all concerned with those particular Images. The Christ-Image is 'kept going' by the 'prayers' or conscious attentions of devotees, and so are all other Telesmics. Into whatsoever Form consciousness is directed, so will it be typified and concentrated. Being Pure Energy, consciousness follows its own laws of manifestation on every level of its differentiations, and we cannot evade or avoid those laws however we invoke them or apply them.

The build-up of an Inner Telesmic Reality in connection with Outer Forms of focus is basic Magical practice and the foundation of all rituals. Methods may change, but principles remain unaltered. In primitive practice, the invocant took his spear, attached an animal head or skull, usually with horns, to the top of it, and drove the pointed end into the earth. This gave a very rough God-Image around which human consciousness wove the pattern of projection for the Power approached Inwardly. Many crude customs grew up concerning this, including the use of human heads, anointment with blood and body fluids etc., but these gave no better results than they deserved—or demanded. Later on, the rite purified itself to the extent of simply setting up a forked staff or stang in the name of whatever Being was invoked, and then dancing around it while calling that Name, or sitting around it invoking meditatively. Sometimes the stang was specially cut in the name of some dead tribal member, and it was believed that their spirit might materialize or manifest by using the named stang as a kind of psychic clothes-peg while they derived the necessary energy from the circulating dancers. Power was also supposed to come from the earth itself so as to bring the dead staff to life. Legend is full of staffs that blossomed.

Tree Symbolism

The 'Spirit-staff' in the earth and its generative symbolism is still with us. The horned Staff became the Crozier born by the Bishop or Abbot as a sign of their authority. Staffs of every kind of office remain from National flagpoles to village vergers' Wands. The Magic Rod of Power is yet borne in Mystery practice, and the Sceptre is the sign of a once Divine Kingship throughout the world. The pagan creates his God-Form about his totem-staff, the Christian creates his upon a Cross-Tree, and the Qabalist makes his up the Middle Pillar (or trunk) of his Inwardly-built Tree of Life Glyph. Different means of seeking the same end— jointure between Earthly Man at the bottom, and Heavenly God at the top. Above an ordinary tree—the Sky, Heaven-Father. Below it—the Earth-Mother. No wonder Tree-Symbolism is used so much in the various Mysteries.

We all project the patterns of what we seek into the inadequacies of what we already have. This is fundamental to human nature and will not be eradicated as long as Man remains Man. It is nicely illustrated in some productions of the pantomime *Cinderella* which is so rich in folklore and therefore possessed of its own peculiar attraction. After Cinders is left alone on stage when her family have departed for the Ball, the girl takes hold of the birch-besom, makes a 'partner' of it, and does a wistful little number with the broom 'standing-in' for the Prince as an Image.

In olden times, country lasses did actually play with besoms in sexual fantasias as they had previously played with their dolls for image-projection. Hence the 'witch' connections between sex-substitutes and unfulfilled females in states of psychic unbalance. Even 'spell-poppets' provided foci for forces directed against individuals with malignant intentions. We make Images all the time in every way. The lad with his 'pin-up' and the lass with her signed 'star-photo' are only following in the footsteps of their predecessors even if they still stumble awkwardly along a Path that has never seemed very clear to them.

When we come to the crucial point or nucleus of everything concerning the Mysteries, religion, philosophy, the occult, or anything of this nature which concerns Mankind so intimately and continuously, we shall find this one issue. What is our Inner

Reality? Do we really have souls and spirits based on immortal principles which operate through dimensions of being beyond our mortal bodies, or do we not? Is there a Divinity responsible for our existence with Which we can relate ourselves or not? The endless, age-old, unanswerables except by experience. How can we possibly deal with these matters except by awareness not only of but *in* them? Ordinary thinking in objective terms is useless for the purpose, uncontrolled fantasy leads to chaos, to deny our Inner promptings results in a spiritual frustration worse than its physical counterpart, so what is left for us? One course only between Wisdom on one side and Understanding on the other—constructively controlled conceptions in and of consciousness. Intelligent Imagery. Cosmation of consciousness. Telesmics. That, or abandon hope all those who choose to live in spiritual squalor and confusion, no matter how successful they may seem in terms of physical advantage.

No Initiate of the Mysteries believes that Telesmic Images of any kind are Absolute actualities. What Form is? Our human bodies and personalities are no more than Images, borrowed for their lifetime to express Inner energies through their conditions of being. They, and Telesmic Images are the vitally necessary X's without which our Universal Problem could have no Ultimate Solution. Providing this is realized, we shall not be guilty of idolatry, which means making the mistake of accepting an Image as an actuality, and therefore preventing ourselves from true progression with our Problem. A major difference between an Initiate and non-initiate is precisely this perception or non-perception past the appearance of Images. The one looks with and through Images, and the other only looks at them. Both types of individual look *for* Images with those different reasons.

The Hermetic Formula

This again is part of the Hermetic formula where we are told to 'separate the essence from the substance', or the qualities from their containers. Suppose, for instance, someone approaches a doctor for medical aid. The Image of the doctor, comprising his body, surgery, drugs, and externalities, will do nothing by themselves. What actually helps are the qualities contained in that

Image. Knowledge concentrated in one man from sources that took centuries to come together. Goodwill, technical ability, interest in work and all the rest of it. The drugs also came from centuries of trial and error, costing perhaps many human lives before perfection in production and dosage became attainable.

None of these factors are actually physical in nature, though we appreciate them through physical Images. We may well ask in the end what really effects the cure—the doctor and his drugs, or the Consciousness producing their Images without which they would not be what they are. Awareness is 'essence' and Image is 'substance'. Once we realize the distinction between them, we may act Hermetically with both.

Suppose again that we are provided with the single power (or essence) of electricity. It all depends what sort of Forms we offer its Force as to what effects occur. Feed it into the 'sub-stance-Image' of a radio and we obtain sonics, into a stove and it cooks our food, a fire and it warms us. Get the Form-Image right for any specific job, and the Force will do it. This is exactly the situation we are faced with in Telesmics. Consciousness is Energy like electricity, though to an infinitely greater degree. If we can discover or design effective Form-Images as mechanisms for Consciousness to operate (or animate), then calculated effects may be obtained to fulfil all necessities. We should be able to build mental and spiritual 'machines' with the same accuracy and skill with which we make physical ones.

In fact these Inner automata ought to be far better in every way than their physical relatives, because they will be able to deal with energies unknown in manifestations of matter. Material mechanisms cannot deal with feelings and awareness. They will not love, inspire, or otherwise react with Inner operations of Consciousness. TIs can and do deal with such typified energies on their own level, and that is their natural function.

Developing True Inner Will

The Magical arts and Mystery practices are intimately con-cerned with the design, construction, making, maintenance, and usage of such Inner Images from minor personal ones to major Archetypes that endure far beyond human limits. It would be true to say that Consciousness is the currency with which all the business of the Mysteries is transacted, and Images are the commodities dealt with. Nothing is easier than to make ignorant assertions that occult work of this kind will unhinge the mind and destroy the soul. Such disasters happen quite independently of Magical practice, and depend upon the nature and character of individuals themselves.

The Mysteries simply provide unique opportunities for developing the True Inner Will of Initiates. Whether this is Cosmic, Anti-Cosmic, or inadequate either way is a matter for human souls to work out by and among themselves. Consciousness is the Primal, and most potent Energy of Existence, and even the attenuated amounts of it available for human use are powerful enough to cause serious damage if misdirected. Comparatively few people have any real idea of what consciousness means, or what can be done with it. At one time only Initiates of the authentic Mysteries could obtain the necessary training and experience to make the most of consciousness while yet functioning in earthly conditions. Although the picture is very different today, the Mystery Tradition still guards the van in the Inner Fields of Action.

Traps to snare the unworthy

It is also a common mistake to dismiss the various rites and customs of the Mysteries which have become 'open secrets' as a lot of childish nonsense and amateur theatricals, or in similar terms of rejection. Such is precisely the impression the Mysteries were designed to give those whose attentions were unwelcome. The most certain safeguard against antagonistic action is to seem utterly unworthy of it and too trivial to arouse the interest of potential enemies. For this reason, the early stages of Initiation are often made to look obviously silly or aimless. Some apparently pointless dressing up perhaps, a few stupid 'secrets', some ridiculous rhymes, a sprinkling of easily discovered errors and inaccuracies. Just enough to convince unsuitable investigators that they are wasting their time in bothering with such rubbish. The best way of protecting valuable information is to write it so large that no one could read it for living on the letters, or so small as to be beneath contempt. Only those taking the trouble to find the correct viewpoint could possibly realize the significance of what lay within their easy reach all the time.

Endless numbers of individuals reject themselves very neatly from the Mysteries this way. Having 'discovered' the nonsense incorporated specifically to trap minds unable to realise its purpose, the disgruntled (or triumphant) discoverers leave it alone, thereby leaving its designers to get on with their work undisturbed by inharmonious influences. The type of enquirer who is 'wanted Inside', recognizes the rubbish as well as anyone else, but also realizes its nature, declines to accept its face value, and examines it most carefully for the clues it holds which lead behind it, behind that again, and ever Inwards towards Truth. The Image behind the Image behind the Image to the Ultimate. Once a genuine Initiate passes this first test-barrier successfully, there are no limits on the Way ahead.

This is exactly the sort of 'Insight' asked and expected of Mystery Initiates. An ability to 'see through' all Images while using each one as a means of perceiving what lies beyond it. To take any physical symbol, living or artificial, and instead of being satisfied with its objectivity or appearance, penetrate past its external portals and consciously enter its mystical depths in search of its Inner Reality.

At the same time it has to be realized that the Image is necessary as an Entry-point without which there would be no available access. Veils are not to be despised or denigrated, but treated for what they are—separators between substance and essence. This is the reason why so much work in the Mysteries consists of meditational and dramatic ritual procedures. Far from being wasted time and effort, it is done for the purpose of conditioning and training practitioners so that they are able to deal conceptually with the Energy of Consciousness directly on hyperphysical levels. Perhaps it will be as well to examine some of these Mystery principles on which they are based. This might help our understanding of Telesmics in theory and application.

CHAPTER II

'WHAT'S IN A NAME'?

In the primary 'Grades' of Mystery Initiation, neophytes are never given adequate reasons for what they are told to think or do, and as often as not are deliberately misinformed or misled, though never in such a way that they would come to actual harm thereby. This is for the specific purpose of persuading them to go sufficiently deep into themselves to discover and then transcend the veils between them and their becoming. Those who accept all the camouflage at face value and are content to play around with it happily, have at least gained some pleasant toys for their spiritual childhood which will help them towards Inner reality later on. They have lost nothing because they are still attaining.

The value of toys should never be underestimated on any level. The playthings of one period become the practicalities of another, and there is plenty to play with in the Mysteries which will eventually evolve into work of the most welcome and important kind. When the growing Initiate begins to realize the toy-nature of his initial Mystery-material, this will grow with him, and the 'toys' change into *tools*. This process is a constant one. No genuine 'Grade' in the real Mysteries is ever 'conferred' or 'bestowed' by any authority Human or Divine. The Initiate simply grows into it as an operation of Nature and becomes of that 'Grade'. Ceremonial 'initiations' act as pattern-formators and power concentrators as Time-Space-Event correlation points. They have their proper place and purpose in the Mysteries, but they no more give automatic ability or spiritual status than a title makes its recipient worthy of its meaning.

Impossible tasks

Initiates are also set tasks or exercises far beyond their personal capabilities. These may be included among a number of activities which are all achievable with varying amounts of individual and collective effort. The 'impossibles' are there to make the Initiates fully realize their own shortcomings and inadequacies as individual beings, and appreciate the necessity for becoming better than they are in order to extend their accomplishments. Such incentives are intended to direct the Initiate towards this very problem of extending their being. Where is all the extra 'being' to come from? How bring it and the Initiate's existence together? What Magic makes wishes 'come true'? The Initiate should have learned by this time that every problem must contain its own answer, so, if his own insufficiency is the problem, he looks exactly there for a solution.

Since it is obvious that the sort of being he is cannot function as demanded or expected, it remains to find out what kind of a being would fulfil those requirements and then make the necessary linkage therewith. This is the reason and purpose for the 'Mystery Name' given to the Inner Self which should be 'born' at Initiation, and 'grow up' Inwardly somewhat ahead of the Outer Self with which it exchanges identities. It is in this respect mainly that the progress of an Initiate differs from that of an average human. Ordinary mortals work in, with, and through the Outer Self as their entity of expression. The results of all this expenditure of energy feed through to Inner levels in the course of time and ultimately return Outwardly as improvements or detriments of behaviour and character. Usually many lives pass before any remarkable changes show up. The Initiate improves on this process by working 'one step back' in and through an Inner Self which is really a TI created by the conditions of Initiation itself. He thus accomplishes with an economy of effort an evolution which would take a more ordinary mortal incalculably more in every way of the 'long run'.

Building up the Inner Self

We must be absolutely clear about this, because it is a very important consideration. The TI of a developing Initiate is not an Astral body, alter ego, split personality, or any such thing. It is strictly 'himself ahead of himself'. Not a separate being at all, except in so far as a head is separate from a foot in one and the same individual. What happens is that the Initiate 'comes to consciousness' (or is born again IN himself (the Kingdom of

Heaven), and builds up his Inner being much as anyone else builds up an Outer one (the 'Temple not made with hands'), according to the plan of perfection he believes in. This is the 'Inner Identity' he will use after death of his mortal body or for extra-material activities Inwardly. When he outgrows this Magical Personality, he will evolve another behind it again as he progresses far beyond birth and rebirth in physical terms on this or any planet. Anyone could do this if they really wanted to with sufficient determination. The Initiate only uses consciousness in a more direct and determined way than most other humans.

One might truly say that Initiation really begins with this Inner birth (or Baptism) of what we might call the Real and Better Self who is, and can always do far more than the ordinary Outer Self manifesting in the material world. Whatever faults and failings the OS has, an IS does not reproduce in itself for an Initiate, but corrects and counterbalances so as to become a more perfect presentation of power. Eventually of course this will 'show through' into the OS unless there is some particular reason for masking it.

Initiates do not usually seek unwelcome publicity in this world. The creation of this Telesmatic IS comes by constructive usage of consciousness as an act of conception. Not only the consciousness at the disposal of the Initiate individually is involved, but also energies coming from every source concerned with such a construction. Fellow-Initiates, 'Adepts', 'Inner Ones', and in fact the whole Hierarchy of Heaven is ultimately behind the Initiate of the Path of Light, though the responsibility for accepting and processing those energies into himself remains his own. Since the whole operation is a 'combined' one it may well be called an act of Concreation or 'making together'.

The Telesmic or Inner Self of an Initiate therefore consists of an Identity constructed with the aid of all other Identities, incarnate or otherwise, from whence the Initiate draws his spiritual supplies. Everyone does this indiscriminately, but the Initiate chooses with care and deliberation what he will build into his spiritual system. Hence the selection of a suitable framework of Inner Images, and the ruling to have: 'none other Gods before these'. It is not that 'other Gods' are right, wrong or otherwise in themselves, but that if spiritual growth and development is to occur along the best possible lines for any being, then Inner conditions must be so arranged to produce those results.

A seed has to be planted in its correct setting before it will turn into a perfect plant of its kind, and a soul must also have its proper 'Garden of Paradise' to become what it should. The real 'Garden of Paradise' for anyone is when they are surrounded by ideal Inner conditions for becoming perfected beings as true reflections of Divinity. Since Mankind 'fell' from the original Garden, we needs must follow the Creative Pattern by making our own to replace it.

All creeds, systems, and other methods of spiritual concreation offer their followers a selection of Concepts from whence to draw the necessary Inner energies for constructing their own Inner Identities and so becoming immortal in their own rights as they grow to Good ('Godhood'). This is similar to a material constructor such as a civil engineer being supplied with a circle of the best contacts for deriving the finest necessities for his project. The Churches offer mainly stock supplies for the public, and the Mysteries cater for 'specialist requirements'. That is the principal difference, and each Mystery System offers its particular set of Concepts for supplying the energies which enable practitioners to become WHAT THEY WILL.

The Qabalist Tree of Life

Probably a reason why the Qabalistic System has its appeal to Western Mystics is because of its basic simplicity and neatness of fundamental Pattern. The Qabalist lays out his Inner Garden of Paradise around his precious Tree of Life with its ten wonderful Concepts of Attainment, Wisdom, Understanding, Mercy, Justice, Beauty, Glory, Achievement, Foundation, and Field of Action. These join with each other by Paths of Power which are peopled by every conceivable sort of individual likely to assist in the overall Plan of Perfection. This amazing Tree grows (like the Rose or Lotus) at the centre of a Circle-Cross Cosmic Chart. Amid this design, the Qabalist lives Inwardly and concreates his 'Invisible Universe'. He does not need to go outside it for the simple reason that all else links in with it through its Concepts. The fundamentals of the various Mysteries and Creeds should engage with each other like the leaves and pinions of the Wheels of Existence they really are. It is simply a question of every soul discovering for themselves what is their best type of Inner Garden for growth during their particular stage of evolution.

The Initiate's job is to build up and become the sort of Being fit for a God to live through. This he does in co-operation with Divinity by constantly constructing an ever better-becoming Image of that Divinity through which It operates and into which he becomes his TRUE SELF. Here again is the difference between idolatry and idealism. An idolator would build up a Deity-Image as an entirely separate concept from himself before which he might stand in awe, fear, or any other separative feeling which would prevent his spiritual progress beyond the limitations of his own immediate imagery. He has not made a God with the aid of Divinity, but an artifice into which he projects his inadequacies and personal shortcomings.

The Deity-Image of the idealist is that of his own ultimate becoming. This was why the Greek God-Images as extensions of humanity lifted their mortal followers to such Olympian heights. The Christ Man-God Image was designed for universal human use, but has been unsuccessful for this purpose because of many reasons, among which is its masculine bias and the misuse made of it. Nevertheless, a large proportion of the human race use it in varying degrees, and only a limited number of individuals are able to deal with the Images in the Holy Mysteries.

The Initiate's Secret Magical Name

At their original and most important Initiation which 'brings to birth in the Mysteries', Initiates receive or choose their 'Magical Name'. This Name is of exceptional importance to them, for it should be descriptive of, or linked with the New-True-Self which they intend (or WILL) to become. The Name literally *is* an extension of themselves Inwardly, and as a Telesmic, what happens to it will happen to them. It must never be divulged to another soul except under necessity of the Mysteries, and then only to those in whom most implicit faith may be reposed. This is no idle gesture for secrecy's sake, but a vital precaution to ensure the integrity of the Inner Being under construction.

Whatever entity, human or otherwise, 'knows the Name' has established a link with it through which a proportion of their energies may pass either intentionally or even automatically. It follows therefore, that the 'Secret Name' of an Initiate must never be revealed to any Entity or individual whose influence or energies would be unsuitable for incorporation into the Telesmic Image of the Inner Self being built up. Otherwise, instead of a strong true Image derived only from the best and most direct Inner sources, there will be a mixture of many undesirable elements which distort and detract from the Image, making it difficult or unsatisfactory to work with.

During its initial stages of growth, a Telesmic Image may be considered as in a state of 'gestation' which needs what might be likened to 'pre-natal care', if it is not to be aborted, miscarried, stillborn, or deformed. Hence the secrecy and caution surrounding its development. Once the Image is stable and strong enough at any level to maintain its own immunity thereon, then it may emerge openly to fulfil its functions if need be.

In a sense we are always being conceived at our deepest levels, gestating at nearer ones, being born Outwardly, and dying from what we pass beyond. This process also works the opposite way (as every Circle must) with our energies returning to their Single Supreme Source. The Inner Image, like the others, is a two-way exchanger, and at any given instant is a compromise between its In and Out sources of supply. This is why the Initiate sets up 'filter-screens' on each side, so to speak, in order to ensure the Image becoming WHAT IS WILLED. The 'Word' does indeed 'become Flesh', or manifests 'as it is made'. Using their 'Magical Names' as nuclei for their concreative imagery, Initiates of the Holy Mysteries may build around these WHAT THEY WILL, providing requisite precautions are taken, and the right rules observed.

Choosing a Magical Name

Choosing a correct Magical Name is not an easy operation. It has to be short, sweet, and complete, so that it becomes an Entity by itself, expressive in its own terms of exactly what the Initiate wills to be. This is why so many Initiates in the Mysteries choose Names meaning 'I will do (or be) so and so', i.e. *Perdur-*

abo—I will carry through; *Scire*—to know about things; *Fidelio*
—I will be faithful, and so on. Latin, Greek, Hebrew, or other
ancient languages are mainly used because so much can be got
into a few keywords as a Motto, but there is no reason why a
Magical Name should not be English, or for that matter a
mathematical formula or symbolic sound. Everything depends
on whether it is capable of producing the purpose of the Will
within it. In Magic, things are intended to become as they are
named.

In usual social practice of course, an individual's name is
chosen for them by the group they belong with, but in the
Mysteries the 'Secret Name' should come solely through Initiates
from direct contact with their own Inner sources. This happens
in various ways. Sometimes it is a 'flash', a realization of 'That's
me!' Otherwise the naming process might be a long and careful series of meditations resulting in the certitude of being
properly linked with what is named.

Instructed Initiates know that this 'Naming' is really a constant effort of their consciousness in an act of continual conception. It has been said that the Ultimate Name of God is unknowable and unpronounceable and this means that no matter
how deeply we go into ourselves and discover what we are, there
is always another discovery to be made behind that, and so *ad
infinitum*. 'Know Thyself' does not refer so much to some in-
incredible final revelation, as to the actual process of 'knowing'
itself. Thus, every Name Initiates find for themselves is a temporary one, in so far as it will lead another few steps along the
Path of Light until the next major expansion of Identity, which
is really all Initiations are. Once any particular Name has been
'outgrown', or accomplished its specific purpose, it may be safely
revealed to others, used as a pen-name, or otherwise shared in
common.

The Unknown Real Name

The 'Name-structure' of an Initiate therefore is an identification of all levels of being. Commencing at the 'Nil-Name' which
can never be 'known' except Ultimately Beyond Being, an
identity projects itself from point to point of its Circle, 'declaring' or 'naming' itself as it goes. The picture of this is beauti-

fully shown by the Qabalistic Tree of Life, wherein Divinity proclaims Itself by different Names on different levels, yet all emerge from the Nil-Name at Zero, and every Name is actually One and None together.

Taking the Middle Pillar as an example, Divinity expresses Itself successively towards Manifestation as: NIL, I AM WHAT I WILL, DIVINE KNOWLEDGE, DIVINE LIFE, and COSMO-CONTROLLER. The Initiate follows this general pattern by admitting that his 'Real Name' can be known to none except the Ultimate, and that a series of substitute 'Names' connect between That and themselves for what they are anywhere. The 'Mystery Name' they choose will therefore be a convenience of consciousness placed at their integral point of Inner development. On the Tree of Life this would approximate 'Death'—Knowledge-Experience —which is built up by the Becoming of Divinity What It Will.

Theoretically, each 'letter' of the Inner Name is an actual quality or 'element' of Existence. Thus, to determine the exact nature of any individual, a Name may be chosen from 'letters' which comprise by their combination the nature and degree of Being required. Just as there are only so many elements of physical matter in existence, and everything is made up from selections and combinations of these, so there are only a limited number of Inner Elements from which our spiritual natures are composed. If each Element is represented by a 'letter', then the Name composed by those 'letters' will express our True Being. To alter or modify this Inner Name, is synonymous with altering the whole nature and structure of an Inner Expression and its relation with Outer Formation. We have a version of this fundamental truth in the belief of 'transubstantiation', in which 'bread' becomes 'body', and 'wine' becomes 'blood', by the utterance of a simple statement to that effect. Magic legends are full of stories about changes brought about by specially arranged 'letters' or 'spells', which quite literally means knowing how to put the right Inner Elements together so as to 'spell out' an actuality which becomes itself thereby.

The Paths of Power

Conscious energies available to humans, initiated or otherwise are unable to achieve this synonymity of Word-Will-Work.

We can and do become What we Will, but through prolonged processes and with considerable modifications and alterations. Nevertheless, Initiates of the Mysteries endeavour to act according to principles so that only power need be connected to make them practical. We do not have enough power at our own disposal to do anything very wonderful. Real Power—actual Energy in its pure state—proceeds from Divinity, not Humanity. Providing we arrange the Paths for Power (or 'letters') properly, and then make contact (or 'invoke') correctly with Divinity at the right level, the Power will pass through the Paths, and an Effect will eventuate. We only wire up the circuit in accordance with the diagram or Pattern we have learned. Until the Energy from Inner Sources of Supply is actually connected to these circuits, they will be no more than fabrications of our ingenuity and efforts. If they should be faulty, then we shall experience the consequences of mishandled energy in one way or another.

Initiates believe with good reason that if a Name is suitably 'uttered' Inwardly, then the energies of Consciousness acting through, and condensing around the 'letters', or components of that Name, will produce whatever is so Named as an Entity of Existence. To what extent or degree that existence manifests and endures, is entirely dependent on circumstances. It is a major aim in the Mysteries to make this process both practical and beneficial in the best possible way. To say what we will be and then become. That is a Magical act with any human being, and the Mysteries are concerned with discovering and perfecting every available method of effecting such alterations.

If considerable secrecy is observed about this, it is for a valid reason. There is no foolproof way of ensuring that only good results will come through the techniques taught. Everything depends on the Will of the user (who may be 'used' by others) as to intentional direction of energy, and there are so many complexities and fallibilities of human nature involved, that it is impossible to guarantee good without ill effects from the workings of what may be called Magic. All that may fairly be done is to set whatever safeguards may be devised around energies of Consciousness which are far more potent than the most lethal atomic pile, and trust in our spiritual Superiors.

It is actually the safeguards and precautions that take most of the time and trouble involved. Like the nuclear Bomb, the only genuine safeguard would be a united human will never to use it, and who would dare presume that possibility at present?

Might an entire Humanity be imagined who were incapable of conceiving any kind of evil, and therefore could not practice it at all? Theoretically and remotely perhaps, but certainly not as an immanent actuality. Yet only a Being utterly beyond wrongdoing would be capable of operating the Energy of Pure Consciousness without destroying themselves. That is why Existence still exists, and why the Magical Image of the Supreme Being is shown as a Right profile, 'in Whom there is no wrong, but only right'. If we visualize a Figure whose Right profile only appeared to use wherever we looked, it would be of someone going round us in a circle the Way of Light, deosil. Godwise. Cosmically. Hence the Mysteries of Light work their circle-dance patterns in that direction to impress basic ideas of 'Rightness' on participants.

Initiates of the Mysteries of Light try to work this 'Right' way, by using their own capacity for rectitude as a control over their capabilities of directing the Energy of Consciousness with True Will. In effect they say and pray: 'Let not mine Enlightenment exceed the rightness of my rule.' In other words, they are making their ability to do good the criterion for Inner Wisdom and power.

Genuine Initiates do not grasp for powers they are unqualified to use beneficially, but they do seek to extend their capacity for rightdoing, so that whatever power comes to them will be properly applied. Once again it is a case of horse and cart. Any determined human may grab hold of energies far greater than their intentions of using them for the benefit of any but themselves. This is eventually bound to act against intentional ill-users. An instructed Initiate with the slightest spiritual sense, has the wits and wisdom to 'seek first the Kingdom of God and His righteousness (which is within you), then all else that may be necessary will be added unto you'. No pious admonition this, but a sound and straightforward piece of practical advice. It is only reasonable after all, to prepare the Paths before connecting the Power. Activating an atomic pile is the last, not the first stage of harnessing nuclear energy. So the Initiate implores the Divinity: 'Do not Enlighten me until I deserve it.' Then works to become worthy.

This Magnum Opus is no less than the concreation of Perfected Being through the agency of the Initiate as an Entity of that Being. A Christian might describe this as 'Salvation', a Mystic as 'Divine Union', an Alchemist as the 'Supreme Transmutation', but it amounts to the same process throughout. An old Qabalistic legend says that Adam was originally perfect, then after the Fall his body broke up into millions of pieces which all became little Adams struggling to exist on their own. If ever they reach a stage of development when they are able to fit themselves together according to the Original Pattern, then evolution will end, and Man will be perfect again. A valuable myth for meditation, because it contains a great deal of essential truth. These free-running 'pieces of Adam', whether male or female in human polarity, are responsible for their own behaviour between the Macrocosm of which they are infinitesmal 'personal pieces', and the Microcosm within themselves which they must eventually 'bring together' into a state of perfection. There comes a point in the evolution of everyone when they become aware of this process in some way, and thenceforth participate consciously in the Great Plan as its concreators—or Initiates. The real 'Degrees of Initiation' are marked by the extent of this Awareness in anyone, and the nature of their concreative activities. Such degrees are only earned in the Lodge of Life Itself.

The Principle of Naming

Once Initiates realize their position as conscious Concreators of Cosmos, they are faced with the task of putting this to practical effect. All the various Mystery Schools have their particular methods and ideas on the subject, but whichever Initiates belong to by belief, they will have to use their own Initiative for fulfilling themselves as the Divine Will in them directs. Initiates of the Western Systems generally use some adaption of the 'Name within a Name within a Name within a Name' scheme for 'knowing' or becoming their True Selves. The rough outline of this is that as an earthly personage they are known by their family name which embodies their ordinary being, behind this they have another name for their mental being, another behind that again for their soul-self, and another again for Spirit. At

'Secret-Centre' of course is the 'Nil-Name' which they will never 'know'. The same being expressed on its different levels. A Qabalist would say that such names were those whereby an individual was known respectively by The Unmanifest, Gods, Archangels, Angels, and Mankind.

The purpose behind the principle of naming anyone or anything at all, is to direct and hold the Energy of Consciousness in some particular way at some especial point or portion of Existence. It is essentially an act of concreation, and therefore Magical. Humanity gives names to whatever exists, while Divinity gives Existence to whatever is Named. When a human being 'utters a name', the object of that name has its primary existence only in their own mind or 'imagination'. When Divinity Utters a Name, Existence manifests wherever it is intended, even in material form, because everything including ourselves IS 'in the imagination of God'. And THAT is far beyond the imagination of Man.

An Initiate of Light simply aims to follow out through his own Microcosm the principles by which he became part of the Macrocosm. After all, he is a focal point (or name) between these different states of the same Existence. Energies exchange each way through him. If those energies are balanced and beneficial through him, well and good, but if not, then chaos and disharmony will certainly cause some kind of damage or disadvantage. So the Initiate tries to equate the energies of Existence operating through his individuality Inwardly and Outwardly. If he be Christian, he would say : 'Thy Will, not mine, be done in me.' Otherwise : 'Let THAT be ITSELF through this myself.' In effect, the Initiate asks : 'What am I?' and spends the rest of Existence seeking an answer. If ever the true answer to that Question were found, Existence, as known, would end. We disappear as we discover ourselves. It is only from our Undiscovered that we may expect Appearance.

Just as an ordinary child of life learns how to become itself first in imagination with toys, and then later on by expression with tools, so the Child of Light in the Mysteries follows this same pattern. All the Rites and practices for dealing with Consciousness at imaginative level are the pre-requisite essentials for power-productions in other states of existence. As in the beginning it was necessary for THAT to produce ITSELF, so at the commencement of human Initiation, the Child of the Mysteries must be conceived like Melchizedek: 'Without father, without mother, without descent, having neither beginning of days nor end of life, but made like unto a Son of God, abiding a priest continually.'

In other words, Melchizedek (Master of Righteousness) is a Pattern-Symbol for a Telesmic Image produced from concepts of auto-cosmation or self-being, using the Divine Image as a Master-copy. The Initiate is told in so many words to become a Master of the Right Way by an act of self-creation after the Divine fashion, thus becoming a perpetual priest or Mediator of Everlasting Energy that ceases not but only changes. As a meditation-contact, Melchizedek can be a most instructive TI.

Using the 'Priest-King' Image of Melchizedek, Qabalists would identify themselves with this at the central point of Harmony, Beauty, Balance, at Tiphereth with its concepts of Priest-King-Victim, and proceed with the Cosmic act of autocreation by relating with the other Sephiroth (or Concepts) disposed around the periphery of the Tree via appropriate Paths. The 'Magical Name', or 'New Identity' will thus be 'born' into the otherwise empty Sphere of Daath, where it should gestate and build until it 'makes itself manifest' in terms of its own entity as an individual. It then becomes the centre of another circle, and repeats the whole process again on higher levels of life, and so Existence continues towards Itself. The 'Mysteries of Melchizedek' are those of Concreation, or making oneself into what one *must* be, with the aid of Those whom one *might* be.

The early psycho-mechanics of this process are of great interest, since they explain many points not generally known about the Mystery techniques for God-incarnating used in primitive times. At one time there was a death penalty for revealing the secret to non-Initiates, but eventually it became guessed at if not entirely discovered, although it finally sank into oblivion through sheer disuse and neglect. In brief it amounted to artificial insemination accompanied by conscious direction of conceptive energy from both Divine and human levels. The broad outlines of the Rite—for such it was—were roughly as follows.

Twelve active and potent males were needed, one for each Archetype or Sign. They had to be as nearly perfect specimens of their kind as possible. In small communities a lesser number might have to serve, one male being chosen for his wealth, another for his skill at hunting, another for intelligence, and so on. Each was required to have some outstanding quality which alone would make him a worthy father, and they formed the circle of seed-donors, or 'God-fathers'. The recipient was of course the Virgin-Bride, specially selected for her moral and personal attributes as a fit Mother of the God-Incarnate. She was AIMA, the Bright Fertile One. The 'go-between' was a Past-Mother, Old Woman, or AMA, the Dark Sterile One.

After considerable preparation over several months of devotion, this group of people assembled secretly at some place and time they believed appropriate for their purpose. A hill-top at full moon of summer was most likely, though by no means invariable. The moment of dawn might be chosen, or even sunset when the sun was supposed to sink into the earth, and Sky-Father entered Earth-Mother. In some way or other, the whole act would be aligned with nature. Either a circle had been previously marked out on the ground to represent the Cosmos, or personal staffs and stones were brought and set up in pattern. Each person took their place by their own staff, banner, or Sign, and the Rite proper commenced.

The men formed the perimeter of the circle, the Maid the centre, and the Old Woman had her peculiar dance-pattern between the two. Procedure varied considerably according to local custom. Sometimes the Maid danced spirally between the men and came to a central rest position embodying the waiting Earth-Womb, or sometimes she was scarcely conscious of the operation at all, being in a state of semi-drugged ecstasy. Elaborations such as music, etc., depended on resources and beliefs. The men might be as still as their staffs, but mostly they evolved a species of on-the-spot sort of jigging movement, possibly accompanied by chanting and drumming.

Each male taking part in the Rite had to work themselves into a condition of consciousness where they were convinced they had successfully embodied their particular God-Aspect. This of course was done by characteristic miming and invocations for as long as might be necessary to obtain the effect needed. Sometimes hours were passed this way before conditions were right.

The Old Woman became very much a Mistress of Ceremonies, going from one point to another with suggestions and commands. She was practically the focus of the group-hypnosis, as she 'wove the spell' with her words and the 'winding up' or bringing to a climax of the whole cyclic charming of consciousness. She might bring attention to bear on one male, saying in effect: 'Thou art so and so! Thou hast the power of such and such. Behave in this way, be this and that, etc.' To the Maid, her suggestions might run: 'Honoured art thou! God cometh to thee. Light entereth thy womb. Thou shalt bear Divinity within thee, chosen indeed art thou as Mother of the Mighty.'

In fact the success or otherwise of the Rite depended very much on the ability of this female Elder to direct the energies involved during its practice. The decision of critical moments and procedural contingencies lay entirely with her. While the others might work themselves into states of ecstasy or semi-trance until they were almost unaware of their physical conditions, the Old Woman had to remain so to speak with one foot on earth and the other in Heaven.

It was the Old Woman who bore with her the Sacred Vessel of the Mystery, an object of particular veneration. This was physically no more than a fairly small phallic shaped horn from some suitable animal with a pierced point normally kept closed during use by the Old Woman's own hand. Otherwise the Cup was waved around, upheld, or gesticulated with as seemed called for. The Gods were implored singly and collectively to pour their power into it as an instrument of doing Their Will on and in Earth. When the time was judged right, the Old Woman of the Cup went deosil around the circle from one male to another collecting their seed into the horn cup as quickly as possible. They donated this not as their human selves, but in the character and on behalf of the God-Aspect they represented.

When the critical moment came, the Old Woman injected this accumulation of seed into the Maid by means of the horn which she blew into from the broad end, thus applying the necessary pressure. This was the 'breath of life' needed for the insemination process.

Object of the God-Incarnation Rite

Once this was done, the exhausted participants 'gave over to the Gods', simply letting their energies drain Inwardly towards the Divine Spark they prayed had been kindled in their midst. They had done everything possible for a human being to encourage the Incarnation of a God amongst them, and the rest lay with Divinity Itself. The humans believed that the child born of such an operation was indeed a complete compendium of every possible human virtue provided by the composite seed of the best available among them. They thought their respective qualities would combine from their Circle of Creation into a common Seed which would produce a Being better than any of them. Physically of course, we realize now this would be impossible, but who shall say what the Inner intentions accomplished?

If the rite succeeded, and in course of time a male child was born, he became the Divine King of those people, having come like Melchizedek to them in a magical fashion. His mission was to bring through the message or intelligence of Inner Divinity to those who had invoked him, demonstrate to them on earth the Divinity they aspired to in Heaven, and finally die for them as a ritual sacrifice on their behalf so that Divine Life would reach them all and raise them even a little nearer their Origin and End. Concreation had been accomplished. Conditions had been fulfilled. No man had touched the Maid, the descent of the King came from the unknown, and he went to the unknowable. A God had incarnated, done His Will on earth, and departed to Heaven. The cycle would be repeated when conditions were propitious.

It is easy for us today amid modern conditions to despise or be disgusted by such primitive practice, but it fulfilled a need which nothing else could supply, and provided sufficient contacts with Inner Reality to bring through the basics of all our most sophisticated philosophies and religions. Ultimately the practice became unnecessary, and once its dangers were realized, suppressed altogether by reputable Mystery Schools except for very rare contingencies indeed. The dangers came from the fact that the Rite was no more reliable than the ritualists themselves. Unless the workers were absolutely 'pure of heart', and quite 'true within their Circle', an imperfect God-vehicle resulted. Moreover if their intentions were evil, a very nasty type of Entity could incarnate. The Rite lent itself to Ill as well as Good. Nevertheless the general pattern is with us even today.

The horn has become a rich Cup, which is still held out to be charged with water representing seed, and wine symbolizing blood. That Cup is yet upheld while imploring the incarnation of the God. Mysteries change method, but the underlying pattern is Eternal.

It is tempting to make many speculations about the unknown details of the ancient God-Incarnation Rite. What happened if a girl resulted? Was she sacrificed? Unlikely, because the primitives did not usually consider a female Victim a valid one. It is more probable the child was dedicated to the Temple for some purpose, perhaps becoming a Maid in her own time, and much later an Old Woman, eventually dying a natural death. To 'die for the People' was a male prerogative at a very early date, and it is difficult for us now to appreciate what an exclusive honour this sacrifice was. Ritual methods of death-dealing varied with century and local custom. Victims were sometimes killed outright, by stabbing or strangling, and sometimes bound to trees in forests and left alone to die of starvation, exposure, wild beasts, or some other 'natural' cause.

The 'scapegoat' was a relic of this custom. One way or another, the Victim must die for his tribe or race, although it was never considered that he had died as other mortals did. He *never* 'died', but 'went to the Gods', 'ascended to Heaven' or any other euphemism for a state of immortality. No word suggesting death was permissible in connection with the Victim's departure from the human world. Nothing Divine can possibly *die,* and therefore the Victim on Earth became the Victor in Heaven. The pattern for mankind to follow became established through Inner and Outer levels of Life, and it is exactly this pattern of procedure which is practised in the Holy Mysteries in modern and evolved equivalents of ancient attempts among Mankind to fulfil the functions of a Divine agency.

The Cosmic Circle-Cross

Each Initiate is responsible for producing the Pattern in themselves, and for playing their own part in it among the Group to which they personally belong, so that ultimately the Whole of Existence will become what It was meant to be at Its inception, and our Pattern of Perfection thus 'come true' at all Life-levels.

There is no particular secret about the Pattern itself, which is the Cosmic Circle-Cross, and the secrets of the Holy Mysteries are simply concerned with discovering the best ways and means of making that Pattern with spiritual energies which will extend throughout Entire Existence and work the Ultimate Will of the Original Word. Initiates of the Mysteries are perfectly well aware of this Universal Truth, and the divergencies among them are mostly due to differences of opinions on methods, terms of reference, systems of symbology, and practical procedures. Since some kind of system and order must be observed throughout any intelligent form of study, we shall confine ourselves to the general outlines of prevailing Western Traditions of the Holy Mysteries.

An Initiate of these Mysteries 'sets up his Circle' within himself for a 'Divine Incarnation' of the Holy Spirit of Life into Which he will Become. The 'God-Fathers' around the perimeter are the Energy-categories or God-Aspects from whence power will proceed to produce the Seed of Light which should result in the arising (or birth) of the new Sun (Son) of God which the Initiate must become. The Maid-Mother in whom this Seed is implanted, is the Initiate's Inner innocence, and Acceptance of Divine Intention in complete confidence and true Love. The Old Woman is the Initiate's devoted skill and experienced Understanding applied to the birth-process of his Becoming. All the Rituals, customs and practices of the Mystery are dramatizations and projections of this Pattern into the various Life-levels.

There are so many ways of producing this same Pattern. We can think of it as a Zodiac-belt of differentiated Energies or Signs combining in a common centre to produce Solar Power. Again we might conceive it as a Round Table concentrating the energies of the Knights centrally to invoke the Graal of Light. With a touch of compassion we might even see it in a few people crouched around their Firemaker making desperate attempts to invoke the only Power which might save them from annihilation by cold, starvation, and savage predators. We can certainly find the Pattern in the Rites of the Mysteries around the Altar of Light served by the Sword, Rod, Cup and Shield linked with the Cord. Where there is Cosmos, there is a Circle-Cross of some kind. It was anciently symbolized by a ball of string or wool, which is a three-dimensional Circle-Cross of Cosmic deosil Right Hand Pattern. These are often found on Celtic Crosses, in combination with the intricate Knots and layouts which told their stories to the initiated. Much of this silent language may still be learned from string-games and cord-practices.

Many of the Mystery Naming principles are to be found in the simple Word-games played by intelligent children. Counting-outs, acrostics, 'Magic Squares', and similar devices of coding consciousness are forms of convenience common to Mystery practice. Anything at all which helps to 'bring through' and build up the Inner Telesmic Entity into an actuality is permissible. The Initiates may see themselves as being surrounded by God-Aspects, each of which donates a single letter of the Mystery-Name to contain their own particular quality, so that its entirety is an epitome of them all. They may do this so long as they relate with Inner and Outer reality by means of their Magical Name associated with the Perfect Pattern of their basic beliefs, this is what really matters. There are so many ways of doing this, that everyone should find their own most convenient method, but an example might not be out of place.

Seven-point Plan of Perfection

Suppose we take the simplest possible method of representing ourselves spatially positioned at the centre of a Cosmos with four Quarters, Divinity above and Humanity below. This provides a seven-point Plant of Perfection with a central Solar nucleus out of which the Seed-self will develop, and six main reference points which may be aligned with specific Cosmic qualities capable of supplying the energies for the Entity-emergence of the Initiate's new Magical Identity. If we ask each point to contribute a letter of the Name for this Image, this will provide us with a six-letter code-name plus the 'Identity initial' at centre. Assuming we have aligned the Quarter-points with Concepts representing the broad principles of Life, Light, Love, and Law, while the top and bottom Pivots are Being and Doing respectively, we may designate a letter to each in keeping with its quality. We might say for instance:

A for my Aspiration in BEING
R for my Rectitude of LIFE
I for my Illumination by LIGHT
S for my Sincerity in LOVE
E for my Experience of LAW
R for my Resolution in DOING.

This gives us the code-name of 'ARISER' with its overall idea of Evolvement from basic to highest matters, and every letter is tied by practical links of consciousness to Concepts of Divinity approachable by human beings. It is, of course, a term descriptive of a being's behaviour, and so another letter will be needed for the central nuclear point indicating the essential nature of the being itself. If in this case we termed such a nature 'Benevolent' ('Good-willing'), then we have an initial 'B' as a symbol for the Seed-self, which amounts to a totality of 'Benevolent Ariser' or any equivalent combination of ideas. If this were a genuine Mystery Name, its owner would be known as 'Frater' (or Soror) 'B. A.'.

Whatever method of 'Magical Naming' is used, the Name chosen as a vehicle must be an adequate one for exchanges of energy between its Inner Sponsors and the Emerging Entity into which the Initiate seeks to identify himself. How do we identify ourselves with our ordinary names anyway? Only by association with them in the material world, and hearing them so often from others as well as writing them ourselves. The same is true of our spiritual Names, but this is exactly why they are kept secret from other mortals, only referred to obliquely by initials when strictly necessary, given in very soft whispers if essential, and all the rest of the seemingly pointless precautions. Inwardly and spiritually, those Names are given clearly and definitely enough. They are for plain use *only* on spiritual Life-levels by those reliable Entities connected with the Initiate's Mystery, so that nothing will find its unwanted way into the Identity being built up, and all energies directed thereto will come from and through these Beings and their appointed agents alone.

When the Magical Name is definitely chosen, and implanted as deeply in the Initiate's being as the Seed in the Maid-Mother, the process of Inner birth through this Image begins. This is why it should be done in some way calculated to reach the Matrix-level of the Initiate's being. Dramatic rituals are the traditional means of accomplishing this, and every System and Mystery has its own ideas on the subject. There is usually some kind of a death-rebirth mime, since the new being must perforce supersede an old discarded one, an 'identification parade' of this being, and a good deal of praying and hoping for a favourable outcome. The one thing that really matters is that genuine and effective contact must be established between the Initiate's true Inner identity, the Name, and those Inner Ones of whose energies it will derive and develop.

Some Systems (like the Christian) attempt this through shock. The church baptisms of modern times are a pathetic ghost of their original vigour and impact. Once the candidate was told to 'die to sin and the world', then forced under the water until nearly drowned, and finally hauled out with a triumphant shout of acclaim from spectators, and the utterance into his ear of his new 'Name in Christ' by the officiant, which only the Initiate was supposed to hear. It was certainly a memorable and effective experience. The Eastern Church still plunges infants bodily into the water while naming them, but unpleasant shocks are likely to cause unpleasant reactions, and most of the Mystery Schools prefer other methods of naming Initiates even though associative shock is undoubtedly the most direct and straightforward procedure of linking Inner and Outer life.

Even one sufficiently effective shock at the right point of anyone's being may alter them in some way for life of both body and soul. Nowadays we call this a 'traumatic experience', and most people realize well enough what it amounts to. It was the aim of the Mysteries to apply such an impact to an Initiate in the most favourable manner to ensure future spiritual growth into a perfected state of being. Moreover, this impact had to be of sufficient intensity to keep the Initiates 'on course' despite any other influence which might have seriously deflected them from it. All kinds of ceremonies were, and are still being devised for precisely this purpose, but no rite can possibly be more than a means for concerting and directing the energies of those concerned with it. If these are 'on contact' and operating freely, then the rite is useful—not otherwise.

The Naming Ritual

There are so many Mystery ways of Naming, that a choice depends entirely on the preferences of those involved. Invariably however, the candidate should be prepared for the event by a prolonged period of study, devotion, and practice. Some Schools insist on a 'fasting and abstinence' period immediately before the ceremony so as to induce a stress-state of anticipation which is likely to favour the acceptance of the impact to be delivered. This is a valuable thing to do, providing there is no danger of the impact being taken the wrong way, or being inadequate to release the tensed energy along the right paths. It would be disastrous for example, to prepare a candidate very properly over many months or years of effort until they had reached their peak-point of readiness for Initiation, and then subject them to such a futile and inept ceremony that their shock was one of disgust and disappointment. True this would constitute an intiation of its own kind if reacted to rightly, but that would depend entirely on the nature of the Initiate, and a good outcome of such a misfortune should never be taken for granted. For that reason, most Mystery initiations proceed along somewhat cautious lines calculated around average expectations.

Sometimes the Initiate is induced into full or semi-hypnotic condition, and the new Name-identity implanted deeply that way. Every conceivable psychological device is used to bring about a realization of Inner Divinity and a sense of identification with It through the magic of a Name. Some methods are crude, and others refined. The candidate might be whirled around a circle dance to a crescendo of chanting which stops abruptly, and out of the sudden silence the Name is echoed. Again the Name might be communicated a letter at a time directly into the candidate's ears by the two sponsors, then uttered in unison by the whole Group present, who 'proclaim it aloud' for the first and only time.

The Elements themselves are occasionally brought into use, and the candidate made to hear his Magical Name in rushing Air, see it in letters of living Fire, taste it in impregnated Water, and feel it solidly in forms of Earth. At one time it was a custom to solemnly 'slay' the candidate in the person of his 'old' self, place him in some representation of a tomb, and then 'call him to Light' in the character of his 'new' self by his Magical Name.

All possible forms of the 'Death to the worst and birth to the Best' drama have been incorporated in the Initiation Rites of the various Mysteries. Their common aim, of course, is the conscious linkage of the Initiate with the Being of his own Becoming through the Telesmic Image born between both as an Energy-exchanger of Entities. The TI is thus a symbolic blending of Divinity's idea about one particular human individual, and that individual's ideas of Divinity in relation to themselves. The critical question to the candidate is: 'What kind of a soul would you really like God to think you were?'

This is indeed the Magnum Opus of every Initiate in the Holy Mysteries of Light. To become what they would be if they were a God thinking a man into Existence, rather than a mere mortal trying to think God out of Existence. Such is the whole purpose of Initiation altogether, a successful synthesis of Divine and Human energies through a concreated Entity. The entire structure of Initiation in the Holy Mysteries depends on this central Concept. Otherwise it would have no more meaning than entertainment value or intellectual amusement. A genuine Initiate of the Holy Mysteries is expected to 'Incarnate the God' into themselves, 'Sacrifice (or crucify on the Circle-Cross) the Self which must die', and so 'Ascend to Heaven the Divine Right-Hand Way'.

It may be tempting to align this pattern exclusively with the Christian Mysteries, but it is a universal one of which the Christ-Concept is a prominent and popular example. The Story of Existence, in which a Creative Divinity whose creatures fail (Fall) to develop exactly as intended, and therefore Divinity must involve Itself (Incarnate) in them to restore the Pattern of Perfection (Redeem via the Cosmic Cross) and ensure Divine Rightness of everything (Sit at the Right hand, etc.) is as old as Existence Itself. The Christian Faith simply presents this scheme in its own way. Since there is but a single Pattern anyway, it can only be displayed according to the beliefs and abilities of those trying to follow it.

The Story of Initiation throughout the Holy Mysteries perforce must be told along the same lines. The sole distinction between an Initiate and a non-Initiate is that the former becomes a conscious participator in the Plan of Perfection as a

Worker of Will, and the latter is either unwilling or unready to do this. The progress-plan of Initiation is simple enough in broad outline. First, the candidate realizes (accepts) his own inadequate human status and determines to alter this in accordance with some set of beliefs. To this end he must identify with Energies capable of effecting such a change, or 'Incarnate the God'. Then what is wrong in him must be righted or rearranged into the desired Pattern, or the 'Cross-Sacrifice' be made in his Circle so as to construct Cosmos. His human fallibilities must 'die' or disappear so that Divine abilities may 'live' or emerge into existence. Only to the degree (or Grade of Initiation) whereat this actually occurs will he 'Ascend to Heaven' or rise upon the Right Hand Path. This is what Initiation means. All the ceremonies, customs, 'tricks of the trade', and other incidentals connected with it through the various Mysteries, are but different people's ways and means of applying themselves to a universal task. Perhaps it might be advisable to examine some of the motives and ideas associated with Mystery workings, and see if they afford any especial advantages to Initiates attempting to achieve a purpose which should be common to the whole of mankind.

CHAPTER III

TECHNIQUES FOR APPROACHING THE WISDOM OF THE MYSTERIES

'And the Word was made flesh and dwelt among us' is the point of the Christian Creed where a momentary pause and solemn genuflection marks an acknowledgement of a Cosmo-creation far beyond the range of mortal minds to grasp as an actuality. Yet it is a simple statement in itself. It indicates very neatly and succinctly the working of a Consciousness that 'thinks true', in the sense that It creates whatsoever It Wills as Entities of Its own energies within Itself. Again we realize: 'All things exist in Me, Not I in them.'

If we consider these laws, we shall find they also apply to ourselves. What we think of objectifies within us. It may never materialize as a physical happening (which is usually fortunate for us), or it may manifest to some degree as a projection into physical dimensions. The relative time-factor is one which is difficult to appreciate. What we think of 'instantly' may take anything up to centuries to materialize (as in the case of flight), or centuries of experience may have been necessary in order to produce a single Concept of Consciousness (as with $E = MC_2$ formula). If it is true to say that the Word becomes Flesh (Spirit materializes), it should be continued cyclically by saying that Flesh becomes the Word (or Matter spiritualizes). The Word, Name, or Concept is the common denominator to both Inner and Outer actualities.

This is the Ultimate of Truth with which the Mysteries are concerned. That which Is What Is Uttered, neither more nor less than the Centre and Circumference of Itself. The I AM WHAT I WILL. Everything of the Holy Mysteries is relative to THAT. As Divine Consciousness 'Utters the Word', or 'Moves upon the Water', or expresses Its energies within Itself in any way, Existence IS.

If such eventuation occurred at human level, whatever we conceived with our consciousness would materialize very solidly around us, and we should 'get what we asked for' in literal lumps, which would be Magic at maximum manifestation. The difficulties and disasters of such a theoretical situation should be obvious. Too many Gods operating against each other and their own existence in a common condition of Creation would rapidly destroy it or create 'instant insanity'.

This was exactly the danger referred to in Genesis when apprehension over the possibility of humans becoming 'as Gods' was realized. There obviously had to be a 'One Creator—one Cosmos' rule if spiritual survival was to be a practicability within the Plan of Perfection. The 'Word-Will' of the One Inclusive Entity had to be con-formated with by all subsidiary entities within It if such Perfection was to be an actuality through every extension of Existence. This is what is meant by the well-known but much misunderstood summation of : 'DO WHAT THOU WILT' used in the Mystery Rites. All Entities working individual wills of the Will from which they emanated. More simply : 'THY Will—not mine—be DONE.'

Will-Words

As we know, such a unification of wills within Will is not a universal phenomenon in our state of Existence. It is not even universal throughout a single human being. The work of Initiation in the Mysteries concerns exactly this process of co-relating Inner energies according to Pattern, whether these operate in one solitary human or a whole Cosmos of Life. An Initiate is expected to live so that what is Willed within him Works as his Word is 'made flesh' or manifests. A real 'Adept of the Good Word' (Baal Shem Tov) would thus 'speak true' in the sense that what 'uttered' would eventuate as (though not necessarily *when*) he 'uttered' it.

Perhaps it is noteworthy that Jesus simply made short statements of Will to accomplish the various 'miracles' attributed to Him. He merely said : 'Let so and so be thus and thus' in effect, and the Work was done as the Will intended through the Word. Such 'miracles' are not nearly so uncommon as might be supposed. To state a will which is subsequently fulfilled by events is a frequent human happening. In the case of an ordinary mortal, this may take years, and work out rather differently than originally meant. The Will-Words of a developed Initiate tend to 'come truer' than that, because they accord with the Inner Will which controls energies beyond the range or reach of average humanity. If an Adept 'uttered' the same Intention, the effects of released energy might seem very remarkable or miraculous to the uninitiated, because of unexpected short circuits in the time-factor or unlikely changes of condition.

A sense of the miraculous is really a sense of surprise and wonder. If the events were fully anticipated and prepared for, there would be no miracle. No Adept ever worked a miracle, nor does Divinity. The miracle is only our lack of understanding concerning the operation of Inner Energies connected with Consciousness as directed through Will-Words.

Old legends of 'Words of Power' which seemed to accomplish Magical effects are based on truth. The secret lay in the focus of Force into the Form of a 'Word' with sufficient accuracy and intensity to make that 'Word' come true or manifest as uttered. This depended not so much on what was uttered, but on who uttered it in what way. An ordinary person might scream 'Magic Words' till their heads fell off, and nothing would happen except noise. A highly trained Initiate 'uttering' the same words with possibly no physical sounds discernible to human ears would cause considerable effects of consciousness. All words are Magic when energized from Within by Awareness directed with Will. The training, exercises, and Rites used in the Mysteries are concerned with methods of extending and deepening Awareness while increasing abilities of Will working within a framework of Wisdom. So is 'The Word of the Mysteries' spoken.

It would be a mistake to assume that such 'Words' were simply combinations of alphabetical sonics. Those indeed may be Symbols of the real Inner Words which are actually associations of pure conscious energies concentrated into Patterns of Power, which may be expressed otherwise than sonically. A 'Word' of any sort is a convenience for condensing and containing these energies of consciousness, and as such, a 'Word' may literally be anything at all. Magic Words may be sensory vehicles of sound, scent, solids, chemical combinations, or more subtle kinds of containers altogether.

As a rule, a Word is a vehicle formed on any Life-level for the containing and expression of energies from other levels. If we accept the conventional classification of Life into the four categories of Spirit, Soul, Mind, and Body, we can see that a 'Soul-Word' would bring both the energies of Spirit towards Mind, and those of Mind towards Spirit. Direction of force-flow depends on the pressure-point from which Will is applied. If again, we follow the 'Word becoming Flesh' through these levels, we shall find it is Originated in Spirit, Created in Soul, Formated in Mind, and Expressed in Body. Such are the 'Four Worlds' of the Qabalist, which, of course, return cyclically back to the point of Origin to complete the Circle of Cosmos.

At the commencement of Initiation therefore, the candidate is made somehow to understand that Consciousness is the 'raw material' of Life, or basic Energy of Being, and out of it may be constructed WHAT IS WILLED. The rest of Initiation is connected with techniques of putting this Primal Principle into Practice, and the true Degrees of Initiation are those to which such Practice becomes Possible. Every Initiate, from the Entrant to the Adept becomes capable of the same abilities and skills with vastly differing effects owing to personal limits and degrees of development. Nevertheless the fraternity of common dedication to their Cause provides a bond between them all, and even the most ineffectual efforts are worth-while if done in a spirit of genuine devotion and sincerity.

How is anyone to take hold of some consciousness and make something out of it? One might as well ask how to take a sexual impulse and make a baby from it. The answer would be the same: a process of reciprocal energy conversion between Entities of consciousness which results in an independent Concept to continue the creative cycle of its own initiative. A male and female, properly applied to each other, produce another of their species whether they are human animals or other types of polarized Beings. The process need not be physical, and it is such Inner (or Mystical) acts of Conception which constitute a vital fundamental of Mystery practice, or what might perhaps be termed 'spiritual sex'. In no sense whatever a mere fantasy substitute for its physical extension, but an Inner experience of energy-exchange in terms of reality beyond doubt by those that have known it, and beyond comprehension by those that have not. Faith, Hope and Love provide the only bridge between the two states of fulfilled and unfulfilled awareness.

The whole question of sexual activity on levels of spiritual consciousness is an exceptionally difficult one to deal with. So much wrong-doing, insanity, unbalance, and downright disaster is liable to be caused through misuse and misunderstanding about this matter, that many Mystery Schools shroud the subject with extreme secrecy and prohibitions. Others are open on the topic itself, but advocate no form of action. Others again, of less reputable moral standards, initiate their members into circles where unusual sexual behaviour produces psychic stresses scarcely comparable with the pure powers of energy-polarities in sublimer states of being. Finally the most degraded types of practitioner pervert the Energy of Existence to the worst possible usage with the most evil intentions. It is all a matter of method and motivation, whether good or ill. Furthermore we cannot avoid the issue. Sex and spirituality are inseparable from each other. A Concept of Consciousness is a sexual act in non-physical terms. However sex is disguised by symbolism, it remains what it is—the Divine Dichotomy of Differentiation. We may neither ignore nor evade it, but must do with it WHAT IS WILLED according to the Way in which we interpret the Word Within us.

The fundamental principles involved are that entities in a state of polarized existence are perforce of this circumstance obliged to engage in some type of sexual activity. Only those in whom polarities are perfectly balanced, or who—like the angels —have no predominant polarity whatever, are exempt from dealing with other beings from a sexual bias. A male on any life-level deals with all else from a male point, and a female like-wise from hers. Degrees of intimacy vary from the deepest, at which conception of another entity occurs, to the slightest, where very mild mental or the lightest emotional energies are all that interchange. The question connected with the Mysteries is precisely how human beings should relate themselves as sexed entities with Divinity.

Open religions usually proclaim a Father-Mother Divine Aspect, with which the devotee may form a most worthwhile type of relationship. A hint is provided of the more intimate degrees to which the Mysteries penetrated, by celibate priests and virgin nuns, the latter being actually referred to as 'Brides of Christ', and formally married to Divinity with a silver wedding ring at their ceremony of profession. All this indicates that an average human being deals with Divinity as a purely beneficient and far superior Power, while Initiates of the Mysteries seek far closer contact than that, rising up a scale of intimacy until Union itself is reached (I and my Father are One). In every Mystery, methods and techniques of accomplishing this Attainment are taught and practised. They start on small scales, and once mastered, are supposed to lead the Initiate higher and higher towards God-goal.

Spiritual Conception

There are two main ways of relating with others so that an effective outcome results from the relationship. The first is conceptually, whereby a fresh entity or energy emerges in its own right, and the second is constructionally, in which already formated energies are re-combined in variations of their previous patterns. Mankind does most of his conceiving on physical levels and little enough on spiritual ones in the way of construction. The Mysteries strive to discover how this lack of balance may be corrected, and a beneficial result ensue for all concerned, human and otherwise. In principle, male humans are taught to connect themseves with Divine Feminine Aspects for conceptual purposes, and Divine Masculine Aspects for constructional ones. As below, so above. Thus Cosmos eventuates.

Inwardly, sex is a matter of polarized energy, and it is possible for pure Being to be either or both at Will. We can do this ourselves as humans to a small degree and also with only small success at this stage of our evolution. There is no real reason why entities living in sex-polarized bodies should not relate with each other from opposite polarities on Inner levels for conceptual or constructional Cosmic purposes, providing such relationships are properly balanced.

Suppose, for example, two inhabitants of male bodies intended to form a conceptual relationship with each other for Cosmic reasons. One would obviously have to adopt feminine Inner polarity, accept the 'seeds of consciousness' projected by masculine methods from the other, develop or gestate these Inwardly, then allow them to be 'born' as an outcome of the relationship. If, however, the energy were diverted into wrong physical channels, it would produce no more than an undesirable homosexual result, which is always a risk in these instances. Everything depends on keeping the energies in their proper paths, working between the Life-levels at the right points only.

Another, and less hazardous way for two or more males to work, would be for them to 'worship a Goddess', or project their energies towards a Feminine Divine Aspect for processing Inwardly. This is the broad traditional system. Females of course would relate themselves with a Male Divine Aspect, eventually 'incarnating the Word' within them, and bringing it to birth as a Concept of Consciousness. In fact, the whole idea of having uni-sexual religious or mystical communities was supposed to work along such lines. The mortal males were intended to devote themselves conceptually with the Fertile Female Divine Aspects and constructionally with others. Female communities worked with the Masculine Fertile Divine Aspects, and eventually 'gave birth' to the spiritual results of the contact. The men, as it were, asked the questions, and the females found the answers via Divine Consciousness. So was contact between Divinity and Humanity meant to develop and increase along spiritual lines until mankind grew beyond incarnating. Theory and practice seem to have grown very much apart from each other in this scheme.

Individual Initiates were taught that they were bi-sexual beings of opposite polarities Inwardly and Outwardly. External Male had its diametric counterbalance of Internal Female, and vice versa. Once the balance of energies became correctly aligned, the Cosmic Circle-Cross was formed. The Mysteries are full of such clues and suggestions. There are the 'Fairy-wives', the 'Spirit Guide' of an opposite sex to the attached mortal, even the Evil Ones produce an Incubus or Succubus on demand. Mythology has endless examples of sexual exchanges between mortals and non-mortals. Many indeed of the 'deadly secrets' imparted under stringent conditions were entirely sexual ones dealing with methods, real or imaginary, for exchanging sex-energy between Matter and Spirit.

At bottom level these methods are, to say the least of it, crude. At top level they are barely recognizable as sexual activity at all, but nevertheless there is an unbroken link of polarized, or sexed energy leading from one end of Existence to the other in a complete Circle. Both the designs of the Caduceus in the Hermetic

Mysteries, and the Tree of Life in the Qabalistic ones, are Master-Glyphs for such Power-Paths.

The Fire of Love

The highest and noblest spiritual energies we might possibly imagine are sexual in nature if polarized, and those who enter the Mysteries discover this one way or another as they attempt to lift the veils between themselves and naked Truth. The famous 'Seven Veils' dance was a practical mime intended to induce such a realization through sheer physical passion. Sexual and spiritual ecstasy are phenomena of the same power separated only by degree and life-level. Any average human is capable of the first, but only highly evolved and trained souls are capable of the second in its sublime state. It is the Fire of Love which blasts the unprepared just as surely as it illuminates those who hold their balance between the Pillars of Purity and Passion upon which rests the Temple of Life. Possibly the most literal truth symbolized in human words is that of 'God is Love'. Fulfilment in and with the Divine Lover is the *ne plus ultra* of the Blessed Mysteries, whether this Ultimate is considered as Love, Light, Energy, or simply I AM. From this Union should be born the new Being of I AM THAT, or a mutual Divine and Human discovery of ITSELF.

The greatest necessity of a living soul is Love. To be 'in love with Love' is a supreme experience, and the supreme experience of the Mysteries is to convert the entire sex-energy with which humans relate themselves together, into a love experience with Divinity in the truest possible sense. This is indicated by the old injunction to 'Love thy God with all thy heart and soul, etc.,' as 'thy neighbour', or That which is closest and most intimate to the essential Being of the individual. This again signifies the most personal possible relationship between human and Divine Entities. Nobody can fall in love with ephemeral emptiness, but only with whom or what approximates their own Inner Reality most nearly. The 'Divine Neighbour' must be *as* (or become) the Self. Cut to essentials, this means very definitely that Divinity must be far closer to any soul than other humans could contact by themselves. Divinity and Humanity being what they are, some kind of 'half way approach' is needed, and this is what the

Mysteries seek by using Images, Symbols, Aspects, Personifications, or other focal points for the Forces of Life both Human and Divine.

Through these Telesmics, the 'Real Presence' of the Powers behind them must be invoked with even greater intensity and actuality than might be found through contact with physical personages or objects. When the Symbols 'come alive', Magic works. Practical ways and means of making this 'coming alive' possible have been experimented with and taught as 'secrets' in the Mystery Schools for centuries. All of them depend on control of Consciousness in accordance with Will in order to adapt Energy for specific purposes, and as such are disciplines and acts of auto-determination, whether they are motivated by good or evil intentions.

With such ends in view, practitioners in the Mysteries have been building up methods of relationship with Inner Entities for a long time in a curious variety of ways. In olden times all forms of sexual intimacies over a wide range of bizarre possibilities were used in quite sincere attempts to relate with Divinity or extraterrestrial Intelligences. Intercourse took place under every imaginable condition in the hope of making contact with suprahuman Life and Consciousness. Arguing that at moments of sexual climax the human state of awareness was at zenith from its 'normal' position, practitioners took themselves to that point and then tried 'jumping off' as it were into Inner Dimensions. Sometimes this appeared to produce results of a kind, but rarely enough of any great value, which is scarcely surprising.

In the case of straightforward 'Temple prostitution', the 'priestess' was supposed to be the medium of the Goddess or Divine Fertile Feminine Aspect. Male devotees were directed to have intercourse with her as an act of worship due to the Incarnate Entity controlling the human female. Their awareness was not to be concerned with merely satisfying a bodily lust, but with love of the Goddess Herself and whatever they expected of Her as an outcome. Needless to say, this practice degenerated rapidly into sheer commercialism and selfish greed. So did homosexual intercourse with the castrated male priests who were in theory vehicles of the God, at least while they were under 'Divine influence' sometimes simulated with stimulant drugs.

Weird forms of sex relationships were tried with all kinds of

inanimate objects which became 'talismans' linked with supernatural life. Possibly the commonest was the broomstick, or
'horse-stick' (which still remains as the 'hobby-horse') for inter-
crural stimulation as a phallic symbol. Both sexes used it. Statues
of near life-size with artificial genitalia were not uncommon.
The 'God-Spirit' was supposed to inhabit the image during a
human sex-act with it. Even stones with convenient holes were
ceremonially used by males, and practically anything of a
phallic nature including live serpents or wriggling fish used by
females. Talismans were consecrated and blessings given by
anointment with the body fluids of blood, tears, sweat, and
semen. Curses were applied with urine, excreta, and menstrual
blood. Spittle might be used in cursing or blessing. Some at least,
if not indeed all and many more of such unpleasant practices are
still in circulation.

Primitive brain-washing

Revolting as they may be to most modern Initiates, we cannot afford to ignore the instincts which prompted their practice,
for there are Keys to Consciousness to be found there which will
reward examination. Experience of life showed that a number of
main factors may be applied to a human being in order to force
awareness far beyond its ordinary limitations in a well-balanced
sensorium. If sufficient stress might be brought to bear at the
right point, proportional results in terms of reaction were proved
to be obtainable. These stresses can be broadly classified as those
of Sex, Starvation, Sleeplessness, Sadism, plus the drug induced
states of either Stimulation or Sedation. All these are made use
of in modern brain-washing techniques, and still affect consciousness along the same proven lines, except that where they were
once largely matters of trial and error, they can now be calculated with considerable precision in order to obtain predictable
results. The erstwhile secrets of many mysteries are textbook
affairs today, but Consciousness is a much deeper Ocean than
any human intelligence has yet explored, and we are barely on
the threshold of Inner Space after all these millenniums of
approach.

Using the skill of applying correct stresses, physically or mentally, mystics learned how to manoeuvre the energies of Con-

sciousness in themselves and others according to will. First of all such stresses were brought to bear on physical levels. Gyratory dances, 'watching and waking', painful inflictions such as flagellation, staring into bright lights, deprivation of food, threats and emotional frights, anything at all to affect bodily chemistry until a state of auto-intoxication induced semi-delirium or visionary effects was and is made full use of. We should remember that in the case of very primitive people with a strictly limited emotional range, drastic methods were about the only ones that worked to any degree. They may sound horrific in our day and age, but ours will seem equally horrible in the distant future.

The basic principles of affecting consciousness by such means are not unlike those of the 'Eat me—Drink me' process in *Alice in Wonderland*. Pressurized polarities, or the good old 'stick and carrot' system. For example, pain might be applied until the recipient was on the very point of unconsciousness, and then restoratives or stimulants counter-applied to sharpen consciousness at that stage to its greatest degree. This was in fact the art of torture used in modified form to obtain contacts of consciousness otherwise unavailable to an ordinary person. In the case of torture, of course, it was used purely to obtain 'confessions' of little value for accuracy, but one rather strange fact emerged after much practice. Most of the babblings from the victim were so much rubbish, but scattered among them here and there were actual germs of truth which they themselves had no knowledge of in their normal state of being. Somehow, under extremities of stress, their awareness had opened up in a different condition of consciousness and 'brought through' information of positive use to the enquirers.

Nowadays we should say that stress-contact had been established with the Universal Mind, and specialized knowledge extraneous to the subject obtained. Eventually, victims were tortured for prolonged periods not so much for the sake of what they knew previously (which might be little enough) but for what their unhappy overstressed consciousness, striving to escape from those terrible conditions, might reach and reveal. Literally, they had been squeezed until the pips squeaked.

The assessment and evaluation of information obtained in such a way is a highly technical business calling for considerable experience and training in the art. Modern techniques have shown that physical torture stresses are not only most unreliable, but cumbersome and unnecessary. Far better results are had by purely mental and emotional stress-procedures coupled with careful dosage by suitable drugs. Nevertheless most results got by such methods are of little or no real spiritual value whatever.

What actual benefits to themselves or other humans were ever achieved by visionaries, saintly or otherwise, who made their Inner contacts through self-tortures and abasements? Conversely, what revelations have resulted from orgiastic excesses and the like procedures? Nothing that has altered the progress of humanity to any great extent one way or another. So little has come from so very much effort, so much unhappiness, and so much stupidity.

Although the 'spectacular stuff' of the Mysteries derives from modifications of stress-induced states of awareness, the material of really deep spiritual value which affects both individual and collective humanity in the most definite way comes through rather different portals of perception than those available on the 'lower levels' of Inner Life. Very few humans indeed are sufficiently developed as souls to have access in their own rights to such Spheres as a natural state of being. Even so-called 'high' Initiates only know those Spheres by simulated states within themselves. A comparison may perhaps be made with either watching a programme on a screen or being actually in the studio taking part in it. The Controllers of Consciousness beyond human range are not only able to present what programme they will, turn it on or off as they deem necessary, but are also rather particular about whom they allow to participate directly in their productions. Our relationship with them either through the Mysteries or otherwise, is an indirect one via whatever media we are able to use for that purpose. All that any of the Mysteries do is to provide such media from past experience, present practice, and experimental issues for the future.

Indicator of Awareness

Anciently, humanity sought its God-Images in the Elements, natural phenomena, and whatever manifested energies affected human life within the comprehension of human consciousness. Man looked for God outside himself. As experience brought wisdom, Man began to seek Divinity inside himself. Now, the Eternal Quest is leading along the sword-edge Bridge between these two states into conditions of consciousness which are so new to us that we are relatively like unborn children trying to guess what life might be outside the familiar womb. Again we have the principle of Inner stress against Outer stress, and our indicator of awareness squeezed as it were between them until it reaches strange heights in purely spiritual states of existence. Here we are trying to hold a balance between the extremities of introverted mysticism and extraverted materialism, and so discover a relative Reality inclusive of both. In effect we are looking for the spiritual content of all physical phenomena, and the physical equivalent of all spiritual principles. The interlaced triangles of the Hexagram illustrate this process adequately.

Once more our 'beginning—end—middle' problem confronts us as it always will. This time it is Consciousness on Divine levels at one end and Human at the other, both needing a middle or medium for their mutual interaction. Most Mystery Schools classify the states of intermediary consciousness in various ways such as 'Archangels', 'Angels', 'Spirits', and so forth. All are agreed on some kind of a Hierarchy reaching between God and Man, though much disagreement seems to arise on other issues concerning them, such as whether or not an individual human has the ability to ignore Inner Hierarchies altogether and deal directly with Divinity outright. Such claims would certainly seem amazingly presumptuous to say the least.

In general, the average Mystery System takes it for granted that a natural and normal progressional Path leads Lightward from human to Divine Life, and tries to plan a step-by-step ascent thereon. Those steps may be fast or slow, long or short, sometimes running, sometimes crawling or even stopping altogether, according to the individual ascendant, but at least they are progressions, and not wild leaps into darkness or serious falls beyond recovery for prolonged periods. Surely steady rising is better than precipitate plunging about.

The whole 'work' in the Mysteries consists of intentional operations with energies of consciousness. This is why training commences with exercises of creative imagination which by drawing materials from the Outer Cosmos to create an Inner one, eventuates an Existence independently and inclusively of both, which is the 'becoming' of Human and Divine Union. Indeed, the Mysteries begin or 'initiate' from such behaviour (for so it is), and continue through its modifications around an evolutionary spiral which is aimed at ultimate perfection. The dual means by which polarized pressure is applied to produce the required outcome along this Light-line are those of Meditation Inwardly, and what is called Magic Outwardly. Thought and Action. Being and Doing. Meaning and Making. Reason and Rite. All Mystery Temples rest on two Pillars with an Entry between them. This is a Universal design, and the Third Pillar forms the top of the triangle at the point of the Sanctuary ahead. We become this Middle Pillar ourselves when we have grown the measurement of its base to apex, or from Earth to Heaven.

In each Mystery Temple should be a complete set of Symbols out of which the entered Initiate must be able to build his entire Inner Cosmos according to the Master-Plan provided by whatever Universal Sign is adopted. Every Rite practised must be constructed from behaviour-patterns intended to achieve this intended outcome. The overall idea has to be: 'If we believe as so and so (the Symbols) and act like thus and thus (the Rites) then we shall become such and such (the Ideal)'. In other words, what each and every Mystery System purports to be is a Procedure for becoming a Perfected Being, in so far as any human creature is likely to achieve such a status.

Naturally there are fairly wide variations among these Systems as to aims and applications, but all adopt basically similar principles for dealing with Consciousness, because as Universal Energy it has to follow its own laws, which were never designed by humanity in the first place. All we can do is operate within the framework of those laws to the best of our ability, which means that we have to both learn and practice them. Such learning and practice should be available within any Mystery School worthy of its name.

Techniques for categorizing consciousness

The first surprising thing most Initiates discover about Consciousness is their own deficiency of it and inadequacy to deal with it. To create such an Inner vacuum strongly enough is the surest way of filling it, but it is advisable to fill it selectively and carefully with properly constructed material. With this end in view, the Initiate is taught techniques for categorizing Consciousness so that everything may be put in place as per plan provided.

It is just as though the various units of Consciousness were components to be fitted together into whatever constructed item was required. Suppose the Image of a Mother Divine Aspect were under construction. From the appropriate compartment of Consciousness we extract all our separate ideas on this point and build them up accordingly. If our filing system is sense-classified, we might produce the Image of a Being as a beautiful female with blue and silver robes, sweet and kindly voice, pleasant perfume, and firm comforting hands. She would, of course, be endowed with all the qualities we associate with ideal mothers, such as understanding, love, patience, good humour, and above all she would care very much what happens to us. Relationship with this Image would be of the most personal kind. Its importance is that as we build it up from our supplies of 'Do it Yourself' Mother-ideas, so it should be energized or 'brought to life' by its corresponding Aspect of Divine Consciousness.

Before any such thing can be done with Consciousness, the Initiate must first learn how to be conscious. We are apt to think that because our physical senses provide us with impressions, and our brains are dealing with our affairs, that we are adequately conscious individuals. Perhaps we believe that our sensations and emotions make us sufficiently conscious to consider ourselves sentient and soulful beings. The fact is that in general humans are only minimally conscious at all. We live mostly in the least possible state of awareness necessary for existence, and command barely enough consciousness to even justify our living. Most people 'get by' on purely material levels of earth-existence and scarcely more. 'Reality' for the average mortal has no wider range than the limits of their physical lives. This is certainly insufficient and totally inadequate for the operations of consciousness expected in practical workings of the Mysteries.

It is usually only extremities of stress that evoke enough consciousness of a correct type and degree from us to accomplish our Inner aims. That is why artificial stresses were applied in olden Mystery techniques, and are still valid though in somewhat improved forms. It used to be said that 'salvation' was achieved between greed for Heaven and fear of Hell, and that is a roughly accurate description of our basic duality of motivation, if not a very flattering one. The Initiate is faced with the task of transmuting these basics into far higher types of drive. Greed for instance may become love, and fear caution. We do not eliminate the energies that incline us to evil, but alter them. The worst in us actually becomes the best and our 'devils' change to 'angels' when the 'Secret of the Stone' is found. 'The greater the sinner the greater the saint' is a very true saying. Only a great sinner uses enough energy to become a saint. No energy is good or evil in itself, for such distinctions can only arise from intentions of use or opinions of results. Old-time Initiates were instructed to 'chain the demons', or in other words harness 'wild' energies and bind them into helpful channels. What mankind has done with external natural forces, modern Initiates are expected to do with their own internal 'wild' powers.

Such a task calls for far greater amounts and qualities of consciousness than any ordinary mortal normally commands. So where is the necessary 'extra' to come from? If the problem were a material one an answer would be obvious—by borrowing. In material terms, anyone wanting to be rich borrows money, uses it, exceeds amount of loan as a return, discharges debt, then continues to capitalize on his own authority. Precisely those principles are followed on spiritual levels in the Mysteries. Since we have not enough of the right energies available in our human selves, we must obviously borrow these from some source of supply. The Mystic believes that 'with God all things are possible', or if sufficient Divine Power could be utilized, anything might be accomplished with it. The Qabalist would agree with this principle, but sees the Universal Energy diverging into ten main categories which balance each other's polarities into a Pattern of Perfection known as the 'Tree of Life'. Others follow the Seven Ray idea of arrangement. Everyone has some method of relating themselves with the needed energies they have to borrow in order to progress upon whatever Path they follow, and most of the methods produce some kind of result.

Just as no financial borrower can obtain more funds than their 'credit' allows, so no one can acquire more spiritual energy than belief permits. Credit of course *is* belief. It amounts to a double faith. First of all the faith of the applicants in themselves, their ideas, and their own ability to handle capital successfully.

Secondly the faith of the lenders in the applicants coupled with their specialized knowledge of related circumstances. The same is true on Inner terms. Not only must the Initiate believe in or give credit to the Divine Sources of Energy approached Inwardly, but Those must also extend credit towards Their would-be human debtor. Belief must be mutual and genuine. The sense of 'Forgive us our debts as we forgive our debtors' can also indicate 'Credit us as we credit Thee'. Everything stems from the mysterious factor we term 'Faith'.

Necessity of faith

There is a lot of loose speculation about the 'Power of Faith'. Faith is not a Power at all, but a disposition or arrangement of conditions so that force-flows through intended channels become possible. In human beings, faith is the adoption of a specific relative attitude between themselves and whatever they expect fulfilment with. Our lives are based on faith, and our expansions of awareness beyond normal physical limits depend absolutely on this Faith-factor. Such, after all, is only an extension of our commonplace faith in very ordinary matters. It is simply a question of pushing past the point where ordinary mortals cease believing because they are willing to accept limitation there. The extraordinary thing about Initiates as a whole is that they plod ahead on a Path which others have either ceased looking for, or refuse to believe might exist. Belief and Faith is an absolute pre-requisite in all matters connected with the Mysteries. We are definitely and clearly told to 'Believe *first*'. For those who say: 'I cannot believe in anything', the rather odd counsel is to believe firmly and positively in NOTHING as an Absolute, and out of This will eventually emerge Everything. *Ex Nihil Omnis est.*

A useful formula in connection with Faith is the well-known 'Ohms Law' one—

$$\text{Amount} = \frac{\text{Pressure}}{\text{Resistance}}$$

This shows in the simplest way the relative factors concerned. To obtain a given amount of faith we must either increase pressure, decrease resistance, or both. It might appear that resistance should be removed altogether, but this would be highly unwise. A proportion of resistance is strictly necessary in order to maintain balance. We are all too familiar with what happens in the case of those who believe unrestrictedly and indiscriminately in anything. Fanaticism, insanity, and all kinds of stupidities arise from blind credulity and unreasoning enthusiasms coming from usually sincere but quite unjustified faith. Belief must always be qualified by discrimination in order to obtain good results. Another way of expressing the formula is—

$$\frac{I\ Will}{I\ Won't} = I\ Might$$

In other words, what might happen is the outcome of Will over Won't.

So while Faith is a vital necessity, it must be effectively controlled with Wisdom if it is to be a practical proposition in working the Mysteries well. The position may be crudely but soundly summed up in the ale-house adage: 'In God we trust—all others, Cash!' We can only afford unreserved, complete, and unresisting Faith in the Supreme Spirit Itself. Towards that Point our Faith-formula should be at minimum resistance and maximum pressure, so that the outcome as an amount is our full capacity for acceptance of Divine Energy. This is like turning a control knob so that power increases proportionately, but only in the case of Ultimate Divinity dare we do this 'flat out' without risk. When dealing with other faith-dispositions, our resistance and pressure must be adjusted suitably to meet each contingency.

Once more it is a matter of degree. When we approach ordinary humans for instance, our faith in them is subject to all sorts of reservations and resistances to belief. We might have faith in one direction but not another. Perhaps some individual may be credited as to their honesty but not on account of their memory. Another might be credited in some particular skill, but disbelieved in for other matters. All this is normal practice in everyday life, but its principles have to be extended Inwardly when applying faith and beliefs along spiritual lines.

In Mystery practice, Initiates are taught to use belief with discrimination. This means specification of faith in order to direct energies along appropriate paths. The principle is to use a formulary such as: 'I believe all Energy is One, but for such and such a purpose the Divine Aspect of So and So operates through this type of Archangel, that sort of Angel, and this particular kind of Spirit.' Then an attitude of faith is adopted towards these Beings as intermediaries of Divine Energy on their respective levels of Consciousness, and an individual adaptation made to them by means of whatever prayer or practice the Initiate may be capable of. Blind belief is not encouraged in the Mysteries of Light except in the Origin of Light, Life, and Love from whence all Energy emanates.

No intelligent Initiate believes that Angels or Spirits of any species are winged people in nightgowns flitting around Inner Space. However their Telesmic Images are shaped as Symbols, they themselves are Active Agencies of Awareness, or categorical concentrations of Divine Consciousness, each existing for some particular purpose in the Plan of Perfection. Initiates of the Holy Mysteries do not doubt the actual existence of such Entities, though of course there is wide disagreement of opinions concerning their forms, functions, and other details. They have emerged through the minds of men in so many ways as to be almost unrecognizable. We may visualize them more or less as seems most appropriate, but fundamentally they remain what they are—Agents of Divine Action and Awareness. It is best to invoke, or concentrate on them by their particular functions, and let them build their own forms around such Inner concepts.

In olden practice, the Name of the Angel had to be concisely descriptive of his precise nature, such as 'Herald of God', 'Light of God', 'Venom of God', etc., while whole Orders of Angels were termed according to their activities as 'Supporters', 'Shining Ones', 'Defenders', and so forth. The Spirit, or individual Inner entity categorically concerned with the matter in question was usually given a relatively descriptive name, such as : 'Finder of Lost Things', 'Conciliator', 'Bread-bringer', or whatever seemed most suitable in the circumstances.

All this might seem rather medieval to modern minds, but it is basically sound enough. A sweep of Conscious Energy takes place from top to bottom of Existence as it were in a complete Creative Cosmic Cycle, connecting the most Abstract Divinity to the most concrete point of mortal life through a definitive series of control stages, each of which processes the Energy closer to its purpose intended by the initiating Will invoking it.

Although this may well be termed Magic, it also happens all throughout nature, and is observable in any radio set wherein the remote energies received from the original power behind the programme are picked up and processed through the different electrical components until the objective of physical sonics emerges from the speaker. That is really only half the cycle, because the sonics evoke mental and emotional responses in hearers which enter their Inner lives to some extent and so modify them spiritually for better or worse according to their reactions.

A radio is considered a scientific achievement, and yet it only operates along the same laws which, if followed in spiritual dimensions, are considered Magic. To every state of being its own energy-systems, and to every age its own means of establishing contact with them.

Of ourselves, as humans and on our accord, we are very limited beings indeed. Our sole hope of ever becoming more perfect is to evolve out of what we become Within. We cannot possibly do this by ourselves alone, since we need to draw our materials and energies from entirely different sources of supply than our own purely personal stocks. Humans just have not enough ability on their own account to ever rise beyond the totality of what they contain. Furthermore we can only exceed our limits proportionately to the degree of our contacts with Consciousness far beyond our normal range. We all depend on extra-human energies for our progression past any point of our existence, and everyone finds their own best means of contacting and using them. Artists, poets, engineers, physicists, romanticists, realists, atheists, cultists, and the 'common man' who thinks there must be something somewhere and if there isn't there ought to be, everyone looks for that indefinable 'otherness' to themselves planted as a fundamental need at the depths of every soul. The Way of the Holy Mysteries is but one way of attempting what everybody in the world is trying to do otherwise.

Magic not for the millions

It has never been claimed that the methods of the Mysteries are either applicable to or advisable for the bulk of humanity. They are highly specialized adaptations of Universal Law which relatively few human individuals are able to deal with, and fewer yet reach any remarkable degree of efficiency in. There will never be 'Magic for the Millions!' or 'Instant Initiation', or any such commercialized travesty of Truth. Sincere but inexperienced seekers are always looking for criteria by which to judge whether various matters connected with the Mysteries are genuine or not, and whether individuals or Groups claiming to represent the Inner Hierarchy are worthy of those claims or otherwise. It is impossible to be absolutely hard and fast on those points, but two sound basics of judgement have stood the testing of many centuries. First, where money comes in, spiritual value flies out. The more money demanded, the less real Inner Truth is offered. Genuine spiritual worth depreciates in proportion to the amount it is held to ransom by those claiming its custody. Spirit may no more be sold in the market than sunlight. Secondly, the higher and more specious the claims made by individuals or Groups to be appointed trustees of some spiritual fund which only they may administer, the falser such claims are likely to be. The only commodity such have for sale is—sensation. No more and no less.

Where working Groups of individual Initiates do operate on earth, the most they may legitimately claim is a common aim at the Universal Ultimate according to methods discovered through Inner experience and practice. They are entitled to share among themselves whatever normal and reasonable expenses arise in the pursuit of their common cause. Any profit-motive automatically indicates un-spiritual incentives which act as cut-offs from higher sources of supply.

The only sincere advice which may be given those seeking contact with the Inner Holy Mysteries of Light, is to be highly suspicious of all demands for money or pretentious claims made on material levels. Offers to sell 'occult secrets', any kind of Initiation, charms, talismans, or in fact anything whatsoever in the way of Inner actualities should be firmly rejected. It is best to avoid commercialism in any form of disguise if genuine spiritual development is sought. No matter what chicanery is used to camouflage money-motives and power-policies, they remain to-day what they always were, traps that lead Lightseekers into confusion and disorders of the worst kind if they are foolish enough to be deceived by these hoary frauds.

Although the Holy Mysteries of Light form the most exclusive Circles of Initiation that exist, no one is excluded from them except by themselves, and the Keys of admission to those Circles are only to be found deeply hidden in the hearts of those applying for entry. Everyone must find their own way In, and the only valid admission fee is the right amount of effort directed in the right manner at the correct instant and point. Once all the wards of the lock line up properly with each other, and the Key is turned, then the Door of the Innerworld will open. Legend says that such an opportunity is offered to every living soul at least once during an incarnation, but is rarely recognized or taken advantage of. Traditionally, there must be no urging or inducement offered to the entrant, who should see no rewards of a personal nature for himself upon the Inner Way opening before him. Entry has to be of entire Free-Will, uninfluenced by any kind of fear or greed. In other words, at exact mid-point between the Pillars of the Portals.

This 'purity of entry-purpose' is very highly important, since it indicates the ability to remain in poise when subjected to stresses which would otherwise lead to unbalance, and it amounts to the sense of 'vocation' so necessary for any dedicated life. A true Initiate does not devote himself to the Mysteries for a single incarnation, but for an Existence. Thus his *raison d'être* as an Initiate is not for the sake of anything except becoming True as That which in him IS. Nothing else should motivate a genuine Initiate of Light, no matter what activities he may be engaged in. All else of life, whether in or out of the Mysteries, must be subject to that single intention of Will which is the Divine Word Within uttering Itself.

Living for one particular purpose only, or directing all energies to one point as a force-focus is a fairly well known 'secret of success', used frequently by anyone seeking achievement of even the slightest objective. The greatest of our intentions are composed of many minor ones pointing the same way like the molecules of a magnet. Men have followed this principle for every kind of reason. To be rich, for political or social power, to destroy enemies, gain knowledge, become famous, the whole gamut of average human 'success stories'. All due to the same factor, putting every power into a single 'Purpose of purposes'. Given adequate extensions of time and energy along suitable channels, this has to succeed in its objective unless frustrated by a nullifying counter-purpose directed against it by a superior organization of Intention.

The Unchangeables of Existence

The vast majority of human purposes, individual or inclusive, are concerned with purely material objectives within the limits of a lifetime or less. There is very seldom an overall life-purpose adopted by human beings as an act of will, and where this happens it is usually too vague or impractical to be of much value. A genuinely dedicated life is somewhat of a rarity, be it for good or ill, but when it does occur, there is generally something outstanding about the individual electing to lead it.

In the case of an Initiate, the life-motive is sufficiently deep and powerful to act as a constant of consciousness through every life necessary to achieve itself. A life based on eternal values is eternal. Lives founded on alterable trivia are ephemeral. Hence the importance of basing a life-motive on the Unchangeables of Existence, such as pure Principles of Love, Justice, Beauty, Wisdom, etc. As we base ourselves, so we build ourselves, and we shall never be firmer than our foundations. If we are truly founded on immortal values, linked with Concepts of Consciousness which are the causations of our Cosmos, then that is what we WILL BE. We become as we believe, which is why belief is so vital to 'living true', and why it is necessary to find beliefs in fundamentals even beyond life itself.

The Initiate of the Mysteries seeks to 'outlive life' in the sense of living consciously, conscientiously, and constantly linked with the Primal Purpose inclusive of every minor meaning. This is the real Magic Circle 'without Beginning or End, Everliving, Everlasting God', of which the inscribed circles on the floors of Lodges and Temples are but shadowy, though effective symbols.

To live properly as a Circle, it is necessary to relate every item of existence with the One Central Point which holds them all together. The Initiate of Light believes this Point to be the Divine Spark inherent in every living soul through and into Which true Illumination is solely possible. With this Unique Ultimate as the Lodestar which guides through spiritual Night until the Sun behind the sun arises in full Glory, the Initiate relates all else in themselves with Inner and Outer reality. Everything in their existence is pointed one way, which is the Divine Direction. Once the primal purpose of the Initiate's Inner Cosmos aligns with That responsible for the Whole Existence of which the Initiate is a single instance, then the Master-meaning of Life may be said to have truly incarnated, and the Word indeed made Flesh.

Such is the 'Primum Ens' for which the Holy Mysteries work. All the apparently divergent Rites, customs, practices, meditations, maxims, and other behaviours of consciousness associated with the operation of what is sometimes called 'Higher Magic' are really angles of approach connected with the same centre. Naturally, each type of practitioner thinks his particular one is the best, though of course all are necessary to complete the courses of Cosmos. However much these differing Ways are needed, it is also essential to pursue but a single Path at a time if confusion is to be avoided. It is an old saying in the Mysteries that they who enter the Ways to gain everything get nothing, and whoso enters the Way for Nothing gains All.

Choosing a System

At the Common Entry examination which every would-be Initiate of the Mysteries should take upon themselves, they are best advised to select very carefully indeed the particular System most suited to their own condition of spiritual development, and then remain absolutely faithful to it despite apparent failures and set-backs. Jumping around from one System to another, joining all possible Groups, mixing Eastern and Western methods indiscriminately, and generally hopping about hither and thither like the proverbial flea brings only one certain result—chaos. This does not mean that knowledge of the various Systems should not be acquired, but the essential information is which System suits which individual Initiate. Hence : 'Man—Know Thyself.'

Systems were made for souls, and not souls for Systems. Therefore the preliminaries before the Portals should be like their Symbol of Janus, a two-way look. One external examination of the Systems available, and another internal examination of the individual soul to decide what makes its best match. In the unusual event of no suitability being evident, such a soul will be forced to invent their own System from Inner resources. No matter which System is adopted, eventually all souls must find their own feet on the Way beyond every one of them, but let none be so presumptuous as to assert an independence they are incapable of supporting for themselves. Otherwise there will be some severe falls indeed.

Responsibility for choice of System must rest ultimately with the Initiate, and very little guidance on such a personal matter can reasonably be expected from other than personal sources. It may be said however, that although all Systems connect with the same Ultimate Point, experience has shown it best for individual souls to follow the Line of Light most closely aligned with their ethnical and cultural associations. There is a spiritual ancestry as well as a physical one, and developing souls usually incarnate somewhere along the broad stream of their Inner inheritance. If a particular person is an Asian, African, or European, there is obviously an especial reason why they belong to those different cultures, and definite purposes for being born as they were.

Each ethnical group has its own suitable Mystery methods and Systems which are products of many centuries and sources of Consciousness. Just as there are various races and families on earth, so there are types and associative groups of soul operating in other dimensions of Life. Each of us has our own 'Inner family' and natural Spiritual Order to which we belong as evolving entities, and it is strongly advisable to build from this basis rather than adopt unsuitable 'foreign' methods for which there is inadequate inherent ability. Asiatic and many Oriental Systems for instance, are not generally advantageous for people whose natural state of soul is in harmony with European or Celtic traditions and cultures. It is for each Initiate to realize the importance of his own Inner loyalties, and remain faithful to the standards of his spiritual heritage.

Principles behind the different Mysteries may be identical, but it is very highly important to preserve their particular styles and types in pure, or unmixed conditions. This is for the same reasons and laws that govern any kind of categorization or discriminative association of energies. To 'breed true' in any specific form of Life means careful selection of stock. When blending colours or sounds there must be discrimination in order to produce favourable results.

Everything in existence has to be arranged in accordance with the laws of its own nature relatively to its contacts, and this certainly applies to energies of consciousness and types of thinking, both of which are major factors of the Mysteries. Each has its especial background, framework, cultus, customs, and even nomenclature to be considered. Some of these are aligned with particular national or racial ethnoi, such as the Egyptian Mysteries, the Vedic, Mithraic, or Druidic. Others, like the Rosicrucian are Occidental by adaptation, or as in the case of the Qabalistic Mysteries have acclimatized themselves to Western behaviour-patterns and channels of consciousness, similarly to the Hermetic and Orphic Mysteries. Most universal (though perhaps the most elusive of all) are the Holy Mysteries of Light.

Whichever System or Mystery is being worked must be kept going along its own lines in its own particular Way. It would be quite wrong, for example, to mix up stylized Egyptian costume with pseudo-Masonic ritual, an assortment of Christian sentiments, some vaguely Oriental music, a few bits and pieces from medieval grimoires, plus a good deal of decorative junk and term all this muddle a genuine Occult Mystery. Yet this mismanagement is not unheard of on earth. Wherever such a lack of cohesion and discrimination is evident, seekers of truth in occult Circles would be well advised to look elsewhere for Light.

The real Mysteries linking with ancient Traditions have all a central Symbol-Pattern linked with themes of thought and channels of consciousness which accord therewith in the style appropriate to its nature. Whatever becomes incorporated into a real Mystery does so in the manner peculiar to it. Not only do earthly custodians ensure this, but the Inner Hierarchy are very competent at safeguarding and preserving the spiritual conventions they stand for.

It is strangely simple to overlook the fact that the great majority of intelligent entities directly concerned with the Mysteries are not incarnate on earth, or have necessarily lived as members of the human race. They have their own *modus vivendi* which differs very considerably from ours, and the Mystery methods and techniques employed on material levels are forms of compromise between the variant conditions of consciousness. The 'Salvation of Mankind' *en masse* is no function of the Mysteries. They do not call the many but select the few. Their Portals must be passed in single file even though the whole of humanity might enter if sufficient Will were forthcoming. Through a relatively small number of focal points on earth, the great streams of Consciousness behind the Mysteries disseminate among Mankind along many peculiar paths and most unlikely ways. All Initiates and their Circles act as relays and components along the energy-circuits of the spiritual Powers utilizing such material media. An age accustomed to bugging and microdotting as mechanical interceptors of awareness should have little difficulty in accepting the possibilities of Mystery Initiates being used as agents of a more advanced type of consciousness than normally expressed through other mortals.

There is nothing very surprising in such an idea after all. The whole purpose of the Mysteries is to provide human beings with opportunities for contacting and working with those beyond or ahead of merely mortal conditions of consciousness. Otherwise they are no more than amusements and pastimes. Maybe if we look at various time honoured and more recent methods of Mystery-procedures for approaching this very point, the problem will appear in a more practical light.

CHAPTER IV

METAPHYSICAL CONSIDERATIONS

The phenomena of what used to be called 'possession' makes a most interesting study and has a direct bearing on the workings of Inner Awareness used throughout the Mysteries, Holy or otherwise. Associated topics of course, are religious conversion, 'mediumship', inspiration, and all forms of what might be termed interference with a more or less straightforward stream of human consciousness.

Man is a self-conscious entity whose awareness is constantly being modified by reactive processes with other beings and entities whether these are physical or not. Moreover, these reactions relate with each other through their different levels to produce an entirety of experience. If our bodies are injured for instance, we do not feel pain unless our minds are involved. On the other hand we can feel pain without bodily injury at all if our 'feelings are hurt'. Different pain perhaps, but pain nevertheless. In each case personal suffering of some kind is undergone. As a rule, hurt feelings are a reaction to behaviour by other embodied beings whose corporeality acts as an objective focus for the forces stimulating such an effect. The average human being reacts mainly in response to stimuli applied through physical foci. As we evolve, so we become able to react consciously with stimuli reaching us directly from non-physical sources or with a minimal extension into physical dimensions.

Uncontrolled forces of consciousness

The Mysteries are not only concerned with supplying and teaching means and methods of making such Inner contacts, but with the more important affairs of controlling and regulating this faculty of consciousness so that it is rightly related with its human users. Asylums for the insane all over the world shelter many unfortunates whose greatest weakness is an inability to control the compulsive forces of consciousness streaming through them into expression. It will be noted that in most cases this consciousness is typified into classifiable categories often associated with well-known human examples, i.e. kings, politicians, religious characters, or others who symbolize major variants of human thought and behaviour. Patients identifying themselves with these and similar figures are common enough. They have become caught into currents of consciousness which have produced the figures they reflect, and short of death, only drastic means are likely to deliver them. Such unhappy and useless confusion is the chaotic opposite of the Inner Cosmoi that Initiates of the Mysteries are supposed to construct.

It is a question of spiritual evolution. Each evolving entity bears with them a Divine potential which is likened to a spark or Seed of Light. This is our Immortal Principle. Either we as individuals evolve with Its increasing illumination until we are able to live eternally in and *as* It, or we do not. If we are to survive and succeed as souls in the right of our own existence, then we are absolutely dependent upon such a development of Divinity through us. Each of us, as an entity, is responsible for this process of Light-growth through our own particular Light-line.

Although the Light may be One as Its totality, the whole 'Picture of Presentation' is built up from an infinity of variated points, each with its own especial value and purpose in the entire Scheme of Existence. We are among those points like the individual impulses that comprise a complete television frame. If every point was exactly as it should be, then the picture would indeed be perfect, but we know well enough this is not so. However faultless the original picture in its 'spiritual studio' might have been, its projection in terms of our active lives in this world seems to have suffered badly from transmission and other faults. We are obviously not shining with Inner Light as we ought to.

The main reason for this discrepancy between the ideal and actual Picture of Presentation, is simply that we absorb and re-radiate already distorted Light from much lower levels than our Divine Inner Source of illumination. If it were possible for us to receive our Inner energies purely from this Supreme Source alone and project them properly through ourselves, then we should present a perfectly true picture of All in All to All. Since we are as yet quite unable to achieve such a standard, we are perforce faced with finding the best available alternatives. This is only possible by working within very carefully chosen systems of selection, so that our incoming spiritual energies are principally derived from sources which at least have proved reasonably reliable so far as human experience and expectations are concerned.

Most human souls, especially young ones in an evolutionary sense, are receptive to extraneous influences of all kinds whether beneficial to them or not. In their natural anxiety to evolve as rapidly as possible, they accept energies of every sort into themselves regardless of consequences, or effects to their own structure. By and large, the majority of souls survive this rough and ready way of gaining experience, and after many incarnations acquire more wisdom through sheer force of circumstances. Such, however, is emphatically *not* the Way of the Mysteries, which is one of discrimination and selectivity the whole time.

The Degree of Initiation

In order to be discriminative and selective in accordance with Wisdom, it is necessary to have some definite ruling or standard by which to work. The standard expected in the Mysteries of Light is nothing less than the highest in every Initiate as expressed by the degree of Divinity controlling their consciousness, which of course is their true 'Degree of Initiation' irrespective of any mere 'Lodge titles'. Perhaps this demands a somewhat fuller explanation.

A primary objective in the Mysteries is to establish a practical conscious relationship between Initiates and the Divine Essence from whence they emanate. This normally results in the compromise of a God-Image or Images which is the closest arrangement by which the two extremities of Existence become aware of each other as entities in their own states. It must be clearly understood that the Form of such an Image is not fixed, but evolves with the Initiate's progress. It is a mutual symbolic convenience of consciousness, and no more, though of high importance in function. This God-Entity is not only a focus of Divine Energy, but as a Being, has Its own code of action and behaviour which again is a compromise between human beliefs and ideas of Divinity, and Divine expectations of humanity. Both God and Man asking each other to be WHAT THEY WILL.

Since most humans ask or expect no more of Divinity than to exist on fairly low life levels as an average standard, they can fairly expect nothing else—if indeed as much. They live close to their bodies of flesh which are the nearest they take to be a Divine Image of any kind, eat, work, sleep, breed, fight, die. Whether rich or poor, their round of life seldom takes them very far away from an earthly existence. A genuine Initiate of Light would find this very boring and unsatisfactory. With all Inner Existence to explore, who would be willingly content to remain entirely earthbound? Yet such exploration has to be along the right lines (or Light-lines) in order to be worth while. Otherwise it is better to stay on the ground and struggle along with the others.

The Initiate of Light, having established contact with a satisfactory God-Image, uses it as a means of setting and accepting standards of spiritual living and behaviour. Literally the Image is there for 'living up to'. It is, in fact, a composite Being, constructed partly from the Initiate's own nature, and partly from Divine Awareness Itself. In theory, the life of an Initiate should become regulated by his own will as an individual, becoming voluntarily aligned with the Divine Will as accepted via his God-Concept. While seldom attaining such an ideal relationship to any great degree of perfection, the practice of these principles will invariably lead conscientious practitioners along the Path of Light as far and as high as their abilities allow. As their abilities increase, so will their progress.

The Path of Perfection

Most emphatically this does *not* mean a complete abandonment of personal responsibility, negation of free will, or any evasion of individual obligations whatsoever. To the exact contrary, it means that these factors increase proportionately to the degree of attainment achieved on the Path to Perfection. True Initiation in the Holy Mysteries is entirely an individual affair of a Divine Becoming through every being. Nothing less, because there can be Nothing more. The full onus of this Operation, however, falls where it originally fell—upon the separated souls inhabiting human bodies. Every one of us must either pick ourselves up and climb the Tree of Life by the Ladder of Light, or remain wallowing in the mire of materialism where we deserve to be if we refuse to recognize our own true potentials. We shall receive all the help we need from Inner sources in proportion to the efforts we make on our own best behalf. The initial impetus towards Divinity however, must arise from within individuals, hence the process is well called Initiation.

This is why the Mysteries of Light are so much against any abrogation of these principles, or the spiritual usurpation of what should rightfully be the prerogative of another individual, regarding compulsion of conscience as a crime against Cosmos. It was mainly for this reason that some Mystery Schools became so sternly set in opposition to all forms of Spiritualism, and forbade their Initiates to consult any kind of seer or even astrologers. To this day such injunctions are still given in some sections of the Mysteries, though it is pointless doing so without fully explaining the reasons. There is no real harm in seeking counsel from any intelligent source, providing it is realized and fully understood that entire responsibility for seeking, accepting or rejecting, and acting upon or ignoring such counsel rests absolutely upon the individuals themselves in agreement with their own Indwelling Divine Principle—which of course should be consulted in the first place before asking external assistance.

That indeed is the crux of the matter. Initially an Initiate is bound by his Oath to look within himself for Light. Should this seem unforthcoming after reasonable efforts, then acknowledgement must be made of personal inadequacy for receiving the required contact, and help sought externally. There is nothing wrong whatever with accepting outside aid when in difficulties. The wrong lies in refusing to 'seek the Kingdom Within' first and foremost before going elsewhere.

Rejection of Divine Authority within the soul is about the worst fault an Initiate can commit. This, in effect, is what happens when an otherwise responsible person loses confidence in himself to the extent of consulting 'spirits', fortune-tellers, astrologers, or for that matter psychiatrists or anyone else, purely for the sake of laying blame on these parties for what has gone wrong with the seeker's own life. Delegation to others of an initiative which should come directly from one's own Inner

Divine Contact is wrong. On the other hand, there is no reason whatsoever why any useful source of information should not be approached in the Light of Inner permission to find fulfilment by outer means. The ethics of the issue are entirely decided by whether or not the True Will of the Word in the Flesh is being done, and this can only be discovered by a faculty once called 'conscience'. Con-science. Knowing 'together with', or something shared by Divinity and humanity through an awareness common to both.

It is for this reason that the Mysteries of Light are normally averse to the general run of trance mediumship, in which an unembodied entity 'borrows' the psycho-physical apparatus which rightly belongs to another being. There are indeed exceptional circumstances which make this interchange of identities a necessity, but it is totally unjustified for other than very serious reasons, and then only under directions from a very high level. Indiscriminate usurpation of another's psycho-physical faculties is not a good idea at all. Fortunately it is not a common phenomenon, and a good deal of what is considered trance mediumship is actually no more than 'undue influence' brought to bear upon a co-operative human being. Little harm is accomplished where there is little power to perform it. In principle, however, no practice involving unconditional surrender of the higher faculties to other than the Highest Power, is permissible to Initiates of the Holy Mysteries of Light.

In olden times it was observed that human contact with non-human types of disembodied consciousness was marked by one of two possible effects on the human side. The receptor was moved from his normal and ordinary state of awareness into a markedly higher or lower condition of intelligence and behaviour. Either he went into frenzies, gabbling a lot of nonsense, or he became ecstatic, losing touch with earth to an extent that made communication virtually impossible. Neither type of experience seemed of real value to the individual himself or his human associates, however fascinating the demonstration might be.

Through the Holy Mysteries therefore, there evolved what might be called the Middle Way of Approach. This was what we now term Inspiration, a condition of consciousness in which a direct line of Inner Light comes from the highest point its human bearer can reach, and shines straight through as it were, so that its nature is evident at all points of observation.

Under conditions of true Inspiration, individual contact with all higher faculties is not lost at all, but to the contrary, very much enhanced indeed. Levels of intelligence, reason, comprehension, and also moral qualities rise considerably because of Inner contacts made by inspirational means. Even an ordinary person of below average I.Q. becomes a much brighter being through the influence of direct Inspiration. What is more, the effects of real Inspiration are lasting, and that is the infallible test of its Divine nature. Although the immediate outcome of an Inspirational contact tends to fade towards the normal life-level of the individuals making it, they never return to precisely their previous level again, becoming fractionally improved by their Inner experience. That is the overwhelming advantage of Inspirational methods. Lesser means of making contact with extra-human beings have either little enough effect worth mentioning, or should the contacts be with sub or anti-human entities, very bad results indeed for those concerned.

Practically everyone has 'moments of inspiration', when at least something from a far higher level than usual 'gets through', and causes a change in consciousness resulting in changes of life-conditions unlikely to have happened otherwise. This is normal enough, if not a common occurrence. It is an aim of the Holy Mysteries to make the whole of life an inspirational experience controlled directly from the highest point of consciousness in every Initiate. Even though this may only be attained in relatively few instances, increasing degrees of success among initiated members of the Mysteries are very well worth the efforts made to achieve them.

Spiritual Reaction Range

Naturally, there is a limiting factor to the extent of Inspiration possible with every individual. This is known as their Spiritual Reaction Range and varies quite considerably among individuals. In a way, it is not unlike the Solar Spectrum of Light to which the average human vision is confined. By the use of special devices, we can extend our perceptions a little way beyond the Infra-red limit at the bottom, and the Ultra-violet at the top of the scale, but our perception is bounded by our own visual abilities in the end.

Apart from these limits as to quality, there is a quantity limit too. If we are exposed to excessive amounts of Light, there may be irreparable tissue damage, as in the case of direct sunlight shining for prolonged periods into the eye. Severe burns are also sustained from Infra-red or Ultra-violet Light. There are boundaries in every direction beyond which we may not pass without peril. All this is true in spiritual Light-terms as well. Not only must we keep within physical safety limits, but spiritual ones too, and if we attempt to exceed them without adequate precautionary arrangements, we shall incur the natural penalties attached.

This is particularly noticeable in the case of sudden 'religious conversion', or any event which forces a human soul far beyond its normal living conditions at a rate exceeding its adaptive abilities. Spectacular spiritual effects are very seldom any more desirable than physical ones. A burning home, and a soul aflame with destructive zeal, mirror the same tragedy on their respective levels. Yet what is a home without heat, or a soul without Light? The problem is to determine the exact degree of spiritual stress which may safely be applied to any soul in order to keep it healthily active and progressing along its appointed Path. If a soul were a physical machine, this would be simple, and its specifications of input/output energy, work capacity, and maximum/minimum functioning would be neatly printed on an attached plate for the user's reference. It is even more important to know the equivalents of those specifications concerning human souls. How can individuals be classified and graded like so many factory products or eggs for market? Also, why should any form of labelling be necessary at all?

The present age delights in fancy labels, most of them deceptive and specious, designed to captivate the consciousness of their readers into acceptance of their inventor's intentions. We also suffer from a plethora of 'aptitude tests', 'psychological programming', and an almost obsessional concern with what are loosely termed 'qualifications'. Everyone must not only be fitted into their appropriate hole but also hammered in and secured there for the rest of their natural lives regardless of their individual feelings or Inner aspirations. That is the terrible Inner imprisonment facing the mass of human souls incarnating into the picture being painted by the anonymous planners of modern socialized civilization. Karl Marx's famous dictum : 'Religion is the opium of the people' might well be answered by the axiom : 'Socialization is the soporific of the soul', and the old cry : 'Workers of the world unite. You have nothing to lose but your chains', might be countered now with : 'Workers of the Will unite ! You have nothing to lose but the world'.

Seldom has true individual spiritual freedom, which the Holy Mysteries of Light offer rightful Initiates, been in greater danger on our human planet, nor have we had such incredible opportunities for establishing the 'Kingdom of Heaven' in Earth. There is a real 'War of the Worlds' going on all around us in which most of the casualties are not even aware what hit them—or even that they have been hit.

Just as it is now becoming customary to blame established religion for the spiritual faults and failings of our forefathers, so in future will our 'psycho-political-planners' of the present be blamed for the state of soul-enslavement creeping insidiously through our modern structure of society. Once more the Mystery Lodges will be needed, with all their cumbrous paraphernalia of security devices, to act as forums of Inner Freedom wherein those whom Light liberates may commune consciously with each other at physical focal levels. It is well perhaps for our world, that the Inner Organization and structure of the Holy Mysteries remains apart from it in the capable control of those whom Truth has proved trustworthy. Blessed indeed are they that not only know their exact spiritual capabilities, but are able to work comfortably within their limits of tolerence for the whole of their existence.

Grading system of the Mysteries

It was mostly for this reason that the Holy Mysteries instituted various systems of Grades. Originally, Grades were in no sense at all a series of promotions bestowed on Initiates as rewards of service, or a set of fictitious honours obtainable in return for money or favour. Grades were what might be termed 'spiritual ratings', like the specifications of a machine, intended to provide an accurate assessment of the Initiate's true spiritual value as an individual. This gave a useful reference figure for the guidance of all concerned, the Initiates themselves most of all. In effect the Grades were supposed to be valuable classification systems, so that everyone in the Mysteries might be fully employed to the best advantage of everyone. Nevertheless the Grades were never meant to be a means of tying labels around the necks of progressive souls to prevent them operating beyond their calculated capacity, or other than decreed by some autocratic spiritual Dictator. In addition to present actual spiritual status, the Grades were also intended to indicate future potentials and the best way of realizing them. One might almost say that a Grade was a practical guide to God-hood.

Suppose, for instance, anyone were suddenly asked what sort of a person they were as a spiritual entity, and had to answer this embarrassing question as neatly and accurately as possible. Had the query concerned their physical condition only, it would be quite simple to give an approximation with the well known A.1., B.2, C.3. classification system. The Grading systems of the Mysteries are attempts at similar codifications on spiritual levels in perhaps a more imaginative way. Probably the best known and the least understood are the so-called 'Rosicrucian' Grades, which for some odd reason are seldom correctly given, and very rarely explained so that anyone of reasonable intelligence can see at a glance how they work. Yet they are really quite simple in principle, being an arbitary relationship-scale between the Divine and human aspects of an Initiate or any particular entity concerned. The method of constructing such a scale is this.

How to construct a relationship scale

At the top of the scale is the highest point of Divinity attainable by Man, and at the lowest point, the depth in humanity at which Divinity begins returning to Itself through its Cosmic Circle. Next, using the decimal system, we make ten equal levels between our two extremities which are really the zenith and nadir of the same Cosmos. We can think of these divisions as percentages or in any way we like, but each division represents a degree to which humanity and Divinity counterbalance each other through the same entity.

It is a question of displacement. If we had, say, a ten ounce measure of water to represent humanity, and then poured in an

ounce of oil to represent Divinity as Light, the result would be
still ten ounces in the proportion of 1 oil, 9 water. Thus an
abbreviation of 1o 9w would be a working symbol for the condition of such a measure. This is the general idea behind the
Grades. They are supposed to show the extent in any Initiate
to which they have exchanged humanity and Divinity in themselves, or the degree of transmutation between Matter and Spirit.
Assuming the 'Descent of Spirit' into Man by ten gradual stages,
and the 'Ascent' of Man to God by an equal number of steps,
this gives us the following general scale to work with.

		O		
	o	DIVINITY	o	
	9		1	
	8		2	
	7		3	
Humanity	6		4	Divinity
becomes	5		5	becomes
Divine	4		6	Human
	3		7	
	2		8	
	1		9	
	o	HUMANITY	o	
		□		

If we identify the Divine proportion of an entity by the traditional circle, and the human amount by a square, we shall not
only link with the Square and Compass symbol, but also realize
what the famous 'Squaring a Circle' problem concerned. It was
not so much a mathematical obscurity, but the major problem
of life itself—inter-relating our Divine and human proportions,
and converting one into the other harmoniously. Thus, for instance, an Initiate with a 3 ∴ 7 rating, would be one who had
achieved a condition of three parts Divine to seven parts of
human nature. The three little dots, so beloved by many who
miss their meaning, signify the principle of balance between
extremities, such as the Three Pillars, three points of the Compass
or Square, three points of the heart, etc. They also mean: 'This
has been accomplished', and may be read as the A of AMEN.
They could equally, of course, stand for Father, Son, and Holy

Ghost, or any Triad intended. Those who enjoy decorating signatures with secret squiggles may read what they will between their dotted lines.

It should be obvious that the Degree Scale described is more of an ideal to be achieved than an actuality to be encountered much in our faulty world. Who could imagine a 9 ∴ 1 type of being? Nine parts Divine and only one degree human! Short of an Incarnate God, none of such a nature could possibly manifest through a human body, yet it must be possible for a being of that degree to exist, or the extremities of humanity and Divinity would not be what they are. Another important point arising, is how to determine Divine and human proportions in any given individual, and who is qualified to do this? What standards are to be used in making such graduations? It is doubtful if these awkward issues have ever been solved to everyone's satisfaction, so the normal procedure in the Mysteries is to accept some kind of representative scale and work with that. Sometimes this is known as the imperfect Index because it indicates the degree to which the individual fails in attaining perfection, and therefore infers their achievements otherwise. This is similar to the British custom of saying a person is 'not bad', instead of claiming they are 'very good'.

Such a scale is the 10–1, 9–2, 8–3, etc., one which is more frequently encountered. It will be noted the digits always add to eleven, the imperfect figure because it automatically commences a new cycle since the preceding one failed to equate 1 with 0 perfectly and so zero out of being. Existence only goes on existing because of imperfection. If perfection were ever attained, there would be no need to exist. We shall find sufficient evidence of this in our most imperfect world. Only in True Zero is Absolute Perfection possible. The imperfect Index commences from a hypothetical double Zero to show that the complete Neophyte is quite outside the Circle of Initiation. At the First Degree, 1 ∴ 10, it is considered that a single portion of Divinity in the Initiate has caused an awareness of a tenfold human discrepancy to be dealt with according to the methods of the Mystery with which the Initiate works, and so up the scale.

The practising Qabalist of course, will relate the scale of degrees with his own decimal divisions of the Tree. Here there are thirty-two Paths or steps towards the Zero-Perfection at the top of the Tree, A 10 ∴ 9 degree to a Qabalist would mean the lowest on the Ladder of Light, at which point an ordinary human having entered the Path of Initiation, is struggling to achieve a sense of balance between the Outer world and the Foundation of an Inner Existence from which stage the Inner Life may be built up. The Qabalist would also admit a 10 ∴ 8 degree, for an Initiate coming to terms with their best intellectual progress, and a 10 ∴ 7 degree for one seeking Inner balance and control of their emotions and artistic capabilities. The Qabalistic Degree System is possibly among the neatest and most practical of all, since it indicates spiritual status with great definition, whereas most of the others are very arbitary, and depend on opinions of necessary qualifications for status rather than actualities.

In the majority of instances, Lodge 'Degrees' acquired on material levels with high-sounding titles and impressive flourishes of fantasy bear very little relation to reality and a great deal of relation to wishful thinking. Generally they are harmless conceits or sometimes sincere compliments, bestowed in a kind of 'nickname' spirit. As accurate descriptions of an individual's average spiritual condition however, they usually go more astray than to the mark. The higher and more elaborate the 'degree', the less accurate it is likely to be. One cannot help being reminded of the classic tale concerning the disappointed members of a Lodge who were informed by a junior Officer that there would be no meeting that evening, because the Past Grand Commander of the Universe and Delegate Divine on Earth had unfortunately been badly beaten up by his wife! In fact among human groupings most closely connected with the Holy Mysteries, fanciful styles of titling deriving from medieval terminology are very much of a joke. Anyone using them to impress the unwary is open to suspicion of many kinds.

Testing a candidate's degree condition

There is, of course, only one practical way to tell the degree condition of anything or anyone, and that is to test it or them by imposing a series of usages to cover a full working range. In the case of a human being, a wide variety of such tests are necessary. Physical ones are simple enough, and mental testing can be carried out by any competent educationalist, but when we approach the Inner realities of spiritual status, methods are considerably altered even though principles may still apply.

The whole idea of the old Mystery Initiations was to determine the Initiate's degree of spirit by applying contrived conditions which necessitated responses from their depth of true being. Perhaps more importantly, this also provided an opportunity for discovering to what degree Divinity was manifestly operative through the Initiate under test. All this enabled a fair assessment of the Initiate to be made in spiritual terms, their Grade known, and future course of conduct estimated. No genuine Grade was ever 'given' or 'bestowed' on any real Initiate of the Mysteries. It was their own acquisition absolutely, whether other members of the Mysteries discovered it or not. In fact, an Initiation enabled other members of the Group to find out which Grade the candidate really belonged to and recognize this among themselves. Humanity being what it is, however, we have fallen away from original intentions as usual.

For these and allied reasons, it is obviously necessary that the candidate for Initiation should be preferably unaware on External levels as to what precise Inner pressures will be applied. Initiation ceremonies were and are kept secret in details for this very purpose. It is essential that the candidate be subjected to Inwardly applied energies to which no Outer reactions have already been prepared in particular form. The general custom of formal ritual responses from the candidate which they are either told previously, or have whispered to them during the Rite is contrary to the original spirit of Initiation. If a standard question was put, an honest individual answer straight from the Inner faith of the candidate himself was expected. Like psychoanalytic free word-association, the candidate's response was supposed to come spontaneously from the depths of his real self, and not from some clever crib supplied beforehand. To ensure smooth working of a sophisticated Rite, it is probably essential to have a number of prearranged responses linking the various sections together, but important keypoints must be presented to the candidate as initial impulses demanding a reactive reply from spiritual levels of consciousness in close contact with Divine direction.

We build up our lives on all levels from our reactions to the energies we encounter therefrom. After a few years of life-experience, we acquire a whole repertoire of ready-made reactions to most classes of energy likely to reach us through our customary environment. With this stock-in-trade we tend to deal with life in general and the fellow beings we meet with. Our reactions have become entirely conditioned to our world, and we seldom if ever seek to extend their range or add fresh supplies to our store. So we stick in ruts, exist in states of apathy and boredom, either continuing complacently, or trying to break out in senseless ways that do no one any good.

When we are young and everything is new to us, we are full of energies and enthusiasms to meet the constantly changing events that challenge our consciousness to deal with them. Life is magic and love is double magic. When the same type of events and their successors become old to us, then we get old with them, because we do not respond to them from our Inner Identity any more, but from the stock responses we have built up like a barrier between our Real Selves and the energies of Life we encounter.

On lower levels of life it is very necessary to construct such a ready-made system of routine responses for ordinary affairs. In theory, this should leave us free above everything else to engage ourselves directly with Inner spiritual energies arousing us to new kinds of life through other than purely physical dimensions. However old our mortal bodies grow, our constant pursuit of spiritual realities through their Inner worlds will keep our consciousness in touch with the Spirit of Eternal Youth, which is the Eternal Enquiry of Existence. We must continually meet fresh Inner forces with new outlooks and approaches which will arouse our reactions on ever higher levels of being and so lift our lives steadily towards the Light of Ultimate Illumination. Ageing physical bodies need not be accompanied by tottering and decrepit souls. Spiritually advanced individuals have always been noted for their qualities of what might be termed Inner youthfulness. This is due to their open Inner approach to the actualities of spirit as a young person might encounter first love with a welcoming wonder.

A great aim of Initiation in the Holy Mysteries therefore, is teaching how to live 'New-True' the whole time so that all life becomes 'magic', because it can never be dull, uneventful, or boring while the Initiate is able to maintain contact with the

Spirit of Creation which ever renews Itself in Its creatures. Such is the I.N.R.I. formula of *Ignis Natura Renovata Integra*— 'The Fire of Nature renews and refreshes'. This is becoming a 'Child of Light' in order to enter the 'Kingdom of Heaven'. It is opening ourselves Inwardly so that the Being behind us can look out through our eyes, and observing with our consciousness the life we are making for its inhabitancy, exert its influence to improve our common conditions. To an Initiate of Light, every day is a new life, every instant a fresh opportunity for coming into closer contact with the Divine Reality his image represents, and no matter how fearsome or difficult living may become, it can never be without Purpose and Point leading inevitably to Perfection beyond our keenest Perception.

The Initiate always encounters fresh fields of Inner activity and expansion. There is literally no end to the opportunities they offer enterprising workers therein. Blessed indeed are those with the faculty of bringing the New Approach of Arising Divinity in themselves to bear upon all they meet with otherwise. The Waking God in each of us reacts to the new Life discovered through our agency and makes of that Life WHAT IT WILL. There is nothing newer in Existence than the finding of Divinity and Humanity in each other. The Initiate of Light seeks to hold the focus of consciousness at this point of revelation.

Impossible questions

All kinds of devices are employed in the Mysteries to encourage this Inner Awakening, sometimes termed the 'Golden Dawn', since it is the Arising of Inward Light. One is the so-called 'koan', or posing a query unanswerable by any ordinary intellectual means, and needing a reply from the Inner Intelligence connecting with the Initiate's consciousness Which naturally is Aware of the whole matter, and will respond according to the Initiate's degree of illumination. Another is deliberately putting the Initiate or candidate into some predicament from which only Divine direction could extricate him. This is often done in minor ways free from any serious risk during Initiation ceremonies.

For example, an ornamental staff is set up in the centre of a circle, and the candidate asked how many degrees a circle has.

After a correct reply, they are then instructed to walk around the circle slowly, watching the staff constantly. On completing this task, the query is then put as to whether they have seen the same staff three hundred and sixty different ways, or whether three hundred and sixty different staffs were seen in only one way. In attempting to grapple with this unlikely problem, the candidate is forced right away from ordinary levels of thinking, and has to seek direct inspiration from higher sources of interior information. The degree of response obtained depends on his own. This is the purpose behind otherwise absurd or idiotic queries such as the famous : 'If God is Omnipotent, can He make a stone so heavy He cannot lift it?' or 'What is the sound of one hand clapping?' They compel consciousness to deal with them from metaphysical angles or else leave them alone altogether.

Once the principles of staying spiritually young and fresh by continually keeping in touch with Inner affairs demanding new reactions from us are grasped, practices making this possible are soon invented. Probably the most direct way of doing this is to ask the Arising Awareness in ourselves for suggestions and then follow along the lines given in reply, once we are convinced these not only come from the right quarter, but can be modified to suit our circumstances. It is quite likely, for instance, that the A.A. in us, seeing all in terms of its own Inner Existence, may suggest a course of action perfectly possible on that exalted life-level, but most impracticable from a mundane viewpoint. So a working compromise has to be reached between the two extremities of Awareness operating through the same individual. This frequently happens during the early stages of their partnership, when each is stimulating the other into responsive activity. Translating Inwardly received stimuli into rational Outer behaviour is not easy at first, but, like everything else, improves with practice all the time, until eventually it becomes a customary process. In the case of an ordinary person, they are receiving stimuli mainly from other mortals with which they react and build their being. An Initiate of Light learns how to react with Divine energies encountered directly within themselves, and so constructs Cosmos from both states of being.

The novelties met with during Initiation ceremonies are only valuable if they are fundamental patterns calculated to inspire corresponding behaviour in the Initiate. The simple circumambulation of a staff under observation for instance, is supposed to instil the idea of approaching things from all angles of a circular field of consciousness embracing every possible viewpoint, and obtaining a series of new reactions to the same subject. Each incident of a genuine initiation should be a symbolic Key of Life, which, if inserted deeply enough into the Initiate's basic being, will provide with him the central control-points to a wide variety of life-situations on spiritual and other levels.

The rule of All in a Cosmos being circularly relative to One which emanates from None is universal. Whatsoever consciousness surrounds, it will ultimately control. A relatively small number of points control vast conglomerations of Creation. The whole of an individual being is kept in control by a single spiritual centre. This is an objective of Initiation in the Holy Mysteries. Not to be concerned with the distractions and side-issues of consciousness, but to make straight for the vital points controlling them all, and become Masters of those, so becoming Masters of the rest in due course. It seems hardly necessary to say that such is scarcely an easy affair in depth, and is only possible after achieving proportional results on a minor scale of what might be called 'rehearsal-reactions'. In the Mystery workings, Initiates should be provided with all needed opportunities for accomplishing this essential preparation of themselves for ever-increasing usage of energy in widening circles. This training takes life-times, and many incarnations may be necessary to shape a soul towards its proper destiny. It is reputed that a minimum of three incarnations affords the barest possibility of producing a competent Initiate of any remarkable degree.

That is the reason why the conditioning periods leading up to Initiations are relatively very prolonged when contrasted with the comparative brevity of the ceremonies themselves. To arrive at exactly the right condition for reacting in precisely the correct way to the spiritual stimuli applied during the ceremony may take a very long time indeed. Unless the Initiate is truly in such a state of being, the entire rite would be no more than a time wasting mockery. Literally anyone at all could be 'put through' all the Initiations the Mysteries have to offer, and experience nothing but boredom and bewilderment.

Genuine Initiations will only affect those who are properly prepared to react rightly with the energies they release. Strictly speaking, no one can take a higher Initiation than they are entitled to, for the simple reason it would have no result on them of any beneficial kind. Until we are ready for them, we just cannot react properly with the Key-points of the higher degrees of Initiation. It is not that we cannot encounter them. They are in evidence all around us in quite casual ways. It is simply that we do not recognize them for what they are, or even suspect the hidden side of their nature, until we are sufficiently developed in ourselves to realize what they amount to, and their real value in terms of Truth.

Importance of Inner Understanding

Let no one imagine that if they were duly pushed through all the Rites of the Mysteries, and met every Master available who told them every secret there was, and whatever teaching they demanded, all this incredible experience would make one iota of difference to their fundamental being by itself. In any case, the genuine Mysteries do not work in such a fashion. Real 'Teaching' comes to and through the individual Initiate himself, via his Inner contacts with sources of spiritual enlightenment. This true teaching and learning cannot come through books, lectures, or ordinary verbal instructions. These may *inform*, but they do not *teach*. Information collects in a mind, but teaching changes an entire soul because it is imparted by Spirit. An informed person is not necessarily a truly instructed one. In 'occult' circles, it is not uncommon to encounter those with books and equipment valued at perhaps thousands of pounds, yet with no real Inner Understanding. Possibly in the same room may be a much more advanced soul with no literary possessions to speak of, or any great intellectual achievements, who, by direct contact with Inner Wisdom has acquired truths beyond the power of death to take away.

This is why it is considered 'un-Wise' in the Mysteries to rely overmuch on written matter and accumulations of what has been lightly termed 'Occult haberdashery'. We lose all our physical properties at death, and our mental stock-cupboard soon becomes exhausted or valueless as we change our nature. Only the Inner Realities of Spirit remain substantially with our souls, and those are to be obtained by our actual accomplishments in their particular force-fields.

At one time, a few of the stricter Schools forbade Initiates to write of any spiritual subject, or even to read about them. This was not for the sake of mere secrecy itself, but to compel the Initiate to seek Truth Inwardly rather than from externals. They were allowed to communicate their traditions orally within a Circle of their own Companions only. This was to ensure that the Spirit of Wisdom which comes to those who 'gather in the Name', did so under the most favourable conditions for its reception.

One of the commonest questions asked in all sincerity by Neophytes is: 'What shall I read to help me on my Path?' Very few would accept the truth that only fractional representations of spiritual Verities can be made in human words, and they would be better employed seeking these within themselves than looking for them in other people's findings and opinions. Nothing except sheer experience of life will get the notion out of their heads that the more they stuff themselves with second-hand arcana the more Initiated they will be. They might as well try to appease hunger by reading an account of a banquet on a menu card, or dress themselves from the illustrations in a catalogue. All that books can do is supply information on methods. They do not, and never have supplied the means.

The craving for sheer information is natural enough to modern Westerners however, though it should be guided into useful channels where possible. Recommending books is always a difficult matter on account of individual needs, but on the whole probably the best idea is to suggest reading that encourages the seeker to look for Light Inwardly, and proposes methods of approaching this spiritually vital problem. Whatsoever deals directly with these topics, and inspires a reader to do, be, and become a more perfectly evolved soul, is worth recommendation. The rest is intellectual entertainment, worth while for mental decoration and display, but scarcely likely to result in betterment of actual being.

This should not signify that intellectual achievements are to be despised or belittled, but they must be placed in proper perspective when seen by the Light of Illumination. They are means and not ends in themselves. If they are sought as useful means to assist the spiritual development of a conscious entity, then they have value in the eyes of Inner Awareness. If, on the other hand, they are acquired purely for personal gratification or advantage, then they are worth no more than exactly that. By themselves they will not lead us along the Line of Light towards Divinity, but only to a simulated state of self-importance. Therefore they should not be sought for their own sake, but for a higher use they might serve.

Once more it is a case of seeking the Kingdom first, and then making necessary additions afterwards. If we face facts honestly, we shall find most individuals are drawn towards the Mysteries by the hope and desire of having new and thrilling experiences of consciousness or gaining superior powers over others. To put matters crudely, they are looking for kicks. The genuine Mysteries have a good way of dealing with such approaches—they offer neither thrills nor unfair advantages over anyone. No wonderful visions, exalted experiences, incredible personal powers, sensational successes with sex and finance. Nothing in fact, except hard spiritual effort with no particular reward except in its own achievement. Faced with such a disappointing prospect, sensation seekers soon abandon the purlieus of the Holy Mysteries and look elsewhere for excitement. Who shall blame them?

None except the most deeply dedicated souls with their Inner Vision truly fixed along the highest Light-line are likely to survive the testing trials applied by the Outer Courts of the Holy Mysteries. What ordinary human being stays very long of their own will in a situation where the pay is negligible, the conditions hard, their companions uncongenial, immediate future most uncertain, problems insoluble, and difficulties in plenty? No fun and games, no obvious reward for effort, and nothing to speak of in the way of tangible benefits. Any employer offering such unpalatable prospects would soon find himself with a one man business, and this is more or less what happens in the Holy Mysteries. Many are attracted into the Outer Courts by the fascination of colourful rites, intriguing companions, new horizons of thought, and all the rest of the obvious inducements. Very few indeed choose to remain after all the entertainment has been exhausted and nothing is left but an apparently empty stage. Who has sufficient courage and endurance to persist invoking NIL indefinitely until ALL emerges? Yet that is demanded of

Initiates in the Holy Mysteries who would progress beyond surface appearances.

Inevitably there comes a point upon the Inner Path where further advancement seems quite impossible and all past efforts an utter waste of time. Everything has become a dead end and a dead loss. Sometimes this is called the Lesser or Inferior Abyss. So-called 'psychic' abilities fail completely, and there may be a quite devastating sense of personal inadequacy and despondency. On ordinary life-levels we meet with this type of impasse frequently enough in relation to normal events. Perhaps some social associations come to a sticky end, or conditions of employment become intolerable. We are all familiar with such commonplace occurrences, and work out our own methods of dealing with them. When we encounter the same sort of situation magnified to spiritual proportions however, the experience may vary between what has been called 'spiritual aridity' to the most shattering of all in the 'Dark Night of the Soul', the Abyss where all seems utterly lost for ever. Whatever degree we undergo, a corresponding change will take place in us, perhaps for better, sometimes for worse, but always for a distinct difference in consciousness as a result.

Chasms of Consciousness

What in fact has happened, is that we come to the point where nothing but some marked alteration of awareness will provide us with opportunities for making progress along that particular Path. It is as if while walking along a road, we came to a river and had to proceed by boat, swimming, building a bridge, or flying across. The Path would be the same, but the means of keeping to it quite changed. This happens when we come to spiritual 'standstill points' where we must either be prepared to change our methods of consciousness and get past the apparent barrier, or wander forlornly around the same circles again, looking for some other outlet. All outlets from those circles would actually present the same problem in various ways.

When we come to these 'Chasms of Consciousness' in spiritual Dimensions, the first decision must naturally be whether or not to attempt a crossing, and the second issue is the nature of the transition. The Great Abyss for instance, is crossed by the Sword-

Bridge, to symbolize the necessity for physical death, the passage of the soul being represented by the Line of Light along the edge of the Sword. Liberated from flesh by the point of the Sword, the soul flies Lightward by way of the Lightline towards the hilt, where it comes safely to the Hand of God which wields the Weapon. The principles of this apply to all chasm-crossing. We must be prepared to 'die', or part from our existing formalization of ideas which bind us to materialized beliefs, so that we may follow the path of pure power straight to its spiritual source beyond the confines of consciousness from which we would emerge into fresh fields of illumination.

Unless we are ready to sacrifice the 'body' of our ideas on the Point of the Sword, and send their 'soul' Inwards to Light, we shall cross no chasms to gain new life among the splendours of resurrection. In other words, when we come to an Inner Space our working consciousness cannot span, we must sacrifice whatever fixed formulations (or bodies) we hold our ideas in, while projecting their 'souls' or principles Inwardly towards the Light of Truth for rebirth in another form (or body) which is suitable for life in conditions pertaining to the other side of the chasm.

In some ways we do this all the time. For example, if we follow an idea so far in words that it will go no further with much gain of meaning, then we might cross a chasm with it, and sacrificing the 'word body' resurrect the idea in a 'music body', a 'sculpture body', or perhaps a 'mathematical body'. We have retained the 'soul' of the same idea all along the line, but re-incarnated it in various forms to express it in different dimensions or conditions of conscious existence. The same principle applies to ourselves throughout our differing incarnations as materialized mortals. We get from one life to another across the Depths of Death, much as we follow a Lightline over any other Abyss.

Crossing the Abyss

In the spiritual dimensions of existence where Initiates of the Mysteries may be classed as inhabitants, very considerable alterations of consciousness indeed may be required between one side of an Abyss and another. So marked a change in fact, that it might almost amount to a reversal of polarity or entire revolution

of nature. This is not unlike the phenomenon of what was called
'conversion', or the acceptance of quite different values, by what
could be termed a 'standing jump' usually precipitated by some
impacting event. One might perhaps be justified in thinking of
this as being kicked or shot over a chasm. Such a drastic change,
however, is not 'instant evolution'. We may become *different*
beings from an expressional standpoint, but we do not become
immediately better or more highly evolved souls just because we
have crossed chasms into other conditions of consciousness. Man
does not reach Godhood with even his wildest leap. The Light-
ning-Flash symbol from top to bottom of the Tree shows the in-
stantaneous contact of Divinity with Humanity, but the spirally
winding Serpent clearly indicates the upward Path of an evolving human soul. The down-pointing Sword symbolizes our means
of bridging the gaps between our differing states of awareness
by voluntarily sacrificing one formation of consciousness for another via the Line of Inner Light.

The Sword Symbolism

In order to illustrate and set the pattern of all this, it has been
a practice in most of the Mysteries to present the actual point
of a physical Sword directly to the breast of Initiates. Sometimes
this is only done during initiation ceremonies, but some Temples
conscientiously do it briefly to all entrants via the Portal. In such
a symbolic situation, it is obvious that no one could proceed
directly without impaling themselves physically. Spiritually, however, the Sword is no hindrance at all. If progress is to be made
therefore, a complete change of approach from physical to spiritual levels must be made to bridge the gap. So a 'Password' is
exchanged in some way to suggest a connecting principle between
the two sides of the chasm, and the transition is made. It is
assumed that the entrant has abandoned a mundane personality
outside the Temple, and by this sacrifice has earned a spiritual
one for the performance of Temple procedures. There is no suggestion that the entrant has advanced as an entity to any higher
Grade by making such a change, but only made necessary
alterations to himself for working according to his Grade-status
in different conditions of consciousness.

It is easy to smile at what seems like rather childish theatrical games, but it might be unwise to do so unthinkingly. Properly performed in a correct spirit, symbolic ritual procedures are capable of setting up soul-patterns so deeply implanted in human beings they will operate for life after life, leading the Initiate to Light by every possible step and across every necessary Abyss. That is the use of ritual which is never appreciated by those ignorant of its principles. As a spiritual drill and discipline, which directs Inner energies along their proper Paths, correctly designed rituals have yet to be surpassed.

Magical rituals are of little value for winning fortunes, raising demons, blasting enemies, or the like medieval motives, but for training and raising the human soul far beyond such motivational limits, ritual methods remain superlative throughout the Mysteries. By their means, mankind has crossed the Abyss of untold centuries, and is poised now upon the brink of perhaps the greatest historical Chasm yet encountered. Shall we bridge it safely or no? The Sword-Bridge itself trembles beneath the weight of that question.

To imagine spiritual progress as an affair of hopping gaily over one chasm after another with ever increasing bounds would be a sad mistake. As in other matters, there are cautions to be observed as far as possible with all chasm crossings. The general rule is to measure the width of the chasm spanned with the Sword by the height of the soul as shown by the Rod or Staff. If these are equal, then the crossing is likely to be a safe one. Should the Staff of the Soul exceed the Sword length, then of course the chasm can be taken in a stride or less, and presents no particular problem. The Abyss of an ant is but a mere crack to an elephant. Size of soul in stature determines the dimensions of any spiritual Abyss. Little souls would be unwise to attempt large leaps on their own initiative, even though they may be carried across by the consciousness of more capable beings than themselves.

In some Magical Traditions, the Rod or Staff was magical because it automatically indicated the exact measure of its owner's soul, or his extent between Earth and Heaven. As he grew, it grew, or as he shrank so it decreased. In practice, Initiates often bore staffs of their own physical height, or a proportion of it such as a third or a quarter. This of course had nothing to do with their spiritual stature, but was symbolic of a relationship between an individual and the standard (or Staff) by which they were spiritually measured.

Measuring one's own soul

How is it possible to know the height of one's own soul so as to judge which size of chasm is safe to cross? Naturally such a question can only be attempted by each Initiate for himself, but a rough estimate may be had from a simple idea. If we remember that the top of the Staff theoretically reaches Divinity, and the bottom of it is fixed in Humanity, this will provide a clue. Taking the individual's highest conscious concept of Divinity as one end, and their most basic belief in Humanity as the other, this will give a broad measure of their soul-stature. If accurate points for these ends are marked, they are likely to be much shorter than might be supposed from wildly speculative guesses. We are seldom as noble as we like others to think we are. It was well said that the Magic Rod must be the closest secret of an Initiate. Only the Greatest God may be trusted completely by the smallest souls. Those without sufficient faith and experience in both directions had better be careful when crossing chasms.

The danger of drugs

The guiding principle of chasm-crossers in spiritual dimensions should be not to cross if possible before sufficient growth of soul has been attained for the attempt, and enough Light illuminates the Way to determine at least immediate conditions on the other side. Wild leaps into the dark from sheer foolhardiness are to be discouraged. This is always a danger in bridging an Abyss without adequate preparation of consciousness. When totally new and unexperienced forces and forms of awareness impact upon a sensitive soul unready to receive them, we may expect nothing but disorientation, confusion, and trouble.

Examples of this can be seen constantly in the results of drug inspired visions and experiences. Those who are trying to break into different dimensions through psychedelic doors come back with badly warped personalities incapable of correct interpretations or evaluation of what has happened to them. They have little to offer but psychic rubbish, which may look glittery and strange but has no authentic value as spiritual material. It is not that what they encountered was worthless, but their own inability to translate such alien energies into terms compatible with human spiritual welfare, make them a menace rather than otherwise upon the Inner Path.

The same is largely true in most cases of 'religious conversion', where a chasm of consciousness has been unduly crossed. Such an experience may be exhilarating to the survivor, but can be disastrous for imitators. It suggests a similarity to someone who falls over a precipice and lands on a ledge with a solitary nugget of gold. In their wild excitement and relief, they shriek for their friends to come as quickly as possible to share an incredible El Dorado, and have genuine regrets that so few seem to have the same luck, or so many refuse the jump. The Holy Mysteries have no place or use for this sort of 'conversion' at all. Every necessary change of consciousness made must come well within the limits of competence and control particular to the changer.

To judge such limits is a heavy responsibility which must fall on the Initiate alone. Even superiors may only advise on the matter, though they may be in a position to isolate an individual so that they harm as few other souls as possible than themselves. By what standard then, may anyone estimate their own measure of ability to cross an Abyss? A strangely practical method for use metaphorically in meditation or literally in ritual is that of the 'raised Rod'. Its principles are these.

Constructing a raised Rod

Using the faculty of creative imagery, construct out of consciousness a Rod which will symbolize the enquirer himself. A good form is the plain black and white Staff with a minimum of ornamentation. With great care and deliberation, press the black end firmly to the ground in fact or fancy, while seeking to know Inwardly just exactly what Mankind means to the seeker. There should be nothing vague or indefinite about any conclusions reached. Decisive definition is the requirement. It is little use, for instance, thinking glamorized impersonalities such as : 'All are my brethren in the family of the Divine Father, and I love them equally.' To make this exercise work properly, it is absolutely essential that a completely honest answer comes from the heart. If the querant really does not like fellow humans in general or particular for any reason, those reasons must be discovered and admitted. The object is to find the most basic actual relationship between the individuality of the enquirer and the rest of humanity. The metaphorical and Magical Rod is used like a probe which is repeatedly pushed into the loose soil of subconsciousness until it meets solid bedrock underneath.

To assist this process, the quiz method is probably about the most practical. Brief and pointed queries are needed, calling for concise replies or a simple yes-or-no answer. It must be remembered that the objective sought is accurate information about the querant, and therefore the questions should be phrased to that end. For instance, it should not be asked: 'Who are my particular enemies?' but 'Who do I consider my worst enemies?' Again it should not be asked: 'Who can I trust completely?', but instead, 'Who do I believe in enough to trust completely?' There is an important difference between these phrasings. We may not ever discover in this life the real truth about any matter or mortal in its own absolute right, but we can and should know our own attitude and standpoint towards them which form the basic beliefs by which we live. It does not follow such beliefs are correct, unchangeable, or should not be modified in keeping with our development as souls. What matters is that we have them, know them, and are prepared to make use of them accordingly. In this instance of Rod-probing, we are looking for a personal Credo to provide spiritual stability for the Cosmos of consciousness we are Inwardly creating. It is somewhat like the force of gravity in a planet. Without gravity we should have no physical stability, and without an equivalent power deriving from principles poised relatively between the pivots of Heaven and Earth or God and Man, we have no spiritual stability worth considering. So our efforts at finding the bottom pivot with a human-probing Rod must be directed to this purpose.

Once a few solid realizations have been made concerning personal relationships with Humanity, the Rod is then raised towards Heaven and the exercise is continued in relation to Divinity. Again the outcome has nothing to do with abstract speculations about Divinity, but should deal entirely with what Divinity means to the enquirer, what ideas they hold on the subject, and how the question affects them in particular. The quiz might well include apparently silly queries such as: 'What do I believe God looks like? Sounds like? Feels like? Tastes like? Smells like?', or 'If I were Supreme Deity, what would I do in such and such a case?' The whole object should be to become as personal and even as petty on the point as possible. Far from magnifying Divinity into an Improbably and incredibly abstract Being, the idea in this exercise is to focus the Infinite right down to the size of a single human in search of himself. This may prove almost as elusive as meeting anything tangible in the air with the white point of the Rod, which makes a good symbolic activity relative to a God-search.

With only a little ingenuity, Rod-raising can be built into a very pleasing and profitable Rite on its own merits. Eventually the operator will become conditioned to associating the simple act of a Rod touching Earth with directing consciousness towards Humanity, and raising the same Rod in the air to Heaven, with lifting awareness in the direction of Divinity. In the end, the symbolic act will function as a Key or trigger causing consciousness to follow its pattern. If it is considered unlikely that a symbolic staff held skyward could lead to contact with Divinity Itself, surely this is no stranger than an aerial rod thrust skywards bringing in radio programmes. It could well be said that in the case of the aerial, it connects with a scientifically designed apparatus to receive the energy impulses and translate them into sensory mechanical terms appreciable to human observers. Just the same may also be said about the raised symbolic Rod. It too connects with an apparatus designed to receive and translate Inner energies into appreciable terms of consciousness. That apparatus is the Initiate.

The entire value of this practice is for sizing and measuring up the soul making good use of it. This enables the practitioner to assess himself with comparative accuracy concerning his ability to cross an Abyss or fulfil any of his proper functions in the Holy Mysteries. It ensures his unlikelihood of tackling spiritual tasks far beyond his natural capacity, thereby suffering a great deal of quite unnecessary unhappiness. So he learns his true degree no matter what fancy title he adopts otherwise, and the real degree of any Initiate is his alignment of Divinity and Humanity through himself in a Line of Light from one extremity of that

Cosmic Circle to the other. The Rod of an Initiate is his own standing in that Circle.

Few people these days believe in (or make a concept of) a personalized Divinity. Even those acknowledging Divinity in principle prefer the idea of an Ultimate Abstraction rather than a personal presentation. For them, to personify Divinity lessens Its distant dignity, and a Father-God Figure would be no more acceptable than Father Christmas. Such thinking falls in an Abyss between two standpoints and grasps neither. For an Initiate of the Mysteries, it is a case of 'Rods up and Swords across'.

Divinity is recognized not only as the Ultimate Abstraction, but also as the most intense Personal Presentation possible. The two Concepts are opposite ends of the same Rod or the closing contact of any Circle. The Abstraction belongs to the Infinite Being, and the Personification belongs to the Initiate. Thus an Initiate of the Holy Mysteries does not believe in Divinity as a personal Being in Itself, but does most emphatically believe in and practises the personification of that Being as a means of mutual relationship between them.

There is nothing really extraordinary about this. We do it all the time one way and another. What with personifications of national figures, commercial figures, and every kind of image imaginable, our whole lives are filled with images and idols of all descriptions. We smile or sneer at the primitive peoples who imagined Divinity in natural forces or personified by mental and material forms constructed by themselves. Yet we accept very solemnly the most idiotic concepts we have made for political, commercial, and social reasons. It has always been simpler to fill a stomach than a soul, though the one is an inadequate substitute for the other. At the same time, it is no more practical to offer a soul insubstantial vapourings than to offer a stomach gas for dinner. Both need solid food in their respective spheres or they will shrink and suffer.

Initiates of the Holy Mysteries are looking for very solid spiritual food indeed. Nothing less than the most personal contact possible with the Entities and realities of Inner Existence. There is nothing vague or impersonal about the intentions of Initiates. In a sense they are entirely selfish individuals, since they seek the Supreme Selfhood of All-Being. They are not content to remain ordinary human mortals living earth-based lives according to man-made rules and regulations. However necessary it may be to observe and comply with customs of conduct controlling human behaviour, the Initiate of Light lives Inwardly by the Laws controlling Cosmos Itself.

No Initiate rejects earthly rewards of riches, fame, and other material benefits without very good reasons indeed. Who seeks Light must travel lightly. Lifetimes on earth come and go, but the Life sought by an Initiate of Light lies beyond the boundaries of mortal bodies. Far from being a self-sacrificing, abnegating soul, the Initiate aims constantly at the Nothing from whence All emanates. The most direct and intimate relationship conceivable is demanded of Divinity in all Aspects. No genuine Initiate of the Holy Mysteries has any use for, or time to consider, some nebulous, ineffective, disinterested Deity of indecision and indifference towards the units of Its own Existence among which the Initiate numbers. There is only one acceptable relationship sought between the Initiate and his Infinity—namely the coming together of each other into a common focal point of consciousness.

This 'Attaining' is attempted in as many ways as there are methods in the Mysteries, and the various practitioners naturally suppose their own particular Systems are best. Blessed indeed are they that find and follow faithfully whichever System is best suited to their condition of consciousness and degree of humano-Divinity. The only One True Path is that of any one soul true to its especial Spirit. True also there are broad categories which may be shared by types of soul, and One Supreme Spirit emanating our entire Existence. As living beings, we are specific emissions of conscious Energy from the Awareness of All. If we are focused upon matter we incarnate. We live as the Consciousness of and in Creation-Cosmos. As Forms we are but mortal, though as Force we belong to Eternal Energy, which is imperishable. Being conscious *with* Force *of* Form, we can simply accept the Forms among which we are focused, or learn how to use our Forces to make the Forms according to the Will within each of us. Initiates of the Mysteries combine both courses.

It is for us to formate the Inner forces operating through us into expressions of their typified energy. We do this in accordance with our own types of nature. We make up our Gods, Demons, and other Concepts of Cosmic or Chaotic Entities out of our own consciousness as impressed by the Entities themselves. Consequently our Concepts are proportionally representational of realities in a totally different set of dimensions to ours. As humans, we must adapt our awareness of other life-levels in the best way we can, and such symbolic means have proved most practical up to now, hence their use in the Mysteries. There is no particular reason why we should not imagine our Gods in any way we like, so long as adequate forms are constructed for the Forces we are invoking.

Conceptions of Inner Energy

The principles of this are childishly simple, and indeed most children instinctively practice them. Whichever type of Inner Energy is required, a suitable Image or Concept is set up consciously to contain and deal with it. Once contact is established between the actual Energy and the Image evoked for it in the awareness of the individual, the force of one operates through the form of the other. In olden times this was fundamentally crude and effective. If ferocity of nature was needed, a Lion, tiger, wolf, or other animal image would serve as a Symbol. Sheer speed and agility might be personified as a deer or monkey. Whatever the quality, so necessary to survival in primitive days, some animal or creature usually specialized in it, and Man summed them all up in himself by symbolic methods. As Man progressed, so did he use more evolved species of Symbol ranging from artistic and poetic to mechanical and mathematical formulae. Primordial Man looked at an animal exhibiting coveted qualities and said in effect: 'That's *me*!' Philosophic Man considered the Cosmos and formulated 'I AM THAT I AM.' A difference of degree only. The principle of relationship between creature and Creator via consciousness centred by a Symbol remains unchanged essentially.

So-called civilized Man makes a terrible mistake in supposing Divine or other Telesmic Images to be nothing more than worthless figments of immature imagination, having no more behind them than purely human origins. Half a truth is worse than a whole lie. Man may formalize Divinities or Devils, but he cannot energize them. Their force must come from the Entities they represent, and These are real enough in Their own realm. Everyone formulates according to their own ideas. Whether we make up Father-Gods, Mother-Gods, Saviour-Gods, Nature-Gods, or the likenesses of our deceased ancestors, we shall provide some kind of Form for the God that in us lies. There is nothing wrong, inaccurate, or undesirable in the fundamental idea of constructing formalized expressions for the forces of Entities beyond and behind our ordinary human state of being. There are just different ways and means of doing this, and the Holy Mysteries have evolved such methods of their own which Initiates practice according to their degree of understanding and ability.

Once it is realized that our formalized notions of Gods and other Aspects of Inner Entities arise from our own awareness of Them, and are simply Symbols of the Energies they really are of Themselves, we can go ahead happily with a clear conscience and use whatever Forms we will for invoking Their Forces. When we are in a position to tell the Inner Ones : 'I know this is not what you are, but it is the way I see you and approach you. Show me a better way if you can,' They will respond through the Forms we create with Their Force. These Forms need not be anthropomorphic in any way, although such is certainly satisfactory from an artistic viewpoint and commonly used in the Mysteries. The Concept of an Universal Spirit, Itself beyond all Form, which is directly applicable to any given human contingency, is a Master-method outside the average means of ordinary mortals, however much they attempt it. Nevertheless this apparent abstraction is a formality of its kind. The further we think ourselves away from the limitations of Form, the more do we exchange one type of formation for another. It is simply a question of level.

Although we are technically free to invent whatever Forms we will, the Mysteries operate with fundamental Forms common to the consciousness of both human and other participants. They are outside ordinary time, so that they will last for indefinite numbers of incarnation, and Initiates can easily follow them life after life whether incarnate or discarnate. Thus they provide spiritual continuity through several dimensions of Existence, linking one type of life with another in their differing Cosmic cycles.

Given the same set of Symbols to work with for many incarnations, an Initiate rapidly retraces previous ground covered in past lives, and not only picks up from the last level of living intelligence, but also adds to it from inter-incarnationary experience. Hence the need of preserving the Symbols faithfully and passing them down their Light-line with the greatest care possible. This is the incalculable value of myth and tradition in the Mysteries. They supply the springboard so to speak from the past, which gives the means of arriving at a worthwhile future. The Chasms of centuries are best bridged by the chains of symbolic correspondences available to those working the Mysteries through all ages and stages of Awareness.

In theory and sometimes in practice, the Symbolic Keys impressed into the consciousness of a Candidate during an Initiation ceremony, will unlock the hidden doors within him leading to his past experience and wisdom gained in previous incarnations as an Initiate elsewhere. There should be no need for verbalized expressions of opinion concerning the Symbols. Once they are firmly grasped by the Candidate, they will reveal their own Inner realities by themselves if they are sufficiently worked with over the necessary period. Everything depends on the quality and quantity of effort expended by the Initiate with his Symbols. The 'teaching of the Grade' comes through them, and not from any talks, lectures, or other trimmings thrown in for makeweights. True teaching comes from Within, via the Paths of Wisdom to which the Symbols are clues, keys, and guardians.

A fair assessment of any individual's actual Inner status can be made by observing how he handles the Symbols given him at Initiation or from other sources. If he shows aptitude in using, combining, and extracting spiritual values from these, he is likely to be of ancient standing in the Mysteries. An example of this is the presentation of Symbols made to an Incarnation of Dalai Lama grade in the Tibetan Bhuddist Mysteries. It is a spiritual 'aptitude test' which reveals the right soul for that particular purpose. The same principles apply to all Initiates in their degree.

Possibly about the soundest advice or injunction that could be given sincere Aspirants, would be to confine their consciousness within the Symbol-Circle of their Initiatory Grade in the Mysteries and attempt working with these exclusively to a point of exhaustion. No matter how tempted they may be to chase around everywhere else looking for knowledge and experience (or thrills and amusement) the first hard lesson a practical magician must learn is to stay in his consecrated Circle and expand its limits from within by means of the Symbols provided. That is by far the best way of making practical progress on any Path of Initiation.

To set up a true Circle, dedicate it, and by working in it invoke 'Gods' and banish 'Demons' is the task of a lifetime or more. The dramatic ritual-representations of this process played in Lodge or Temple are the shadows of a much vaster Drama lived in reality on the spiritual Stage of Inner Life itself. Yet they are the shadows that lead to Substance, the Unreal pointing to the Real, the False that indicates the True, if only we use them wisely and interpret them rightly in the sense of going rightwards as the Way of Light.

The concept of a magician in his circle with perhaps two faithful associates, engaged on a Magical Operation of summoning good spirits to overcome evil by means of Magical Names and Symbols is a fancy based on absolute spiritual and psychological fact. Its fundamental pattern is perfectly sound, and an essential part of the design incorporated as a theme throughout the Mysteries. Since it shows how to set up and operate the 'Magical Microcosmos' in and through which the Initiate relates himself harmoniously with all else, there is every reason why we should take it seriously enough to study carefully and find out what its Forms and Forces amount to.

It should be remembered that our progress is cyclic around a spiritual spiral like the Serpent and Tree, so that we always repass our median Lightlines on higher levels. The truths we first grasp in a child-like way instinctively, later become folklore and fairy tale, then eventually scientific fact and ultimately spiritual certitudes. A child accepts Father Christmas as a personal Being, an intelligent adult treats the same entity with amusement or indifference, but an Initiate realizes that Consciousness is a Force that can be focused into Form, and therefore the entity of 'Father Christmas' is a valid one as a Concept. One complete cycle of belief, disbelief, and re-belief.

On a broader scale, much the same is happening on the 'Occult Front'. Having thrown all previous beliefs in Divinities and Demons on to the scrap heap, Mankind is now carefully decorating the vacancy of his disbelief with fragments of their broken images. As a whole, we have not yet reached the point of their reconstitution into Concepts commensurate with our evolutionary ends. When Man and his Gods meet personally again it will be a cause for celebration by both, and the degree of mutual recognition may be quite startling. Who knows where and when this will occur? Perhaps the most likely point will be within a Magical Circle, however this may be termed in the phraseology of any period. If we call it a cyclotron at present, why should we be surprised at any projection it may become in future? Providing it leads to our Ultimate Enlightenment, there is no reason why our forces should not encounter Divinity in any form of Circle imaginable. A Magic Circle may be made in many ways, let us examine a standard pattern and discover what we can of its design.

CHAPTER V

HOW TO BUILD A MAGIC CIRCLE

Almost every book purporting to deal with 'practical Magic' gives formulae for making and consecrating Magical Circles, but none seem to give very precise reasons for such an activity, or suggest further developments and uses in connection with it. Yet it is indeed the basic exercise out of which everything else must come for the practitioner. The Circle of Zero, as it were, defining the Nil from whence emerges All. To an outside observer ignorant of the process, few things might seem more ridiculous than an adult person making rings round themselves and attaching mental labels at the intersections like some childish game. In fact, however, the principles behind the practice are as sound and scientific on spiritual levels as any form of designing on physical ones. To 'set up a Circle' properly is a highly skilled affair, and no mere mumbo jumbo at all. If we consider what is happening from an Inner observation point, this will soon become evident.

To construct a Magic Circle is to create Inner Cosmos according to Intention. Although imagination is the method used for the construction, the forces which focus through it are very real energies of consciousness deriving from sources other than the operative arranger of their symbolic forms. Naturally the individual ability of the operator is a decisive factor, upon which the efficacious degree of any circle depends. Circles do not put themselves together without a directing will, whether they are Cosmic creations of a Divinity, or the personal cosmoi of human beings, both of which a genuine Magic Circle should intersect.

We live in circles of all descriptions. Family, social, political, economic, religious, and every kind of circle imaginable. We may be born into them, coerced into them, or enter them for any reason whatever. Why should a Magic Circle be any different in principle? The answer is because while other circles are so to speak 'ready-made', a true Magic Circle has to be set up by individual Initiates themselves of their own will in relation to their contact-points with what might be termed the spiritual world around them. No one can make a Magic Circle for any-body else, though we may all be included in those belonging to others. Until Initiates are capable of creating the circles of Cosmos around themselves, they will not be admitted into the wider circles of Inner Reality that exist beyond the usual limits of human awareness. Nor will the substitute of a mere 'dream-world' as an escape-sphere from disliked external conditions be acceptable to the Inner Guardians. Such is not a Magic Circle, but a refusal to realize the responsibilities of an awakening soul. An authentic Magic Circle is the strange anomaly of being a construction of imagination designed to relate both Inner and Outer realities together through the symbolically channelled con-sciousness of its maker. When properly formed, it will do exactly that.

The first thing any mortal child must learn is orientation and adaption to its physical world and the phenomena encountered therein. We must discover the spatial dimensions of up, down, back, forth, left and right in order to make sense of our bodies. Then we must gain a time sense of past, present, and future, so that our minds are able to work.

In those circles of space and time, events happen. In sensing the significance of events we exercise our souls. There we have the Three Rings of Cosmos, a representation of which is made by every correct Magic Circle. Literally we are being born again into new dimensions of Inner being, and have to go through another type of orientation and adjustment on those levels. They too have Time-Space-Event equivalents to those of mundane life, though very differently indeed from our limited edition of exist-ence on this planet. Nor is the type of consciousness used in one state valid for another, being quite different in application and expression. To operate in a human world we have to use human consciousness, and to operate in other states of being we must use the necessary kinds of awareness proper to their limits. If, while we yet inhabit human bodies, we would work otherwise, then we must find some means of adapting our consciousness from one condition to another and back again safely. Hence the need for, and value of, a Magic Circle.

The Triple Magical Circle of Cosmos

The seven co-ordinating points of the Triple Magical Circle of Cosmos are Heaven, Earth, the Four Quarters, and the Centre. Otherwise, Divinity, Humanity, the four Archangels, and the Initiate. These define the symbolic limits of the Inner Dimensions with which the Initiate is attempting to make a stable relationship on the principles of a gyroscope establishing self-gravity by its own rotation.

All the ritual procedure connected with this process is for the sake of acquiring poise, balance, orientation, and the most favourable adjustment between Initiate and Innerworld. It sounds easy enough when described in books—a gesture to each quarter, an uttered Name, and the Circle is supposed to be there in theory. In hard fact no Circle can possibly be built in that way without an enormous amount of time and effort spent in developing it to such a point of amenability.

Any Initiate capable of establishing a true Circle at an almost instant rate would admit that it existed around already, him and he was simply directing his attention to pre-prepared points arranged in his consciousness. For this to be possible, many a long hour of meditation and work will be necessary. No Name of Power is worth more to the utterer than the amount of energy he has charged it with himself. It is useless calling on Angelic or other Names unless sufficient conscious effort has already been put into them by the magical means of meditation and mediation. All a Name does is to evoke at one instance what has been accumulated bit by bit over prolonged periods. A Magical Name is not unlike a filing code that selects a card in a moment providing data which has maybe taken many years to build up into a collection of consciousness.

Rulers of the Quarters

The Names of the Archangels or Rulers of the Quarters then, should be Keywords, each to a typified quarter of the total Circle of Consciousness the Initiate aims to centre around himself. That is to say, if we took the whole of an initiated human awareness and sorted it into four major categories of a distinctive kind, the descriptive name of each quadrant is magically termed 'Archangelic', and personified as such. Furthermore, if each segment is considered as part of the whole Circle and given an individual 'letter', the four in combination will 'spell' the Divine Name controlling, creating, and cosmating them as One. To 'Utter the Name' is thus to invoke or call upon the totality of Being, whether it is the Ultimate Divinity, or an individual soul. The overall picture of Magic Names is of the One Name co-ordinating the four 'Archangels', their Names holding their particular Angelic Orders together, and so on right down to individual spirits and souls. Not unlike the schoolboy address system of reaching any person from the Infinite by writing:

> John Doe Esq,
> 14
> Any Street,
> Anytown,
> England,
> Earth,
> Solar System,
> The Universe,
> Creation.

Nine steps from Existence to a single individual by a series of Names directing consciousness from one stage to another, establishing a relationship between them all. Magical Names should provide equally reasonable linkage throughout the stages of Inner Existence.

The Names and attributes of the Rulers of Quarters vary according to the Mystery System, but for Western workers there seems little doubt that the most practical Concepts are those of the four Archangels Raphael, Michael, Gabriel, and Auriel. They are well established by Tradition, and have characteristics entirely in keeping with our culture and ethnological developments. Familiar figures as they may be to many, it might be useful to recapitulate their idiosyncrasies here, and perhaps learn some additional data or gain fresh ideas thereby. To paraphrase a proverb, there are many new tunes to be had from old fiddles.

Although there are endless speculations on the natures and beings of Angels, Arch or otherwise, such can be a very time-wasting and profitless occupation. So far as average Initiates are concerned, Archangels are personalized foci of typified conscious energies with an existence of their own as Entities operating through Inner Dimensions. They are major fulfillers of specified functions in the construction and continuity of Cosmos. Each is a 'heading' as it were, under which all other allied aspects of awareness and action are grouped. Though they have Inner reality by themselves, Initiates are responsible for building up their TIs at the quarters of their personal circles, because it is through those TIs that Archangels interact consciously with Initiates, and the Initiates in turn participate fractionally of the powers inherent in those incredible energies. True, the individual fraction of power temporarily acquired by an Initiate is probably a very minute one indeed as compared with its source. The Initiate is unlikely to accomplish anything very spectacular in physical terms by means of these forces, which must be applied through spiritual and mental paths for the most practical results. This of course will eventually produce physical results if those are an ultimate requirement of the directing Will, but the decisive factor is the mediatorial ability of the Initiates themselves.

Just how well or otherwise are Initiates able to mediate the energies they contact through their Circles, depends on the degree to which they have worked therein, and this again ties back with the basis on which that Circle is constructed. The Archangels of the Quarters being our basis in this instance, let us meet them in person, commencing from the East according to the Way of Light.

Raphael

Raphael ('Healer of God') typifies the youthful enthusiasm and 'go-aheadness' we need to make progress on our Pathways. He is the rising of the Inner Light in mankind, and heals the hurts we encounter both from circumstances and each other in our eagerness to follow where he leads us. (Though Angels are referred to as 'he' or 'she', it must be remembered they are non-reproductive and therefore sexless to us, and may be dealt with from either polarity.) Raphael personifies our natural curiosity and desire to know all about everything. To some extent he equates with Hermes as leader of souls and instructor of minds. His Key-Symbol is the Sword and Arrow ('Keen as a Sword, swift as an Arrow to its mark'). His Element is Air as signifying

Life, and of course he is a winged being to indicate Aspiration and Faith. Like Hermes, Raphael is patron of travel and most enterprises of adventure in human activities such as commerce, inventions, theatricals, and the like. As a healer of hurts he bears a golden vial of balm, which is not to be interpreted in the sense of gold being sufficient payment for any hurt. It may, however, be taken to mean that compensation for whatever injuries we sustain in our spiritual struggles will eventually come to us one way or another. If this reaches us via Raphael, it is likely to be in the nature of new opportunities or abilities to overcome old difficulties.

Raphael is usually visualized as a young being with brown hair and grey eyes, lively voice and engaging disposition. His colours are associated with Springtime and the dawn, pale blues, delicate greens, etc. His robes are of these tints in the traditional angelic pattern, and his girdle is deep blue. It is technically possible to visualize the Archangels in modern dress of any description, but this would be a bad aesthetic and magical error. They should be seen as timelessly as is practicable, linked by the natural colours of the Solar cycles and seasons in combination with the elements, so that we associate them with the creative energies around and within us.

Michael

In the South, Michael ('the Godlike') stands in full mid-day splendour, a familiar figure in armour, commonly pictured as spearing a symbolically evil monster. He shows the power of Light over Darkness, and is figured as being at the Right Hand of God. This in fact is his position at his Quarter of the Magical Circle to an East-facing Initiate. He is the Right Hand Angel who tells us what we ought to do, while his colleague on our left (Auriel) warns us what not to do. Michael appointed himself as mediator of Mankind before the Throne of God, and promised to stand by even the worst mortal as long as they had the slightest good in them. He is thus the Champion of Cosmos over Chaos, and definitely a Solar Angel. Occasionally he is shown on horseback, the horse being a Sun creature, and Apollo in the Sun-chariot equates with an equestrian Michael.

It is Michael who cures diseases of humanity arising from unbalance and disorder of natural forces. He typifies our inherent longing to be 'Right' in every way, and if we ever achieve any degree of such an objective, it will be with his help. Michael's Key-Symbol is the Rod, or spear-staff, his period full noon, and his Season Summer. For that reason he is visualized with golden hair, brilliant blue eyes, a commanding voice, and a wholly admirable nature. The kind of superior officer whose orders would be obeyed without question, and in whom may be placed entire confidence. Michael is indeed the Grand Master of the Mysteries of Light.

Fire is Michael's Element, and as might be expected, his colours align with Summer and Noon, being deep greens, vivid blues, bright yellows and the red of roses. His girdle or belt is golden-yellow, and there should be a Solar Symbol on his brazen breastplate. Usually his armour is quasi-Roman in type, with a kilt, but he may well be thought of sometimes in off-duty uniform. He is patron of sports, athletics, and open-air pursuits, and in his capacity of Judge of Souls, hopes for high standards of performance within the principles of fair play from humans.

Gabriel

At the Western Point, Archangel Gabriel (Javriel the 'Potency of God') rules. He is the Fertility-figure, the Lord of Resurrection who triumphs over Death by the Potency of Love. He personifies Compassion and feeling, tenderness and strength combined. His Key-Symbol is the Cup or Horn with all its significance, and he is visualized with chestnut hair, amber eyes, a friendly and sympathetic voice, together with a completely congenial disposition. He typifies our great need of loving and being loved, desire of conviviality, and our deepest necessity for true spiritual sustenance, without which we might as well not live at all.

Since Gabriel is at Sunset-Autumn position, his colours match up accordingly. Reds, russet-yellows, and similar hues. His girdle is red. His concern is with the kinder side of humanity, and he is represented as a mature being connected with our more peaceful pursuits, consolidation of gains, and enjoyment of existence. He directs our attention to the moral as distinct from the intellectual side of the Mysteries, and presides over the companionship that should prevail in every Circle.

His Element being Water, Gabriel is a pervasive Angel, cooling hot-headedness, soothing irritations, and generally dissolving most difficulties capable of solution by such means. The tears of Gabriel wash away the sorrows of our world, because they are tears of sympathetic and understanding love. It is Gabriel who provides confidence to face death in no particularly brave or heroic manner, but quietly and normally as part of our Eternal Existence. Gabriel convinces us that Love is immortal, and as products of it—so are we. However many times our flesh bodies die and are dissolved in the Ocean of Life, our souls will be safe in Gabriel's keeping while they continue along the unseen edge of the Cosmic Circle to re-emerge into material manifestation again until we are sufficiently developed as individuals to exist otherwise. The Cup of Gabriel is also the Cauldron of regeneration.

Auriel

Lastly, at the Northern Station, Archangel Auriel ('Light of God') presides. Unless properly understood, he might seem rather a dark Angel indeed. His robes are sombre, being aligned with Winter and Midnight. Blacks, dark browns, greys, though lightened by the sparkle of frost and the shining of stars in brilliant moonlight. He is represented as a kindly Elder with greying black hair and beard, dark eyes, and a deep deliberate voice. His girdle is black, but relieved with silver. His Key-Symbol is the Shield and Mirror, and his Element is Earth.

Auriel is very much an Angel of Light. He is the Light shining in Darkness, that the Darkness did not understand and could not extinguish. Consciousness in Unconsciousness, Knowledge in Ignorance, Being in Unbeing. He is the Light of Experience and Wisdom, shining brightly in the Dark Womb of the Eternal Mother. He typifies the Seed of Light that manifests in us as living beings, and which we bear from life to life that it may grow ever brighter until it becomes an Inner Sun of its own System, and we become Solar Logoi in our turn.

Auriel is associated with all the tolerance, wisdom, and development that should come with sheer experience of life and death until a soul grows enough to take such matters in its spiritual stride and seek better forms of being. He rightly belongs to Earth, because when we live on Earth as we should in Heaven, our object as humans will be attained, and both Heaven and Earth will 'pass away'. An unlikely event in our predictable future, but attainable in individual instances. Humanity will never achieve 'salvation' *en masse,* but only in single file through the narrow Gates leading to Light. Correct Pillar passage in any Temple should be for one person only.

The Magic Mirror of Auriel reflects us to ourselves, showing up our mistakes, and picturing whatever we should learn. Occasionally Auriel is shown with a Book of Wisdom instead of the Shield. His Shield however, is supposed to protect us from adversity by cushioning our consciousness against shocks and blows, or sparing us from knowing what would hurt us needlessly because we had no means of dealing with it. Auriel is a kind Angel, who attempts to enlighten the Children of Light, but sees no advantage in allowing them to suffer senselessly. It is he that tries to stop us making the same mistakes over and over again. Altogether, Auriel is the Light of Law and Learning, without which we shall never grow up in Spirit.

Location of the Quarters

Such is the briefest possible outline of the Archangels at the Quarters of our Magical Circle. The more they are thought about and worked with, the more real and meaningful they will become. It is a matter of constructing their TIs from all the 'spare parts' provided by the checklist. As they are assembled, a great many other details will fill themselves in and drop into place. It will be discovered for instance, that if their girdles were tied together in a circle, it would form a Circle of Light spectromatically, with red at the bottom end, yellow in the middle, blue at the top, and silver-black connecting through the invisible bands. Apart from the Seasons, the Archangels are recognizable as the Ages of Mankind, and about everything else divisible into four. The normal Magical relationship to them as a team is facing East, but of course all Quarters are faced individually for various reasons. The basis of East-facing is much older than Christianity. In Hebrew the Quarters are definitely indicated by the words :

Yamin   Right, or South.
Kedem   Front, or East.
Shemal   Left, or North.
Achor   Behind, or West.

In the Ancient Egyptian Mysteries, the Quarters were aligned with Osiris and Ra on the North-South axis, and Nepthys—Isis on the East-West median. This was supposed to be a closely guarded secret, and the text runs: 'Let no outsider know this. Do it not in the presence of anyone save thy father or son or alone with the Gods, for it is a Great Mystery known not to man.' The father or son referred to, would of course apply to seniors or juniors in the same Mystery workings. Sometimes the picture of Isis was painted in the bottom of a coffin with arms stretched up sideways, so that the corpse lay enfolded in the 'arms of the Goddess' from behind, since the souls of the faithful were 'taken West' with the Boat of the Son. The affairs of the living were worked along the East-West Light line, and those of the dead along the North-South magnetic axis, since Osiris was the God of the Dead and governed the North.

We must remember that in equatorial countries the North wind was the blessed one, since it brought coolness and comfort from the scorching heat, whereas in Northern latitudes it was an accursed wind bringing ice and sterility with it. Even so, the North of our Magic Circles is still the Place of the Dead with Winter, and we guide ourselves by the Pole Star, sometimes represented above Auriel, or on his headdress.

With the Christian Mysteries, the central Christ-Figure into which Initiates attempt to identify themselves, joins Divinity above and Man below into a single personification. There are no definite Quarter-Concept personifications, since the Christian Mysteries are based on Triadism like those of the Druids. However, the Quarters may be associated with such Quarternities as the Four Events of the Saviour's Birth, Life, Death, and Resurrection, the Four Arms of the Cross, the Four Gospels, etc. The Elements of the Eucharist consisting of Salt, Wine, Water, and Bread, are common to other Mysteries than Christian. So are the Passion-fluids of seed, blood, tears, and sweat.

If we consider the four main headings concerned with agriculture, sowing, tending, harvesting, and clearing the Earth of its crops, we shall see the Cycle of Cain. If we take a quarternity of herding, breeding, rearing, slaughtering, and consuming the animals, we shall have the Cycle of Abel. Everything fits somewhere into the Magic Circles of Time-Space-Events which Initiates of the Mysteries are expected to construct around themselves.

It might well be asked why an Initiate or anyone else should go to the considerable lengths and amount of effort necessary to cast, or construct those Circles of Consciousness in which they will live, move, and hold their Magical Being. What possible advantages can there be in playing such games with oneself in one's own mind? If our Gods or Demons are no more than projections of ourselves into our own awareness, what benefits can they bring, or why need we fear their antipathy?

It is probably impossible to over-emphasize the importance of the fact that in creating forms for and of Inner Entities, we are simply making conveniences of consciousness to establish mutual relationships. The actual Energies concerned are beyond any form we know or can imagine, therefore they must be translated into our terms. They bless or blast us depending on how we relate ourselves with them. Electricity will bless us from a lamp, or blast us if we stick the wires thereto in our mouths. More subtle Energies in what we term 'spiritual' dimensions will either bless us by cosmating our consciousness into harmoniously formed Circles (or cycles), or else by wrong relationships will blast us by causing chaos in our consciousness through fragmentation of force into anti-patterns of discord. Need anyone doubt such effects when they are to be encountered so often in this world?

Correct relationships with the Energies of Life and Existence are of paramount importance to us all. Divinity is more than an idea in anyone's mind. It is the Difference between our Being and Non-Being. So far as we are concerned, It is Who, What, Why, Where, When, and How we ARE. Our Eternal I AM. Those who cannot see the importance of relating themselves reasonably with an Energy so vital to their own actuality are obviously 'lost to Light', because they are utterly blind.

Initiates of the Mysteries are well aware that the 'Gods and Demons' they work with via their Circles are what might be called 'Inner Art Forms' energized by actual Forces derived from and directed by what Jung calls the 'Collective Consciousness', which of course includes their own. To some extent, this is not unlike painting a picture or writing a story, and then having the characters come to life of their own volition like Pygmalion's statue, though scarcely for the same reason.

Nevertheless, these characterizations of Inner Energy will only behave according to their specific terms of reference. That is to say, a Michael-concept will always be and act as a Michael-concept should, its essential nature remaining unaltered throughout its existence. What has happened is that a Michael-concept becomes a focus for energies of what might be called the 'Michalean frequency band' only. Just as a pre-set crystal will only permit electro-magnetic energy of its own frequency to pass through it and manifest otherwise, so does a pre-set Michael-concept respond to its particular modification of conscious energies received from any source. Hence the need for a comprehensive set of concepts covering the widest area of Awareness with the fewest practical number of changes. The Four Archangel-concepts are intended to personify and present this coverage of Cosmos.

Each Personification provides the Initiate with access to that specific type of Consciousness as far as they are able to reach through It into the Collective Consciousness It typifies. If we try and imagine the CC as a literal Ocean containing all the Awareness there is or ever was, and every kind of different species of Awareness as fish within it, we shall have a useful picture to play with. Suppose the fish to be of all different sizes, colours, and descriptions. How could we depend on landing any particular sort of fish we might need? Obviously by using only bait and tackle to catch it in precisely the right way. Say, for instance, we were after green fish of one species alone, and nothing but a green bait shaped like a pothook, attached to a yellow line at a depth of thirty feet during the night of a full moon would catch the creatures? In other words, to arrive at any given sort of conscious energy, we must operate through whatever prerequisites may be called for to effect the contact. The Archangel-concepts fulfil that function at the Quarters of our Magical Cosmoi. Most so-called Magical Formulae are in fact prearranged patterns, which, if followed faithfully, should result in exchanges of Inner conscious energies with a definite input-output relationship.

This is the practical purpose of rituals, even of the nastiest kind. If any of the unpleasantly insane rites from medieval Grimoires were scrupulously carried out, the consciousness (and conscience) of the operator would have been subjected to such a horrible conditioning, that it would infallibly make contact with Inner entities of the worst description. True, these might not reach objective levels immediately or dramatically, but their influence would be none the less real for that. Their reality would certainly be demonstrated well enough by the human operator's behaviour and changes of character. The 'Formulae', or conditioning process of consciousness laid down in Magical procedural patterns are perfectly valid exercises of Awareness, whether they are laid out for good or evil purposes. Once set up the course, and chase an individual consciousness around it often enough, and the soul becomes conditioned accordingly. It is the aim of the Holy Mysteries of Light to set out a circular course that will direct the dedicated souls therein to the Creator of the Cosmos they are trying to copy.

The main question at issue concerns the relative realities of Inner and Outer Cosmoi. We are familiar enough with the exoteric so-called scientific, materialistic, 'humanist', or otherwise termed viewpoint which denies reality to whatever is not in objective evidence and observable by outwardly polarized awareness. So too, are we familiar with the 'all is Maya—illusion' esotericist who takes the opposite line of everything being 'in the mind' while the Supreme Spirit is 'Ultimate Thought'.

Between these Pillars of Extremity the Initiate of Light seeks the Middle Way out of the problems proposed by both antagonists. In the old Egyptian Mysteries, one of the candidate's experiences was to pass between Pylons in which concealed priests hurled opposing queries and epithets at him, as well as trying to prevent his progress with all sorts of snares, barriers, and other devices. All this had to be overcome, and the candidate sail serenely through the test along the median Line of Light. At a ceremonial Initiation of course, prepared stimuli and responses were provided, whereas in real life, whether Inwardly or Outwardly, we have to find our own answers to the Problems of the Pillars.

Dweller on the Threshold

Here we have to decide just how real Gods, Archangels, or other Entities are in their own right or in relationship to ourselves via the Telesmic Images we propose to make for and of them. It seems a fair question to ask that if these Great Ones are indeed real, why do they not manifest directly to us in objective fashion and speak for themselves in our language? Why should we have to do all the work of making vehicles for them before we can establish conscious contact with their awareness? Why does there seem to be no evidence of their existence which we may appreciate with our ordinary senses, which we presumably derive from our Creation?

These, and allied queries meet us fairly and squarely at the Portals between which we cannot pass until our solution of them permits us. Once, this barrier was called the 'Dweller on the Threshold', which consists of whatever in ourselves refuses admission to the Inner Adytum of Spirit for that part of us which seeks evolvement away from our purely earthly projections. Each must deal with their particular 'Dweller' in their own way, for every one is peculiar to the individual concerned. The struggle with the 'Dweller' is always a solitary one, and usually a most distressing experience, since it amounts to practically civil war in a divided self.

At an earlier period of our Inner development, the 'Dweller' was frequently shown as some kind of a foreign fiend determined to prevent our slightest spiritual progression. A terrible shock awaited pure minded Initiates with a noble opinion of their souls who discovered the 'Dweller' to be part and parcel of themselves entirely opposed to all that seemed best within them. A sort of Anti-God as it were. With the best intentions, they 'summoned the Dweller' which often appeared to the Inner eye as a most unpleasant sort of fiend, and attacked it with every weapon suggested by self-righteous virtue. To their amazement and horror, they found themselves sustaining every injury they inflicted on the monster, which made them realize they were wounding themselves, and the monster's hideous face was really a distortion of their own. Many a mind broke under the impact of this appalling revelation. To see the worst of oneself focused into a personalization is a most demoralizing affair.

The problem of the 'Dweller' for an individual is the same as that for the whole human race on a world-wide scale, but the only solution is a personal one, each unit of humanity being responsible for his own contribution to the general question. When we learn how to deal with the worst of ourselves both individually and collectively without the insanity of destructive warfare, we shall have overcome our 'devils', and 'Dwellers' in the most valuable way. The wise Initiate does not waste useful energy in combat with his 'Dweller', but converts this entity into a 'Doorkeeper', an office which changes a predator into a protector. This is largely accomplished by the realization that the Dweller was only fulfilling its natural function of excluding from the higher Spheres of Inner Life what is unfitted to enter them.

It may seem odd perhaps, that what we consider our noblest nature is prevented from passing into what seems to us its proper Heavenly habitat by our own worst propensities acting in the interests of Divinity. Yet in effect, this is what happens. We may not abandon our lower natures and enter Paradise independently of them because they are part of us and must be included with us wherever and however we proceed as persons. They are to be 'redeemed' or re-directed, not destroyed and extirpated. We should not consider our Dwellers as antagonists, but as our own inadequacies and imperfections preventing our progression beyond a certain point as much for our own good as anyone else's. We may feel that we should be able to fly, but unless some indwelling type of consciousness convinced us that we could not, many would perish by leaping from a height with unfounded optimism.

Just as our best intentions save us from the worst in us, so does our worst side save us from our good intentions paving a Hell-bent path. We cannot afford to be without either Pillar of Personality, because together they must ultimately merge into the Middle Pillar of Poised Power, which is the becoming of our True Being. All the noble motives and good intentions we have will not get us anywhere worth reaching without the sheer basic energy and crude force of our lowest Life-contacts.

Just as our material progress and evolution depends on refinement of raw basics into highly specialized products to accomplish intentions decided by our degree of social development, so does our spiritual evolution depend on the same process applied through our Inner Dimensions of being. Whether we call it transmutation or transubstantiation makes little difference to the arts of Inner Alchemy that must be practised in order to convert Saturn into Sol, or the peripheral planet of a System into a nucleus for another.

It is an interesting thought that our nuclear explosions which are miniature Suns, derive from elements named after our known peripherals of Uranus and Pluto. In spiritual terms this signifies changing our 'Dark Dweller on the Threshold' into a 'Sun of God' providing power for new aeons of living consciousness. The 'Devil' redeemed into a 'Deity'. Chaos turned into Cosmos.

How is such a Magical miracle to be worked? In the same way that purely physical matter is processed into perfection. The bulk of any raw mass is subjected to whatever selective treatment may be necessary for categorizing its contents, isolating its required principles, and making molecular adjustments so that the product obtained is suitable for the purpose demanded. The operations of commercial chemistry may quite well be translated into spiritual terminology and applied to non-physical states of being. Alchemists knew this well enough, and sought to learn from their physical experiments methods of spiritual procedure for obtaining equivalent Inner results. They also realized the possibilities of continuing this cycle so that techniques learned in spiritual states might be simulated physically with profitable results.

Refining the raw material

The Operation of the Magical Cosmic Circle is thus the first practical processing of raw conglomerate conscious material by directing it into four selected streams personified as Archangels linking the Principles of Divinity and Humanity through the being of the individual Initiate arranging this Pattern of Perfection. Once this is properly done, subsequent selective work and refinements to required limits may proceed quite normally. Entire instructions for this advanced type of magical practice are only obtainable from sources of consciousness contactable via the Archangels or other Telesmics reachable by Initiates in their Cosmoi. Furthermore, each must receive his own particular instructions for himself through his personal contacts.

The 'Received Teaching' (or Qabalah) is essentially what every Initiate receives individually. Hence the need of personalizations in practical Magic. The so-called System of Abra-Melin (probably from ABR MLAIM—'powerful consecrations') is based on these premisses. All Initiates can be trained or instructed by others up to a point where they should be able to make their own Inner Contacts for themselves. From that point on, their Enlightenment must come through those Contacts alone. The 'Holy Guardian Angel' has to take over from the Initiates' fellow-human Sponsors, or the personified Higher Self must walk its lonely Way of Light towards Ultimate Truth.

How indeed shall we ever know if Gods, Demons, Angels, Spirits or any immaterial Entity has reality, or whether we simply make them up out of nothing? For that matter, we ourselves and our whole Cosmos have been made up out of Nothing, so why should our existence have reality?

The materialist screams for 'proof' entirely on his own terms, and the mystic is inclined to consider all material phenomena as aberrations of the Divine Mind, demanding virtually impossible expansions of Spirit for himself as 'evidence' of Divinity and Inner Life. The one is asking 'Heavenly' conditions demonstrated with earthly materials, and the other is expecting 'Earthly' experiences to be manifested by Divinity. They typify the Inconvincible in search of the Incredible. Both are demanding energies from entirely differing Dimensions of Existence to manifest beyond their natural Laws of Limitation without any or adequate means of inter-connection. Both are making the same mistake in opposite ways, insisting on 'evidence' of Existence which could not be supplied without automatically negating itself. The only point either extremist 'proves', is their own personal refusal or inability to pass beyond the perceptual limits they have accepted as their conscious periphery.

To demand objective or phenomenal 'proof' of Inner Existences is not only a waste of time and effort, but shows a sad misunderstanding of the entire question. No amount of even the most fantastic phenomena would prove or disprove any such issue. The hard core of this whole controversial matter is this. Either a given consciousness is able to operate through different Dimensions of Existence and maintain a balanced relationship with them all—or it is not. Either we accept our own evidence of

Inner Life from experience and intuition, or we do not. One or the other. The outcome either way is entirely an individual affair. As Outward facing humans, we are individual souls directing our attention into a field of commonly shared mundane consciousness, but as Inward facing beings, we are separating from our Group-Soul as solitary Spirits whose individual consciousness is only shareable with others of comparable condition. The Initiate of Light strives to achieve poise between both polarities.

Few pastimes are more futile or productive of wasted human energies than our age-old attempts to demonstrate or deny the Existence of God and other states of Conscious Being other than our own. Wise Initiates do not enter this controversy between other investigators of imponderables, but concern themselves with the more important Magnum Opus of constructing their own Cosmos from what might be termed 'crude consciousness'.

They do this because they know that only from and through such a creation of theirs will they ever reach and realize the actualities about which those outside the Circle are likely to argue and quarrel for ever more. Full well do genuine Initiates appreciate the necessity for acquiring means before any end may be achieved. Therefore they proceed quietly about their business of getting such means together and developing their abilities for using them. Whether this takes one life or many, is relatively unimportant so long as it is done in the most practicable way.

A properly instructed Initiate also knows perfectly well that he must not reveal his Inner workings to the uninitiated or make any attempt to 'convert' or unduly influence others towards the Holy Mysteries. None must be persuaded against their True Will. It is most important that the Mysteries be approached by all from Within themselves of their own True Will. The veritable Holy Mysteries are beyond price since they are unreachable by any currency save that of consciousness itself. The most that human money will buy is admission to expensively equipped private theatre-clubs disguised as Temples or other places of occult entertainment.

Real Mystery Temples are *not* 'made with hands', even though it may be pleasant and practical to make use of their symbolic counterparts in material form. All Initiates must build their own Temple for both work and worship, making it from their minds, hearts, and souls, acting by the Spirit of the Indwelling One in Whose Name the Temple is being built. All the money in the world would buy no more than a few art-representations suggesting designs for such Temples, and those need cost no more than the necessary visits to any average public library. No soul of the right determination and ingenuity is ever denied access to the Mysteries. In fact such is the actual 'admission fee'.

Apprenticeship to a Master

This was partly the reason why it was insisted on, and is still desirable, that Initiates made as much as possible of their physical Magic robes and instruments with their own hands. It was to accustom them into habits of converting raw materials into constructed creations. If they learned to cosmate physically, then they could do the same on other levels of life. The true Initiates are Craftsmen of Consciousness, whether working physically or spiritually. Who then, teaches them their trade? None but instructors able to reach them on whatever level their work is to manifest. The material details of craftsmanship are best learned from human specialists, but the finest spiritual craftsmanship is best learned through apprenticeship to 'Masters' who make contact with the soul in its own proper sphere.

These so-called 'Masters' and 'Teachers' are neither more nor less than spiritual potencies of various types which maintain life-linkage with humanity as a whole or as specified sections and even individuals. Many, though not all, have evolved through the human incarnationary cycles themselves, and are continuing their existence through states of consciousness far beyond the reach of average mortals. Their motives for intentionally relating themselves with earth-existent souls incarnating as humanity vary a good deal. By no means all are concerned with our noblest ends or highest capabilities. Many might be described as benevolently neutral to us, neither helping nor hindering our spiritual advancement. Others, for their own reasons, are malevolently opposed to humanity as such or in particular instances, and will do what they can to spoil our chances of over-reaching their spiritual status. Others again concern themselves with our truest welfare as living souls and do their utmost to help our progress along similar Paths to their own. Whether we regard such beings as good, bad or indifferent, none of them can compel us into any course of life or activity against our True Wills. Our degree of Divinity in us decides the outcome.

Initiates of the Mysteries seek to make and maintain contact with, Inner Schools of transcendental training which will afford opportunities for living beyond their bodily bonds to an incarnate identity. What is more, such Schools and their attached Teachers must be of the right kind, aligned with the Initiates most direct Light-line between themselves and their highest aims. Not all Circles are dedicated to what we call 'Good', nor are the 'Good' ones all suitable for any kind of Initiate. To each, his own. Every individual Initiate must sooner or later take his proper spiritual place in whichever Circle of Consciousness will prove of most benefit to him and where he can be of most value to others. How is this position to be achieved?

It is a well enough known saying that 'When the pupil is prepared, the Master will accept him'. This is literally true. In the genuine Mysteries, when the pupil-Initiate has done the correct preparatory work of his own initiative, an appropriate 'Master' will infallibly establish Inner contact with him. The Initiate will be recognized for what he is in himself, and dealt with accordingly.

Such recognition is relatively a very simple matter from a spiritual viewpoint, the status of the Initiate being easily known by the patterning of his Inner force-fields. This, of course, is determined by his behaviour and condition of consciousness. None of this may be disguised in any way from those whose awareness is directed from an 'overseers' angle of vision. As we believe and behave, so do we automatically set up force-fields around ourselves which have definite rhythms and patterns associated with our basic beings. We might say for instance that such and such a person radiates this, that or the other sound and colour effect. That would only be their person-pattern projected in ways appreciated by physical eyes and ears. These would also have equivalents perceptible by spiritual senses, and this is how individual souls are singled out from higher life-levels when they are ready for advancement thereto.

Group Angels

All humans radiate force-patterns which are recognizable and classifiable by observing Intelligences from other than human states of being. Just as we become accustomed to rapidly classifying our fellow humans under general and specific headings such as: 'Male middle-aged Asiatic Islamic doctor', which would provide considerable information about such a person, so can Inner experts (or 'Masters') estimate our spiritual condition from the patterns we present in the Light of their perception, and realize exactly what sort of a soul we are. General categories of humans are more or less mass-guided by what are sometimes called 'Group-Angels', or Intelligences associated with racial and ethnical or religious circles of humanity. As souls evolve away from their root groupings and individualize themselves, so do they receive increasingly individual attention from those 'Inners' who are concerned with human progress (or otherwise) along the particular lines of interest. 'Masters' of all descriptions who are willing to deal with incarnate or earth-based beings, are constantly alert for the spiritual signals that indicate a soul prepared for their particular ministrations. They are not likely to miss this call-sign any more than a guided missile misses homing on its target.

Everything depends on the type of signal we send out spiritually as to what sort of Inner contacts we are likely to make. Apart from our own natural frequency or pattern, there is the superimposed symbolic design of whatever System or Order we are working with, whether of the Mysteries or not. Just as a Nation is recognized by its Emblem or Flag, so are spiritual Systems recognized by their Symbols. It is for that especial reason Initiates are carefully trained by ritual and other procedures in the production and use of their particular Symbol.

Qabalists for example formulate the Tree of Life in a variety of ways, and most Mysteries use the basic Circled Cross. Such Symbols sent into spiritual dimensions via the consciousness of the Initiate will automatically attract the attention of 'Masters' concerned with what they represent.

Only by so working within a Circle characterized by the Symbol-pattern of whatever spiritual sorts of consciousness we intend associating with, may we feel any assurance of making such contacts. This is where the Initiate of the Mysteries scores over others who merely seek 'Spirit Guides' or echoes of departed relatives. For those content with pleasantries and platitudes, these facile comforters are usually harmless enough or even mildly beneficial. They are very easy to obtain. Any kind of human group meeting together in some sort of a circle for the purpose will achieve some measure of contact with types of consciousness other than their own. Whether they use devices like tables, ouija boards, pendulums, or human mediums, they will get results comensurate with themselves. Probably about the worst thing possible for them, is to sit around with amiably open minds awaiting an impact from whatever type of entity shows sufficient interest in them to make it. Fortunately for these experimenters, they are unlikely to provide the slightest interest, except in the most general way, for entities with any great power to injure them.

Initiates of the Mysteries differ from 'spirit-seekers' in several important ways. They are discriminative, selective, and deliberate in making their Inner contacts from levels of living consciousness at the precise spiritual state to which they direct their True Magical Wills. Furthermore, those levels are somewhat closer to Inner Reality than the more easily reached ones most immediately behind physical manifestation. It is the aim of Initiates to work much more deeply in the Ocean of Consciousness than at what used to be called 'Lower Astral' conditions. This is why the older practitioners of Ritual Magic used to operate especially 'tuned' Rites in which all the appurtenances, etc., were aligned with whatever single Keynote or frequency accorded with the Will behind the operation. It was not a question of mere harmonious decoration, but of using every possible means to keep the Operator's consciousness 'on contact' with the specific type of Inner Consciousness invoked for some particular reason consistent with its nature. It is this concentrated polarization of conscious power which operates the processes of practical Magic, much as a radio transmitter and receiver must remain tuned to each other's natural frequency in order to exchange energies.

Contacting Intelligences

Here the logical question presents itself—does this mean that any sincere soul who takes the trouble to arrange themselves into specified Magical Patterns with the requisite amounts of effort, will make contact with the Intelligences directing what are known as the Holy Mysteries on Inner Life levels? The answer is yes, it means exactly that. If anyone considers the efforts worth while, and is prepared to devote himself whole-heartedly to the work, he will indeed come into eventual consciousness contact with the Powers behind the patterns they project towards Inner Space. The nature of such contacts depends upon the individual spiritual condition of those making them.

It is highly unlikely for instance, that contacts of consciousness made on deep Inner levels will take the form of materialized or vividly imagined personages in superhuman guise issuing man-dates and messages of momentous import. Any such happenings should be highly suspect. We must remember that Inner Aware-ness inverses polarity with Outer, and therefore the order of consciousness is diametrically opposed between the Dimensions of Life.

As a simple illustration, let us consider what happens in an ordinary way. We meet someone or a group of people who pre-sent their consciousness to us in some form such as conversation, pictorially, or otherwise. We experience the impact of this, react with it, and subsequently alter to a certain degree in consequence. Now supposing the order of these events were turned around so to speak, and our objective awareness became activated accord-ingly. In the first instance we should be conscious of a change in ourselves, then of various factors associated with that change, and last of all the persons or individuals responsible for initiating or directing the causative energies towards us. That is analogous to the workings of Inwardizing consciousness. It is not that events really happen backwards, but that our Inner senses register them along a very different time-scale to the one accepted on earth.

Initial contacts with Inner Existence are normally in the nature of a growing certainty that not only does such a condition of Being actually exist, but that certain changes in ourselves and our consciousness are definitely related therewith. As we progress, we may discover what those changes amount to. Later, we may be led to finding out how they take place. Eventually we might even find out what Entity or Entities are responsible. Finally, it is conceivably possible we shall be able to direct those Energies of Existence by our own True Wills.

Anyone thinking that Magic or other Rites will promptly produce Appearances or the like psychical phenomena for their entertainment or edification is doomed to sad disappointment from the start. Yet, because of our inversed Inner-Outer Existences, we have to commence our Magical careers by using creatively constructive imagery concerning the Ultimates we seek in Spirit. If we are not prepared to work from the False of our own making, we shall never arrive at the Truth which makes us, and constructs the Cosmoi in which we live.

There is nothing very extraordinary in this. After all, we have been working that way for many thousands of years, during which, beliefs we assumed as absolute truthful facts have subsequently come to be regarded as fables and unrealities. In Magical practice we must operate the other way around, commencing with concepts which we accept as representational symbols of yet unreached realities, by means of which we hope to attain those actualities with ever-increasing degrees of True Light. The initiated Magician realizes perfectly well that the forms and figures he works with are necessarily false and incorrect from an ordinary standpoint, but that nothing can possibly be either false or inaccurate unless a Truth exists to make it so. Thus the Initiate of Light accepts apparent fables very gladly indeed for the sake of the Inner Realities which only they can contain. It seems odd that if we want Truth we must look for it in the heart of a Lie, but this is a method of Magic none can afford to ignore.

A really practical Magician does not worry about the existence or non-existence of Otherworld Beings, nor waste time speculating on their natures, possibilities, and idiosyncrasies. He goes ahead and creates his own concepts of whatever Beings he would believe in if there were any. Those will eventually put him in touch with the actualities of consciousness they stand for. It is as simple as that. The old legend of the boy Jesus and his companions making clay birds for a prize which He won because His models became living birds and flew away, is a literal instruction of how to work magic. The other boys' birds remained nothing but clay, because they only thought of them as such. Those boys believed their birds to be false images of a living reality, and so, up to that point, they were. Jesus however, continued the cycle of consciousness beyond this limit. He demanded

His images to produce the life-truth without which they could not be false, and so they did—for Him. Lesser Initiates must expect proportionately lesser results, but may be quite assured of results nevertheless.

Does this mean that Initiates are supposed to have faith in Concepts they might not believe in? Yes. It does. That is even the secret. To believe in the impossible until it becomes improbable is the first step from Zero to One. Perhaps we may not, like the White Queen, believes in as many as six impossible things before breakfast, but Initiates would do well by heeding her advice to do it for half an hour a day. How else has Mankind made any advance along the various Paths of progression? It is not our recent so-called scientific discoveries which have led us towards enlightenment, but our original fantasies and exercises in exploring the Universe of our Unconsciousness. Without the second we should not arrive at our present position of making the first.

Man neglects or despises Myth and Magic at gravest peril to his progress. Man the materialist says: 'I will not believe in anything until I have fully experienced evidence of its existence in relation to myself and other humans.' Man the Magician says: 'I will believe in the Nothing out of which anything may come into contact with me according to the Will that in me Is.' There is an infinity of difference between the two viewpoints, and as usual, the Initiate of Light seeks the Median Way. Let us consider some of the methods made use of by magical ritualists for this reason.

CHAPTER VI

SYMBOLS, PRACTICES AND ASPIRATIONS

To sort the whole of our consciousness into six different categories relative to the seventh factor of ourselves is a major Magical Opus. It sums up our entire being into a single Word, each letter of which designates the crossing points of polarized power. Just as the Divine One 'Uttered the Name' which created Cosmos, so must Magical Initiates 'utter' their own Names which will create their own Cosmoi. So again must the same activity take place in the cosmation of Magical Groups. Whether for one individual or a number of separate souls, the principles of creating Cosmic Circles are the same.

The unit-cell of Cosmos on which all is based presents a simple enough picture. In the centre the individual 'I AM'. Bisecting the centre from top to bottom is the Divine-Human polarization of consciousness. Bisecting once more from front to back is the Life-Love axis, while from right to left is the Light-Learning co-ordinate. These polarities produce the Three Circles of Cosmic Consciousness. We might say that one is an awareness of being a soul in a human body, the next is a feeling awareness of a love relationship with life, and the last is awareness of intellectual thinking processes in relation to self-existence and whatever is not self. Being, feeling, and thinking.

The entirety of consciousness has to fit this frame, be it a large or small one. Whatsoever consists of consciousness, (and what does *not*?) must align with some angle between the centre and surface of such a spherical Cosmos. Once we define the main axes of our Inner Universe, it becomes true to itself and relative to all else. Instead of being like a sphere rolling chaotically about anywhere, it becomes auto-dynamic, setting its own Cosmic course according to its inherent pattern of consciousness.

Forming a Circle

When an Initiate of the Mysteries is capable of cosmating himself, he is entitled to form into Circles with others of a similar condition. Here again, the same pattern is simply repeated on a greater scale. A concept of Divinity as the highest ideal shared in common, a human social concept as a basis, the preferable minimum of four Initiates who are able to typify the Quarters, and a central Spirit will become an Entity in the midst of them.

In the rare event of a Holy Spirit manifesting through some particular human Initiate, such will be the nucleus of the cosmating Group which may extend to a circle of twelve individual members. This figure of thirteen has nothing whatsoever to do with a witch or any other kind of 'coven' (from co-venire = to come together) but is the natural figure of the most practical Cosmic circular association. If a single sphere of any size is to be completely surrounded by similar spheres in contract all together, the resultant figure will be that of twelve spheres around one. A Sun and its Twelve Signs. No properly cosmated group of Initiates should exceed this maximum. If, indeed, this figure should be reached, then the Group ought to be considered as a whole Unit ready for cosmation among much higher circles than human ones. In such a case, one member of the Circle at least would be responsible for commencing another new Circle elsewhere, and so Cosmos continues.

It is not common to find many properly constituted and cosmated Magical Circles of Initiates working efficiently in this modern human world. The theory of their formation is simplicity itself, but in practice such a Circle is rarely encountered. Occult Societies and Brotherhoods with 'Secret Chiefs' and elaborate hierarchies are very wide of the Cosmic Pattern. So are groupings around a purely human Initiate, no matter how advanced their development.

The central point of a cosmated Group must always be a spiritual one. Furthermore, the Initiates constituting the Quarters and perimeter must be exactly the right individuals for their office. It would be hopeless trying to cosmate a Group with unsuitable people, and this is the usual reason why so many Groups fail. No one except suitable Initiates should attempt cosmation in the first place, and absolutely no one should be allowed into the

Circle who does not fulfil the strictest specifications. It may be interesting to see how those specifications are interpreted in a modern magical manner.

Officers of the Circle

The axial Officers of the Circle are designated by the Quarters East, South, West, and North, as at a card table. There is no rank, but only office and function. This is shown by the Four Instruments of Sword, Rod, Cup, and Shield, connected by the Cord who patrols the perimeter as a link between all points. These of course are personalized by the Archangels, each of which must be characterized by one of the Initiates much as a role is assumed by an actor. There is this important difference between an Initiate 'mediating' an Archangel and an actor 'interpreting' a role. The actor is cleverly adjusting his parts so as to portray a distinctly drawn human personage. The Initiate is using the natural frequencies of his own character to harmonise with and project Inner Power from whatever category of consciousness is represented by the personifying Archangel, who is the Key-Symbol for making contact with that particular Power.

Thus we have to consider a sort of Inner Circle consisting of the actual Archangelic energies, and an Outer one made up of their human Initiate-agents. It is interesting to imagine what the ideal types of people for such a task would be, supposing them to be even available and willing to work together. Since they have no titles, they are best designated by their Instrument-Symbols.

The Sword, or Officer of the East, whose function is to mediate the Air Archangel Raphael, should preferably be a young male. Of an intelligent enquiring nature, able to inspire interest and enthusiasm in fresh fields of enquiry. His duty to the Group is to actively keep it free from undesirable contacts, maintain keenness and alertness among its members, look for new ideas, and generally supply an element of liveliness and vitality which is so necessary to any enterprise.

The Rod, or Officer of the South, who mediates the Fire Archangel Michael, calls for a mature male. He has to be the 'shepherd' and in some ways the leader of the Group. Must be of an upright nature, setting the best possible example to others, a good disciplinarian, fair minded, and with all the finest quali-

ties of an honoured and respected commanding officer. He is
perhaps a Father-figure. His duties to the Group include the
making and keeping of rules, regulating conduct, pointing out
paths and possibilities, and being a kind of 'backbone'.

The Cup, or Officer of the West, mediating the Water Arch-
angle Gabriel (Javriel), is best represented by a young female.
She should be lovely in herself, and capable of great love for
fellow humans and creatures. Her function with the Group is to
inspire affection and kindliness among members, pouring out
compassion to all, dissolving difficulties between individuals by
affectionate good humour and sympathy, acting as conciliator
and softener of hardened hearts. Her kindness however is not
of the 'permissive' sort, but must be resolute and strong enough
to overcome whatever fears, hatreds, or other disintegrating
influences may threaten the cosmation of the Group.

The Shield, or Officer of the North, who mediates the Earth
Archangel Auriel, ought to be a senior female. She is the one of
experience and common sense who is the friend and counsellor
of all, providing dependable advice, clear insight, and a solid
basis for acting on beliefs. She guards tradition, records, and the
general teachings adhered to by the Group. She may well be a
Mother-figure, acting as confidante, consoler, encourager, or
whatever may be needed from a wise and beneficent woman
seeking to help her fellow humans.

Each of these Officers may have up to two Companions who
are qualifying for that Office or capable of deputizing in the
absence of the regular Officer. These might well be younger
people who in any case should take their occasional turn of duty
at ceremonial or other Group gatherings. Their place in the
Circle of course, is on the left and right of their Officer. Should
there be only a single deputy, they are to be stationed on their
Officer's right hand.

Officer of the Perimeter

The last human member of the Group is the Officer of the
Perimeter whose Symbol is the Cord and whose Archangel is
Sababiel (Savaviel) the Turner or Circler of God. This Officer
may be of any age or either sex. Their function is liaison around
and among all members, and to provide linkage with other

Groups. They must be a good 'all-rounder', capable of filling in any awkward gaps, acting as the Group's agent or Messenger in external affairs, keeping members in touch with each other, etc. The Cord is the Zero-Figure surrounding all others while being equitable to each.

The Controller

Centrally in the Group is the Controller. This is a purely Spiritual Being who will definitely make his presence felt (though unlikely to be seen) in the midst of any properly constituted Group of cosmating Initiates who fulfil at least some measure of their required functions. There will be no doubt about the existence of a Controller, because all or most of those in the Circle will be aware of such an Entity among them, and their impressions will agree with or complement each other's findings subsequently.

The duty of a Controller is to co-relate the Group not only in itself, but also among all others operating in the Holy Mysteries whether incarnate or otherwise. The Controller should be of a Spiritual Order sufficiently advanced to be capable of affording mortals an opportunity of realizing that Divinity is indeed among and in them. No merely earthbound human soul or average discarnate individual is able to do this any more than they could when in the flesh. True Controllers are very specialized Spirits, and do not devote their attention to Groups incapable of response to their direction. Like other Officers they have a working Symbol—the central Light—however it is arranged.

The material and social difficulties of bringing just such a right number of the right Initiates together for the purpose of cosmating a Magical microcosm are enormous. It must always be remembered however, that it is the actual qualities which are of paramount importance, rather than the precise type of human possessing them. Providing the qualities are available, and are forthcoming among the right number of people, a Circle can work with at least average success. For example, the Sword might even be an elderly female, or the Cup a mature male if they had exactly the right qualifications for office, and no other individuals were available.

Everything depends on suitability and fitness for each particular task, combined with correct numerical proportions. Sheer numbers in quantity are not only valueless but disastrous. Correct Cosmic proportions must be scrupulously kept within limits. An overloaded or badly unbalanced Circle 'explodes' or disintegrates just as certainly as critically massed plutonium. The Circle must always be balanced as perfectly as circumstances allow, and the better the balance, the more worthwhile results will be.

A single Initiate is responsible for his own cosmation. Two can work together if each is capable of mediating two of the necessary Quarters. Three may work if the 'odd one out' is capable of functioning as Cord. Four is the minimum for best Group working. Five will give the Quarters and a Cord, which makes for good average cosmation. From this point on, the cross-quarters must be filled in with those capable of qualifying in one direction or another. If it were possible to choose ideal types, the SE position would be held by a Sword-Rod sort of person, the SW by a Rod-Cup, NW by a Cup-Shield, and the NE by a Shield-Sword. The last four types to complete the Circle would have a positive bias towards some one particular Instrument, and a lesser bias towards its neighbour, such as SWORD-rod, ROD-cup, etc. A complete cosmated Magical Circle of individuals would thus read; SWORD, SWORD-rod, Sword-Rod. ROD, ROD-cup, Rod-Cup, CUP, CUP-shield, Cup-Shield, SHIELD, SHIELD-sword, Shield-Sword. Connecting all these, of course, is the useful and ubiquitous perimeter CORD.

How is anyone to know which Quarter they are best suited to? By their dominant characteristics which remain unequated by their personal efforts at cosmation. No matter how we try to equilibrate ourselves as individuals, there is generally an overplus of some qualities and a deficiency of their complementaries. For instance, a surplus of Cup qualities often means a deficit of Sword and Rod potencies. In an associative Circle, the various Instruments should supply each other's deficiencies from their surplus stocks of categorized energies, and a condition of balance should arise among them all which permits their Controller to set their course dynamically towards Divinity. So much is a question of mechanics as much as Magic. The aim of cosmation is always the achievement of a perfectly balanced state of harmonious and equilibrated energy which may be put to any purpose by the controlling Will of the whole.

Such a state is only attained by a great deal of effort and arrangement. Even if suitable Initiates of the Mysteries agreed on mutual cosmation along the natural lines of the Quartered-Cross Primal Pattern, they would still have to find methods of relating their energies with each other through the paths which the Pattern provides. The Pattern is like an electronic circuit which affords a behaviour system for the electro-magnetic power connected to it from appropriate sources of supply, in this instance the Initiates themselves. Since their energies are derived from the raw material of Consciousness, we must seek means of adapting and utilizing this universal commodity in the most practical ways possible. This brings us back to our basics of Reflection and Ritual, or Meditation and Magic. These are yet the fundamental means in the Mysteries for collecting and controlling the almost unbelievable energies available from the Consciousness behind and within our creation as Its effects.

Aims of ritual Magic

Ritual Magic is a sadly misunderstood and usually misapplied art. Its reality is only barely related to its frightfully distorted image that grimaces at us from the grimoires of the Middle Ages. As a means of raising demons or other supernatural agents for doing whatever dirty work might be needed to gratify human whims and unjustified demands, ritual Magic is an entire waste of time, money, and effort. For the production of energy-patterns in the force-fields of living consciousness which are definitely relatable with intentional Inner effects that might even conceivably materialize, ritual Magic is unique, unrivalled, and quite invaluable. Once this is sufficiently realized, and competent practitioners devote the necessary amount of attention and devotion to the work of constructing Rites linking modern procedures with the most ancient Traditions and basic beliefs, Magic will be reborn in the happiest way among Mankind.

Rightly reconstituted, Magic has an even greater part to play in our present and future than it had in the past. As humanity reaches saturation point of satiety with mechanical and material marvels, so will there be an increasing Inner urgency for expansion into spiritual dimensions. Man, the eternal explorer, will embark on the greatest Magical venture of all time. Whether our spiritual heirs will be honest enough to acknowledge the sources of their legacy, or will disguise it under some pseudo 'scientific' euphemism such as 'Internalistic Activationism' remains to be seen. Blessed indeed are those with sufficient strength of character to accept a truly Ancient Art for what it is, and continue its practice according to present day standards of knowledge and behaviour.

The art of Magic is acquired rather than taught. Since it means so many different things for so many different people, definition of terms is bound to cause disagreement in all directions, but this is relatively unimportant because Initiates must work the Way Within themselves, and where enough of these are available to form a complementary Cosmos with each other, let another Circle of Light co-exist with the rest.

For practical purposes, let us suppose Magic to be the ability of handling Consciousness like any other basic energy and putting it to whatsoever purpose may be required. If we consider Consciousness as an energy like electricity, and our Magical Symbolic devices like the various mechanisms which electricity works for our wills, we shall have a useful analogy to play with. Furthermore, we should realize that within our natural limits of consciousness as human beings, all we can do of ourselves is to construct mental mechanisms. These will not come to life and activity until they are powered by the consciousness of more potent entities than we are. We, and our magical productions, are only agencies for energies beyond the direct control of our consciousness. Hence the necessity for working within a force-framework affording us the maximum spiritual safety.

Selecting a thought system

Just as the first exercises in any art consist of familiarization with materials and the elements of construction therewith, so must aspirants to Magical adepthood learn how to treat consciousness as a tailor with cloth or a plumber with lead. In effect, we have to take lumps of our ordinary consciousness and deal with them so as to make serviceable items for the use of Inner Intelligence. Before we can supply any quantity of good-class commodities of this nature it is only reasonable to assume that a considerable amount of training and organized effort will be needed. This is indeed the case, and is the reason why there are relatively few ritual magicians in practice. The apparent lack of rapid return for expenditure of effort and capital is enough to discourage all but the most deeply dedicated souls.

For most apprentice practitioners the problem is where to start drawing their circle or including themselves into existing ones. There are large numbers of 'thought systems' available for study, many of these so unnecessarily complicated and woolly minded as to be virtually useless for practical purposes. As esoteric entertainment most of them are little more than 'time-killers' and harmless amusements. They all help to develop conscious skills of one kind or another, as any form of mental exercise would, but unless the operator is prepared to accept a firm measure of self-discipline, avoiding inessential distractions and keeping very much to the fundamental Pattern on which the System is based, there will be very little real spiritual progress made. If any 'thought system' cannot present a clear and definite Pattern of its whole structure to an enquirer, it is best left alone, for it is unlikely to have anything worth finding in it.

Pseudo-mysterious affairs throwing out tantalizing hints of the tremendous powers to be gained by those attaining higher degrees for higher fees should be avoided like plague spots. Any workable or worthwhile System should be expressible as a recognizable Symbol which contains the whole System in itself, and therefore cannot be the exclusive property of any particular Group.

This is why the most usual Systems prevalent in Western Mystery workings are the Qabalistic, Rose-Cross, and Solar (or Celtic) Cross Patterns. Each presents an entire Way of Inner Life readily acceptable and practicable for human souls living the way we do, to follow faithfully and obtain useful spiritual results from. What is of great importance, but rarely grasped, is that the Symbol itself holds the System, and not any particular human Group claiming to represent it. In other words, any soul of good intention at all is perfectly entitled to apply himself directly to a Symbol, asking its Inner Guardians for instructions, and if the application is sincere, such teaching will truly be forthcoming.

There are no especial human Groups with exclusive rights to

System-Symbols other than those arising entirely among themselves for private use. All that any Mystery-Group does is to work out means and methods of dealing with whatever System they follow, and offer companionship to suitable souls who would walk the same Way.

It is true that basic groundwork and approach to any Symbol is easiest acquired in company with others, but after a certain stage is reached, Initiates, like journeymen of old, have to go forth by themselves and operate as Originators rather than copyists of Consciousness. No genuine aspirant however, need feel deprived because no Mystery Lodge exists around the corner clamouring for new membership. The first stages of Initiation, like much later ones, are best taken outside Lodges on this level of life. All that is needed is a firm and definite approach to the chosen Symbol, a positive request for admission to Inner Life through it, then application and practice with it in every way it suggests to the enquirer. Seek, ask, knock—in that order. Since there can scarcely be a simpler System than the Cosmic Cross Pattern, let us continue dealing with that. It holds all that any other does, but in a different display-design.

Once the general lay-out is appreciated, it should be a fairly straightforward job to construct Cosmos around ourselves both individually and collectively. A good way of starting anything is in the beginning, and since the basics of our bodily being are its constituent Elements, we might as well deal with those from a spiritual standpoint. They are of course the distinctions of Inner conditions, which, if they were physical, would best be recognized as Air, Fire, Water, and Earth. It should be scarcely necessary to say that the Inner Elements are not in fact such material phenomena, but do bear a representational relationship to them, as might the energies of Heat, Light, Electricity, and Magnetism bear comparison with the Magical Elements. If we think of them as the first four distinct divisions of otherwise undifferentiated Existence, this will serve well enough as a commencement-code. At all events, they must correspond with the Four Major Points of our Magical Cosmos, where they will associate with the Archangels and other attributes.

The Cosmic Diagram

Seated in a comfortable Western meditational position, we sketch a quick Cosmic diagram around ourselves. This is similar to the Christian Sign of the Cross, except that we mentally draw the Three Cosmic Rings, the first being vertical around head and feet from front to back, the second horizontal from right to left via the back, and the third laterally over head and feet again from left to right. All three are thus doesil. They start and end from the central point just below the heart. The standard formula is: 'In the Name of the Wisdom (up), the Love (down) the Justice (Right), and the Infinite Mercy (Left) of the One Eternal Spirit (Circle) AMEN (Heart).'

Having 'Uttered the Word' that has brought Cosmos out of Chaos, we now proceed to fill in our dotted lines. Mentally moving simultaneously towards head and feet from our Central Spiritual Seed within us, the axis of rotation is made between an accepted Infinity of Divine Intelligence above us, and an Infinity of Human Innocence (or Ignorance) below us. At this stage it is sufficient to take these for granted rather than make many speculations about such Unknowables. They are the Pivots between which we shall set up our Centre of Spiritual Gravity. The power which will keep our Cosmos poised and functioning dynamically has to be derived from the Elements of course, so they must now be thought up.

The Air Concept

Reaching out mentally again from the Centre in a forward direction, we try and create an 'Air state' with which we identify that quadrant of ourselves. The objective should be to 'become an idea of Air' rather than visualize ourselves doing anything particular with it. All sorts of associative ideas will immediately present themselves for use. Air is atmosphere, lightness, life, freshness, uplift, exhilaration, freedom, and the like. Only the best possible ideas should be chosen. Unpleasant suggestions such as evil smells, hurricanes, etc., must be firmly rejected at the commencement if we are to create a Cosmos worth living in. Nothing but the finest and purest qualities that can be imagined into an 'Air-Concept' are fit to incorporate into our Inner Cosmoi.

These must be dwelt on to a degree where we actually feel and experience an Inner sensation of identification with the properties of the Element being dealt with. With Air, it may be a feeling of lightness and expansion, a pleasant perfume, or a 'young and fresh' impression. Whatever it is, it should be a very definite Inner experience caused by the concentration of our consciousness for that particular purpose. The degree of intensity will depend largely on the individual Initiate, but it should always be kept at controllable levels. When some success at Air is met with, we mentally turn to the Fire Quarter of the South, and invoke its Element.

The Fire-Concept

Here, Fire is thought of as Light, Illumination, clarity of consciousness, equable temperature, Inner vision, the Divine Spark shining, Heavenly Radiance, and so forth. Let the pure Inner Element be as perfect as possible, free from all the fears it suggests to us as mortals. Again we must work until an experience of radiance, clarity, or suchlike is actually undergone inside ourselves. Then, going West, we encounter Water.

The Water-Concept

'Inner Water' is not wet, cold, or anything that might be unwelcome. It is flowing, friendly, protective, sustaining, amenable, powerful, rhythmic, and anything else of a beneficent associative nature. When we have sufficiently 'waterized ourselves' to obtain a definite experience, we may turn to the North for the last Element of Earth.

The Earth-Concept

Here we meet with objectivity, solidity, gravity, weight, fertility, mass, incarnation, definition and so forth. When we feel properly 'Earthed', we should come back to the Centre again, and from there contemplate the Cosmos around us as a dynamic construction driven by its own Elements. As a crudely effective analogy, we may think of a mythical perpetual motion machine wherein Air blows Fire, which boils Water, which dissolves Earth which becomes Air and so on and so on. The end-product at this stage ought to be an Inner experience of being a balanced entity around a Central Point of Poise, with an Elementary Cosmos in working order humming happily on its Divine-Human axis to the Keysound of its own Name. We should hear this in ourselves, and even hum it under our physical breath as perhaps 'UmmmmmmmmmmEnnnnnnnnnUmmmmmmmmEnnnnn' or the rightly resonated AMEN.

No attempt should be made to go beyond this framework until it can be built up rapidly and satisfactorily as an easy exercise. Even to achieve this may take more material time than might be supposed. The exercise has to be persisted with until we become aware that such a state of cosmos has actually been built up around us and we are indeed living in it as a natural everyday condition.

The Control-Symbols

Once the Elements of Consciousness have been successfully differentiated into their four categories, anything at all may be built from them by combination and arrangement. It is a question of using the correct formula for the intended construction, which is no simple matter. When it is realized that every type of individual existence must necessarily be compounded of the Four Fundamentals in some manner or other, we shall at least have a notion of making a general approach to any particular kind of being.

For example, in the creation of a life-form from raw consciousness, its respiratory system would derive from 'Air', its natural heat and associative functions from 'Fire', its fluidity from 'Water', and its solid portions from 'Earth'. All kinds of materials and artifacts have elemental linkages, and abstractions such as circumstances, environments, emotional states, etc., may be traced to their elemental sources. Human temperaments are easily aligned with elemental equivalents. When we have learned how to handle with any degree of skill the very Elements of our Awareness themselves, the best beginning to the remainder of Magical Arts will have been made.

11—ITOM * *

In order to control and manipulate our Elemental Consciousness as required, it is necessary to apply their control-Symbols of Sword, Rod, Cup, and Shield, connected via the Cord. These Symbols are really procedural principles related directly with each Element, indicating the main method of Magical dominion over their energies.

On purely physical levels for instance, the Sword might well show control of Air energy by suggesting pressures brought to a single point as with a jet. The Rod could be a fire-bar, or the control-rod of an atomic pile. The Cup on a grand scale is in a sense like a hydro-electric dam. The Shield presents a picture of anything from a blue-print to a brick wall or even a television screen. It is the principles of the Symbols that must be sought for rather than their external appearances or literal make-up. Every Initiate is responsible for discovering the Inner values and applications of these Symbols by meditation and experience. They can be applied in the most surprising ways, and the only possibility of finding these is by personal investigation.

When some practical Inner meanings to the Magical Symbolic Instruments have been made, they must be associated with Elemental control, and therefore we plod around the Magic Circle again, this time attaching each Symbol to its Quarter. The exercise might be commenced by mentally evoking the Air Element, then directing a Symbolic Sword at it so that it conforms with whatever is Sword-willed. Perhaps a jet of Air follows the Sword-point and does exactly as this indicates. Any such ideas will serve, so long as the key-ideas of 'Element', and 'Symbol' are firmly associated with the basics of 'Control' and 'Competency'. Fire may be approached with a Symbolic Rod in the form of a lamp-standard, a blow-torch, or any Rod-means of Fire-control except an extinguisher or eliminator of Fire. We need to use the Element, not annihilate it. The Cup and Water should be easily associated with control, and the Shield can turn into an enormous variety of Earth controls, from a mason's trowel to the lay-out of a city.

The Archangels

We have now got to the stage of a Cosmos with an inexhaustible supply of Consciousness at its centre, the Universal Energy of which is directed into four principal Elemental categories, each of these being controllable by the Symbolic Key applicable to it alone. Control obviously implies a governing intelligence, and the question at this point is what sort of Intelligence should control the Elements? The answer to this one of course, is the Archangels. They personify the ideal type of Being to control the energies of the Elements in such a way that an absolute minimum of damage, and a maximum of beneficial effects will result throughout the Cosmos under construction. The next Magical task therefore, is to formulate and evoke these Archangels, while handing over to them the direct control of the original Elements by their Symbolic Instruments. Once more this is achieved by Reflection and Rite.

The Cosmic Scheme

The general scheme for creating Cosmos in a Magical manner should now be apparent. First the Central Seed or Nucleus divides from within Itself, and the equators of Existence appear, within which all else to follow will expand endlessly. Then Energy differentiates into four distinct Elemental categories. Next controlled regulation of these energies is applied. After this, a suitable individualized Intelligence of an Archangelic (or Abstract) Order is evolved for the specific function of controlling the Elements.

As the Cosmator brings each stage of Cosmos into being, the next stage must be built up around it in order to adapt it with the rest of Creation. Our Infinitely Expanding Universe through Inner Dimensions is thus made with its Centre in the proverbial Nowhere, and its Circumference Everywhere in Consciousness. So we must Magically work from the Divine Spark within us. As we create each item of Cosmos correctly, so should it become 'ensouled' by the Inner Actuality it represents. We make the moulds, 'They' fill them up for us! When we connect the correct Cosmic circuit together, the Inner suppliers of spiritual power will switch it on so that our work 'comes to Life'.

Ritual practices for this purpose have to be evolved according to whatever Mystery System is being used. Each has its own nomenclature, customs, costumes, and variations of behaviour, though all operate on the same Cosmic basis. It is like the national and even local ethnical traditions in this world which make us what we are, even though everyone has to live on the same planet—as yet. In either scale of practice, it would be a stupid mistake to mix the Systems hopelessly together to nobody's advantage and everyone's detriment. Although every practising Group of ritual workers usually regard their own rites as exclusively authentic, or possibly the only valid rites in the Mysteries, such suppositions are nonsensical. The really important part of any rite is its fundamental pattern, and this is freely available to all Initiates who care to look for Archetyptal Symbols which are common to all Systems. The only claims for Uniqueness a group is entitled to make for their rites are those in connection with actual scripts written by their members for private circulation. No more than any claim for an author's copyright is worth. Since much material in current rituals is composed from quotes taken from existing literary sources, there are few really original ritual scripts available.

Even supposing an entire set of rites, well scripted and based on sound patterns, were placed before any would-be ritualist, this in itself would not guarantee the slightest value in them. Everything depends on what is done with them, in which manner, by whom. A single utterance and a gesture by a competent operator, is worth considerably more than the most faultless ritual script misread through by some fumbling and uncertain amateur in the art.

Why so many people without ability, experience, or aptitude for ritual performance or procedures, seem to think that all they have to do is recite a few lines in the worst possible way and miracles will occur, remains the greatest mystery among the Mysteries. Nothing but the amazing vagaries of human vanity can possibly account for it.

Mimetic Magic

An efficient ritualist has to work simultaneously on a number of levels, living what is uttered throughout. Very primitive rites indeed were simply mimed descriptively in the pattern chosen as being appropriate for the purpose. For instance, if a Rain-Spirit were being invoked, a lightly dancing approach might be made to the West, then inviting gestures made towards the dry fields or wells, while drummers imitated rain falling, and the whole tribe chanted the Spirit's name with an ululation calculated to sound like wind and rain. One might almost call this mimetic magic Elemental Ballet. For those unable to operate more sophisticated and modern rites, it is best to keep ritual along those early lines which are quite effective within their limits.

Providing the operator feels at home with the ritual form being used, and is capable of expressing himself into it as fully as possible, magic may be made out of almost anything. The necessary release of Inner energies is only possible via the most central, and therefore the most Elemental part of a personal Cosmos. A primitive individual has established only a few inadequate controls around this spiritual nuclear pile, and so it needs little activity to objectify into an energy-overspill which seldom accomplishes any very useful purpose.

As our training and evolution develops, we set up so many internal resistances to our 'Force-Source', that it becomes very remote from our direct control through what is termed 'normal' consciousness. Many Western Initiates tend to have this condition of Inner inhibitory congestion. This usually results in their being perfectly competent along purely intellectual and moral lines, but otherwise not very effective in fields requiring considerable pressures of sheer spiritual energy to obtain directly positive outcomes.

Primitives encounter very little trouble in releasing their Elemental energies, even though this has small effect beyond immediate explosive outbursts. As much might be accomplished by racing around a kitchen table banging it heartily with a large spoon and shouting some reiterative slogan. No matter how far we develop away from this stage, and however complex our Cosmos becomes, the most sophisticated Initiate and the least advanced tribesman must derive their Inner energies from the same Elemental central Force-Source in themselves. As individually evolving entities, we are not, nor ever were all 'equal in the sight of God'. We are, however, equally dependent upon a single Source of Divine Energy within each of us in order to make personal progress along the Path leading to Ultimate Light, whatever That may be. As we Will, so will we Be.

The primitive releases Elemental energy via his noisy and violent rites for a single valid reason. His external activities are related to his Elemental Inner energies by the shortest and most direct route with no particular inhibitive resistances in between the circumference and centre of his Cosmos. This is comparable to joining the poles of a battery together by a short conducting wire which rapidly heats up and burns out in addition to damaging the battery. Nevertheless a drastic effect has unquestionably been produced.

In the case of more civilized Initiates who depend largely upon verbalized concepts and exercises of controlled consciousness for ritual workings, contacts between their centres and circumferences are established by much more devious routes, and frequently unsatisfactory ones. This cuts down available energies very considerably, and often far below the point necessary for obtaining valuable results at all. Thus we are faced in one direction by primitives with direct access to enormous Elemental energy but unable to do anything very useful with it, and in the other by sophisticates with possibilities for working quite well if only they had not blocked up their power supplies. Initiates of the Middle Way of Light seek as usual to find the balance between both extremities in themselves.

A good deal of the difficulty encountered with modernized ritualism arises from inability to associate actualities of experience with their verbal symbols. Words are uttered that arouse no particular reaction in their hearers, and therefore cannot act as levers to release Inner energies. This is scarcely surprising. We are so bombarded with words from all possible angles, press, radio, advertising, other humans, not to mention vast quantities of irritating noises from mechanical sources, that most of us have had to build up defensive screens in ourselves against these threats to our sanity. As a rule, the older we get, the more 'word resistant' do we become, and the less able to make experiences for ourselves out of verbalized concepts whether read or recited aloud.

The most wonderful ritual in the world would be of no use to those for whom it proved only a meaningless amount of uninteresting noise, or just a lot of boring words repeated in a dull, unattractive voice. To ensure enough of the right reactions by participants in carefully constituted rituals, we must either find means to avoid reliance on words altogether, or else discover ways of relating ourselves successfully through them with the necessary Inner energy to work our Will in the Word uttered.

It is perfectly possible of course, to gain much from Group Rites celebrated in foreign languages, and therefore without immediate intellectual effect on the guest-participant. This however, pre-supposes a performance by expert ritualists on sonic and visual levels. Lacking such, there is little likelihood of any favourable response from anyone. If it were possible to achieve the fullest reactions along verbalized channels of consciousness in addition to the others, then modern magical rituals would be the most effective yet designed. Experience shows this to be an acquired art rather than an automatically natural one.

Human reactibility to and with words is so diverse and individually different, that only those skilled in dealing with them and capable of controlling their own responsiveness to specified verbal stimuli are likely to benefit at all from rites mainly dependent on a verbalized structure. Other types of ritualists would be well advised to build their rites chiefly from sonic rhythms, significant movements, and associative visual and olfactory stimuli alone. In fact they will do better without verbal components to confuse their issues of concerting consciousness around form-foci they can handle adequately.

Those committed to the use of verbal symbology in ritual practice should consider very carefully their capabilities of bridging the Inner distance between their Elemental Life Energies and the perimeter of their outer awareness by means of words. To what degree of reality can they raise themselves in consciousness with words alone? For instance, if they mentally framed the formula: 'I am wet', could they actually experience a similitude of feeling and being soaked either pleasantly or otherwise according to specification? How real to themselves can they make what they say or hear? Just how much of what they say in ordinary conversation with other mortals do they genuinely mean from their Inner Being, and how much is said to mislead or simply mean nothing special apart from mechanical superfluities? How far do their words represent their True Wills? What are words really worth to them? All these and other relatable points demand honest answers from ritualists hoping to use words as media for Inner energies.

If we cannot achieve Inner reactive experiences with ordinary human words, we must either invent sonics that make this possible, or else devise some kind of exercise which will lead to a similar state of affairs by means of our existent vocabulary. Both are possibilities, and the latter course has the advantage of being a practicability also. Thus it seems quite worth while examining the idea at least in principle.

Before any trial efforts are made, it should be realized that word-reaction with our deep fundamental elemental energies is not particularly helpful or desirable in our present conditions of civilized living, except in protective circumstances such as ritual procedures or other duly guarded occasions. If, for instance, we went around during our everyday lives reacting deeply and elementally with every word we read, heard, or uttered, our lives would be a most excruciating and exhausting experience.

From a Magical viewpoint, we must not only choose the subject matter of our Inner verbalizations very carefully, but also fit them and ourselves with some kind of a defensive device which will prevent our response at depth except in favourable conditions, and also facilitate this same response as much as possible. A sort of spiritual valve as it were, combined with an ignition key! Fortunately such a contrivance is available like the Pavlov bell, and works very much on the same lines.

The Link-Lock Signal

What is needed will be a species of contact, agreeable to our ordinary outward consciousness, and our deep Inner Awareness alike, which will link energy between the two extremities as and when conditions are suitable to the Will bonding them together. Once this covenant or bargain is firmly established, relationships between centre and circumference of our individual Cosmoi are bound to improve considerably, because the same Words will unite them. On the one hand the Centre promises not to supply Elemental energies for wasteful or stupid reasons, and on the other, the Circumference agrees not to let harmful or distressing influences from the Outerworld get through Inner defences and upset the delicate equilibrium of the Cosmos under construction.

The position is not unlike two guardians on either side of a communicating door between variably hostile conditions which should not be opened except during propitious moments. A mutual signal is thus decided for the purpose. Submarines and spaceships demonstrate this well enough, and we ourselves are in a similar state as entities existing between Inner and Outer conditions of consciousness.

The really important factor about this spiritual security mechanism is that it must NEVER be abused or misemployed. If this happens to any serious extent, it will automatically negate itself and be useless ever after. This is why the Ancients made such an issue about 'taking the Name of the God in vain'. If the Names by which we reach our deepest Inner realities are 'profaned', or rendered valueless, how can we ever hope to employ them for our greatest advantage? The injunction against profanity was not given so much from religious motivation as from pure common sense.

The actual form of this Link-Lock word arrangement depends entirely on the users. Above all, it must be a formula which is absolutely accepted and believed in by Inner and Outer consciousness alike. In olden days it was usually the Name of a God at the commencement of an Invocation. Once that Name had been uttered, contact was established between the utterer and the deep Inner Awareness represented by the God-Concept. This, of course, did not happen unless both ends of the same entity had implicit and unquestioning faith and belief in that God-Being.

There would be small point today in using old God-Names in rituals unless they really and truly meant what they implied to the invocant. To overcome this difficulty, the Christian faith used the formula of the Trinity, 'In the Name of the Father, Son, and Holy Spirit', with or without the Cross gesture. Muslims adopted the 'In the Name of God the Merciful and Compassionate', while Jews kept to their traditional: 'Blessed art Thou, O Lord our God, King of the Universe.' All are brief formulae of belief and relationship between Outer and Inner Being, common to the consciousness of both. Practitioners of modern Mystery Rites lack agreement among each other concerning any such formula, but probably one of the most effective is that adopted by the 'Companions of the Cosmic Circle', consisting of a Cross and Circle gesture which has already been described on a previous page. It seems unlikely that any genuine Initiate would find those terms for Infinity related to the individual unacceptable or unbelievable, since they present change-less values however they may be interpreted.

Working formulae

When the working formula for one Initiate or a whole Group is definitely adopted, every single exercise, no matter how simple and brief, or solemn and complicated, must be prefixed and terminated therewith. To distinguish between a beginning and ending signal, the Companions of the C.C. found it practicable to conclude the opening formula with an opening hand gesture from centre line to right and left as if throwing apart the leaves of a double door, and to conclude, after the Sign is made, the hands are brought together in a shutting movement. Such a procedure is invariably carried out with even the least meditative or magical work, for without it, the highly conditioned consciousness used by its practitioners will not function effectively.

Neither this, nor any other formula is an automatic 'Open Sesame' instantly admitting its user to some Inner Treasure Cave of improbable delights and wonders. It may bring us to the threshold of our Innerworld, but we have to advance therein step by step perhaps as uncertainly and with all our effort just as much as any baby struggling to its feet for the first time in a young unco-ordinated body on this earth.

Since the first necessity in entering any world is to be convinced of its reality, our first experiments at 'word experience' as we enter our Inner Magical world should be confined to simple and undeniable phrases connected with it and ourselves. As each phrase or word is uttered, there must be a maximum effort made to identify with it and express in ourselves what it implies. It must be felt as a truth, a reality, and an actual accuracy beyond the least suspicion of doubt. It must be as genuine to us as our own bodies, minds, and souls, and virtually as integral to our existence as the consciousness which makes it possible for us to think and speak it.

The importance and significance of the words must grow and grow with every utterance. They must come alive to the degree where we can almost see and feel them resonating around us. They have to be lived with all the intensity of which we are capable. Nothing but practice will develop this art for those in whom it is not already a gift, but it is certainly possible to acquire quite a reasonable technique with persistence and regularity of effort.

As an initial exercise, it is a good idea after 'signing in' with the Cross formula, to align ourselves directly with our Inner Elements by something like the following arrangement. With closed eyes, think centrally 'I AM', then project awareness above the head uttering or thinking 'DIVINE', below the feet affirming 'HUMAN', then forward (E) with 'I BREATHE' (Air), while breathing, then rightward (S) with 'I SEE' (Fire) as the eyes are opened, following this to the rear (W) with 'I DRINK' (Water) and then to the left (N) with 'I EAT' (Earth). Real food and drink may be taken if wanted at these points. Next a complete circle of consciousness is established deosil connecting all four points with the affirmation 'I EXPERIENCE'. Lastly, all is balanced in the Centre again with the statement 'I CONTINUE'. When the exercise has been repeated several times until a sufficiency of effort becomes evident, it must be terminated by 'signing out' with the Cross formula.

Anyone encountering this exercise for the first time is easily forgiven for thinking it an idiotic waste of time in emphasizing the obvious. There is considerably more to its structure than that. The practitioner has related himself categorically and specifically with Inner and Outer Life by means of nine fundamental affirmations arranged as verbal formulae which link Centre to Circumference of Cosmos by the most dependable and trustworthy bridges imaginable. This is not an inconsiderable achievement. It is a remarkable feat of 'Inner engineering'. In old parlance, it was called 'pontificating', or building workable bridges between the different Dimensions of Existence. Because these bridges had to be reliable, the verb took on its present connection with infallible pronouncements, which all too often prove nothing of the kind.

Mankind needs to Know himself with a species of Divine desperation. If our Inner Lives were as real and important to us as our Outer ones, then we should become what we were meant to be, and follow the Master Plan for our perfection as spiritually produced individual entities. To KNOW WHAT WE ARE Inside ourselves, it is only natural to make comparisons and relationships with Outside phenomena. This is what the exercises suggested are aimed at achieving. We do not need to ask ourselves whether or not we breathe, see, drink, and eat. We KNOW so much, in so far as any human being ever knows anything. From this known, we are reaching towards the Unknown and finding an equivalent Reality in which we are able to Live. The simple exercise has within it the essentials of a Communion service. We have identified the Elements of breathing, seeing, eating and drinking, with a definite relationship between Divinity and Humanity summed up in the entity of the invocant. Those are the Keys of the Operation. The rest consists of elaborations and facilities.

In an Outerworld like ours, so crammed with confusions and uncertainties, indifferences and bewilderments, all humanity with a spark of soul left in it cries pathetically for even a single solid spiritual actuality to grasp for the sheer salvation of its own existence. We instinctively need to be *someone*, a real live feeling soul, and not just among a mass of figures stuffed into a computer. We want to be *alive*, and not a depersonalized programmed mass of indoctrinated semi-morons sold into spiritual slavery for some obscure group of controlling anti-humans who are clever enough to stay on the outside of these conditions.

Every one of us first and foremost needs to be *ourselves* before we make our contribution to the rest of humanity. How can we possibly prove to ourselves that we are real? Only by establishing undoubted contacts with the fundamental 'ME' in our Central selves. Anything and everything along those lines is of more value now than perhaps ever before in human history. If we lose ourselves—our souls—that will be the end of us. At the same time, we have to lose what we are in order to become what we ought to be. Only a good grip on the Elements of our Existence will give us the strength to make this exchange successfully.

This explains the otherwise peculiar preoccupation with so many people concerning sexual and functional bodily behaviour. Those are undoubted fundamentals linking us with Outer and Inner Life via the Elements. We exhale or break wind (Air), perspire (Fire), emit fluids such as seed, milk, and urine (Water), and excrete (Earth). Even though the intelligences directed at us from the Outer world fill us with fears of being less than dust before an all-destructive atomic blast, these commonplace abilities of our poor human bodies convince us of our own reality in spite of everything. So a large number of people hang on to them with tragic desperation, because they are all that seem genuine among such treacherous and unreliable surroundings. To those incapable of grasping any other fundamentals, the elemental physical functions with Inner connections are about their sole hope of sanity and individual expression. It is true there are many other and probably nobler ways of achieving the same ends, but all must act according to their capabilities. Elements are Elements, and we recognize them as our degree of Light shows them to us.

Word Concepts

The next stage of arrangement is to make out a brief associative list of verbal concepts directly linked with our Elements on higher levels than physical ones, and operate with those. It is very important that individuals obtain such a list from inside themselves out of their own resources, because this is the essence of cosmation. The commencement of this categorization might read—

Element	Air	Fire	Water	Earth
Existence	Spirit	Soul	Mind	Body
Action	Being	Feeling	Thinking	Doing
Characteristic	Vivacity	Brilliance	Depth	Stability
Quality	Aspiration	Insight	Adaptability	Patience
etc.	etc.	etc.	etc.	etc.

Few people's lists would be identical, nor is it essential they should be. What matters is actually doing the work and being intelligent enough not to start stupid squabbles over individual differences. The over-riding factor is for every Initiate to make his own Elementary attributions which he believes relates himself in particular with Indwelling Divinity at his Nil-Nucleus. It is easy enough to write long 'Tables of Correspondences' along Elemental lines and consisting of external objects and phenomena. Those are useful when making up ritual invocations and patterns, but they should be kept as a kind of supply-store for the purpose. The paramount collection of Elemental verbalizations is definitely the one providing the closest links between point and perimeter of a personal Cosmos.

When a workable assortment of Word-concepts has been obtained, they should be systematically experienced. This means they must not only be meditatively dwelt on, but more especially dwelt *in* and *with*, which involves a process of 'getting inside' the concept itself in such a way as to assume its nature for that instant. No easy exercise except for those with an inherent ability for it. Others will have to practice it the hard way, and there are quite a number of pet theories how this should be done. Some may be helpful, and others not. It remains for the individual to experiment and find what is best for him. Here at least, are a few of the devices which offer scope for investigation.

Since it is necessary to keep the attention and concentration of consciousness on a single word or phrase for a period of time which may last for even several minutes or longer, all reasonable means for ensuring this should be adopted. The simplest of course is to write the word or words down, screen everything else from view with the hands or a cardboard visor, and then begin meditation. This has the disadvantage of being rather fatiguing and eye-straining.

A somewhat better way is to put some minutes of the reiterated wording on tape, and then listen to it while meditating with it while eyes are closed and Inner visualizations are proceeding. It helps if the phrase is intoned or chanted as its natural rhythm suggests, or according to whatever plain-chant system may be preferred. Failing a tape recorder, the mouth may be connected with the ear by cupped hands, a stethoscope, or similar means, and the wording softly repeated directly 'mouth-to-ear' fashion. This can be made more intense still, if done by another person, especially one for whom a high regard is felt.

It is probable that the words having the most marked influence on anyone are those either whispered into the ear by a lover or bawled in a frightening tone by those who inspire fear. Both extremes register to maximum depth via emotional channels. Since the bulk of our life-experience is relative to sense-data, words with sensory connotations will naturally be easiest to experience. Early experiments in these exercises are likely to be most successful if sense-appealing words like 'perfume', 'warm', 'tasty', and 'snug' are used as Element-links. There is no reason why fear-evoking phrases should be used at all for sense-stimulation. If an Inner Cosmos is being built up, it may as well be a pleasant one, free from the horrors we already associate with our external world. Indeed, if enough Inner Cosmoi are constructed in a really worthwhile way, they will ultimately produce beneficial effects upon the Outer.

Mantras

Since we recognize words chiefly with our eyes and ears, while most of our ritual reactions to them follow their intonation and resonance, the repetitive 'mantram' is still among the most practical methods of word-experience. A mantram need not be a pious or abstract expression at all. It may be any word or phrase whatever, since in itself it is neither more nor less than a means of holding external consciousness captive in a circle so to speak, while Inner awareness uses this like a launching platform for setting out on a Cosmic exploration of its own.

The mantram is sometimes classified in a slightly contemptuous way as 'auto-hypnosis', but deserves far more consideration than that, being one of the genuine 'old reliables' in mystical practice, and common to most Faiths and Systems under various names. Though almost everyone has heard of or read about it, nothing but actual experience will demonstrate its use, and few modern people are prepared to spend the necessary time for the practice, which may consume an hour or so at a session. Nevertheless it is well worth devoting at least some effort to the ancient art for the sake of an experience gained thereby.

Selecting a suitable Mantram

When deciding on the make-up of a mantram, it is useless at first to pick some high sounding or incomprehensible phrase. A familiar or easily understood terminology evocative of a welcome concept is best to start with. The more readily it is possible to form personal relationships with the subject of a mantram, the better. It should certainly consist of a preferably harmonious phrase with which the user is in full agreement and has a definite affinity with.

Other topics may be tried at a later period when a reasonable amount of experience has been gained with 'mantra-muttering'. Despite Biblical injunctions against 'wizards that mutter', this rhythmical resonation of the mantric phrase is an essential part of the exercise. Quite apart from its hypnotic effect, the physical frequencies of the utterance, modulated by the vocal variations which give it meaning to the mind, ensure that the mantram is not only produced by a mechanism of consciousness, but is in fact responded with and uttered by the human organism as a whole. Though framed with lips and pharynx in obedience to the Will, every molecule of the body eventually picks up and resonates with the mantric message.

With sufficient persistence, we are practically unified with the mantras throughout our entire being. There is a build-up of cumulative energy on the principle of slight rhythmical impulses applied to a heavy pendulum until it eventually swings through a considerable arc. Given enough time, the mantram is theoretically capable of achieving effects with human consciousness which might well be considered magical, and of a higher order than those attributable to auto-suggestion or repeated self-admonitions.

The idea behind the mystical mantras was that by uttering a Divine Name often enough the invocant would eventually unite with that particular Deity. Sometimes this was complicated quite unnecessarily by the supposition that a definite number of invocations, usually running into hundreds of thousands, would achieve such an aim. Thus, to the utterance of the mantras themselves, was added the complication of keeping a mental account of their total. This may have exercised the Inner faculties of memory and vigilance, but the practice led only too frequently to a useless obsession or a compulsive habit leading to little of real value.

Occasionally the developers of religious observances intimated that substantial gains in spiritual real estate were to be had by mantric utterances. Hindus postulated that every mantram became a sort of scaffolding up which one might climb to the otherwise Unattainable, and Christians accepted the notion that officially approved mantras would buy them so many days remission from suffering in Purgatory. Grasping and lazy souls even paid hard cash for others to utter such mantras on their account. So do many genuine and beneficial Inner disciplines become debased by human indolence and greed.

An Initiate of the Middle Way of Light, seeks to use the

mantric practice as a convenience for controlling consciousness in accordance with whatever purpose this method will serve. Its primary function is specifically a technique of adapting Inner awareness with itself on different operational levels. As a superstition it has nothing to offer, but as an Inner skill of an intelligent Initiate, it has very great possibilities indeed.

How to intone a Mantram

Having selected a suitable mantram and settled into a comfortable meditational position, proceedings are commenced by arriving at the most favourable chant, pitch and rhythm. This may be done by trial and error, or simply common sense and instinct. Either the chant has to fit the mantram, or more practically, the mantram should be arranged to fit the chant. Strange to say, the almost universal schoolchild's group-chant of 'La de da de, DA de' makes quite a serviceable rhythm. Whatever rhythm and tone is chosen, it must be hummed or intoned quietly by itself until it feels right.

Generally speaking, a deep tone is preferable, that is felt tingling as far as the fingertips if possible, though this need not be especially loud. The purr of a cat makes a good guide-image to work by. Experts bring a little 'secret' into play here, by manipulating the muscles of the throat so that the passages to the ears open slightly, and even the smallest humming sounds like a high powered roaring in the head. This results in a maximum of internal sonics for a minimum of effort, but is not easy to achieve by catarrhal people or heavy smokers. The trick is to keep the lips closed with teeth apart and a fair volume of air in the mouth, exhaling via the nostrils while regulating the chant with the tongue and larynx. The intellectual sense of the words are then superimposed on these basic sounds by the mind. To an outside listener, only a confused hum would be heard, but inside the head the mantric message should be loud and clear, excluding all other thoughts. The lips should be kept closed all the time, inhalation being done through the nostrils in rapid intakes between sections of chanting.

All this of course, is the purely mechanical component of the exercise. When it is organized and under way, the more important Inner complement may be attempted. This consists of treat-

12—ITOM * *

ing the mantram much like a door or Portal which can literally be entered and access gained to the particular condition it typifies. To promote this experience, the entire field of Inner awareness must be voluntarily limited to the content of the mantram, much as attention is confined to the specific field of a telescope, microscope, or even a T.V. screen. So far as possible, the whole sense of the mantram must be brought to life Inwardly by the use of constructive imagination, and felt as a reality related to the investigator.

Suppose we are trying to relate ourselves with the Elements of Air and Fire in a pleasant way. A useful mantra could be: 'I will feel fresh and light.' The phraseology is put that way in order to link in the very important consideration of individual intention between fulfilled. While the phrase is being intoned, the entire and whole-hearted concern of the operator must be with the ideas of freshness and lightness directly applied to themselves. Perhaps a brilliantly lit seascape might be vividly imagined, while a sense of oneness is sought with the breeze and sunshine. Only the actual concepts of a mantram must be experienced. This is highly important indeed, as otherwise control cannot be established over the channels and categories of consciousness, and everything is liable to blur and go wild.

Any visualizations or impressions in harmony with the concepts may be admitted, but all others must be resolutely dismissed and screened out. Once the mantram-category has been chosen, it must be adhered to for the duration of the exercise. If it is to be changed deliberately, this is quite permissible by means of a new mantram and a fresh start. All must be worked by Will.

The object of such exercises is to give a new depth and meaning to the realities of Inner Dimensions though the Media of human verbalizations. With practice, words can be used as keys to unlock an entire Universe which might otherwise remain unknown to us as an actuality of experience. That is the true Magic of words. When a word is uttered, we must learn the art of constructing its meaning in ourselves as a state of being, if indeed it is our geninue Will to do so. Since any sensible Initiate seeks to build up a Cosmos of Consciousness which is reasonable rather than a mere rubbish heap, only the soundest and most satisfactory concepts should be admitted to it. Hence the careful approach by chosen channels under conditions safeguarded as much as possible by the regulation of ritual rules.

An extension of the mantram practice is the deliberate prolongation of at least the Keywords in any rite, such as Divine or Angelic Names, in order to give the users a chance of focusing their Inner faculties and awareness through that particular wording. Tradition has always said that Names of Power should be chanted at considerable length, and this has often been taken to mean that only this insistence is likely to reach the 'ears' of the Intelligence with which contact is sought. The real reason however, is to allow purely human consciousness the necessary time for adjustment and alignment with the type of Archangelic or other Inner Awareness sought. Few human ritual workers are able to switch from one state of consciousness to another in the split fraction of a second. Therefore, when it becomes necessary to divert the attention from comparatively ordinary wording to a verbal symbolization of a totally different category of being than their own, a brief pause for breath and a drawn-out intonation of the Name-Symbol affords the best opportunity for making such a change.

If the operator were painting a picture with oil colours instead of words, this would correspond with putting down the brush being used for basic colour, selecting another special brush with a different colour, placing some important detail in the picture with it, then returning to base or background again. In fact there is such a similarity between word and colour painting, that one art is quite understandable in terms of the other.

A good practice exercise using this technique is to take an entire invocation and work through it in very slow time indeed, a whole exhalation of breath being devoted to every word, and a brief pause made between words. While the words are being intoned, every effort must be made to experience them and relate them together as a series of concepts coming towards a common purpose. When that purpose is announced as an achievement, the sonic symbol of a gong-stroke is suitable for a transition from physical sound to Inner resonances beyond human vocalization. Such a deliberate method of verbalization is reserved mainly for extremely solemn ritual passages such as dedications and consecrations, when an absolute maximum of concentrated categorized consciousness is called for. In this instance, every separate word is treated as if it were the focal point of a cone of consciousness, which carries the weight and force of every associated concept included in the mass of the cone.

Associative Concepts

To appreciate this idea, let us imagine in theory or construct in practice a light and hollow 45° cone with a tungsten steel or diamond tip capable of penetrating most materials. The size of the cone must be extensible to requirements. If this structure is rested point down upon, say, thin sheet zinc, it would have insufficient weight (or mass) to even produce much more than a faint scratch upon the zinc. Now suppose we commence filling the cone with some heavy material such as molten lead, or perhaps sand. The greater the mass brought to bear (or focused) upon the point by its conical extension, the more will be its power of penetration into the zinc. In order to penetrate tougher or thicker metals, much more mass will be needed, but theoretically the formula of relationship is applicable whatever the circumstances.

If we take the whole of this analogy, substituting a Keyword or 'Name of Power' for the penetrating point, its associative concepts as the mass or amount of consciousness behind it, and the cone-structure determined by our means of focusing the force of the mass on the form of the fulcrum, this will show the principles of 'Magic Words'. Project our familiar Symbol of the Solar or Cosmic Circle with a central point into three dimensions, and a cone will appear. Again and again in Magical practice we meet the same message of centre-circumference relationships. Even the term 'Mass' in the sense of a religious ceremony conveys the idea of relating a cyclic mass of spiritual concepts with the central point of Divinity penetrating the nuclei of our existence.

The greater power we can put into words, the more Magical they will become, and the closer relationships with Inner actualities we shall be able to form with them. Countless ideas and experiments have been explored with such an aim in view. Some workers were of the opinion that common usage of words lessened their impact on individuals, and therefore prolonged silences eventually broken by a single Utterance offered the best opportunities for Will-working with words.

Certain extremists took vows of practically perpetual silence in the hope that eventually Divinity Itself would make an Utterance through them perhaps at the moment of their physical death, one Word from that Source being worth infinitely more than any human might speak in a lifetime. There seems no evidence whatever that anything even resembling such an incident has taken place, or appears remotely likely to. Nevertheless, the balance of silence with utterance is of considerable significance.

The old admonition of thinking before speaking is a major maxim of Magic. Most of what we say in ordinary conversation or stock situations comes from our computer-banks of stored verbalizations which is like a supermarket of speech. Real Words of Power must come from far deeper levels and much closer to our True Being than those casual commodities. Each Magical Utterance should be a Force-Fiat proceeding directly from our Inner Identities. This is not an easy matter for those who spend their lives making trivial and unimportant remarks about matters in which they are neither wholly interested, nor with which their Inner attention is fully engaged. For this reason, monastic communities adopted a working scheme of silent periods during the day when nothing must be uttered unless it is absolutely essential. When the recognized period for verbal contact arrives, anything uttered is supposed to be the product of careful thinking during the silence, and therefore worth listening to. The principles behind this practice apply very strongly to Magical procedure, and similar disciplines should be adapted to suit requirements.

A simple exercise constructed along these lines consists essentially of conceiving an idea, associating all necessary mentation with it, then ultimately giving it birth in the shape of a verbal utterance. The process need not take a great deal of physical time, but must be carried out very conscientiously and sincerely, otherwise it will be ineffective. In a way, it is not unlike self-applied psycho-analysis, but with a difference. Armed with pen and pad while in a customary meditative attitude, the experimenter evokes any desired condition in himself without words, and directs the effect of this as deeply as possible Inside himself towards the Reality he believes will reply. This must be done with an intended implication that the response will be directed through the stockpile of words in his own mind, where a suitable one will be selected and conceived in terms of clear consciousness as an objective verbal entity.

Eventually, after maybe only a few moments, there will be a sense of a returning answer, and a concept will emerge from Within as an unspecified impression rapidly taking shape and character until it names itself with a definite verbal description. Once this happens, it must be imagined as becoming louder and louder with an insistence that leaves no room for anything else in the forefront of the mind. There must be only one way to get it out of the mind—by giving birth to it with the mouth as an utterance. This should be duly done with all the sense of a deliverance, and the word also written down so that it even has a physical body on paper.

Those are merely the bare bones of the exercise, and nothing but experience and experiment will reveal the rest of it. There is more to it than might appear on the surface, and it should pay quite good dividends in return for work and effort expended. In addition to controlling consciousness through an Inner-Silence Outer-Sonic cycle of intentional events, it opens up very useful paths of contact between our ordinary persons on earth and what we really are behind those beings.

Apart from these considerations, the exercise considerably increases skill with words and vocabulary on purely material levels. It is of the utmost importance that the energies of consciousness pushed back as it were into the individual mind towards the Collective Consciousness should be unverbalized. The feeling of this is similar to being at a loss for a word in connection with a known condition and seeking among a purely personal stock of memories for an apt description. We must go much further than that, striving for a contact with a Consciousness far greater than that limited to a single human brain. If the replies received seem odd or even inappropriate at first, this will only be because of inadequate means in ourselves to express what we receive in better terms. All that any human can do is to offer what he has in himself for use by the Higher Intelligence contacting him Within. The better we provide ourselves with Inner facilities, the better will be the type of response we elicit.

Images of the Sephiroth

Some practitioners find it very helpful with this sort of exercise to visualize a Divine Aspect or other personification of Intelligence in keeping with the condition for which a verbalized contact-symbol is required. Qabalists using the Images of the Sephiroth will be on familiar ground here, and others will have to use whatever Aspects or Images apply to their particular System. Interesting results may be obtained by directing the same intentionalized condition towards a number of different Aspects.

Qabalists will discover a good deal of fascination in wandering around the Tree of Life by its Paths and obtaining at least ten varied replies concerning a single proposition, all of which should relate with each other to form a whole Concept of Consciousness. To make the exercise even more practical, the specific responses from the Sephirotic Intelligences should be written in the appropriate places on a Tree-plan, and subsequently studied carefully as a meditative exercise by itself.

Other workers might try the Circle-Cross plan, or whatever their basic Symbol suggests. With practice, reliable channels of communication should be established between the human and Divine levels of consciousness contacting each other through individual Initiates, and direct information should be obtainable through those channels in terms of comprehensible words in human language.

When some ability to use ordinary words like any other material of art is gained, they will prove most valuable in ritual practice. Devising exercises in word-realization can be quite fascinating and rewarding in itself. Every ritualist ought to work out a series of these for himself, much as a musician constructs his favourite little practice-pieces. A lot of such exercises can well be done at odd moments during an average day, perhaps while travelling, in the bath, or at any instant when the mind is not absolutely needed for focal attention to essential duties.

For example, the physical senses make interesting verbal realizations possible. Going through them in order, we might take touch first, then think of the word 'smooth', and imagine ourselves handling some smooth surface until we can practically feel the skin-contact. Taking 'peppermint' next with taste, and 'rose' for smell, we evoke these by mouth and nose. Sight and hearing should be stimulated by uncomplicated words with very clear meanings such as 'book' and 'gong'. All these words of course, will cause reactions to be drawn from memory-banks. At a much later stage of development and skill, more advanced magic may be made with inventions of words intended to carry consciousness beyond the average limits imposed by ordinary human experience.

Most of the so-called 'Magic Names of Power', 'barbarous Names of Invocation', and even 'Enochian tongues' are attempts in this direction. Every one represents a human effort at extending the range of consciousness into unknown Dimensions of Existence and forming intentional relationships with other than human species of entity. Sometimes such efforts are successful, and sometimes not. In the case of a purely human language, many individuals will accept similarity of meaning concerning single words, but this is not yet so with 'Inner' language which every Initiate has to learn for himself in his own 'words'. Hence the 'Magic Words' peculiar to any particular Initiate or Group may be of no value to others unless they are able to attach a similar spiritual significance to them.

Until mankind as a whole is able to converse together by means of a common Inner vocabulary (and that lies in the unforseeable future!) we must rely upon what reaches us through existent channels formed during centuries of effort by the enquiries of enterprising souls operating on both sides of what is loosely termed 'The Veil'. As yet, the Inner speech of Humanity is comparable to the early attempts of an infant to communicate with its elders, but contact between the differing types of consciousness is definitely established *per se*, and the rest is a routine matter of development through the Time-Space-Event Circles. At the present stage of our Inner evolution, it is very much a case of 'every little helps'. Our tenuous linkage on this planet with Inner Life must be improved and strengthened by the efforts of every single willing worker in whatever way is most natural to him, his common aim being unification of Inner and Outer Life to the point of making 'Heaven' and 'Earth' a 'Whole Kingdom', or the shared experience of human souls dwelling therein.

When those operating ritual methods of procedure are more

concerned with developing and perfecting their own systems than criticizing or condemning the faults of others, a much happier state of affairs will exist throughout the Holy Mysteries on earth than at present. One major complaint from would-be ritualists who are unaffiliated with any particular organized Group within the Mysteries, is that no reliable Rites are published for them to perform. Either they are faced with medieval rubbish, or very dubious amateur concoctions with a limited sale and as little practicality.

It seems useless pointing out to those in such a dilemma that almost anything they do of their own accord straight from their hearts in search of Inner Reality, is much better for them and everyone else than a whole welter of wordage which does nothing but muddle their minds and stupefy their souls. They simply would not believe such a plain and straightforward statement. Moreover, they have some right on their side. What, indeed, *is* available?

Naturally no Rites could possibly be written or arranged which all types of Mystery worker would find equally acceptable. Bearing this in mind, let us now examine the structure of an actual Rite published for the first time, which is based on Qabalistic and Circle-Cross Tradition. It is operable by one or more individuals up to twelve in number, and it can be made as simple or elaborate as required. Even though it will not be usable in its present form except by those who subscribe to its ideas and for whom its terms have meaning, its formation and basic arangements are applicable to a much wider field. Study of these should prove interesting.

CHAPTER VII

HOW TO ARRANGE A RITUAL

The fundamental secret of putting rituals together is to do so around an appropriate Symbolic design. If this is expressible as a Glyph on paper, so much the easier for the constructor. Once the basic Plan is drawn up, it only remains to meditate on it sufficiently, and decide what type of ritual act or intention fits best where, having regard to the overall purpose in mind.

Symbolic Design

Suppose for instance, a Rosicrucian species of Rite is being considered, and the long-shafted Cross with trefoil finials, having a Crown at centre, and chaplet of seven Roses is being used. This Symbolic group will provide at first glance a Quaternity, Septenary, twelve Stations, and a Central unit. Immediately this suggests the Elements, Planets, Signs, and Creator or 'Faithful King'.

Working the design inwards from its periphery as a Rite of relationship between humans and their Divine Principle, many possibilities and opportunities present themselves. By means of the Crown Symbol, we can accept this Principle as the central Being of our Cosmos, and then approach It by the Four Elemental Paths in turn, varying each approach three ways according to the Zodiacal Cardinal, Fixed, and Mutable Signs associated with each Element. This may be simply done by just a change of thinking, or accompanied by banners of the Signs, special chants, or whatever is wanted.

The Seven Roses may be treated as Planetary presentations of their Spirits and personified with invocations and even action-dances or hymn verses. The culmination or climax of the Rite might very well be a silent attempt at 'Crowning', when if there is more than a single officiant, all kneel in a close circle, held together with each other's arms and heads bent forward until they touch each other all round. During this brief period a real Inner effort must be made to reach the Highest possible Divine contact attainable by the combined energies of all those coming together in such a manner for that common reason. After this, some closing procedure will be needed, and an orderly procession with a chant may lead away from the working area by the long arm of the Cross.

This, of course, is just a very rough outline of one type of Rite suggested by a particular Symbolic lay-out. Designing a Rite is like designing anything else. Obtain a practical blue-print (or Symbol), specify the materials to be used in construction, select the specialist operatives for the task, organize a work-programme, and so forth. There are, after all, only a limited amount of ritual materials available to human beings intending to practice Rites within reasonable limits of dignity and decency.

Theoretically, any description of human behaviour and attitude can be ritualized. In the case of low-grade, depraved, and vicious individuals, beatings, copulations, and other un-lovely activities are indeed ritualized into so-called 'Black Masses' (which they rarely are), 'Witches' Sabbats' (depending entirely on the class of practitioners present), and similar arrangements of human group-association. Materials for rituals are therefore limited by the standards demanded on the social, cultural, or other levels of approach. It will be assumed in this instance, that only good general standards will be accept-able for ritualization. Everyone ritualizes according to their own spiritual, ethical, and educational abilities and status. By their Rites are these recognized, and the higher the standard and quality of any Rite, the greater demands will it make on those who would practice it.

Literally, if we adopt and practice Rites from a somewhat √ higher Life-level than our own for a sufficient length of time, they are bound to raise our whole beings accordingly. Con-versely, the practice of degrading or peurile rituals will result in the practitioner ultimately falling to such lowered standards of behaviour. It is always a temptation with otherwise good quality ritualists to 'experiment' with Rites and practices of very inferior natures to their own natural levels. There is no real justifica-tion for this whatever, and any pretexts advanced for such experiments are likely to be self-excuse screens to cover personal inclinations towards misbehaviour.

To avoid being over-censorious, or self-righteous, it is well to remember that no human being is able to work any kind of Rite beyond the scope of his own individual abilities and state of development (or 'Degree') upon the Inner Path. There are many species of ritual which to cultured souls appear either silly and inept, or perhaps downright indecent. Yet these are absolutely the only ones practicable for those who have not risen above such primitive means of cosmating their consciousness. If nothing but fear of punishment in some direct form will restrain people from wrongdoing, and only immediate rewards of sex and food will induce them to make any effort at all at evolutionary advancement, then those crude means must be applied whip-and-carrot fashion in Magical Rites as in life itself.

It is no use therefore, condemning out of hand ill-constructed clumsy, illiterate, and sex-motivated Rites which are put together or practised by souls incapable of more worthy efforts. If that is indeed the most they can do and all they have learned, they are surely blameless if their intentions are honest, and not directed against their fellow-beings. Some day they should grow into more advanced methods. If anyone is deserving of real blame and condemnation, it is those who, with every advantage of status, training, and Inner awareness, decide to practise ritual procedures of a much lower grade than their proper entitlement, for the sake of amusement, cheap thrills, or maybe much worse motives. Unfortunately these abusers of the Holy Mysteries do indeed exist in some numbers, and present a serious problem to others who would uphold far higher standards of spiritual behaviour.

Direction of intention

To be of real value, every genuine Mystery Rite should have built into it some factor or other which is designed to lead its practitioners ultimately out of it into even better, nobler, and much finer forms of ritualism beyond any practice confined to purely human consciousness. Even the crudest, clumsiest, and otherwise most futile Rite may contain this.

Somewhere within the structure of a Rite there ought to be

a direction of intention towards a more perfect expression and vehicle of Inner energies put into patterns of power. A few words, a gesture, or a mutely offered prayer will do. Anything practical which makes the ritualists realize their necessity for rising above and beyond their present position on the Path, is an essential in all Magical Rites which deserve to be considered 'White', or beneficial to human spiritual progress. Either we regenerate ourselves or else degenerate, and it is sad if the latter course is taken.

Ideal Magical Rites therefore, should be of a standard compatible with the highest capabilities of the workers on all or most life-levels, preferably a little above their average competence, requiring a real effort to perform properly, and so resulting in a genuine sense of achievement and attainment when carried out correctly. Unless there is a true feeling of their worthwhileness and a really deep satisfaction obtained by carrying them out, no Rites are likely to be of much value to those engaged with them.

Building A Rite

With all this and somewhat more in mind, let us take the base-Symbol of the Cosmic Cross, Circle-Cross, Solar Cross, or Celtic Cross, however it may be called, and build a Rite with it. It provides us with ideas of Elements, Instruments, Archangels, and everything else that fits into this fourfold formation. It also gives a pleasing dance pattern, circumambulation, and most of the fundamentals from which reasonable Magical Rites are constructed. Furthermore, it can be worked by any number of operators from a full Circle to a single person. Equipment may be very simple and elementary, or quite elaborate, though it can scarcely be emphasized enough that nothing used or present should be either unnecessary or incongruous.

In good ritual practice, only essentials to the Rite, compatible with its nature and allowing for the means and circumstances of the workers, ought to be directly associated with it. There is no reason why any Temple should be stark, bleak, or uninviting, but there is every reason, aesthetic and otherwise, why it ought not to resemble a junk shop or collection of occult curiosa. The Temple or working area is a Symbol in itself, and if it appears to be an untidy heap of miscellaneous bric-à-brac suggesting confusion and disorder, such an element of Chaos will infallibly enter whatever Rites are worked. Unless we are aiming at this very pointless result, it is best to operate otherwise.

Symbols

We will assume therefore, that a clear working area or at least minimum size is available. In olden times, such a circle was derived in the case of a single worker by setting his staff upright in the earth, looping an end of their girdle-cord around it, then with a knife at the other end of the cord, tracing a complete circle around the Staff. This gave a circle of roughly nine feet in diameter, though it might quite well be less if circumstances so dictated. It there were a number of people present, hands were simply joined and the circle made that way.

However a circle is described, whether in chalk on a floor, an arrangement of string, a knife-cut in the earth, or a properly inscribed floor-cloth, it must be set up in reality or imagination with indication-Symbols at the Quarters, and Centre. These may be merely the Signs of the Elements on cardboard, or their actual Instruments of Sword, Rod, Cup, and Shield. Whatever suggests the Attributions of the Quarters will serve, though of course properly made and dedicated Symbols are best. Even a feather in the East for Air, a lighted candle in the South for Fire, a glass of water in the West, and a flower pot with a growing plant for Earth in the North are valid Symbols. Anything definitely linking the consciousness of the operator with its objective is suitable, but naturally the more care and consideration has been devoted to any Symbol, the more useful it will prove.

The Staff

The central Symbol of the circle is an upright Staff representing the most direct Path from Earth to Heaven, and also acting as a sort of 'armature' around which the Inner spiritual Controller of the Circle is supposed to align himself with the consciousness of the working Group on earth. Although such a straightforward idea may seem primitive, it is still dependable, being so closely related to the deep basics of human experience, and with such a long history of use from early times until today in all kinds of manner.

Theoretically, a Staff should be about the height of a tall man, with an iron or spear at one end, and some means of light at the other. There are countless variants of this nature with every sort of carving imaginable, or decoration of ribbons and bells that might be described. Probably one of the most practical for our present purpose is a plain ash-staff not exceeding an inch diameter and six feet high, with a point or suitable spike at the bottom, and a Light-Symbol such as a glass knob or Solar Cross at the top. A real flame in the form of candle or lamp may indeed be used, but this proposes an undue fire-hazard, and is not advisable in most circumstances. Undoubtedly some modern workers are bound to think of a battery or inductively powered electric bulb at the top of the staff, but this is quite wrong in principle. However, electricity may be used for background lighting, working amplifiers, and other purposes in modern Magical practice. The Flames forming integral parts of the basic ritual Pattern must always be 'living' ones, dependent on the same atmosphere we breathe ourselves. This is a most definite ruling.

The cords and bell

There must, of course, be some means of setting the Staff upright in the centre of the Circle. A heavy wooden block with a sunken socket is most convenient, but a suitable container full of sand makes a substitute. Ideas suggest themselves according to circumstances.

To improve the symbology of the Staff for little extra cost or effort, four coloured cords are attached to the bottom just above earth level. They are laid to the Quarters, acting as markers, and are best secured at their free ends in some way affording a quick release. These cords must be long enough to wind around the Staff as many times as circumambulations may be made, finally being fixed to the top by a clip or an easily untied knot, leaving a tasselled or ornamentally knotted end dangling. The colours of the cords must suggest the Quarters somehow. They can be light blue for Air, yellow for Fire, dark blue or green for Water, and brown or black for Earth. A pleasing arrangement is that of the Light spectrum, blue being for first light of Dawn at East, yellow for the sun at Noon in the South, red for sunset in the West, and black for Night in the North.

To add another permissible touch of symbology to the Staff, a bell or bells may be fixed to its top beneath the Light-Symbol, so that a slight movement of the Staff causes a ringing noise. We thus have the primary forces of Creation represented as Light and Sound. The whole Staff now depicts the Tree of Life, or Serpent-ascent of Man on Earth to God in Heaven. What could be a more appropriate Glyph, standing like an unspoken prayer among us? Perhaps some symbologists may see it as a Maypole in reverse, but there seems no reason against such an idea providing it is developed past that point.

Lighting and incense

In addition to an appropriate Symbol, the Quarters of at least, E, S, and W, should have also a Light to signify their natures, while the N Quarter is either left dark, or allowed a tiny flame in a blue glass to represent a Star, unless a Lunar type of illumination is required. The simplest Lights are coloured candles, but more beautiful effects are to be had with properly coloured glasses.

A stool for each worker is a great convenience unless it is proposed to perform the entire Rite standing and kneeling. Stools are more useful in this type of Rite than chairs, which take up a lot of room and are easily knocked into with painful consequences likely to disrupt any atmosphere. This completes the 'property list' apart from incense, which may be kindled in a burner at the S, or, if a thurible is used, offered at each Quarter (two swings) during the actual working. Since the Rite is an 'Office', plain robes, or habits with girdles and raised hoods is correct wear.

Music

A great asset is recorded music to be used with discretion, and a reasonable gong or bell. Failing this, any suitable chant-sequence may be sung or hummed, and gavel knocks given. In all ritual, the Pattern is the main thing, and methods of adherence to it depends entirely on the means available to the ritualists. None need be deterred from ritual practice because they lack costly or difficult equipment. The real Symbols exist in the consciousness anyway, and their physical counterparts are only pegs to hang an image around. If a true ritualist has only an old pocket-knife to show physically, yet constructs the most wonderful Magic Sword about it Inwardly, the Symbol of the Sword is present where it ought to be.

Most Groups these days are scarcely so impoverished that no kind of recorded music is possible, and ritualism without appropriate music is a rather stark affair. For the 'Office of the Four Archangels' strong and lively organ music makes a good prelude and finale, while quieter and more delicate background music is recommended for the meditational phase unless silence is required here. The Office has been especially written for a straightforward plainchant rhythm familiar to most workers, and the few song tunes will suggest themselves along already existent lines. Full resonation is called for in utterance of the Office, except where mutations or other effects are indicated. No difficulty ought to be encountered by any ritualist with even modest experience in the Western Tradition.

In practice, no insuperable objection seems to present itself if the entire Office is recorded, and followed through by the workers in mime, with uttered responses and singing. In fact this is quite a pleasant way to carry it out, providing it is actively worked on Inner levels, and not merely listened to as a species of entertainment. Dyed in the wool traditionalists apart, there seems every likelihood of recorded Rites becoming a standard procedure of the future, once operatives become skilled in their proper usage. One main advantage is that removal oɪ 'donkey-work' or sheer mechanics from the Rite, leaves participants with much greater Inner scope and freedom of experience. Nevertheless, this appears applicable to already expert ritualists alone. Beginners should still learn the hard way of practical performance, before they attempt launching themselves into Inner Dimensions without having acquired auto-stability therein.

The dance-sequence

The dance-sequence is simple enough if only one person is working the Office. It consists of a centre-circumference approach to each Quarter in turn, with identification gestures. A graceful combination easily remembered and applied, are to the E; left hand over heart, and right arm into side with extended forearm and hand held as if gripping a sword-hilt at the 'carry', to the S; left hand still over heart, but right hand raised as if holding the top of a tall Rod or Staff, to the W; both hands brought together outwards and downwards as if holding a Cup and actually cupping the palms as though to hold water, to the N; the cupped hands brought up and flattened either with palms inwards like a book or Mirror, or outwards as if to Shield the face. These gestures run one into the other quite naturally and freely, making good junctions between the Quarter-concepts.

If four or more operatives are present the dance is probably best as an on-the-spot affair unless there is sufficient space for more complicated manoeuvres. Since there is only one four-line chant and a chorus, it may be reiterated as often or as little as required. There should aways be some degree of flexibility in every Rite which the ritualists can set for themselves according to requirements, and dance-sequences, meditations, circle-chants, and special invocations are good opportunities for this factor.

There should also and most importantly be an 'X', or 'random' factor provided for in Rites, whereby the Unknown Entity or representative of Divine Energy may 'link in' according to Its own Will. The most usual way of doing this is by means of the hushes and silences between sonic passages, but it is also (though less commonly) introduced by what is known as the 'Holy Hiatus'. This is a sudden, unpremeditated, and complete cessation of sound and action on the part of whoever conducts the ceremony at that instant, because of an Inner inhibition coming from the Direction responsible for those higher life-levels on which the Rites is being correspondingly worked. These breaks are likely to occur without the slightest warning, and be of only short physical duration. During that opportunity, all present should direct the whole of their Inner attention towards the cause of the Hiatus, and strive to make individual contact with it as well as they can.

The obvious warning on this point of the 'Holy Hiatus' is that so many workers may wittingly or otherwise misuse it. There is a strong temptation to introduce it deliberately in order to call attention to whoever does so, thus falsely giving an impression they are in better contact with Inner Entities than others in the same Circle. Any attempt to do this defeats the whole object and value of the Hiatus. It must come entirely from within of its own accord, and no one should be more surprised by, though not unprepared for it, than the one it happens to.

Everyone taking part in the Rites ought to be prepared for such a possibility, yet neither insistent upon its occurrence, nor disappointed by its absence. The constant possibility of its happening will maintain an inward alertness and attention to the Rite throughout its entire course. In the case of recorded Rites however, the Hiatus will not take place, and this should be remembered when any work is planned in advance. Although many 'live' Rites may be worked without any genuine Hiatus happening, when it actually does eventuate, there must be an understanding among the ritualists as to what action must be taken should it seem inordinately drawn out. Most Groups soon develop an instinct about these matters, knowing exactly how and when to set the run of the Rite going again. There cannot be any entirely hard and fast ruling, except to suggest that no Hiatus is likely to be of any great value after a few moments of our earthly time. Once an Inner contact has positively been established and 'flashed over', there is no point at all in throwing needless time and space from our dimensions of existence after it. We cannot make it more or less than it actually amounted to of its own accord, and we shall add or subtract nothing to or from it by juggling with our earthly availables.

These 'X' contacts are of the utmost interest and value. Although they occupy perhaps the barest fraction of our time, enough actual Inner energy in terms of condensed consciousness may reach us to keep our normal awareness busy for maybe months and years of earth-time to come. It is as though an 'instant film' were made inside us which would take a considerable amount of our time to run through a projector and follow.

To some extent, the 'X' contacts are like the secret 'high speed' codes transmitted at such a rate that to ordinary ears only a rapid screech is received. Recorded on tape, and slowed down many times, a long and intelligible message in clear language is heard. In the same way, the briefest 'flash' received during a Rite (or otherwise) from Inner Intelligences, will probably prove sufficient to enlighten our earthly lives for quite a while. That is why they are so well worth waiting for, and working to obtain.

If we perform the basic tasks of our necessary meditations and exercises, we shall build up inside ourselves the necessary mechanisms for translating the 'high-speed' contacts of coded consciousness from Inner Dimensions into terms we can deal with on our ordinary levels of life. Although rituals are by no means the only way of making these contacts, they have certainly been a well tried and established system for many centuries past, and with an even greater future potential.

Commencement of the Rite

Assuming that all these and associated conditions are being kept in mind, and that we have processed around the Circle by the right to our appointed places, where we have seated ourselves and put our Inner states into good order while listening to the introductory music, the Rite proper commences. It does so with four slow gong-strokes, this being the basic figure. The principal Official will naturally lead the chanting, but those parts of the Rite relating to any one Quarter in particular should be dealt with by the proper Officer of that Quarter. The leader 'signs in' with the customary:

IN THE NAME OF THE WISDOM, AND OF THE LOVE, AND OF THE JUSTICE, AND THE INFINITE MERCY OF THE ONE ETERNAL SPIRIT. AMEN.

P   BLESSED ARE THE FOUR BY WHOM OUR FAITH IS FIXED UPON THE CIRCLED CROSS OF COSMOS.

R   BY WHOM THE EDGE OF OUR EXISTENCE IS

RELATED RIGHTLY TO OUR SPIRITUAL CENTRE.

P HONOURED BE THEIR NAMES AND BLESSED BE THEIR NATURES UNTO ALL BELIEVERS IN THEIR BEING.

R AND UNTO THE ETERNAL ONE IN WHOM ALL BEINGS BELIEVE.

P COMPANIONS, LET US CALL INTO OUR CONSCIOUSNESS, THOSE GREAT ARCHANGELS WHO PRESENT TO US IN PERSON THE FOUR PRINCIPAL DIRECTIONS OF DIVINITY MADE MANIFEST AS MEANING. LET US CONSIDER THEM CONNECTED WITH EACH OTHER AND OURSELVES UPON THE COSMOS CROSS.

Induction Narrative

This is the 'Story behind the Rite' recited for the purpose of aligning everyone's consciousness with the principles connected with the action as a whole. It should be recited by whoever is best qualified for the task, because it will 'set the tone' of what follows.

BEFORE ALL BEING BEGAN WAS NOTHING SAVE THE SUPREME SPIRIT. UNDIFFERENTIATED IN ITSELF, UNMANIFESTED, UNEXISTING. THE WORD OF WILL WAS UTTERED (gong stroke). I AM BECAME WE ARE (gong stroke). LIFE, LIGHT, LOVE, AND LAW CONSTRUCTED COSMOS (gong stroke). CONSCIOUSNESS EXPANDED EQUALLY AROUND ITS SACRED SEED OF SPIRIT, AND THE CIRCLES OF CREATION CROSSED EACH OTHER AS TIME-SPACE EVENTUATED INTO INDIVIDUAL EXISTENCE.

COMPARABLY WITH OUR CONDITIONS, THE POLAR POINTS ARE REPRESENTED BY DIVINITY ABOVE, HUMANITY BELOW, AND THE PRINCIPAL ARCHANGELS AT THE QUARTERS. IN CENTRE IS THE ALL SUSTAINING SPIRIT WITH ITS NUCLEUS OF NIL.

SUCH IS OUR CONCEPT OF CREATIVE CONSCIOUS ENERGY ITSELF AS EXISTING COSMOS. SO

DO WE CONCEIVE ALL IS FROM NIL, FORCE FLOWS INTO FORM, THINGS COME FROM THINKING, AND BIRTH BEGETS US ON THIS EARTH. AS ABOVE, SO BELOW. WHEN THE PLAN OF HEAVEN IS PUT TO PRACTICE UPON EARTH, AND THE HOLY WILL IS WORKED BY HUMAN HEARTS AND HANDS, WE SHALL PRESENT THE PATTERN OF PERFECTION UNTO ONE ANOTHER.

LET US THEREFORE, ADDRESS OURSELVES TO THE ARCHANGELS WHO CONTROL THE QUARTERS OF OUR CONSCIOUSNESS THROUGHOUT THE COSMOS WE ARE WILLING TO CREATE AROUND THE HOLY SPIRIT WORKING IN US AT OUR ORIGIN, THIS MOMENT, AND FOREVERMORE. AMEN.

The AMENS are echoed and chanted at length by all.
All echo these chants.

P   BLESSED WITHIN US BE THE ONE WE ARE
      BLESSED ABOVE US BE ETERNAL GOD
      BLESSED BELOW US BE EVOLVING MAN
      BLESSED BEFORE US BE THOU RAF—I—EE—EL
      BLESSED RIGHTWARD BE THOU MIK—I—EE—EL
      BLESSED BEHIND US BE THOU JIV—RA—EE—EL
      BLESSED LEFTWARD BE THOU AUR—RA—EE—
      EL

   SO MOTE IT BE AMEN.   *All echo the 'So Mote it*
                                        Be's' throughout.

The Litany

All sit or kneel.

O THOU FAITHFUL FOUR WHO REPRESENT TO US THE POINTS AND PRINCIPLES OF OUR AWARE-NESS IN EXISTENCE, BLESSED BE THOU UNTO US FOR EVERMORE AND EVERMORE.

WE INVOKE THINE IMAGES, AND CALL UPON THEE FROM OUR HEARTS, BECAUSE OF THE DIVINE NECESSITY IN US WHICH ONLY THOU MAY FILL. BE THOU INDEED WITH US O MIGHTY ARCH-ANGELIC ONES, AS WE APPROACH THEE IN OUR

MINDS AND SOULS, PROCLAIMING THEE ALOUD:

THOU TRUE ANGELIC ARCHETYPES
MOST RIGHTEOUS RULERS
SUPPORTERS OF THE SOUL
CONTROLLERS OF CREATION

Response is
BE ONE
WITH
US
through-
out

THOU CORNERS OF THE COSMOS
UPHOLDERS OF THE UNIVERSE
PILLARS OF PERFECTION
TETRARCHS OF THE TRUTH

KEEPERS OF THE KINGDOM
DISTINCTIONS OF DIVINITY
HELPERS OF THE HOLY HAND
OVERLORDS OF ORDER

BEATITUDES OF BEING
REVEALERS OF REALITY
PROVIDERS OF PURPOSE
PRINCIPLES OF POWER

GREAT ONES OF GOD
LEADERS OF THE LIGHT
GOVERNORS OF GOOD
DEFEATERS OF THE DARKNESS

LORDS OF LIMITATION
MAKERS OF THE MANIFEST
QUESTORS OF THE QUARTERS
SPIRITS OF THE SEASONS

EQUATORS OF THE ELEMENTS
MARKERS OF THE MEDIANS
EXTINGUISHERS OF EVIL
DELIVERERS FROM DEATH

PRECEPTORS OF PERCEPTION
CHANNELS OF CONSCIOUSNESS
INSTRUCTORS OF INTELLIGENCE
ARCHANGELS OF AWARENESS

THOU FOURFOLD FORCEFORMS
CATEGORIES OF CREATION
COMPASSORS OF THE CIRCLE
COSMATORS OF THE CROSS

LIVE THOU WITH US O GREAT ARCHANGELS OF THE COSMIC CROSS. SPEAK THOU WITHIN OUR SOULS, IMPART INTELLIGENCE INTO OUR MINDS, MAKE THYSELVES MANIFEST THROUGH OUR MORTALITY. MAY WE BECOME INCREASINGLY AWARE OF ONE ANOTHER, COMING INTO COMMON CONSCIOUSNESS TOGETHER IN THE NAME, etc.

P   LET EACH ARCHANGEL BE APPROACHED AND HONOURED.

R   ACCORDING TO THE RIGHTEOUS WAY OF LIGHT.

Here, each Officer of the Quarter should invoke the appropriate Archangel while facing outwards, then making an obeisance should invite the Entity into themselves, stand erect, face inwards to the centre and utter the Archangel's words in the character of that Being. It should be as nearly as possible as if the Archangel really said them (which in effect is so). While the rest of the office is in chant-form, the Archangel's words are given in a natural voice with the best possible diction and appropriate characterization. In general, Raphael speaks with a young and eager voice, Michael in a firm commanding tone, Jivrael in a friendly and affectionate manner, while Auriel speaks in a senior, deliberate way. The East commences.

E   HAIL UNTO THEE ARCHANGEL RAPHAEL AND ALL THINE ATTRIBUTES.

R   MAY WE RELATE OURSELVES WITH THEE BY WORD AND WILL.

THOU ART RAPHAEL. HEALER OF HUMAN HURTS AND TEACHER OF THE HIDDEN WISDOM. THOU GIVEST US ENCOURAGEMENT TO SEEK FOR TRUTH WITHIN OURSELVES. THY SPLENDID SWORD DELIVERS US FROM OUR SELF-MADE ENTANGLEMENTS OF INDECISION AND DECEIT. THOU ART LIGHT ARISING AS A SHINING DAWN ABOVE THE DARKNESS OF OUR IGNORANCE.

THINE ENTHUSIASM MOVES US TO MAKE BETTER PROGRESS ON OUR INNER PATHWAYS. THOU ART AN INSPIRATION TO US IN THE HOLY

MYSTERIES, AWAKENING IN US A SPIRIT OF EN-
QUIRY INTO EVERY SECRET SCIENCE.

THOU FIGHTEST FOR OUR FREEDOM TO
SUCCEED AS LIBERATED AND ENLIGHTENED
SOULS IN SEARCH OF OUR APPOINTED DESTINY,
DECREED BY THE DIVINE ONE AND DECIDED BY
OUR OWN DEVOTION. INSPIRE US THERETO
ALWAYS.

I AM INDEED RAPHAEL. BE AROUSED BY ME, AND
LOOK AHEAD FOR LIGHT TO OVERCOME OBSCUR-
ITIES ON SACRED SUBJECTS HIDDEN FROM PRO-
FANE PERCEPTION. BECOME AWARE OF INNER LIFE
AND ITS IMPORTANCE TO INITIATED SOULS.
REALIZE THE FULL RESPONSIBILITY OF INDIVID-
UALS FOR CONSECRATING AND CONSTRUCTING
THEIR OWN COSMIC CIRCLES. FEAR THIS NOT, FOR
I WILL STRIVE TO HEAL ALL HURTS AND INJURIES
SUSTAINED IN SERVICE TO THIS SUPREME CAUSE
OF SPIRIT. ACCEPT ALLEGIANCE TO IT WITH A
WILLING HEART AND KEEN INTELLIGENCE, PRE-
PARED TO FIND THE POINT OF WHATSOEVER MAY
BE PENETRATED BY THE PIERCING SWORD OF
TRUTH.

R ACKNOWLEDGEMENT TO THEE O BLESSED
RAPHAEL. MAY THOU BECOME TO US SUCH
QUALITIES WITHIN OURSELVES, THAT UTTER-
ING THY HOLY NAME ALONE WILL RAISE THEM
TO REALITY IN US WITH THEE.

SO MOTE IT BE AMEN.

S HAIL UNTO THEE ARCHANGEL MICHAEL AND
ALL THINE ATTRIBUTES.

R MAY WE RELATE OURSELVES WITH THEE BY
WORD AND WILL.

THOU ART MICHAEL, PRINCE OF HEAVENLY PER-
FECTION. MOST EXALTED LEADER OF THE HOSTS
OF LIGHT. WITH THY ROD, THOU GUIDEST US
UPON THE RIGHT HAND PATH TOWARDS ETERNAL

GOODNESS. THOU ART THE EVER GLORIOUS SUN OF INNER TRUTH, REVEALING ALL TO THEY THAT ASK FOR RIGHTFUL REASONS.

THOU DEFENDEST US AGAINST THE DARK ONES, DISMISSING OUR DISEASES AND EXPELLING EVILS FROM US. THOU HAST PROMISED FAITHFULLY THAT THOU WILT NOT ABANDON US UNTO OUR ENEMIES WHILE YET THE SLIGHTEST SPARK OF GOOD REMAINS WITHIN US. WE DEPEND ON THEE FOR OUR DELIVERANCE FROM SPIRITUAL DANGERS. BE THOU OUR CHAMPION FOREVER.

I AM INDEED MICHAEL. BE ENERGIZED, UP-LIFTED, AND ENCOURAGED BY THE SPIRITUAL STRENGTH I SEND TO SOULS THAT SEEK THE UPRIGHT WAY OF LIFE. ALWAYS BE STRAIGHT-FORWARD, LEVEL, AND DIRECT IS DEALING WITH DIVINITY, HOWEVER HUMANS MUST BE MET ACCORDING TO THEIR MEASURE. LET THE SACRED STAFF STAND EVER TRULY IN THE CENTRE OF EACH COSMIC CIRCLE, AND WE WILL PROCLAIM THE HOLY NAME OF GOD AT THE PERI-METER.

I WILL NEVER FAIL WHOEVER ASKS MINE AID AGAINST THE ENEMIES OF RIGHT AND LIGHT. HAVE FAITH IN MY DISCRETION, AND BE FAIR IN JUDGING MATTERS THAT DEPEND ON GOOD DECISIONS. NONE SHALL BE WRONGED THAT TRUST ME TO DEFEND THEIR CAUSE BEFORE THE HIGHEST COURT OF HEAVEN. RELY UPON MY RIGHTEOUS ROD FOR REASONED RULERSHIP.

R ACKNOWLEDGEMENT TO THEE O BLESSED MICHAEL. MAY THOU BECOME TO US SUCH QUALITIES WITHIN OURSELVES, THAT UTTER-ING THY HOLY NAME ALONE WILL RAISE THEM TO REALITY IN US WITH THEE.

SO MOTE IT BE AMEN.

W HAIL UNTO THEE ARCHANGEL JIVRAEL AND ALL THINE ATTRIBUTES.

R MAY WE RELATE OURSELVES WITH THEE BY WORD AND WILL.

THOU ART JIVRAEL. POTENT AND COMPASSIONATE ART THOU BY NATURE. THY CUP OF LOVING KINDNESS OVERFLOWS UPON US. THOU LEADEST US TO EVERLASTING LIFE PAST PERSONAL EMBODIMENT OR INCARNATION. THOU ART LIGHT DESCENDING ON US GRACIOUSLY WITH ROSY RAYS THAT PROMISE PARADISE AS WE ATTAIN PERFECTION. THOU ART THE SACRED OIL OF TRUE ANOINTMENT AND ILLUMINATION.

THROUGH THEE COMES LOVING CONFIDENCE THAT CASTETH OUT ALL FEARS FOREVER. THOU ART THE MEDIATOR OF SUPERNAL LOVE THAT KNOWS NO LIMITS SAVE OUR SPIRITUAL MEASURE TO SUSTAIN IT. THOU FILLEST US WITH FAITH, AND COMFORTETH THE SOULS OF THEY THAT COME TO THEE FOR CONSOLATION.

THOU BRINGEST BLISS BEYOND BELIEF TO US, AND SURE BEATITUDE WILL BE BESTOWED ON THOSE PARTAKING OF THY POWER. CONTINUE THOU TO CARE FOR US.

I AM INDEED JIVRAEL. BE ASSURED OF LOVE BY ME, AND REALIZE THAT IT AND LIFE ARE OF ONE ORIGIN IN UNIVERSAL SPIRIT. EACH SINGLE SOUL IS BEST BELOVED BY THE ONE IN WHOM THEIR BEING BEGAN. LOVE IS THE CAUSE OF COSMOS, AND THE TRUEST MEANING OF MANKIND.

WHOEVER HAS THE LEAST CAPACITY FOR LOVE NEED NEVER FEAR EXTINCTION. LOVE IS IMMORTAL IN ITSELF, AND IS THE REAL ELIXIR OF ETERNAL LIFE. THEY THAT LIVE IN LOVE WITH THE DIVINE ONE SHALL NOT PERISH, BUT WILL ONLY CHANGE CONDITIONS OF AWARENESS AND EXISTENCE.

TAKE HEART THEREFORE, AND CALL WITH ME ON OUR COMPASSIONATE CREATOR. BE SUPREMELY HAPPY AND CONTENTED IN THE CUP THAT BRINGS COMMUNION WITH OMNIPOTENT BENEVOLENCE.

R ACKNOWLEDGEMENT TO THEE O BLESSED JIVRAEL. MAY THOU BECOME TO US SUCH QUALITIES WITHIN OURSELVES, THAT UTTERING THY HOLY NAME ALONE WILL RAISE THEM TO REALITY IN US WITH THEE.

SO MOTE IT BE AMEN.

N HAIL UNTO THEE ARCHANGEL AURIEL AND ALL THINE ATTRIBUTES.

R MAY WE RELATE OURSELVES WITH THEE BY WORD AND WILL.

THOU ART AURIEL. THINE EXPERIENCE EMBRACES EVERYONE AND EVERYTHING EVOLVING THROUGH EXISTENCE. THY SHIELD PRESENTS US UNTO ONE ANOTHER, YET PROTECTS US FROM THE FULL EFFECTS OF OUR INJURIOUS INTENTIONS.

THOU ART THE LIGHT NO DARKNESS MAY EXTINGUISH, THOUGH IT BE A SOLITARY SPARK WITHIN A SINGLE SOUL. THE WISDOM OF ALL AGES IS THE HOLY HERITAGE WE HOPE TO SHARE WITH THEE. THOU GIVEST US GOOD COUNSEL IN THE SPIRIT OF DUE CAUTION, SAVING US FROM FOLLIES AND STUPIDITIES. THOU REMINDEST US OF WHAT WE SHOULD REMEMBER, AND ADVISETH WHAT IS BETTER TO FORGET FOREVER.

THY MAGIC MIRROR SHOWETH US SUFFICIENT REASONS FOR REFLECTING INNER TRUTH PROPORTIONATELY TO OUR LIMITED PERCEPTION UNTIL WE ARE MADE READY TO RECEIVE IT IN REALITY. ENLIGHTEN THOU US EVERMORE.

I AM INDEED AURIEL. MY WHOLE EXPERIENCE IS MEANT TO HELP MANKIND EVOLVE AND UNDERSTAND THE LAWS OF LIFE. I AM THE SPIRIT OF SOUND SENSE AND CAREFUL CONDUCT. I ADVISE REFLECTION AND RESTRAINT CONCERNING LIFE ACTIVITIES ON EVERY CONSCIOUS LEVEL. CONSTRUCT CREATIVELY WITH CAUTION AND CONSIDERATION. DARE WITH DISCRETION AND DISCERNMENT. BE LED BY LIGHT, NOT DRIVEN INTO DARKNESS BY DESTRUCTIVE INCLINATIONS. ACT NOT IMPULSIVELY FROM IGNORANCE, BUT ALWAYS BY INFORMED INTELLIGENCE.

PERFECTION IS ACHIEVED BY PATIENT AND PERCEPTIVE APPLICATION OF ABILITY. MY SHIELD SAVES REASONABLE SOULS, NOT RASH ONES, NOR HAS MY MAGIC MIRROR ANY MEANING FOR THE INATTENTIVE OR THE UNINITIATED. LOOK. LISTEN. LEARN, THEN LIVE. I WILL EVER BE WITH THEY THAT ASK MINE AID IN THE OMNISCIENT NAME.

R ACKNOWLEDGEMENT TO THEE O BLESSED AURIEL. MAY THOU BECOME TO US SUCH QUALITIES WITHIN OURSELVES, THAT UTTERING THY HOLY NAME ALONE WILL RAISE THEM TO REALITY IN US WITH THEE.

SO MOTE IT BE AMEN.

P O LET US SING AND DANCE OUR MEASURE OF DIVINE DELIGHT.

R MAY HEAVEN AND EARTH ALIKE REJOICE WITH US FOREVER.

Hymn of the Archangels

E RAPHAEL, THY SWORD UPLIFTED
SEVERS US FROM PAIN AND GRIEF.
MAY WE LIKE THYSELF BE GIFTED
TO BRING HEALING AND RELIEF.

Chorus

HOLY ART THOU. HOLY ART THOU.
FOUR ARCHANGELS OF THE LIGHT.

S MICHAEL, THY ROD DIRECTING,
GUIDES OUR PATH FROM WRONG TO RIGHT.
BE THOU POTENT AND PROTECTING,
LEAD US IN OUR WAY OF LIGHT.

Chorus

W JIVRAEL, THY CUP CONTAINING
LIVING LOVE ETERNALLY,
GRANT US GRACE, OUR SOULS SUSTAINING
UNTO IMMORTALITY.

Chorus

N AURIEL, THY SHIELD PROTECTING
EVERY BEING FROM THEIR BIRTH,
SHOW US LIGHT AND TRUTH REFLECTING
IN THY MIRROR HERE ON EARTH.

Chorus

P LET US TREAD WITH JOY OUR CIRCLE OF THE
QUARTERED COSMOS.
R WITH LIVELY MOTIONS, LIGHTSOME SPIRITS,
LOVING HEARTS AND LEARNING MINDS.

The Dance

E LIVE RAPHAEL, THOU RISING ONE, OF SPIRI-
TUAL SIGHT.
S LIGHT MICHAEL, THY SPLENDID SUN, OF
BEAUTY, TRUTH, AND RIGHT.
W LOVE JIVRAEL, THY GLAD DESCENT, MAKES
BEAUTIFUL OUR BIRTH.
N LEARN AURIEL, THY STARS ARE MEANT, FOR
GUIDANCE ON THIS EARTH.

Circling Chorus chanted as bells.

RAPH AI   EE EL
MIK AI   EE EL
JIV   RAI EE EL
AUR RA EE EL

(*At conclusion.*)

P   LET US REST AND REALIZE WHAT HAS ARISEN IN US.

R   SO MOTE IT BE AMEN.

Here all sit and meditate either silently or to suitable background music for a short while. A knock or handclap recalls to order.

P   BLESSED BE THOU FOUR MOST HOLY ONES UPON THE QUARTERS OF OUR COSMOS.

R   RESPECT AND RECOGNITION BE FROM US TO THEE, O GREAT ARCHANGELS OF THE LIVING LIGHT.

P   WHO AND WHAT IS CIRCULATING CONSCIOUS ENERGY AROUND EXISTENCE?

R   SAVAVIEL, THE CIRCLER OF GOD, WHOSE SACRED SYMBOL IS THE CORD, AND WHO ADAPTS CREATION TO ITSELF BY COSMIC COMPROMISE.

P   BLESSED BE THOU, ARCHANGEL OF THE CORD, SAVAVIEL. SHOW THOSE AMONG US WHO ARE TRULY WORTHY, THY MOST PRECIOUS SECRET OF CONNECTING COSMOS POINT BY POINT FOR ITS OWN PURPOSE. TEACH US HOW TO CAST OUR CORDS AND CAPTURE **WHAT WE WILL** WITHIN THE COMPASS OF CREATIVE CON-SCIOUSNESS.

LIBERATE US FROM THE SNARES OUR SENSES SET FOR US. DISENTANGLE US FROM OUR DELUSIONS AND DECEPTIONS. FETTER THOU US NOT, BUT FREE US UTTERLY FROM FALSE-HOOD AND BLIND BONDAGE TO BELIEFS THAT HAVE NO BASIS IN ETERNAL VERITY. BE THOU OUR LINE OF LIGHT THAT LEADS US THROUGH THE MAZES OF MISUNDERSTANDING TO THE CERTAIN COMPREHENSION OF OUR SPIRITUAL CENTRE.

SECURE US UNTO STANDARDS THAT ARISE DIRECTLY FROM DIVINITY. TRIP US NOT UPON OUR PATH, BUT REPRESENT REALITY TO US

ACCORDING TO THE PATTERN WE PERCEIVE THEE WEAVING IN THE PERFECT TAPESTRY OF ALL REVEALING TRUTH.

P BLESSED ART THOU SAVAVIEL, OUTLINING FOR US EVERYTHING WITHIN EXISTENCE.

R SQUARE THOU WITH US THE COSMIC CIRCLE, THAT WE MAY BE FOUNDED ON THE TETRA-FORM OF TRUTH.

Squaring the Circle

Here those at the cross-quarters reach out their arms in turn so that a square is formed with its corners at the Quarters. The chant is the same as for the dance.

S.E. FROM RAPHAEL TO MICHAEL WE LIVE THE PATH OF RIGHT.

S.W. FROM MICHAEL TO JIVRAEL WE LOVE THE WAY OF LIGHT.

N.W. FROM JIVRAEL TO AURIEL WE LEARN THE LOVING LAW.

N.E. FROM AURIEL TO RAPHAEL WE LIVE AND LEARN ONCE MORE.

ALL ALL SQUARING OUT, IS FORM THROUGH-OUT.

P. LET US CIRCLE SPIRALLY OUR MEASURE OF THE MYSTIC MOUNTAIN.

R FROM OUR PRESENT BASIS OF BELIEF UNTO OUR APEX IN ETERNAL LIGHT.

SO MOTE IT BE AMEN.

*Here the officers of Quarters (if all present, or by gesture if a single officiant), take hold of their cords attached to the staff, and keeping these taut, process around the Staff until the cords are wound to the top and secured there. The Officers give the words of the Chant, and others softly intone the Back-Chant, which consists of the vowel sonics—**EE II OO AA HU-U** in that order. This Back-Chant may be continued as long as it may be necessary for winding the cords.*

Circle Chant

BY THE EAST, SOUTH, WEST, AND NORTH,
WE SEEK THE WAY OF LIGHT SET FORTH.
DAWN, NOON, DUSK, AND MIDNIGHT HOUR
WE SPIRAL ROUND OUR POINT OF POWER.
FIRE AND WATER, EARTH AND AIR
ARE THE ELEMENTS WE BEAR.
SWORD AND ROD, CORD, CUP, AND SHIELD,
ARE THE SYMBOLS THAT WE WIELD.
THE FAITHFUL FOUR WITH ALL THEIR MIGHT
DIRECT US UPWARD TO THE LIGHT.
AS WE RISE, SO SHALL WE SEE
OUR SERPENT PATH AROUND THE TREE.
GOD ABOVE, AND MAN BELOW,
AROUND OUR CIRCLE-CROSS WE GO.

(*when completed, and all are close together in the centre*)

ALL ALL CIRCLING IN IS FORCE WITHIN.

P BLESSED BE THE ONE WE ARE WITHIN, THAT
WAS, IS NOW, AND EVER WILL BE AMEN.
ALL AMEN.

Final Hymn

GLORY BE TO THEE
O LIVING ONE OF LIGHT.
MAY WE FOREVER BE
UPON THY PATH OF RIGHT.
DIRECT US FROM ABOVE,
ACCORDING TO THY LAW,
AND MAY THY BOUNDLESS LOVE
BE WITH US EVERMORE.
LET THY SUBLIME DESIGN,
THE CROSS OF GOD AND MAN,
REVEAL THY PERFECT PLAN
BOTH HUMAN AND DIVINE.
AMEN.

P SO MAY OUR SACRED CIRCLE EVERMORE BE
DULY CONSTITUTED AND CONSTRUCTED.

R AS WE COMMENCED, LET US COMPLETE IN PEACE PROFOUND BETWEEN OUR CENTRE AND CIRCUMFERENCE OF COMSOS.

P PEACE TO THEE ABOVE US GOD.

ALL SO MOTE IT BE AMEN.

P PEACE TO THEE BELOW US MAN.
SO *etc.*

E PEACE TO THEE BEFORE US RAPH AI EE EL.
SO *etc.*

S PEACE TO THEE RIGHTWARD MIK AI EE EL
SO *etc.*

W PEACE TO THEE BEHIND US JIV RAI EE EL
SO *etc.*

N PEACE TO THEE LEFTWARD, AUR RA EE EL
SO *etc.*

P PEACE TO THEE WITHIN US, THOU THAT ART **I AM.** SO *etc,*

P IN THE NAME OF THE WISDOM, AND OF THE LOVE, AND OF THE JUSTICE, AND THE INFINITE MERCY, OF THE ONE ETERNAL SPIRIT,

AMEN.

This last chant should have everything put into it in the way of feeling and expression that the officiants are capable of. There should be no lag between the phrases, each coming straight out on the heels of its predecessor so that the sound is practically continuous until the last diminishing 'AMEN'. After a short pause, the music strikes up, and everyone processes silently around the circle and out of the working area. No general conversation ought to take place until after disrobing.

To read a ritual in cold print and perform it in practice are two very different experiences. Ritual is an art like any other in so far as constant endeavour is necessary in order to achieve good working standards. Few Magical practitioners are sufficiently experienced as ritualists to qualify for what might be termed professional competency. This is often because in their case ceremonial practices are a 'spare time' occupation to which they have not devoted sufficient basic exercises so as to gain expertise.

It is only necessary to contrast the average ritual techniques of any orthodox religious Order such as the Benedictine, with the painfully inept and badly arranged affairs of many 'Occult Temples', in order to make this point plain. The one is a highly finished and powerful professional product resulting from a centuries old Tradition and painstaking training, while the other is not only a poor imitation, but even inefficient amateur theatricals. There are indeed Temples of the Mysteries to which this does not apply, but for every one of those, there are many that fall short of even the lowest standards.

What constitutes a high standard of ritualism? The same factors as with other practices, mainly discipline, devotion, and attention to detail, based on a true sense of dedication resulting in knowledge of the subject.

These requisites have nothing at all to do with expensive equipment, wonderful robes, lavishly decorated Temples, and suchlike outer trappings, Those luxuries will no more guarantee ritual competence than valuable tools and materials will produce skilled craftsmen by themselves. A ritual does not consist of showing off collections of arcane curiosa, but in actual Inner behaviour symbolically related with Energies and Entities beyond the average range of human awareness. Just as there are certain standards and codes of behaviour for regulating our conduct towards each other in this world, so do the equivalents exist in regard to our dealings with those in other states of existence than ours. As we behave to them, so may we expect to be treated in return. Indifferent, slipshod, irregular, and poor quality ritual work will result in similar rewards. Careful, meticulous, and painstaking ritualized effort is bound to produce an outcome worthy of such devotion.

Every Rite should be approached with the technical ability and detailed management of no less a degree than an ordinary theatrical director would consider normal with the most ordinary production. All the run of the mill queries must give satisfactory answers. Is the stage properly set? Lighting correct? Entrances clear? Music cues right? Props in place? Are the actors ready and trained in their parts? Do they know their moves and responsibilities as they should? Can they cope with emergencies? Who is most likely to give trouble? Why? Who is the strongest of the cast? The weakest? Are the stage crew dependable, and what are their potentials? All these and a thousand such questions have to be tackled as routine matters of stage direction, and yet would-be ritualists exist in considerable numbers who expect to succeed in their art without any attempts to organize its practical points properly.

None of those necessary jobs get done with no one to do them, and a primary essential for every working Group is a clear and agreed understanding concerning who does what, is responsible for which, and a mutually acceptable code of behaviour in connection with the Group's aims and activities. In other words a clear-cut Rule, such as the Great Orders base themselves upon.

Whether a practical Magical Group consists of one, or a full complement of individuals, some form of Rule (which is a Rite in itself), must infallibly be not only drawn up, but also adhered to faithfully. The simpler the Rule, the better, providing it allows for contingencies of conscience and flexibility of interpretation. Extravagant and improbable promises or bindings are quite out of keeping with modern practice. For instance, it would be pointless to swear dramatically: 'I will, (or will not) do so and so, under pain of five arrows through my heart should I fail.' That would have no meaning in our times, and unless a Rule has genuine and definite meaning, it is worthless. To say instead: 'I will try my utmost to direct myself in such and such a manner, and if I neglect this trust and duty, then I shall lose the confidence of my Companions, the respect of my friends, and the Inner guidance that I value, etc.,' puts the picture into much truer proportions. Only wording which tends to emphasize the spiritual principles involved, and makes the hearer realize precisely what is at stake for him personally, should be used in framing Rules or Resolves.

A Rule is not a Code of Ethics (which all members of Groups or Orders are supposed to have anyway before they associate together,) but a Code of Conduct aimed to further the Common Cause of such an association. Every Group or Order is responsible for working out their own, just as each individual Initiate must formulate their personal Code, which obviously ought not to clash with those of any Grouping they tie themselves up with.

Rules are alterable at the will of those who make them, and individuals are free to alter theirs at any time, even though those binding a whole Group together can scarcely be changed except by mutual consent. Initiates do not normally bind themselves by such rigid rules that they cannot be changed for good reasons or on the other hand by such vague and undecisive rulings that these have no binding effect in the first place. The course adopted by most Initiates is to set up their own personal Rule, incorporating in it some clause which permits change in specified circumstances. This is by far the wisest plan if it only applies to matters within the Initiate's personal control which may be linked in with those involving associates.

It is adherence to such rules governing behaviour and conduct that makes all the difference between good and bad ritual practice. For example, there may be a rule of silence during the robing prior to a Rite. This is never done for the sake of harshness, but to afford an opportunity for getting into the right frame of mind for the Rite itself.

It might be done just as well if everyone sat and meditated for a while after robes were assumed, but if the two essentials of robing and meditating can be combined, a good deal of valuable time is saved, which is a useful consideration these days. The purpose of every rule must be abundantly clear, and no rule without entirely sound reasons understood by all should ever be applied. Discipline without purpose, meaning, and full acceptance, is no discipline at all, but sheer oppression and stupidity. Those who find rulings unacceptable are best excluded from the circle of those who maintain them. No compulsion of conscience or coercion of conduct is permissible in genuine Mystery Group-associations. If loyalties are not pledged and observed by free-will motivated by love and respect, they are not worth having and can be well dispensed with.

There are no infallible rules for ritualized behaviour beyond those which would normally apply to courteous conduct, and the punctilious performance of ordinary duties. What is important both to individuals and Groups, is that such standards are not only set up but also complied with. Persistently bad, unreliable, or undisciplined behaviour should no more be tolerated in a well-run Temple than anywhere else. Discourtesies like unpunctuality, non-attendance for inadequate reasons, breaches of confidence, inattention to duties, careless and slipshod practice, dishonesty such as removing ritual scripts without permission, and untruthfulness in speech or implication, all merit expulsion from Circles dedicated to eliminating these propensities among members.

No one is to be blamed for honest mistakes or character deficiencies they are trying to compensate for, but deliberate disloyalty and betrayal of principles around which Circles are constituted, calls for exclusion of these elements if the Circle is to survive in any worthwhile form. Hence the necessity for abiding by a set of governing Rules which are firm enough to deal decisively with those who endanger stability, but flexible enough to even re-admit these individuals should altered circumstances make this advisable.

Practising membership with almost any constituted Group on earth bearing even remote relationship with the Inner Mysteries has a marked effect of bringing out both the best and worst propensities in human Initiates. This is particularly noticeable during the immediate post-initiation period. Almost like a vaccination causing reactive rashes and other unpleasant symptoms, so Initiation seems to bring about Inner reactions resulting in character deficiencies and instabilities. These appear most evident in the field of the Mysteries themselves.

For example, hitherto honest and reliable people in regard to their work, families, and social lives, suddenly develop peculiar double standards as regards their lives inside and outside the Mysteries. They may perhaps retain script copies of Rites which are only on loan to them, or should not leave the Temple premises, swearing they have never had these, or they have been lost. Those same people would not dream of stealing any valuable ornaments or fittings from their Temple, but only Rites which they mistakenly believe possess power on their own accord. This seems to be a not uncommon failing, and experienced Temple officers watch for it with amusement—and pity. Sometimes impressively titled but practically unworkable pseudo-Rites are deliberately left as if unguarded. Anyone removing these for personal use has only himself to blame if things go wrong.

Another not uncommon likelihood is that an antipathy may arise between the new Initiate and their Initiator, sometimes amounting to considerable hostility, or at best merely a loss of interest and a growing indifference. This may sound surprising, but is really nothing much to wonder at. If a genuine Inner contact has been established with a positive source of Energy by two individual human entities, there must necessarily be a certain amount of risk during the reaction. The deeper and more powerful the contact, the greater and more widespread the risk. Human nature being what it is, if no particular reactive changes are observable following an initiation, one might be tempted to suppose a failure of contact. Most Initiators are screened to a certain extent against adverse effects by their Inner Guards, but even so, in some instances they must accept possibilities of injury in the course of their duties as they would have to in the case of most professional practice. The fact that such injuries are spiritual rather than physical does not lighten their effects. Those who are actively engaged in the Mysteries must expect to incure liabilities comensurate with their reponsibilities.

Safeguards against accidents

All sorts of things can go wrong with ritual working which are unlikely to appear on the surface immediately, but may materialize in various ways later on. Initiations reactions are often fairly rapid, and by no means always unfavourable. In fact bad reactions are much in the minority, which probably makes them more noticeable when they do occur. A spectacular failure is always remembered and marked far more than a long run of modest or average successes. No matter how carefully safeguarded any Rite may be, there must always be an element of risk if genuine Inner Power is actually present in the Rite-pattern. The moment that electricity or gas is connected to a house, its fire-risk automatically increases because of those amenities. The most certain risk of death is to be alive!

Initiated members of the Mysteries are not saints or immune from ordinary inclinations and passions. They are normal human beings, with all our built-in weaknesses and fallibilities, yet dedicated to the cause of cosmating themselves into beings more closely resembling whatever Pattern of Perfection they believe in. Because of their specialized knowledge and practice, they are liable to make mistakes on a more serious scale than the average mortal muddler. 'The greater the grace, the greater the guilt,' and the profounder the nature and scope of any Rite, the more drastic spiritual consequences may result from failure among its human or other components.

As the best safeguards against physical accidents and unpleasantness are sensible rules and procedures codified into directions for behaviour, like the 'Rules of the Road' for instance, so the equivalent in spiritual terms must be some kind of directives like the Ten Commandments. Just as these have never been surpassed as moral criteria, so the old Magical formula of 'Know, Will, Dare, and Keep Silent' still remains paramount throughout the Mysteries. We might phrase it 'Comprehension, Intention, Action, and Caution' for greater clarity perhaps, but as an overall coverage for Magical procedures in general, it is unequalled, and can scarcely be improved on as an axiomatic concept. Each of the four points are utterly dependent on the other three, and all are equally interdependent upon each other as true Quarters of any Whole should be. Whatever we read into the detailed meanings of those Master-Words, they deserve to be inscribed in large letters on the walls of every Temple. Comprehension fits the East with its arising Spirit of Enquiry, Intention applies in the South in the Spirit of highest Illumination, Action is fitting in the West governed by the descending Spirit of active Love, and Caution is proper to the North with its Spirit of careful Reflection. We may very well indeed surround ourselves with such admirable counsel.

Most Individual Initiates and their associative Groupings will have their own ideas about interpreting the extensions of the Great Magical Maxim, but those a trifle uncertain of the issue might do worse than draw up a series of 'DO's' and 'DON'Ts' concerning ritual practices. These could run perhaps in this way.

DO	DON'T
1. Realize the individual degree of limitation, and always work within it while seeking to increase ability.	Work any Rite against clear convictions of conscience, and basic beliefs concerning the True Will of a Beneficent Supreme Being.
2. Work under the direction of trustworthy Inner patronage, or those affording good evidence of their probity and capability.	Work any Rite that is not clearly understood in principle and reasonably possible in practice.
3. Work each Rite with the deepest possible sense of relationship between the human operators, their objective, and the Inner Ones holding that in common with them.	Take part in any serious Rite with others, unless a Circle is truly possible which commences with complete confidence, and terminates with full trust among all.
4. Motivate even the smallest Rite with an adequate purpose agreeable to True Inner Will.	Ever work even minor Rites for entertainment or idle and improper purposes.
5. Work all Rites according to definite plans and patterns conformable with Cosmos throughout Inner and Outer life-levels.	Attempt any major Rite for purely personal motives without adequate and evident authority from superior sources of direction.
6. Study and practice dutifully and consistently the elements and exercises of ritual principles.	Neglect the small details and arrangements out of which the greatest Rites are constructed.
7. Make every effort to ensure	Profane the Rites by foolish

that individual responsibility in any Rite is realized and fulfilled.

abuses of their Spirits or Symbols in any way.

8. Believe wholeheartedly and sincerely in the value and validity of the Rites being worked.

Work among inharmonious or unreliable company, or under conditions inimical to the fundamentals of the Rite.

9. Prepare for at least the major Rites properly, carry them through conscientiously, then finalize them faithfully.

Work any other type or grade of Rite than those compatible with somewhat above average standards of ethical and ethnical status.

10. Keep close counsel concerning the Rites, speaking of them to none save those properly entitled to deal with such confidences.

Take part in any major Rite while in bad physical, mental, or spiritual health. Strive first to regain harmonious balance.

Ten 'Do's and Don'ts' to cover ritual practice over a broad spectrum. Doubtless there will be those who believe various vital points have been missed out—which is not impossible. Their immediate concern should therefore be to fill in these deficiencies for themselves, probably discovering a few extra ones in the process. A most useful Magical exercise.

Rites and rituals may be as old as humanity or as new as we can bring them up to date, but unless they fit in with our absolutely fundamental relationships with the Absolute Itself, they will not be very much good to us. That was, is now, and ever will be the primary purpose of ritualized behaviour. Nothing less, because there can be Nothing more.

Early mankind evolved Rites intended to make the closest possible contact between themselves and the Entities of Energy behind their ordinary earth-existence. This was the driving motive, and the hoped for resultants of fertility, safety, happiness, and all the rest, were what we would now term 'fringe benefits' stemming from the main source of Spirit Itself.

Reach That, and everything else cosmates around It. We are still, and always will be, faced with this basic problem of 'seeking the Kingdom first'. It is the inescapable point into which we are inexorably drawn by the tightening of the invisible Circle-noose around us so that the Knot ultimately makes Nil, the Nucleus from whence proceeds all the powers we shall ever possess. Some consideration of this issue seems called for at the present instant of our studies, and should be very helpful in relating Magical theories to their projection into practice.

CHAPTER VIII

RITUAL IN THE DAILY LIFE OF AN INITIATE

The entire structure of the Holy Mysteries, Magic, and indeed all else concerned with the metaphysics of Mankind rests on a common, simple basis. Taking our own existence for granted, does indeed a Supreme Being exist with which we are really able to relate ourselves however remotely, and if so, are we truly able to extend our own existence beyond the limits of physical bodies? No matter how we wrap things up and invent the most high-sounding and misleading phraseology to cover, it always comes back to these same fundamental points which comprise the bedrock of our very beings. Put into its most primitive nutshell, we might as well ask: 'Is there really an Eternal Living God? Can I relate myself as I am with That Being? Can I exist as myself apart from my body? Can I unite with Divinity into Everlasting Entity?' If even the possibility of positive responses to these vital queries exists, then mankind is fully justified in all the efforts he has made in that direction. If, on the other hand, there is a negative reply all the way around the circle of our Inner Quest, then our existence is the greatest waste of energy and effort we shall ever encounter. Why should we bother to be if we have no becoming worth arriving at? Despite his playwright, Hamlet could no more answer our Perpetual Problem than the rest of us.

No amount of intellectual reasoning, argument, critical calculations, or objective approaches from purely human sources of information, will be the slightest use in solving the Sphinx's riddle: 'What am I?' Few human endeavours are so futile as those attempting to 'prove' or 'disprove' the Enigmas of our Existence. One might as well eliminate the entire earth by denial of its very being, rather than demonstrate the presence of Divinity by any amount of discussion. Every one of us must find our own Faith-Fundamentals for ourselves. No one can put these into anyone else any more than they can eat, sleep, think, or live for that other person. Our Basic Beliefs of Being are a condition we Become, just as we are born into a physical body which no other human completely shares with us while we animate it. We are built on a 'Be-it-Yourself' basis which is the true 'Philosopher's Stone' of our establishment; we must fill the 'Grail' with the blood of our very being, distilled drop by drop from the point of the Lance by which we experience Existence.

Absolutely nothing but the ABSOLUTE NOTHING which IS the Ultimate Nucleus in us, can emane anything or everything we want to BE. This is the True Will in us which is referred to in the summation of Law : 'DO WHAT *Thou* WILT', which has nothing to do with the little petty wishes, whims and ill feelings of our personalized projections, but is the Real Reason in us that makes us WHAT WE ARE. The Quest of Light is seeking to establish the clearest and most direct channel of connection between this True Will within us and its outer representation through our human expressions. Best described perhaps in the Lord's Prayer as the Heavenly Will being done in Earth. Divinity emanating out of Itself via Humanity and returning again in a Circle of Light undistorted by any imperfections arising from our interference on its course. It is obvious that we are far from such a state of perfection at present, though this is no reason why it should not remain an inspirational incentive for us providing we are prepared to follow it in faith before we find it in fact. To achieve, we must first believe. To believe, we must first SO WILL. Will WHAT? THAT is the Eternal Question again, and WHAT THOU WILT is the inevitable Answer.

It is appropriate that the first traditional question demanded of every entrant Initiate at the portals of the Temple is : 'What is your Will?' Everything in our existence, and our existence itself, began with that same Query. Our most recondite Name of God signifies 'That Which Becomes What It Will'. (AHIH). Everything depends on which way we follow the conceptual cycle. If we say : 'I will be What I Am,' this implies no more than inert acceptance of *status quo*, but when we affirm : 'I Am what I Will Be,' we indicate the Directing Energy of Creative Will constructing whatever Cosmos is called for by the Master-Word of its Manifesting. Humanity says : 'Let me be as I am,' but Divinity commands : 'I Become What I Will.' The Initiate of Light who is conscious of individually evolving from one state to the other, says : 'DO WHAT THOU WILT,' or 'Thy Will be

Done.' This is no abnegation of entity or rejection of responsibility at all, but the raising of spiritual standards from lowest to the highest possible point from whence Will may direct Energy through that individual.

Humans, as such, are not immortal beings, nor can they become so in human guise. The Divine Spark, (or Spirit) in each of us, belongs to Itself. Our bodies belong to the Elements of which they are constituted, and from whence they come and go through the Birth-death cycles. We 'borrow' our minds through the channels of consciousness which existed before our births, are fractionally modified by our life contributions to them, and will be available for our further use if we re-incarnate in these dimensions again. What does that leave we might call our own? Only an entity created as a resultant resonant energy between Spirit and Substance which we term 'Soul'. This is all we are which we have any right to call 'ours' in the sense of being 'me' or 'I' as an evolving human being, exercising independent Will.

This ability of limited auto-determination which developed by our original 'Fall', much as a seed becomes an independent Tree by falling from its original attachment to a branch, is 'our' will as distinct from the True Will which emanates us as extensions of Itself. Either we align 'our' wills with the Cosmic Energy Patterns produced by the True Will operating through us, or we do not. We have that option up to the point of our degree of development as entities, but no further. Since this depends on our evolutionary efforts, it is capable of extension to yet unknown possibilities.

Our 'Souls' are not immortal of themselves. Nothing but Pure Spirit is really Immortal. We are thus faced with very few alternatives of action. We may align ourselves as 'Souls' with the Cosmic Pattern of Perfection so that ultimately we share Its Identity and thus Its Immortality. On the other hand, we may set up 'Anti-Patterns' of our own, evolving into unstabilized entities liable to ultimate 'explosion' and resolution into 'primal power potential' again. Unguessable incarnations and existences may be necessary for the eventuation of either ultimate. Alternatively again, remarkably few humanized entities may ever get very far in either direction. The bulk of them may never develop enough Will of their own to continue as evolving Souls past a certain degree of expressed existence. For single individualizing human souls to go steadily on for one incarnation after another, gradually evolving towards a higher order of being by the efforts of their own Will is not so common as might be imagined.

The greater percentage of human Soul-entities probably do not survive as such for more than a few incarnations—if that. There are plenty more where they came from to take their places. Nothing wipes them out of existence, or annihilates them. They simply have no individual will to continue as Souls, and therefore the True Will automatically relieves them of this unwanted responsibility, reduces them to fundamental force, and then uses this for fresh productions. We only stay in being as Souls while our individual wills associated with our Soul-principles determine so. Souls may survive bodily death, but this is not true immortality at all, being as transitory and variable an existence, though in different terms, as life on any expressed level.

It may be difficult to imagine why any Soul experiencing individualized existence should determine to discontinue itself or commit spiritual suicide, but there are many motives for this, ranging from utter indifference to ultimate refusal of entitized life. We only live if we really want to. Whatever life-entities reach human expression have obviously willed this, but whether they succeed as Souls, or revert to what they were, depends on their efforts of will entirely. It makes no difference whether they believe consciously in any kind of 'otherlife' than in physical bodies. Their decisions to cease or continue being Souls are taken on much deeper levels of awareness than those of ordinary human communication.

There should seem nothing very strange in a cessation of Soul-entity. Nothing is actually lost except a temporary individuality which may have fully served the original intention behind its creation and then dismissed itself of its own accord. Every component of its construction is used in the creation of new entities, even its memories. No energy is ever totally expended, but simply transformed and re-constituted. The old *Ignis Natura Renovata Integra* formula was a good general outline of the regenerative circuitry responsible for Creation as a Whole. Nevertheless, in a Creation like ours, having an inbuilt Pattern of Perfection, whatsoever fails to achieve its function in that Plan must be re-used *ad infinitum* if need be until it 'comes right'. The wills of All must operate as the Will of One if Cosmos is to be complete, and this cannot truly be unless each individualized entity with an ability of auto-determination voluntarily aligns itself with the Power-Pattern behind its being. To find and follow that Pattern of True Cosmic Will in themselves, is the dedicated aim of all Initiated members of the Mysteries of Light.

If matters were as straightforward as that alone, we should have reached perfection long since. Once humanizing Soul-entities realized their capability of choice in producing whatever power-patterns they pleased within their own spheres (Knowledge of Good and Evil) trouble entered Paradise with a capital T for transgression. The more intelligent humanity grew, the more dangerous it became to itself and the Intention of its Origin. Nevertheless, Law being Law, all must be worked to its conclusion according to its Rules. Highly developed and individualized Initiates with opposing wills are still bound by the same Laws. It all depends what they do within those Laws because of their wills.

Knowing their ability to exist as entities for as long as they maintain self-will to do so, those Souls who may be termed 'Anti-Cosmics', or perhaps 'Chaotics', set up their own power-patterns entirely for their own purposes and the extensions of their existence into a state of autonomy which might be described as Undivinity. If this was all they did, they would constitute no very serious menace to the Cosmic Corpus, since they could be easily isolated and finally fade out of existence from lack of life-motive and cessation of will. They can no more continue existing without regeneration of energies than anyone else however, and this needed supply of power they divert to themselves from other souls who afford it willingly either from insufficient experience and wisdom, or because they fancy some advantage to themselves in the process. No power can be obtained from anyone without the consent of their individual wills, but it would seem from the most casual observation that the mass of humanity needs remarkably little persuasion to sell what souls they have for pathetically poor returns. There are very shrewd buyers in the Soul-market too!

The Cosmic Pattern of Perfection

Although we have been assured from various sources that the ultimate and decisive outcome of this dichotomy will be favourable to Cosmos, this in no way alters responsibilities for individual Initiates. We must assume nothing except our own obligations to the Cause we have chosen to serve. The best way to advance this Cause is to establish and develop the Cosmic Pattern of Perfection in ourselves before we attempt introducing it to others, in whom it exists embryonically anyway.

We are all individual cells in the Cosmic Corpus, and first and foremost our duty is the arrangement of our own structure according to its specifications in the Divine Diagram or 'Drawing Board'. If every Initiate would only attend to his own development before seeking to perform all sorts of activities far beyond his capabilities, the Mysteries would be much more effective among humans than they are on earth at present. Good intentions are insufficient substitutes for good sense.

The basic beginning of Initiation in the Holy Mysteries of Light, in common with all Faith, is an Intentional relationship of the Individual Soul with Identified Infinity by means of a Mediative Symbol. The human entity wills of his own record to relate himself for whatever he is with Eternal Entity, whatever That Is. The means of this unique relationship is obviously whatever will link such extremities of Existence with each other, and this has to be some kind of Symbol, whether physical, mental, or any combination of conscious construction. This is the primal purpose of all Great Symbols like the Circle Cross, Tree of Life, Rose-Cross, Wheel of Life, etc. That is why it is so important for any and every Initiate of Light to build up and establish within themselves at the very nucleus of their being, whatever Symbol of Cosmos they feel is essentially theirs. This is accomplished by every means and practice of Ritual, Meditation, or any exercise whatever that is calculated to create such a state of Cosmos according to that particular Pattern. The Symbol must be taken again and again and again, as often as possible and convenient, until it becomes as solid an Inner reality as the earth beneath Outer physical feet, and then much more solidly than that. Solid enough to stand the journey of a Soul through any number of separate individual lives that may be necessary, and hold its stability amid all kinds of disintegrative influences.

Spiritual Nuclear Energy

In effect, this is an operation of Spiritual Nuclear Energy. None of us will ever find Divinity or the True Will therefrom, excepting through the Nil-Nucleus at the focal Point of our own deepest existence where our Un-being becomes our being. This, and none other, is the Single Source of All we shall ever be. No matter what evidence we have, or think we have, of Divinity elsewhere in Creation, we shall only receive Absolute confirmation of It, and our other Major Queries *in ourselves*. Nowhere else. At the same time, unless we perceive some reflections of It in others, it is unlikely we shall realize those reflections are mirror-images of our own potentials, no matter how distorted they may appear.

There is only one final authority which will definitely decide for us the vital issues of whether a Divinity exists, how we can relate ourselves with It, and if we ourselves can exist without a physical body. This authority arises entirely from our own valid experiences. Every soul must make its own decisions on Divinity and associated issues. Only when we learn how to rely upon the authority within ourselves are we likely to discover anything of Divinity at all. All else is opinion, tradition, supposition, teaching, or whatever we care to call it. Valuable to the degree alone that it encourages each one of us to make that vital voyage Within to seek Truth. There is NO OTHER WAY save that. Those unwilling to seek this Supreme Venture may willingly resign themselves to non-entity, or what used to be called 'losing the Soul'. Why should this matter to anyone who denies their own entity as a Soul in any case? That was and is the 'sin against the Holy Spirit which cannot be forgiven'. Unforgivable because the self-disintegrated entity does not exist any more to forgive.

Basically, we ARE, because we want or WILL to BE. If we cease that WILL, we shall Not-be. If we insist on being what we ARE beyond physical limits of body and mortal manifestation, then we shall BE. Otherwise NOT. Since we are Souls, we have earned the right to decide our own destiny. The *Baghavad Gita* puts it neatly in the phrase: 'Higher than Indra's shalt thou lift thy lot; or sink it lower than a worm or gnat.' If, for whatever reason, we lose all True Will to exist, have no real will to relate ourselves with Divinity, and no genuine intention of going any further as an entity in our own right—then we cease continuity in Creation, and That is That. This of course, has no reference to ordinary physical suicides because of grief, pain, unhappiness, or the like. It relates specifically to those who deliberately refuse Life altogether. What point would there be in expressing such useless entities into further existence?

The Initiate of Light accepts Life and individualized evolving entity as a responsibility reposed in themselves by a Divinity with Whom relationship is sought along the most direct lines of contact, consciously or otherwise. Realizing the vital importance and use of Symbols for this purpose, Initiates of the Mysteries have no hesitation at all in exploiting them to the utmost degree. Having found, adopted, or even invented a practical Base-Symbol, they start associating others with it which will produce other Symbols again out of themselves on a higher level, and so on until an Ultimate may be attained. That is how the Mysteries work. If Symbols are followed inside themselves deeply enough, they will alter their expression, though not their essential nature, and admit the adventurer into perhaps unsuspected extensions of their Inner reality.

An Initiate is taught to regard his ordinary mundane personality and expression on earth as a Symbol of the Soul he is. Viewed in this Light, quite a lot of possibilities and opportunities occur. Symbols may be related with each other in order to make sense together, and this is precisely why Initiates seek to relate themselves in a right way with both Divinity and Humanity in general and particular by ritualistic or other Symbolic methods. They try to make Patterns of Power with people, places, objects, and all physical projections of Inner energies, so that if these were letters of some spiritual alphabet by themselves, they would spell something together that made important meaning in the Spheres where this was the proper language.

These are the real 'Words of Power' which are represented in rituals by various sonic arrangements. A genuine magical word of power is not of itself some 'Barbarous Name' intoned by even the most accomplished ritualist alive, but the living projections of individualized energies associated together in the right order so that they 'spell' WHAT THEY WILL as an actuality among them. The importance of the 'Name' uttered during the Rite, is that it ought to indicate the exact Way this 'Utterance' is made actively in other Life-Dimensions so as to accomplish the Intention or Will within it. Every Initiate is their own 'Word', or 'Magical Name', which composes a summative 'Letter' for use in a larger sense of 'Language' among others, and so the 'Language of Life' is spoken or uttered throughout all its Spheres or levels. Yet there is little purpose in uttering any Name during even the most recondite Rite which we are not prepared to live ourselves into otherwise.

The initiative in seeking responses from Infinity to our incessant demands for demonstrations of Its Existence must come from ourselves. That is why Initiates are so called, because they have indeed taken the initiative in the Great Quest. It is a question of energy-direction. The spiritually unawakened entity says in effect: 'There is no Divinity, nor am I more than animated flesh, nor are there other states of existence than mine, because I have found nothing to make me believe so. It has not shown Itself to me.' Poor reasoning to start with, because non-attainment of any objective does not indicate impossibility of its existence, but only a lack of personal ability in achievement. The fool does indeed say: 'There is no God,' while the wise person in a similar position would remark: 'I cannot discover Deity.'

An Initiate of Light changes the direction of this conscious-energy-current, and rephrases it: 'I cannot discover Divinity any more than another human—but I will cause Divinity to discover Me!' This may sound the most amazing piece of egotism, but is really nothing of the kind, being simply an acknowledgement of horse-and-cart relationships between Entities at such extremities of Existence.

Man, seeking Divinity in externalities is going the wrong way all the time, travelling as it were in a centrifugal direction outwards and ever away from the vital Nucleus in a laevo-rotary anti-Light manner. Divinity seeking Humanity acts in a centripetal way, drawing us towards the Spiritual Centre with a dextro-rotary Lightward motivation. To follow the first course, it is only necessary to drift aimlessly along with no attempt at central control of consciousness, or else deliberately evade and avoid the currents of Cosmation. To follow the second course, the individual will must be set up in such a way that it acts in much the same manner as a radar receptor which picks up signals from the Control Point, and from that initial impulse sets every directive device so that they automatically bring the whole concern on to the True Course—and keep it there. This not only takes considerable determination and initiative, but we are all aware of the erratic and irregular course resulting from divergencies between the individual and the True Will operating in the same Soul.

Regularity with the Rites

For this reason, a sincere Initiate cultivates regularity with the Rites, and precision in their performance. Both factors are of the highest importance. Once we find our Master-Chart, Symbol, or Plan to follow through towards our aim of Perfection, (whatever That may be) we must keep ourselves applied to it with no less diligence than a space-rocket that comes under constant course-correction throughout its journey to wherever the Intention (or Will) of its directors has decided. Given a clear aim, reliable Rites, and a dependable Master-Symbol, there is no reason why an Initiate should not become WHAT IS WILLED in the course of eventual existence through sufficient amounts of Life and Entity. Even orthodox Faiths have tried to inculcate a sense of regularity and re-directive course correction in their followers by insisting on routine services with daily, weekly, monthly, yearly, and other time-sequences. Unless Initiates of the Mysteries are prepared to do even better than that, they may as well remain with the bulk of their human brethren following more commonplace Creeds and customs.

Calendar of the Mysteries

A major strength of the Christian Church (which it inherited from the Mysteries, and without which it would fall apart) is its Calender. The major weakness of most modern Mystery workers is that they do not sufficiently follow out the cycles of the Divine Drama with a sense of its importance and value to themselves. Whether or not they are associated with any particular Group is of relative unimportance here. What matters is that they should relate themselves individually with the Cosmic Cycles by means of some suitable Time-Space-Event programme. In olden times this was a simple matter with all the various festivals, fastings, seasonal events, and other activities connected with the Mysteries. Nowadays only the tattered remains of these are yet with us, and the preoccupations of material life threaten even those vestiges.

The problem of how to earn a living and deal with family and social affairs overshadows the more leisurely pace of the Old Mysteries, and yet in those days the affairs of Inner and Outer life were not separated from each other by the artificial barriers now encountered, but were inseparably part of each other as a whole-meaning existence.

Initiates of olden days met with reflections of Divine Energy in themselves wherever they looked in the Mirror of Nature. Thunder echoed Inner voices, rain told them of freshness and fertility, stones spoke to them of endurance and firmness. Every creature had its own message, lions of strength and magnificence, foxes of cunning, birds of aspirations and freedom, fishes of darting thoughts and quests in all directions. Each and every life-symbol in the Outer world presented an Inner meaning of its own which helped to mould the Soul of Man for what this has become today.

In place of natural world-components, we have manufactured artificial ones. Can these produce the same or better effects in us on Spiritual levels as their natural predecessors? How can our Souls react with modern machinery and methods in such a way as to evolve towards Benificent Being? What are we making to tell us of beauty, compassion, tenderness, graciousness, understanding and love? Shall we learn of kindness from a computer or love from a laser-beam?

Commonsense alone should inform us that unless we discover how to make our modern artifices into mirrors which reveal new splendours within our spiritual depths, we are in danger of losing what Souls we have evolved already during our earthly existence. Perhaps, given sufficient time, this may indeed be possible. Our ancestors needed many centuries to reach their levels of spiritual achievements which we have inherited, and it would be stupid of us to expect 'instant Evolution' now.

A really pressing need of the Holy Inner Mysteries as represented on Earth at present, is a practical Calendar of Events by which the Mysteries may be experienced both Inwardly and Outwardly in terms of up-to-date reference, yet maintaining all the essential linkages with the oldest traceable Traditions, and affording opportunities of alteration into whatever equivalents or extras the future may hold for us. This is a Magnum Opus well worth the attention of serious workers. It is unlikely to be the outcome of any one particular mind, but would indeed be an outstanding achievement of whatever System might succeed in introducing it for general usage. In the meantime, there is no reason why individual Initiates should not arrange their own Calendar cycles for Group or personal purposes.

Since the rough divisions of the Solar Year of Light are Days, Weeks, Months, and Seasons, we might imagine a fair distribution of attention among these as being:

The Day. Dedicated to each individual for his personal progress as he sees fit.

The Week. Dedicated to the 'family' of a very few close associates, working according to their Wills together.

The Month. Dedicated to the 'Group' of a number of 'families' coming together every month for mutual co-relationship.

The Quarter. Dedicated to an entire 'System', when the major Systems of the Mysteries hold their respective gatherings in spirit, body, or both.

Annually. Dedicated to the Holy Mysteries as a single Cosmic Spiritual force of cohesion among the whole of Mankind and associative Entities. A yearly recognition of this at 'top-level'.

Within this framework, which provides for combinations of consciousness-contacts leading along all Lines of Light, every kind of activity is possible, and a sense of genuine Inner importance of concerted effort among every true member of the Mysteries is gained. Each type of Rite could very easily be co-ordinated with the others to produce an incalculable amount of Inner energy directed towards the ultimate benefit of every practitioner. All Initiated workers in the Holy Mysteries would operate in their individual, ethnical, and Traditional methods as they should, yet the total effect of this spiritual power would, via a common Calendar, combine co-ordination into a really worthwhile result for the totality of human and other beings involved. It only needs 'bringing through' into actual practice, rather than remain a remote ideal.

Daily ritualized routine

Suppose Initiates are given a day of earth-life, and told to do with it WHAT THEY WILL. There are bound to be variations, depending on personal circumstances. Some will plan out just how they can acquire even fifteen precious minutes entirely for their own use in meditation and making Inner contacts, yet without injustices to other people. Nothing whatever gained by injustice or undeserved treatment of others is of value in the true Inner Mysteries.

Other Initiates will devote each day to some particular objective or Key-subject, such as a Planetary Spirit, or Sephiroth, or whatever they mean to make contact with that day as part of a systematic Scheme. They will seek contact with that specified subject in every possible way amongst all they encounter during their ordinary activities. They will treat anything and everything (including everybody) met with during this dedicated time, as agents or Symbols for leading them towards the Inner aim they have chosen by Will.

Other Initiates again might work a four-point plan of beginning the day with a brief and intensive meditation on some single topic from a planned series, making an almost momentary Inner Invocation at noon, then a few minutes reflection in the evening during which ideas and constructive communications from Inner intelligence may be noted, and finally just before going to sleep a deliberate effort of Will at directing the Soul towards higher levels of learning during physical unconsciousness.

There are many different ways for Initiates to spend their days, but all of them are relative to some definite systematic arrangement of attention which Initiates find useful for relating themselves directly with Inner Reality via Outer available means. That is the common denominator, though everyone must supply their own figures.

The Weekly Incident

This daily ritualized routine is a highly personalized and individual affair, but the next stage of a weekly Incident among Initiates should result from a combination of several conscious entities. The nature of this is for those entities to decide, or Will, among themselves as a joint effort.

There are many forms of Rite suitable, but those incapable of constructing their own Rites or adopting one from existent patterns are unlikely to progress past this point. That, in fact, seems to be a major difficulty among very many otherwise valuable workers in the Mysteries. They have little trouble in figuring out minor Rites to suit their individual needs, and can quite well fit themselves in with the Rites of comparatively large Groups, but when it comes to associative ritual proceedings in co-operation with two or three others, disagreement and discord arises all round, and more harm is done than good. This is mostly due to lack of care in nuclear construction, and indiscriminate association of inharmonious elements.

It is absolutely useless attempting associative ritual work unless the co-ordinating elements are suitable. If the proper pattern of Officers is put together as their Symbols indicate, any Cosmative Circle of the Mysteries will work. Otherwise it is best to operate as individuals.

The Monthly Contact on Inner Levels

The monthly combination of the smaller Circles is simply a large presentation of the same problems. Possibly its best solution is still the ancient one of active work being done by a single representative of each Circle, while the others supply a reservoir of energy for the purpose. Whether an actual physical meeting and ceremonial takes place, or whether token gestures are made by those concerned in whatever way is best available to them, a monthly form of contact on Inner levels of life should most definitely be made and kept going. Old Traditions held these at full moon, not only for fertility reasons, but because it provided Maximum Light. Eventually the 'Goodies' met at full moon because they had nothing to hide, and the 'Baddies' met at dark of moon since they had everything to conceal from Gods and

Man alike. There seems no reason why the full moon tryst with Inner Light should not continue. A common point of meaning might easily be found in association with the appropriate Zodiacal Symbols which cover the whole of Creation over a broad band by their annual Circle. If each monthly contact were aligned in purpose, type and nature with whatever ruling Sign prevailed, the Mysteries might be enabled to improve relationships between Micro and Macro-Cosmos quite considerably.

The Quarterly Rites

The Great Quarterly Rites are probably the most familiar among Initiates of all Systems, although there is divergence of opinion as to whether these should be at the Solstices and Equinoxes, or the cross-quarters commemorated during February, May, August, and November under various names. It seems logical to suppose the former more appropriate to those who base their Systems on the Solar Cross of Light, and perhaps the latter for those who work by Lunar fertile tides and periods. If we are prepared to accept the Spirits of the Four Seasons as overall Concepts, the spiritual equivalents of Spring, Summer, Autumn, and Winter can scarcely be objected to by any System. Spring with its seed-time connotations of sowing our germinal ideas, aspirations, and intentions of Will, Summer with its care and tending of the same, Autumn and its harvest results from our Trees and Fields of Life, Winter and its clearing away of debris followed by preparation of our Inner Fields for another Cycle of Creation. However the Seasons are imagined, they present us with ideal opportunities for linking 'Heaven' and 'Earth' through ourselves at least four times a year, and should never be neglected, however much other occasions may regrettably fall into abeyance.

The annual Time-Space-Event

Annually, there should be some special Time-Space-Event at which the Holy Mysteries as a Whole, regardless of System, ethos, or Entities involved incarnately or otherwise, are recognized as a diversified Power-Pattern projected from a Single Spiritual Source for our cosmation into an Ultimate Perfection at present beyond our conception. Although this should fill the background of our beliefs all the time, it may be focused into the foreground of our combined consciousness at a minimum of once a year. Again there is variance of practice among the Systems themselves as to this very laudable intention behind Initiation. Some believe New Year is most fitting, others find May favourable, and there are those who prefer combining it with Maximum Light at Midsummer. If ever agreement is truly reached among even the majority of Mystery Initiates throughout the different Systems, such a state of genuine Mystical Unison will become so much nearer Attainment for us all. In the meantime, let everyone be and do WHAT THEY WILL towards the Great Achievement, providing they at least WILL it not less than once in a Solar Cycle.

In case any imagine or believe this Ultimate Union to be some species of supreme spiritual automation wherein all entities comprising the One Entity are completely uniform in being and behaviour like the wildest dream of an ultra-communist Creator, let this misconception be exploded at the earliest opportunity.

The Unit of Existence is the Individual, be it what it may, or WILLS TO BE. No individual, or even the largest grouping of individuals on earth, has the right to demand, coerce, or suppose all other Souls away from their particular Paths proper to themselves into spiritual subjugation by the self-appointed dominant Section. We may be parts of the same Cosmic Pattern of Wholeness, but as Souls we are *specific* parts with a *special* purpose in each of us and a function to fulfil for what WE ARE. The true purpose of Initiation is the achievement of right relationships among ALL, that each may BE ITSELF, and so ALL BEING ONE—NONE IS SUPREME. Ultimate Being is NONE, save That Which Wills to BE ITSELF. From our present viewpoint, this means we must complete our Cosmoi by the Will within ourselves for one another.

So long as humans are compelled together against their Wills by sheer force of circumstances, whether natural or man-made such as economic, political, commercial, religious, or other dominant factors, Cosmos cannot truly complete Itself. The one and only integrative energy which Cosmates in the real sense of the Word, is what we might as well term Absolute Love. All producing a common Power-Pattern together from sheer True Will in themselves towards each other, and THAT IS ALL. No inducements or compulsions to influence individual Will, because the instant these are altered, that Will reverts to what it *is*, and unless it IS TRUE, it cannot Cosmate truly.

This is why the real Mysteries of Light seem so elusive and individual, not having enormous Temples erected on earth and a powerful organization of 'Do-good Directors' and a vast network of Civil Service-like executives dedicated to making everyone else fall into line with the thoughts and opinions of the 'Top Brass'. Nothing would be calculated to destroy the Mysteries more efficiently than this type of efficiency which automatically bears the seeds of its own destruction within it. Fortunately for the future of Mankind, the genuine Mysteries never could, nor ever will, operate among humanity on Earth in such a way. The contact-points on Earth sought by Those responsible for maintaining the Divine Mysteries lie in the heart of every human Soul as an individual entity. True, where some of these Souls come into physical range of each other, Circles and even Temples may appear in material form, but these are ephemeral and transitory. True Temples exist on Inner levels where they are best safeguarded from destructive forces. Nevertheless, their representations and projections into physical dimensions do indeed serve some purpose while they last, and Rites practised therein for Right reasons do help towards human harmonization. Therefore they are to be encouraged while they further the Cause of Cosmos, but allowed to disintegrate themselves if invaded by anti-cosmically inclined entities.

No Temple on earth, no matter how well guarded, can guarantee security from the enemy within for indefinite periods. All that can be done on Earth is whatever True Will through Man makes possible. As one Line of Light becomes obscured, so another must open up elsewhere, as it infallibly does in fact, and often with much greater intensity.

A principal reason for the existence of the Holy Mysteries for what they are, is not so much to demonstrate in any way the Being or Doing of Divinity and other than earthly types of entity, as to provide human beings with means and facilities for making their own discoveries in this direction of Light by their own efforts—or 'Intiate -ive'. This is precisely what they do through the various Systems of Symbols, teaching of consciousness-techniques, and the Inner contacts established therewith.

By a suitable Calendar-Scheme for instance, Time-triggered methods of contact between Inner and Outer awareness are arranged. With a Symbol-Scheme like the Masonic Tradition, Initiates become accustomed to finding Inner realities through the commonplace tools of their everyday trades. That System might well be extended into all possible professions. Unless we learn how to find and deal with Inner energies by discovering their reflections in even the most ordinary things around us, we shall never be really Initiated into the Mysteries of Light.

Of all forms whereby we Finites attempt relationship with the Infinite, the mass of humanity seem to be mainly interested and intrigued with sexuality, taken on physically functional levels. Just as most ordinary children are usually fascinated by sexual topics and can scarcely wait to discover what lies factually behind their fancies, so do most Souls in a state of spiritual childhood seem chiefly preoccupied with sexual possibilities in Mystery practices. Providing they are honest with themselves and others concerning this important issue, few serious problems are presented, but if, as is frequently the case, they disguise otherwise straightforward sexuality behind cloaks of pseudo-religion and unecessary dramatics of justification, all sorts of trouble ensues, causing endless complications which scarcely ever appear to clear up completely.

The roots of the matter lie in expansion of awareness and enhancement of experience which every Initiated Soul instinctively seeks to complete their cycles (and Circles) of Consciousness. The three time-honoured extenders of consciousness and experience beyond the average human range are Sex, Pain, and Drugs to which may be added Illness of mind or body. Any or all of these will produce stresses of Soul resulting in extensions of perceptiveness due to exaltation or excruciation of the human sensorium. Pain and Illness are seldom pleasant or very welcome, though many unhappy Souls make use of them if other means fail. Drugs are unreliable, with often terrible side-effects on health and character. Sex is a natural function compatible with physical pleasure, emotional delight, and (apart from dangers of disease) no particular risk of much damage, provided the partners involved are not causing distress elsewhere by their act. The morals of the issue must rest within the framework of whatever creeds and conventions the practitioners subscribe to, but the mechanics of the matter, so to speak, remain on a much broader general basis.

Sex, Pain, Drugs, and Disease, have something in common. They are all productive of a separating condition between Soul and Body so that awareness of this state gives rise to a resultant stress-consciousness with an ability to discern each extremity via the other and thus realize an independence of both suggestive of a distinct spiritual entity. The principle is not unlike applying pressure along one axis of a crystal in order to produce an electric potential along another. Apply physical stresses to a bodily axis, and a corresponding Soul-potential develops. The greater the pressure the higher the potential within limits of nature.

By pushing a human Body and Soul apart as far as possible short of actual severance, all sorts of unusual consciousness-fields are encountered, and these have all been exploited in the past and even the present under one form or another for reasons connected with various branches of the Mysteries. How far they were or are justified is a very controversial issue. Mankind still remains an Ass in search of a Rose, attracted forward by Pleasure, and impelled from behind by Pain. Our time of total transformation is not quite yet at hand apparently.

Pleasure as Joy of Being

Unluckily for humanity, we react most definitely to Pain from so many sources, but how often do we ever reach an equivalent degree of intensity from pure Pleasure? We should be very careful before replying too readily to such a query. By pure Pleasure, its second-hand substitutes such as greed, complacency, glee, and other doubtful delights are not meant at all. No. The pure Pleasure indicated is sheer and absolute Joy of Being, or the incredible Inner Happiness of being in Harmony with That Which is Peace poised as Perfect Power. How many humans even realize or suspect such a condition of Consciousness might be possible for them? How many reach the slightest fraction of it, and how often in their lives? All too few and too seldom for world welfare. No matter what possessions men acquire, or how well they live on a purely material level, no money will ever purchase this particular Pleasure, whatever synthetic imitations it makes available in the most enormous quantities. The True Happiness we instinctively seek is not a condition of *having* more, but of *becoming* more, or expansion of entity at the most basic levels of our being. Humanity becoming fractionally nearer Divinity.

This is a very rare experience for an ordinary human being, usually of a momentary nature. Perhaps we encounter it during some kindly activity, or at those strange instants when everything and everyone around us seems so wonderful and magical because we are 'at-one' with it all for maybe only those few minutes. Most Mystical Systems aim to find a scheme of life whereby this expansion of entity comes under the control of Will, and can be experienced as a continual progression rather than 'flashes'. How far they succeed can only be assumed from results observed. All Systems have their merits and demerits for various types of individual.

Probably the most common expander of experience connected with pure Pleasure and available to the vast majority of Mankind is sexuality. Being a polarized exchange of energy, the male and female components have rather differing viewpoints on the issue. The male experiences a 'peak' expansion Inwardly when contact is felt between himself as a human entity and the Source of Life Itself, whose incalculable power he is proportionately projecting through his personal means. At that instant, he is acting directly as an agent for the energy of Existence, and is bridging entirely different Dimensions of Being. This makes him as near a God as he is likely to reach for a great period of evolution, and possibly as much as he may ever achieve personally. No wonder he 'feels good' for those pathetically few moments, during which he was not just one man, but millions of them! A much magnified 'Me' as it were. Whether he acted rightly or wrongly, moralists must judge from circumstances and instances according to standards of behaviour. All the man knew was that he enjoyed the experience and probably means to do it again when opportunity occurs.

The female sexual experience commences with the conceptual act during which she expands Inwardly while anticipating an increase of entity via the incarnating ego seeking attachment to a fertilized ovum. Should this not take place, she has still had her moment of expansion into Inner Dimensions. If pregnancy occurs, she has the entire programme of producing another entity through her own which provides its particularly unique opportunities for Inner contacts. When born, her child becomes a living proof of her ability to materialize a living Soul by means of motherhood.

Both male and female partners enjoy their sexual experiences for the main reason that they feel bigger and better for them, even though they could not possibly explain why. Their acts give them some kind of an Inner assurance that there really are states of Being beyond their purely physical conditions, and therefore the possibility might occur for their more permanent projection into those Dimensions. They thus obtain an inkling of immortality, and probably a suspicion of their spiritual potentials. Although their sex act as such is a physical performance, their enjoyment of it is not physical at all, but very much emotional and even spiritual in nature, unless of course, they happen to be of a low-grade category on the evolutionary scale. Even at the lowest life-degree, humans still expect some kind of inexplicable 'thrill' from sexuality, and unless they anticipated this, they would scarcely bother to copulate.

Since sex offers an almost infallible means of achieving one major objective in the Mysteries—awareness of and contact with Inner states of Existence—it is scarcely surprisingly that sex practices have been included in various Mystery procedures from time immemorial. The variations of sexual behaviours experimented with, or in current usage for one reason or another associated with what might be termed Magic, are scarcely credible. Whatsoever human ingenuity can arrive at, or is possible within the limits of our wildest performance has undoubtedly been tried in fact, or contemplated in imagination. By and large, it is often assumed that all sexual acts in the Mysteries must necessarily be those of Black Magic or evil in themselves. This is not quite the case, for there is a sexual element at all Life-levels which appears very differently on higher ones than on lower, even though there is a common connective link.

It is Motive, Method, and Means, which decide whether or not sexual activities are being employed for evil purposes within a framework which we may as well call the Mysteries of Black or Chaotic Magic. Everything depends upon the particular type of Will directing the energies obtained either at first hand, or as side issues from, human sexual behaviours. Certain behaviours lend themselves more specifically to one type of Will than another, and so both benignant and malignant Wills relative to Humanity, have worked out their most suitable techniques.

In olden times, when humans met in their Circles of Stone, made their sacrifice of a dedicated life, ate their fill, then copulated cheerfully with a general invitation for any congenial Soul seeking a body to join them then and there, they achieved just what they asked for—more ordinary folk like themselves incarnating as their Children. Simple, straightforward, and satisfactory. Later however, when intelligence increased, and mankind learned how to harness other than purely physical energies for specific purposes, sex potentials were diverted from procreative to other channels of intention. Moreover, this was absolutely necessary if we were ever to rise above the most primitive stages of evolution. Man must do more than reproduce himself like a rubber-stamp image. He must reproduce something better than himself in continually ascending cycles of life around the Tree thereof. The sex-act alone cannot accomplish this, so the secret of 'sex-plus' was sought and found.

Sex between human males and females produces only another human being. Superimpose upon that act a close contact with an Entity of a higher order willing to share human conditions of living consciousness, and the resulting offspring became human-plus whatever degree of Inner Entity aligned itself with this mortal manifestation. In time, given enough opportunities and incarnations, the purely human element ought to breed out, and the Inner Identities breed into evolutionary Existence until the necessity for it passes away into Perfection for ever more. So should the 'Race of Gods' absorb and exchange identities with the 'Race of Men', not as a conquest or invasion from Inner Space, but as a steady spiritual development affording mankind its only ultimate opportunity of survival as living Souls in a super-physical state of being. As humans, either we evolve into these Inner Entities which have been termed 'Holy Guardian Angels', or 'Higher Selves', or else devolve into far less pleasing species of life until extinction deals with us. We have our choice. It will be WHAT WE WILL in the end.

'Sex-plus' in principle is a human act of sex while the individual Wills of both parties are placed at the disposal of whatever Higher Entity is invited towards incarnation. Naturally there are great differences of degree in this practice depending on participants and circumstances.

All the different Mystery Systems had some kind of 'sex-plus' arrangement either built into their Rites or incorporated into their philosophies in clear or coded terms. In early days the procedure was elementary enough. The human male 'personified' the God by dramatic mime while surrendering personal Will to the Spirit invoked, when this process seemed ready, coupling took place with the female half of the partnership who had been 'personifying' the Goddess. We should now say they were acting as trance mediums for whatever entities were able to establish contact with them and influence the material results of the copulation. In theory this is perfectly possible, since human souls and bodies must come from *somewhere* in Inner Space, and *someone* has to be associated with them if they are to live in our dimensions. In practice however, this dedicated copulation carried out by unsuitable practitioners literally threw the doors between dimensions wide open for entities of all descriptions to form close links with incarnating souls, or even in very special instances, to incarnate themselves in material bodies.

Unhappily for humanity, it has mainly been the least desirable type of entity (not necessarily evil at all) who seems most eager to live under our Earth-conditions. Those entities in more advanced states of being than ours who are prepared to form direct links with us and our consciousness, do so at considerable cost to their own convenience and entitlements of Existence. We owe them a debt we can only pay with the same compassionate coinage when our turn comes to offer it.

Once 'Spirit-sex' became an established custom in the old Mysteries, it became ritualized in every fantastic form available to humanity, and practically defeated its own purpose. A chief 'trademark' of the genuine act was that no personal pleasure in it was experienced by the human beings involved, for the simple reason that they themselves were virtually unconscious of what took place through their bodies. All they actually felt was a strangely detached sense of Inner Peace, and when they 'came to themselves', a sort of reverential awe and wonderment. Such a happening was very far from common indeed, and eventually the artificial insemination method became the closely guarded secret of those who sought the best beings of both worlds. Later their lines of enquiry led them to processes of spiritual linkage with Inner Entities which might almost be called superphysical sex, and it seems safe to say that in general we have not yet reached the full possibilities in this direction by a very long way.

Meanwhile, spiritualization of sex offered no attraction at all to the overwhelming majority of those humans who remained quite content with its physical thrill component, and momentary elevation to an exalted position of power they could achieve no other way. Ordinary people coupled like any other creatures, but those who were more advanced or Initiated into Mystery practice, ritualized their sex habits into definitely procedural patterns, some beneficially, some ridiculously, and some disgustingly and viciously. It all depended on the sort of people they were (or Willed to Be) in themselves as to what they did. It still does.

In broadest terms, the more advanced Mystery procedures practised their sexual approaches to Inner Life on symbolical terms physically and real relations spiritually, the worst and most depraved practitioners worked physical actualities of sex and violence into anti-Cosmic symbol-patterns, and the rest mostly muddled along with fantasies and futilities which might lead almost anywhere. If they got nothing else from their operations, at least they derived some sort of entertainment—or afforded it to others watching their antics.

Chaotic Inner Darkness

Ask an average enquirer what is the very worst and nastiest type of Ritual that may be imagined, and they will almost inevitably reply : 'The Black Mass' in suitably shocked or salacious tones. It is surprising what they seem to know about this reputed Rite, considering that none will admit to ever having attended one. For them, it concerns a sacramental copulation with the female uncomfortably draped over an altar clutching a black lighted candle in each hand, balancing a chalice of blood on her belly or therebouts, while the priest performs his athletic advances as best he may with such a contorted concubine. Leaving these highly theatrical and improbable details aside, there is a very terrible reality indeed behind this horrible conception.

The horror lies not in the sex act itself, or the ludicrous

arrangement of it which could be bettered by any competent brothel keeper, but in the motivating Will responsible for it, and the possible results among humans if that Will achieved its aim. This Will behind the 'Black Mass', (which has many forms other than its popular presentation) is no mere mockery of established religion, or an ineffectual insult to a Divinity far beyond the worst malice of men, but a deliberate attempt to incarnate in physical form the most anti-Cosmic species of entity obtainable from Chaotic Inner Darkness.

Whether we call such entities devils, friends, or anything else makes no difference to their nature, which is fundamentally opposed to human development towards Divinity. Our gain would be their loss as it were, and vice versa. The more energy they can illicitly divert from our spheres of life to their conditions of existence, the better for them and the worse for us. Nevertheless they would obtain nothing whatever from us unless we allowed ourselves to be so depleted by one way of consent or another. Humanity always invites its own destruction upon itself. It is AS WE WILL.

Anti-Cosmics are in their way as much part of the ecology of Existence as we are. Their function is the breakdown of whatever becomes unsuitable for continuance into Cosmos, and its reduction to a state of 'universal usability', so that it may be remade otherwise into the Supreme Scheme. Thus the Chaotics are as necessary to Creation as an excretory system is vital to our human bodies, and they serve much the same purpose while they work as they ought to. The real answer to the childish question: 'If God is really good, why doesn't He destroy the Devil?' is: 'Because as things are made, this would destroy us too.' There is nothing wrong with the Plan for Perfection except our idiotic and intentional interference with it, for which none are to blame but ourselves. It is useless and pointless to dwell on and recriminate about past guilts and responsibilities for our present predicaments.

Those able to work the Cosmic Wheel of Life must do so with all their might while the rest follow as they may—or Will. The higher we evolve, the more discriminative our Will becomes, and the less likely are we to deal with Anti-Cosmics except as agents for disposal of our imperfectibles, which is the proper way to treat them. Once they get out of place they become like dirt, which is only matter in its wrong environment. If we persist in treating Anti-Cosmic entities as favoured friends and welcome acquaintances, we shall thoroughly deserve the degrading messes they make with us, since this is their natural propensity and they cannot do otherwise. We could—and should.

The real evil of the 'Black Mass', therefore, consists of the humans involved not only accepting Anti-Cosmic entities as equals and superiors, but actually inviting these into the closest possible association with humanity, even to incarnation itself so far as that might be achieved. Practitioners of the 'Black Mass' in any of its forms automatically declare themselves the enemies and betrayers of their fellow humans all over the world, and are guilty of ethnicide in the worst way, since the race they would destroy is their own. For what reason? No more than their temporary material gains from a symbiotic association with their Chaotic Companions. For so little is so much abandoned.

To practice the 'Black Mass' it is not essential to procure the ritual trappings of girl, altar, candles, etc. Even with those means available it may still be impossible to perform. Fake 'Black Masses' with real copulation are produced for sufficient money inducements paid over by wealthy degenerates. Although such spectacles must certainly attract ill-intentioned Inner entities as well as human ones in physical bodies, there cannot be maximum energy-exchanges between Outer and Inner Dimensions unless the operators are Initiated to a degree which enables them to make actual power-contacts on very deep levels. This would be most unlikely in the case of mere money-grabbing imitators, though these can work quite enough serious harm on their own account without assistance from experts. Apart from them, enthusiastic amateurs seeking 'kicks' or 'sex fun' are perfectly capable of causing very bad spiritual effects having widespread repercussions, with their senseless parodies and 'party-piece' productions of what they think is a 'Black Mass' just done for amusement to show how silly the thing is.

Young people in particular who have more money than sense are very apt to play such a dangerous game. All they are likely to encounter in the first instance is disappointment at the lack of immediate results. No demons appearing, no exciting phenomena, little else but a sense of being let down by their own stupid behaviour. Subsequently, over perhaps a protracted period, there will be a different story to tell. Having willed evil and invoked those interested in practising it, the participants are certainly to be followed one way or another by those on whom they called, and they cannot expect otherwise. They may claim they worked in unbelief for a joke, but this obviously cannot be true, since a genuine unbeliever would not work a Rite at all. The fact of being concerned in even the wildest travesty of a Rite shows some degree of belief in it however that might be denied on the surface. It can scarcely be stated often enough or emphatically enough, that any attempt at imitating the 'Black Mass' for whatever reason, is bound to cause ill-effects dependent on circumstances.

On no account should the Rite be even contemplated by those intending to stay clear of trouble. Script-writers for stage or screen who are aware of this, usually omit key-phrases, change procedures, or insert some invalidating clause in any representation of the 'Black Mass' included in a dramatic production. Even so, many actors dislike working with this type of art.

The genuine and most horrific 'Black Mass' Rite has a number of authenticating marks without which it is invalid. First it must be worked by those fully dedicated to the Anti-Cosmic Cause, and who are Initiated to the degree of ability in making Inner contacts to the required depth and intended direction. For this reason an apostate priest was once considered the ideal officiant, since he would certainly be opposed to a Beneficent Being, and would also have the necessary experience of Inner workings. Given such qualifications, there is no real need for an ordained ex-minister of any established Faith. Providing the operator is sufficiently ill-intentioned to follow the creed of 'Evil—be thou my Good', and has the required capability for manoeuvring Inner energies, he will be fit for service of the Dark Ones. Incidentally, such entities are termed 'Dark Ones', not because they are essentially evil in themselves, since Evil is a matter of Will, but because their functions and natures are associated with Interior Darkness much as the organisms of our bodily intestines exist and operate in conditions that exclude the Light of Day we associate with Life. So do the Dark Ones concern themselves with devolution away from the Living Light.

The second mark of the authentic 'Black Mass' is wilful murder of an innocent or undeserving victim, usually an infant or young virgin of either sex. The object of this is to provide the invoked entity with elemental life-energy for linkage with the operators on physical levels. The Spirit of the victims cannot be injured of course, and neither can their Souls be further damaged than by the trauma of bodily death through violence, but the energies inherent in their growing and healthy physical bodies may indeed be projected Inwardly by the Will of the killers and the 'Want' of the entity seeking this unholy contact with human life.

This is where the 'know-how' comes in, for the force-focus is only a very brief and difficult one at this point, which we might liken to a minute but significant hole being pierced in a separative membrane, through which forbidden fluids will first ooze, then gradually flow with greater and greater intensity as the original hole becomes a rupture. Unless this initial penetration between the Dimensions is actually achieved, the object of the Rite will fail also, although great enough evils are sure to occur, principally to those engaged in the act. That is a calculated risk they have to take. If their primal act of brutality and injustice is not committed with sufficient skill, they must take the consequences upon themselves. To some extent they are like hunters with a single shot aimed at an advancing menace. Once that shot is fired, their fate is fixed. A hit in the right spot and they survive and eat. A miss, and they get eaten.

The third component of this abomination is the so-called 'communion' with the blood of the victim which has been caught in a ritual dish. A general assumption has been that this is drunk with glee and gusto by the assembly, which may perhaps take place in some instances, but is not a correct procedure. Cups or other vehicles of intoxicants and drugs certainly enter the proceedings for obvious reasons, but the sacrificial blood itself is smeared into the genitals of all 'communicants' both male and female, especially the females. Ceremonial copulation then takes place between the partners, now in a condition of being 'all of one blood'. The object is to bring the Dark entities as close to incarnation as possible, for the sake of making personal gains from the transaction at the expense of human evolution otherwise—regardless of ultimate outcomes.

These Dark ones however, are no happier in conditions which might expose them to direct Light, than the Shining Ones enjoy existing in conditions of Chaos and obscurity. They at least have their own inextinguishable Light which Darkness cannot injure, while the Dark entities dare not extrude themselves into spheres of Light without the protection of adequate screening, the strongest of which is but a temporary measure. Direct incarnation into a human body is therefore a risky, though not an absolutely impossible act for them to accomplish. In general, they feel much safer working from behind screens in co-operation with the Wills of their human partners, which, since this is inclined in their favour, is a relatively simple affair.

The fourth and possibly worst essential of the 'Black Mass' is its sequel following through the conception, gestation, and birth of the incarnating entities, especially the principal one conceived on the altar. Theoretically, the pregnant female should be kept in near-dark conditions for the whole nine months, or as much away from light as possible. Sunbathing for example would be forbidden, and excursions made chiefly at night or during the dullest days. Conditioning along mental and other Inner lines is in keeping with this photophobic process. When and if the birth of a living child takes place, not only must this infant be dedicated to Darkness by its human and other sponsors, but it must be reared and trained in the service of its Dark Overshadowing entity.

Such is only the ritualized form of the 'Black Mass'. Its elements of vice and corruption among humans are unhappily common in this world. All that the Rite itself does is to focus and specialize those energies for the exclusive purpose of circles which might well be called an 'Efficiency of Evil'. Small circles with a widespread seepage effect which is far from easy to control, since almost as fast as affected areas are cleared up, the Wills of 'permissive' humans allow re-infection otherwise. The 'Black Mass' in its greater implications throws a shadow not only over those who practise it in Ritual formation, but an entire group, race, or world who practise its principles among themselves as behaviour-patterns. That is what makes it so essentially evil. 'Black Masses' can occur on a national scale as well as a private one, though the two instances may have very close connections.

The Holy Grail

Leaving the unpleasant subject of the 'Black Mass', let us look at its 'White' equivalent, which has the same elements of the Conception-Birth-Death-Rebirth cycles, or the Life-Death Drama of Existive Being, but put together in a very different way and for an entirely different reason.

All the Mysteries had and have their types of 'Mass', or ritualized relationship with each other in the Eternal Entity through the Hierarchy between IT and every I in Existence. There is, of course, a basic sexual motif to the Rite, however this may be concealed, as for example it is in the Christian version. Behind that Rite is the story of Divinity mating with Mortality in the person of Mary (the Bitter Sea) through whom a human bodied Divine King is produced and dedicated to his holy purpose. At the appointed time when he has reached the top of his Tree via the 32 Paths or annual cycles, his human life is sacrificed upon a Tree-altar and he resumes his Divine position. His followers, by sharing his human elements of flesh and blood, also partake of the immortal and Divine essence with which he has impregnated these material components of his continuum, and so they too are offered an opportunity for eventually reaching his state of spiritual Inner Reality. The tale is Eternal, and told in so many ways we often fail to recognize it when we meet it in other than ritual form.

If we analyse the symbology of the 'White' Mass even casually, it will start leading us to deeper levels almost at once. How many people attending Masses ever bother to do this? How much Light is lost from sheer laziness? Still, the story being endless will follow them always. It starts with a surprising conception, namely that a single touch of Divinity to one womb on earth produced results capable of passing on that Divine contact to the whole human race forevermore. Not even a physical contact, since the Divine-King-Child left no human descendants of his own on earth. The implication is that the least connection of Divine Light with humanity is capable of leading all human Souls to Itself providing they follow the Pattern It traced for them in the process. It is almost as if the Light photographed the blue-print for Perfection deeply into the consciousness of

Mankind by one Flash, and we have been endeavouring to reprint it ever since.

Such is the Legend attached to the Mysteries Of Light. An Original Radiance impinging upon living matter developing on Earth. It impacted on all, but only a certain type reacted with it in such a way as to evolve towards it according to its inherent nature and the Image that Radiance impressed into the receptive reproductory system of cells. That Life-type of course became Man, and it is reputed that this Original Image is in some way imprinted into human blood, not so much physically, but as a spiritual content.

Like all Life-types, humanity developed several distinct strains, the best and highest of which became known as the 'King's sons', 'Children of the Gods', etc. These individuals both male and female became selectively evolved into the most advanced species of Life incarnate on earth. Their qualities were transmissible not solely by physical reproduction, but by their line of the 'Blood Royal' possible to inherit spiritually by an Inner contact which would be a sexual one if it occurred in material terms. This 'Blood Royal' is otherwise the Sang Real, or Holy Grail. Those who 'achieve the Grail' are thus those who have come to partake of the 'Holy Blood', or otherwise become included in the most direct Line of Light relative to our Divine Initiating Impulse.

To maintain this linkage and renew the purity of our 'Blood Royal', the ancient custom of Divine Kings continued contacts through the centuries. These Kings were willing victims, acting on behalf of their people, offering themselves and their blood as a focus for Eternal Energies, which, at the cost of their physical bodies and earthly personalities, used their Spiritual components as projection points for reproducing the Divine Image among humanity again. Technically the Divine Kings really did 'die for the sins of their people', since, had the Image not been obscured and distorted by human fallibilities, there would have been no occasion for the King's service. No vengeful Deity or any such monstrosity demanded their sacrifice as a punishment for human sins and offences. They were strictly volunteers in a Cause they believed in implicitly, namely keeping at least their own sections of humanity in touch with the most Ancient Ancestry of all, in order to carry that Line to its Rightful Destiny.

Much as selected individuals in modern times put their lives at risk to link us with other Life through Outer Space, so did the old Divine Kings offer their lives in the exploration of Inner Space and Spiritual Dimensions to ensure an Immortal Heritage for those humans capable of accepting it.

At first this blood-contact was only available among a small percentage of people, but as with all innovations it eventually increased, until today it is achievable by almost whosoever devotes themselves to the Quest in the Right spirit, and with enough determination to overcome obstacles. The Grail Legends tell the tale truly enough in allegory, and the Symbols of Cup and Lance with a drop-by-drop blood contact should be too obvious to need explanation.

Such is the story behind the 'White' Mass. The officiants do not offer any lives but their own, freely and willingly, as a means of making Inner contact with Divinity in accordance with True Will. The type of sex action involved is not physical but spiritual, its material manifestation being signified symbolically, yet none the less actually as an experience of Inner Life.

From a male viewpoint, a Seed of Will must enter the equivalent of a Divine Womb, gestate there, and ultimately be brought to Light as a Concept clearly recognizable by Inner sight as a true 'Child of Light', capable of spiritual activity on its own account. From the female angle, an impregnation ought to take place Inwardly which after gestation is ultimately 'born' among mankind so as to 'come to Light' in human Dimensions of experience.

Thus, human agents send 'Seeds' into spiritual states of being which mature there through 'Divine Motherhood', and spiritual 'Seeds' are received here from their Inner Origin which mature through the Motherhood principle in humanity. Moreover, the physical sex of human individuals does not decide the issue. Spiritually we are a combination of both polarities, and it all depends which we apply Inwardly as to what happens—if anything. Humans may be barren or infertile spiritually as well as physically. Nor may they produce any very remarkable offspring in either set of Dimensions. The Blood-Royal does not run in all veins, nor has the Grail yet been achieved by the majority of mortals. Perhaps it never will. Its unique survival-pattern in Spiritual Space probably applies to the selective species who evolve a means of continuing their conscious existence apart from physical being when human life becomes impossible on this planet. We cannot stay here forever in flesh-forms, nor are they our only containers of consciousness.

The Mystery of the Grail, or the 'White' Mass contains our survival instructions as spiritual entities against an evolutionary epoch when we cannot be physical ones. Each human Ethos has its particular 'Plan within a Plan', and the Western Tradition of the Inner Mysteries is especially connected with the Grail. Though we are humans as a Whole, all will do best to follow their especial Ethnical Paths, each with its 'Blood-Group' leading to the same Light. Just as mis-matching physical blood-groups can cause serious harm and even death, so does spiritual mis-mating bring similar dangers in its train.

Dramatic ritualizations of the 'White' Mass vary with Traditions, but the fundamentals are general. Recognition of Supreme Spirit, Acceptance of True Will, Offering of Victim, Sacrifice of Self, Entry of Divine Entity in Elemental Form, Sharing of Spirit by Common-union, and Continuance of Cosmation, are main points of a 'White' Mass. Human officiants offer up their little lives to the Larger Life, identifying their Wills therewith, so that by sharing the Brotherhood of the Blood-Royal they may lift themselves even the least degree towards Divinity. That is the object of 'White' Masses, all else being side-issues necessary to that end. The Blood-Royal being spiritual, is symbolized by wine, as bread substitutes for flesh. In the light of modern information, it is perhaps interesting to note the hallucgenic properties of alcohol in the wine, and ergot, or L.S.D. in the bread, which should always be made from rye. In proper combination the original forms of these should control each other, leaving the way between them clear for the superimposition of consciousness from Inner Intelligence.

It seems clear that in the first place the Elements of bread and wine were meant to be taken in more than ceremonial sips, and certainly when in a fasting condition so as to be maximally effective. Since this induced a confusion of normal consciousness which could only be dealt with and supervened on spiritual levels by a very highly trained and accustomed Soul, it was only suitable for this type of officiant in close collaborative working with a comparatively small Circle of Companions, which, of course, was the early way of operating the Mysteries.

Despite this implication, the 'White' Mass is emphatically *not* based on a drink-drugs foundation. The chemical constituents of the Eucharistic Elements were chosen for their Symbolical rather than their physical natures, even though definite links existed between the two. The very slight 'lift' obtainable from the physical side of the Elements was only meant as a kind of 'take-off thrust' for an earth-based consciousness seeking extension or projection into Inner Dimensions. No more. All the rest of the power must come from Inner Sources through the Entrant themselves. Otherwise the Rite failed its purpose. To project a human entity Inwardly by means of toxins alone, is like firing them from a gun whereby an inert projectile is hurled through space by the force of an initial explosion in a line determined by the gun setting at that instant. The shell has not the slightest control over its course, and may fall very wide of its mark.

The type of Inner projection intended by the method of the 'White' Mass in the Mysteries is like a guided missile with a self-determining authority in control. It goes AS IT WILL. The initial 'aided take-off' was simply for convenience of achieving separation from the gravity-field tending to hold consciousness among earth conditions. Once those have been transcended, Inner adventure becomes a simpler affair. Thus the 'charge' of the 'initial impellent' had to be very carefully calculated indeed to a fine degree, and this took a good deal of experience and experiment, since few human reactions are absolutely reliable under varying conditions. The obvious criterion to aim for here is to obtain maximum Inner response to a minimum Outer stimulus, and that needs an expert judgement, both in adjusting the dosage and reacting to it.

While this particular Mystery practice remained in the hands of trained Initiates, all was well. Once it spread beyond the confines of their Circles to an imitative but uninitiated following, drunken and degenerative orgies with sexual excesses increased to scandalous proportions, as might indeed be expected among undisciplined and uncontrolled masses of mortals. Even the Christian Mysteries, which were responsible for releasing spiritual procedures among sections of humanity utterly unprepared for them, and in terms of evolution, unfitted to use them, had to withold the Cup from the laity in the end. It was never intended for the unworthy in the first place, and to make it universally available for anyone in a totally indiscriminate manner has been a very bad error indeed among branches of the Christian Church.

We may remind ourselves of the Grail Legend relating that the Hallow was removed from Earth because of human misuse, and while available in purely spiritual Spheres, is unlikely to manifest openly among Mankind until we become truly worthy of its Mystery. Meantime, Initiates may continue their celebrations of the 'White' Mass in sacred secrecy, and keep the contacts of 'Blood-Royal' according to their respective Traditions.

There is very much more to the meaning of a 'White' Mass than making Inner contacts which could quite well be established without the Rite or its larger Life-Pattern. The Divine Aspect or other Entity of Inner Energy invoked should identify sufficiently with the officiants to become a mutual experience between both ends of Existence, and so complete the Circle of Cosmative Consciousness in Common-union. This might truthfully be described as Supreme Sex on a spiritual scale, though only possible to the individual degree of each Initiate. If Telesmic Images are used, the Officiants should relate themselves with whichever Aspect completes or complements the personal polarity they are projecting Inwardly. This may or may not be the same as their physically manifesting personality. Spiritually, a Soul can operate as either sex, once it passes a certain point in evolution, but its predominant polarity is always WHAT IS WILLED, and ultimately it should reach a state of being beyond necessity of polarization. Sex relations are rhythmic affairs after all, and the more evolutionized they become, the higher their natural frequency until they pass physical limits altogether, ultimately culminating in the Supreme state of Zoic Zero.

Eternal Life and Love are the pivots between which the movements of the 'White' Mass are poised. This should be a theme of Deathlessness demonstrated by existence of entity beyond bodily bounds. Of old, the Divine Kings were expected to manifest themselves in some way after their bodies had been sacrificed. Exactly how they did this is now conjectural. Whether they appeared to seers, made themselves known in dreams, or produced what is now called 'psychic phenomena', their human

associates were undoubtedly convinced of their extended existence independently of the physical framework they had seen
sacrificed with their own eyes. Perhaps the best known instance
of this is the Christian Resurrection, and the most unspectacular
example the re-incarnation recognitions of high ranking Lamas.
Although these individuals follow the line of Divine Kings into
our time, their Tradition does not call for bodily sacrifice other
than by physical existence itself in service to its Cause. This
seems undoubtedly the most practical Pattern to follow at
present.

Without an assurance of ultimate Immortality, if such is
indeed the Will of the participant, there is little meaning to the
'White' Mass. How that assurance is received rests with individual efforts at this stage of our evolution. In the larger sense,
all Souls seeking Cosmation are part of the 'White' Mass, but
those operating its various forms of Ritual declare by their deed
alone that they are Willing to become Immortal entities in their
own right. Otherwise they would not be officiants. Whether or
not they take part in stylized Rites at Lodge, Church, or Temple,
or work out the basic Pattern of the Rite in terms of their ordinary lives, or best of all on both levels, Initiates of the different
Mysteries share the common aim of Ultimation as Entity. In
the words of one old invocation : 'Thou art God. Thou art Man.
Be What Thou Will as ONE.' The entire structure of the 'White'
Mass turns on this point. Since it has kept turning for a very
long time and shows no signs of cessation, very many human
Souls indeed must have found what they sought within its framework.

Ritual Travesties

Apart from either form of Mass, many other types of Rite
include sexual themes in various guise, some innocent and others
not. All that is fertile is necessarily sexed in some way, and unless
we are fertile in Inner fields we shall reap a very poor spiritual
harvest. This does not mean however, that unless we copulate
physically there will be no Inner outcome. Many have fallen
into this trap, not altogether unwillingly. It is as old as Eden.
With the simple aim of human sexual enjoyment for the sake
of its thrills in view, this plain objective is dressed up (or un-

dressed!) in so many odd shapes as to be almost unrecognizable under its cloaks of rationalizations, justifications, and religious formalities.

It is doubtful if a single sexual possibility of any description at all, has not been ritualized for the benefit of some thrill-seekers, no matter how small in number. Behaviourists and psychiatrists solemnly note these down and classify them, gutter journalists produce them as periodic 'Exposures of an Evil Cult' for the titillation of an even dirtier-minded readership, and everyone makes what capital they can out of such a perennially popular subject. As manifestations of the genuine Mysteries, these rituals are all too frequently but tragic travesties.

Their best known and most frequent elements are nudity, buttock-beating, bonding, copulation, masturbation, flagellation, and defecation. An odd point is that none of these human behaviours *per se* is particularly vicious or wrong given correct conditions, intentions, and applications. For example, we must be nude for a bath or to pose for a picture, an occasional whack at a child's bottom is a useful corrective, a dangerous captive may be tied up, copulation between consenting partners free to practise it is a very common human custom, most children or lonely people masturbate, remedial flagellation may be found in any sauna bath, and we must all defecate or die. Taken by themselves, those practices are normal and commonplace enough in their right contexts. When worked up into so-called Magical Rites however, they present a rather different Pattern.

It all depends upon the basic motive. If this is neither more nor less than sensory self-satisfaction, or the purely personal establishment of petty power over other Souls even more disorganized than their director, then the picture is merely one of a few fools footling together. If there are more unpleasant motives of fraud, blackmail, extortion, or other coercions, then the same Rites may become much more sinister in character. The main danger is that Rites which seem innocent enough or perhaps only mildly 'naughty', can easily be given a much deeper and dirtier slant towards Darkness. There is a whole line of 'sales talk' given quite glibly about why it is essential to 'work in the nude so as to raise power.'

Now there is nothing especially nasty about a healthy human body, nor is there anything very vicious in dancing around nude in the sunshine or rain. Few people except the most purient-minded object to nudity as such. For those to whom nudity is a normal condition accepted naturally, ritualized devotional dancing and behaviour may be quite a proper performance. Attitude of mind and Soul is the decisive factor. A nude person (unless a trained karate or judo expert) is a very defenceless being, both physically and psychologically. Any internment camp guard knows this. So does the esoteric exploiter. People without clothes are at a disadvantage against an armed individual. As a rule, the leader of any nude-working Group may be naked like the rest, but bears some mace-like sceptre, scourge, flail, or other weapon. Whether this is used practically or symbolically, it still implies and usually obtains domination over the Group by its wielder. All too often Groups of this nature permit power to the wrong people, though generally little enough. Most members of such Groups desire to be dominated anyway.

From that point on, it seems to be a matter of finding out just how far certain humans are willing to be ill-treated, ridiculed, degraded, impoverished, deceived, and otherwise misused, yet still come back for more with outstretched hands.

It is almost incredible what indignities these people will not only endure but appear to enjoy. Especially at the hands of expert exploiters who know just how far to apply pressure short of severing contact with their victim's co-operative will. The fringes of the 'occult' world in the twilight are unduly cluttered with these odd 'Groups', 'Orders', 'Temples', and the now popular 'Coven'. Mostly these simply supply eager entrants with a means of misbehaving in the way they want, while assuring them it is not only good, clean fun, but a very pious and religious activity as well. It is surprising what may be made to look virtuous and holy by clever decoration. Did not the Thugs sincerely believe murders committed in accordance with their Rites to be a pleasing act to their Goddess who would protect them from punishment? Did not Christian Inquisitors implicitly believe that burning heretics alive was pleasing to the Most High God? People will believe WHAT THEY WILL, but they prefer it wrapped in the way they *want*. Let them copulate, masturbate, defecate, and be tied, tried, or fried as they please, providing they are told the Great Goddess approves of all this in Her Children, and they are very likely to oblige as a welcome religious duty. There is seldom a shortage of applicants for those Paths.

It is difficult to particularize about the average Group claiming to represent the Mysteries in any way. If the entrant has not the sense and discrimination to distinguish one sort from another, they are only likely to discover the difference through bitter personal experience. In general, if ritual or other customs and beliefs in a Group offer offence to, or violation of, human dignities and decencies, there is something fundamentally very wrong with its foundations. Those working by the purge, scourge, and urge, are not likely to lead any further than lavatory levels.

Any Group unwilling to declare its principles uncompromisingly, clearly, and positively, leaving applicants free to decide for themselves whether to support these or not, should be suspected of at least chicanery. Despite the present tendencies towards 'impersonality', and 'looking higher than the human element', one of the best ways to judge any Group is still by estimation of its leaders in terms of character and ability. No matter what the Inner Contact may be, this has to work through the focal points of its Earthly agents, and if these are unsuitable in themselves, the power controlled by that Contact will have to be projected elsewhere.

So a good question for anyone to ask themselves, is whether or not the human leaders or focal points of any Group are worth associating with. Are they in fact intelligent, sincere, trustworthy, beneficent, and worthwhile Souls? Do they have reliable qualities of leadership, or do they not? Impossible questions to answer truthfully without considerable experience of them, but quite possible to make a fair estimate of by sound surmise assisted by Inner guidance. This should infallibly be done before association with any Group. Should its human directors hide modestly behind screens of high-sounding titles, or refuse to reveal their real identities to those entitled to enquire, then something serious accounts for such subterfuge, and they are best left to the privacy they prefer.

No one is authorized to make unwarranted intrusions into any private proceedings among Groups of Mystery operators, yet at the same time, every single applicant for entry is fully entitled to complete assurance that those proceedings are in the care of responsible and competent people in whom confidence can be placed. If the applicant cannot be assured of this essential factor, he would be wisest to let his enquiries rest there.

No matter what wonders may bewilder the brains or snare the senses of entrant-Initiates to the true Mysteries, one finalizing fact ought to keep their Inner instincts pointed in the right direction. If their object in approaching the Holy Mysteries is (as it should be) to find the most practical Path between themselves and Divinity, they should be constantly conscious that this is only attainable by their own energies and efforts in their own entities. Initiation is an individual progress to Perfection, however parallel our Paths may be. The Kingdom is indeed Within, and every Soul has his own Key thereto somewhere about his person. He will not find it in anyone else's possession. All he may fairly find elsewhere are helpful search-suggestions, plans for procedure, or 'Magic mirrors' for reflecting his image so that he can observe his successes and failures by inference. Self-stabilization as a consciously cosmating Entity is an Initiate's principal responsibility.

Once a right relationship is established between the central Nil-nucleus of Spirit, and its peripherals of Soul and Mind based on bodily manifestation, everything else will relate in its own way—eventually. They that seek right relationships with other Souls, ought first to find that happy state in themselves.

If contact with the genuine Mysteries is sought for lesser reasons, such as sheer curiosity, hope of material advantages, possession of undeserved powers, or unjustified authority and satisfaction of desires regardless of results, they will evade every attempt at entry, and the invader will encounter just what he merits. Deception, fraud, waste of time and money, misdirection, and in fact a loss of valuable life-energy altogether, if not worse. This is no exaggeration, but a plain and straightforward statement. The world has many Souls in it who complain bitterly about how earnestly they sought 'Truth' in the Mysteries and found nothing but falsity and maltreatment from charlatans and credulous cranks. No doubt at all they did experience such unhappy encounters—but—were they really innocent victims, or self-deceived, ignorant fools? They must face both possibilities in the end, and progress past them through the Portals leading to Light beyond either state. Let us see if we can obtain a glimpse of what may prevail there, so that we may decide whether or not it is worth while asking admission.

CHAPTER IX

THE SIGNIFICANCE OF MAGIC IN A NUCLEAR AGE

If anyone asks what is the use of Magic in the twentieth century, the proper reply is that it has the same use as in any other era, for intentional and intelligent work with metaphysical energies on Inner causative levels of consciousness. The outer formalities of Rites and customs alter like any other fashions that change with time, but their principles are as sound now as they ever were—or will be. This age needs real Magic far more than the average mortal might suppose, and the sooner the Sacred Mysteries become available in modern manner to those of mankind on Earth with sufficient spiritual stature to safeguard them, the better it will be for us all.

We have reached our present state of evolution today because of the 'Light-Patterns' our ancestors set up long ago which have led us here along those lines. Should we be reaching the Moon physically now, if they had not reached for it symbolically in their rituals on the hill-tops? What relationship does a cyclotron bear to the circling dances around the central fires of primitive people? Would we have aircraft unless the behaviour and nature of birds had been imitated in old initiations? How much of our modern medicine do we owe to the sincere, if usually unsuccessful, attempts of early medicine-men at alleviating and curing human ills? If enterprising and Initiated Souls had not reached out far beyond their purely human capabilities in those early days, and made contacts with a type of Consciousness Which was (and is) relatively Omniscient to ourselves, we should never have achieved even the little advances we have bought so dearly with our blood through the centuries.

Remembering the old Sacred Kings who were ritually slain for the welfare of the tribe, we think now: 'How stupid' or: 'How Wrong'. Do we consider our modern parallels with literally millions of dedicated victims sacrificially murdered during our two World Wars? How many of our recent scientific developments came out of their blood? The Christian Church commemorates and Deifies a single Jewish Sacred King slain on a Tree-altar in a few hours. What honour do we give the six million of His modern race-descendants who perished far more horribly for a much longer time? We are in no position to criticize even the fiercest Rites of antiquity when we can more than outmarch them with contemporary barbarity.

By establishing their Rite-Patterns, and extending their awareness by Magical methods into a much more advanced condition of Consciousness than their ordinary human levels, the early Initiates of the Inner Mysteries set the spiritual seeds which are even now only just beginning to show signs of flowering and fruiting among us, the scarce-worthy inheritors of a Tradition we would be utter fools to abandon. The very least we might do is to re-establish the modern equivalents of those Rites with acceptable practices based on the Original Patterns. This would be not only for our own sakes, but particularly for our descendents—if indeed we are to have any! Our Rite-Patterns at present will eventuate into the realizations of the future, and if we are to ensure worthwhile spiritual legacies of progressive and peaceful living towards Perfection, our time to set up those Rite-Patterns of this vital objective is *now*, while we still have the chance.

Why should Magic be especially valuable for such an overwhelmingly important purpose? Mainly because it affords unique opportunities for individualizing entities to apply maximum energies in their own way of their own Wills. This is the especial secret. What other Systems of behaviour as Beings on any life-level offer such incredible degrees of Inner freedom for each Soul, with unlimited scope of entity-expansion towards Infinite Ultimation? Magic is for those Souls who are strong enough and brave enough to direct their own destinies according to the Will within them. Otherwise, humans have to be content with whatever compulsory arrangements are imposed on them by the manipulators of mankind.

Freedom through the Portals of Perception

In our time, we have only to look at the two apparently opposed Systems of Communism and Commercialism between which the Soul of Man is being rapidly bound to the Pillars of

Compulsion and Coercion. Both Systems are dedicated to a single Cause, the imprisonment of individual Souls in artificial cages of consciousness constructed around them. As might be expected, the bulk of human beings on earth are by no means unwilling victims. They may be as blind as Sampson, but do they have his legendary strength to break their chains and pull down the Pillars? More importantly, do they realize they have such an ability, would they be willing to use it, and could they build a better Temple if they tried??? Who is wise enough among us to answer? In any case it would be fatal to release the whole human race from its accepted bondage all at once, for this would mean an auto-destructive explosion. There is only one reliable way to full Inner freedom of spiritual status, in single file through the Portals of Perception, each Soul by itself in proper procession. The old Mystery processions of Symbols showed the correct Order of advance.

Towards wider Awareness

The purpose of Magic in our days is thus the same as it always was, to allow individually evolving Soul-entities among mankind a Way ahead to even wider Awareness. There were other means years ago that man could adopt if he chose. The Arts, religion, philosophies, and suchlike approaches to Inner Dimensions of Life. The once-open doors from these directions are being rapidly closed to every sincere seeker of spiritual identity in other than merely Earth-life. If any activity is likely to lead enterprising Souls towards genuine Inner Identity, the Communist System will proscribe it, and the Commercial System will purchase its controlling interests, if possible. So what Way of Escape from Earth-bound spiritual slavery remains yet open, and how long will it be before this becomes too diffcult for the struggling Souls of Light-seekers to negotiate? Only those responsible for guarding the Gates of the Mysteries might hazard guesses on this point.

There is no purpose at all in approaching what might be termed the Magical Mysteries in a sort of crusading spirit and with even the best intentions of freeing fellow humans from their state of unenlightenment. Attempting this will result in Inner Portals being carefully shut in the enthusiast's face until he learns more sense. All must find Light for themselves of their own Will. Light shining from Inside, illuminates everything, but shone from Outside, only blinds and confuses. We must each learn that distinction for ourselves. The proper way to help our fellow mortals from within the Mysteries is by making as much personal progress as possible, and setting up Inner Patterns that may be followed advantageously by those who Will make use of these on their own accounts.

Before we are in a position to give, we must first have something to offer, and our first duties to others should be to improve our own abilities and facilities for helping them to help themselves. This is why the old Mystery rule was, and remains true today, that no candidate, however promising, should be invited or urged into personal association with any Lodge or Group. The initiative for requesting direct admission to any Circle or Temple, has to rest with the entrant, and the right of inclusion or exclusion remain with the Group itself. As a rule, some hints are generally made to enquirers concerning the likelihood or otherwise of their welcome, but the first of the traditional three knocks on the Portal must come independently from outside, the second knock is made by the opening of the Portal from inside, and the last knock comes from the Portals being closed again. Whether the adventurous Soul is then on the Inside, or remains Without, depends on what has transpired upon the Threshold.

The Magical Mysteries are emphatically NOT for those Souls who are unwilling to make any efforts on their own behalf at evolving towards a higher state of entity than a merely human existence. Nor are they intended as refuges for eccentrics and 'drop-outs' with nothing to offer except disorganized personal peculiarities. The genuine Initiate does not parade around in odd clothing attracting unwanted attention by outrageous behaviour and strange conversation. Beyond perhaps a very few closely trusted companions, none are likely to have any inkling of an Initiate's Inner interests or identity. In this world, an Initiate of Light (or Darkness for that matter) usually appears as quite an ordinary unspectacular person, engaged with very mundane affairs, earning a living like everyone else. Some Schools and Systems traditionally insisted that their Initiates were all trained in some trade or calling at which they obtained their living expenses, since they were utterly forbidden (and still are) to make money from any form of spiritual activity.

Let none doubt the practicability and value of the Magical Mysteries in our times and for those to come. By all means let us smile at medieval methods of concentrating the energies of Consciousness, itself the most remarkable Energy of all, by the rather crude contrivances described in 'Grimoires' and elsewhere. Let us also remember that better means were available at that time to the more advanced Souls who accompany every age as sponsors of the ages ahead. Most of all, let us try in our turn to do what they did, put Patterns of Power-Paths together in Ritual or other arrangements, so as to make further progress possible for those Souls Willing to come forward in the Light of their own spiritual perceptions.

Anyone inclined to suspect the feasibility of this proposition has only to consider the implications of present day political propaganda and commercial 'pressurization'. Literally millions of human beings live, work, and die according to the dictates of the relatively few nameless individuals responsible for running these Systems, ostensibly opposed to each other, but actually coming close to a mutually acceptable agreement as to methods of 'carving up' future civilizations to suit very private purposes. Between them, they are succeeding where the Churches failed, in casting a wide enough net over the world to capture almost every Soul alive. Eventually, only well-instructed Initiates may know the tricks of slipping through the meshes into a far nobler Way of Life, unless, of course, the sheer unwieldy weight of the masses breaks through the Systems somewhere, and scores a Pyrrhic victory for a while, before survivors are rounded up into other captivities of consciousness.

Authority fears spiritual independence

There is nothing new about all this. Small circles of highly concentrated consciousness have always produced decisive though temporary effects over very wide fields of human living. We can see this in practice wherever we look on any level.

Ultimately One Will is considered to be responsible for the whole of Existence, and extensions of this Primal Principle are naturally everywhere eternally. The One, or the few, projecting energies of Consciousness influencing the activities and entities of All or many. The vital Question to ask here is, Why? What for? What is the Will Within? In the case of political, commercial, and generally established religious Systems, the answers are obvious even to their most apathetic acceptors. For the sake of the powers, money, positions, and other material advantages obtained by the administrative entities of those establishments.

Fortunately for humanity at large, not even the most domineering directorship on earth has ever devised a System which retains every single benefit for their exclusive enjoyment while those whose efforts produce such benefits remain utterly deprived of them. Something or other has to be shared with other Souls, however grudgingly, or they would be unable to make their contributions towards the general funds of force which the ambitious administrators intend to control. The more enlightened among those select few, have come to realize that the more fringe benefits they arrange for the masses they manipulate, the better is bound to be their own status. Ostensibly, the carrot has the lead over the whip. Nevertheless, the common factor feared most by authoritarian administrations is the entire spiritual independence of Souls inhabiting their spheres of influence, especially if such Souls acknowledge an Inner Authority which may not entirely agree with purely Earthly authorities, and with which these enquiring Initiated Souls have actually made conscious contact, mainly through the Magical Mysteries of Light.

This fulfilment of individual freedom as Souls living normally and naturally in a state or condition of consciousness far beyond the jurisdiction or dictatorship of any Earth-based authorities, wherein every entity cosmates with the rest purely because of their Will towards each other, or a universal Love together, is an acknowledged aim of the Mysteries of Light. An absolutely uncompelled or coerced cohesion of consciousness among Circles of Souls bound by nothing but a force of Love undreamed of by most mortals, yet nevertheless implanted as an instinct in their fundamental depths. No matter how humans try to cover this up in themselves or suppress it in others, sooner or later its energy breaks through somehow with good or ill effects depending on circumstances. If unable to cosmate, it disintegrates, causing degrees of damage consistent with its particular form and force.

The Holy Mysteries in general, and those of Light in particular, provide facilites for releasing energies which are uncosmatable earthwardly, into Inner Dimensions where they will be put to their proper purposes. Instead of wasting these valuable forces on earthly frustrations, irritations, and other adverse reactions, they are fed through appropriate channels into Inner Spheres where they can be converted into whatever is needed for the construction of Cosmos on those levels of living. Another use for Magic in the twentieth, or any other century! A long time ago it was called 'laying up treasures in Heaven'.

The time and effort spent in working out and setting up basic Projection-Patterns of Consciousness by means of symbolic Rites, which contain them and relate them with Inner and Outer Existence is very far from wasted, nor is it no more than idle wishful thinking. To the contrary, it is mankind's highest and most practical method of applying Power to Purpose (or Word with Will), at the point where Humanity rises its nearest to Divinity, and therefore stands the best chance of spiritual success, which may even materialize subsequently in suitable earthly equivalents.

This was one reason why the ancients held many of their Rites on hill or mountain tops. Apart from a sense of 'away-from-the-world-god-likeness', the altitude conditions of decreased air-pressure and increased electrical potential considerably assist our 'other-than-physical' awareness. Divinity Itself may be everywhere, but we are not, and there are definite Time-Space-Event co-incidents which bring us more closely into contact with Inner Consciousness than others. Hilltop Rites by Circles of Initiates at propitious moments were reliable in old times, and indeed remain so, though in modern circumstances, even modest Temple conditions if suitably situated in freedom from disturbance by inharmonious influences such as noise, bad feelings, etc., may be made to serve the Mysteries at any altitude. Still, it would be most unwise to abandon all opportunities for direct contacts amid natural conditions, and the Elemental Cross of Sun, Air, Water, Earth formation, is likely to be our most convenient power-supply in immediate Inner workings for a very long while yet.

The Inner equivalent of Nuclear Energy

Magic might well be defined as a metaphysical means of putting Power into Practice through a Plan for a Purpose. The fact that all this takes place in extra-physical Dimensions prior to projection into material manifestation if intended so, does not make the process either more or less real than it is. Suppose someone asked the straightforward question: 'What is this "Magic" aiming at that may be understood from an earthly viewpoint, and what possible benefits can it bring us?'—how might this very fair query be answered? Simply by telling the truth, that a major objective in Magic is the Inner equivalent of Atomic Energy as it is now called in physical terms, and that what may be accomplished with this Energy among us in mundane ways may not only be equalled, but immeasurably surpassed throughout spiritual Spheres by analogous methods of application.

Initiation is a multi-lifed process of acquiring sufficient spiritual status and Inner intelligence to evolve Souls capable of dealing with that incredible Energy as directed by the Controlling Consciousness we loosely recognize as Divinity. We shall not achieve this entirely by ourselves, any more than nuclear energy in its present form was discovered and developed by human brains alone. The co-operation of conscious entities existing in other states of Cosmic continuity is needed to suggest our lines of approach and direct our researches towards the right quarters. Whether we call those entities 'Archangels', 'Angels', or any other name matters very little to them. Our symbolic concepts of them serve as a means of mediating the intellectual and other influences they direct to us through channels of communication at present termed 'Magical'. Until these are superseded we must continue using them, and improving their design.

As to what might be accomplished with nuclear energy on spiritual levels of life, we may gain some faint ideas of such possibilities from what we know of nuclear energy on earth in our days. Once properly controlled and adapted to human needs via the proper paths and suitable apparatus, this energy is likely to do for us on earth WHAT WE WILL, purely in mundane ways. It will not bring us to life, make us happy, or improve us in ourselves in any way at all. We may expect no more from its earthly expression than physical facilities.

How we react with these remains our own affair, and we are little different in ourselves for the use we have made of them. If equivalent Nuclear Energy might be released from a spiritual Source via the spiritual channels affecting human Souls, a very different story might be told. Assuming that we were able to react with this Energy and still function as Souls, we could literally BE WHAT WE WILL. Our mode of Existence might be so entirely changed, that we would only remember our old human habits with amusement or relief at our transcendence over their troubles. No one need suffer anything unless he wanted to, none need die in the sense of discontinuation of Life as conscious entities, unless they chose.

Why should we bother with remaining as earth-based entities, conscious over a very small spectrum, bound to flesh-formed bodies that age, deteriorate, and then die, putting us to all the inconvenience and interruption of identity through the painful process of re-birth? Moreover, those bodies have to be fed, rested, cleaned, and serviced in so many ways. Our homes, and indeed most of our civilizations are designed around them. All that amount of effort might not only be saved, but put to much better advantage in a Sphere of Life powered by Spiritual Nuclear Energy.

Just suppose we were able to eliminate all our present bodily necessities, and simply LIVE in one another's awareness with an intensity of conscious experience far beyond our modern reach or even realization. No need to eat, sleep, breathe, excrete, re-produce, or do anything other than BE WHAT WE WILL. Our code of living would be: 'We Will it—We ARE it.' We would, in fact, live in a condition once termed 'Heaven'. Not only possible, but absolutely practical with the aid of Spiritual Nuclear Energy. It would revolutionize our Existence to a barely imaginable degree, and indeed the Will of Earth and Heaven would be One.

What prevents us from becoming such supersouls? Little else than our entire incapacity and unsuitability in general for dealing more than fractionally with the forces needed to energize a Sphere of Existence wherein entities we might consider super-souls share their conscious continuum in Cosmos together. On the Whole, as average humans, we just are not yet ready or fit for living such an intensified Light-Life, any more than primitive men were prepared for atom bombs. The same Spiritual Nuclear Energy that might make conditions of Heaven for us is also capable of erupting into the most horrible Hells. It all depends how it is handled, as with any Energy whatever.

Individual human Souls however, do evolve to a point where they become increasingly able to sustain adaptations of S.N.U. and eventually utilize it for themselves or others. Unhappily, there are no moral or ethical qualifications needed to acquire this ability, and ill-disposed entities may just as well learn how to gain powers for their own purposes as beneficent beings. As with the earthly Bomb, the same problem of how to blast others without being blasted back exists, and so the Great Deterrent is rather more than a purely mundane consideration. It applies in other Dimensions as well, fortunately perhaps for our fate as a collective species.

Forbidden fruit

How did Nuclear Energy arrive on earth during our generation? Actually it always was here. We have been reaching out for it into Inner Existence ever since we got here ourselves, and modern mathematicians have only continued what the ancient magicians commenced with their rituals. Those were the first Symbols of the complicated formulae which have recently placed the fingertips of mankind in contact with the forbidden fruit we have been looking for so long. The Rites have done less than half their work. If they do not now lead us much more deeply towards Divinity than our present position, we had best have left them alone in the first place. Individually or altogether, we dare not discontinue our Magical Path of Progression. We have inherited part of our legacy from Original Light, but without the remainder, we shall never live to spend what we have just received.

Atomic Nuclear Energy was suspected in theory for a very long time before the first trial explosion ever rocked the history of our planet. This only occurred because the minds and Wills of highly specialized Souls probed beyond the limits of normal human consciousness along a Line of Light which led to their objective. They did this by means of Symbology related throughout itself by a series of extensions into states of Existence utterly outside their experience and certainly beyond their personal beliefs as materialists. The concepts with which they had to deal were much more incredible than most concepts used in Magical practice. Those scientists did not particularly believe in their concepts because they wanted to, but because they *had* to in order to make any progress into conditions of Consciousness previously unreached from that direction by human explorers. In addition to those problems, the highly important one arose of how to construct on physical levels the necessary apparatus for utilizing this Energy with relative safety on earth. Nothing of the sort was in physical form at the time, and it all had to be worked out in theory on Inner levels before anyone dared to connect up the Energy in practice with its physical control-channels. Any major mistakes might have been fatal, not only to those directly concerned, but over a very wide field of human life.

Control before power

The interesting part of this is that it happened in the opposite order to Man's general utilization of natural forces. As a rule, humanity makes firstly very faulty and ineffectual contacts with power-sources, such as Water, Oil, Gas, Electricity, etc., then steadily improves the methods and mechanisms for relating this power with human purpose. In the case of Nuclear Energy, the control-systems had to be adequate in the first place prior to direct contact with a power which was still theoretical. Otherwise the experiment could literally have blown up in everyone's faces. Perhaps this was one of the first times in human history we have attempted to relate ourselves with Energy in the proper order, capability of control first, and power last. Eliminate or reduce error to minimum in terms of physical productions, then link up with the operative energy so that everything works as it should. If only we had been as careful and painstaking in spiritual ways as we were in scientific ones, we should be far more evolved Souls than we are on the average at present.

The story and difficulties of the mathematicians in search of their Nuclear Energy Grail to put Heaven and Hell into the hands of Man on Earth, is paralleled by that of Magicians seeking the same Eternal Inner Energy with which the same Mankind may alter not so much his environmental equipment, but his actual essential entity itself, which will entirely change not only conditions of consciousness but the whole of human living-methods as well. This again may result in Heaven or Hell depending on how it eventuates. Whether in or out of incarnation, we must eventually decide the issue for ourselves.

Like the mathematicians, the magicians are satisfied that the Nil-Nuclear Source of Energy can be reached on spiritual levels just as it may be approached on material ones, and the process is a similar one either way. Instead of working with mathematical concepts however, the Magical Initiates use Symbolic procedures and ritualized formulae involving patterned processes of consciousness among specific individual Soul-arrangements, relating mutually for this precise purpose. Where the laboratory scientist co-relates standard pieces of apparatus, and computerized information to achieve results, the Initiate of the Mysteries sets up an equivalent pattern among living entities, incarnate or otherwise, each co-ordinating with the rest in a Cosmic circuit energized by the Will of every one. This, at least, is the present position of the Plan.

It may very well be asked why, if this is the case, we have not noticed any vast improvement in the nature of mankind over the last few thousand years, during which the Mysteries were supposed to be in operation. The answers are all to be found in our modern parallel of Atomic Power production. Just what percentage of the whole human race were and are actually engaged on this project directly? Less than a tiny fraction of one per cent. The same would be true in the case of genuine Initiates of the Holy Mysteries who might be compared with our nuclear physicists. A very minute minority concerned with power-problems affecting the fate of massed millions. The few brain-cells making a decision which will save or lose the life of an entire body belonging to the being they share in common. A big job, and an utterly terrible responsibility. We all depend on the issue. The atomic scientists' main concern was and is to find just what is best fitted to contain and convey the Power they have reached, so that it will serve the human race. They know quite well what will happen otherwise.

The spiritual 'scientists' are presented with exactly the same problem on another scale. Their concern is to discover which species of human, or arrangement of Souls, may best bear and distribute the incredible Energy obtainable from the spiritual equivalent of the Nil-Nucleus Itself. Do such people exist on earth? Are there sufficient of them? Will they arrange themselves? Can they carry the Energy safely? Even if this is possible, how far may others be damaged? An endless list of such questions constantly confront the Directors behind what might be called the 'Cosmic Control Commission'. Even their Intelligence has its limits, and must be supplemented by cautious advances in the experimental field.

We have seen some of the results from such experiments for ourselves. Now and again special Souls with strong Nil-Nuclear contacts are put into circulation amongst humanity much as radiant-energy particles are introduced among a mass of near-inert molecules in order to produce reactive effects.

Possibly one of the most spectacular instances of this is shown in the case of Christianity. After over two thousand years of discharge it can scarcely be considered as an unqualified success, nor yet a total failure. None can deny the force of its impact, though many may regret its disruptive and destructive influence among Souls quite unprepared to use it for peaceful and constructive purposes.

Had he lived today, Paul would have certainly have been branded as a 'defector' in no uncertain terms. Instead of the original Circle (or Cyclotron), in which the Power was contained, developing the Energy quietly and progressively for perhaps a century and more until reliable circuitry became obtainable through living links, Paul's insane enthusiasm blew everything apart at just the wrong moment, pouring the Power in all directions just as an escape of Nuclear Energy into the atmosphere does today. The natural result was that spiritual 'mutations' took place which we have not succeeded in 'breeding true' even today.

Christianity sparked off all kinds of dramatic and spectacular effects among Souls for better or worse with every variety of chain-reaction. We are still living in the aftermath, and attempting to re-arrange the necessary integers for the next experiment in such a way that a similar or worse mishap will not follow. Can we succeed? Events alone will ultimately show.

A circuit of human Souls

There are many who sincerely believe that another great Avatar, Messiah, or Christ is imminent on earth. This would actually be the greatest risk we might encounter as an entire life-species. Should the human race be exposed to the radiance from such an Energy-Particle-Personification while we are in our present unstable condition, the results might be disastrous beyond belief. We need stabilization and cosmation, rather than Impact from an Entitised-Energy more than likely to push us past critical mass into the most Soul-destroying explosion ever known on earth. Direct contact with Divine Energy suddenly striking an unprepared humanity would just about write 'Paid in Full' across our long-standing account with Destiny.

What is needed on Earth this time is a thoroughly reliable apparatus and circuit arrangement of human Souls capable of containing and distributing the Energy from Its Source so that it should benefit all in major ways, and harm none except in very minor ones through their own faults. At the moment this is asking an impossibility, but there is no reason why it should not be perfectly practical in the forseeable future—if enough 'John the Baptists' with high qualities are forthcoming to 'prepare the Paths and make straight the Ways', or in our modern terms design the circuit and lay out the components accordingly. Even though we have no Herods, these fore-runners are still likely to behead each other if we may judge from some of the self-advertised samples running around in their small circles like headless hens. The genuine article will have to do better than that!

Associative Cosmation

Instead of waiting around hopelessly and helplessly for some Soul-shattering Messiah to come sailing out of the clouds formed from our wishful thinking, the immediate responsibility of every awakening entity on earth is to commence associable cosmation first and foremost in themselves, and then with other suitable Souls. The worst mistake would be to rush into unstable Group formations purely for the sake of company. Unless a Group is able to balance itself on Cosmic principles, it will injure all its members in the long run. Everyone is bound to fit in *somewhere*, and it is a question of finding a proper place with the proper people. Should this not be available on earthly levels, individuals would be well advised to balance themselves as such, and seek complementation Inwardly. Remaining in unhappy harness with inharmonious Circle companions is more than stupid—it is positively dangerous to all.

If a really reliable set of Circles can be established among humans on earth, and if again these can be connected Inwardly with each other so as to form a circuit capable of dealing with, and dispensing Energy of a truly Divine nature from Its Source, then indeed a suitable 'Avatar' may close the contact between that Source and Circuit through the mediation of their own Being. On this next occasion, it is most unlikely to be done in any very public or spectacular way, in the full glare of T.V. lights and a howling mob of press photographers all set to record the next miracle.

In fact the personification of the Avatar among humans might not be known by the general public during their Earth life-time at all, but only to those entirely trustworthy few who are able to absorb the 'contact-shock', and communicate its effects through prepared and reliable channels. It may be wondered in that case, how the rest of humanity would ever know such a Soul had reached Earth. They would discover this eventually, because strange things would happen to human nature itself all over the world rather than in any particular locality. Without quite knowing why, humans would feel well-disposed to one another, avarice and greed lose its hold on them, warfare become unthinkable, and people would discover they wanted each other far more than things they made to buy and sell. Persons would become much more valuable than property, and their health and happiness of greater importance than what they possessed or performed. Money, social position, and all the things we consider so vital at present, would cease to mean very much as distinctions. Our sense of values would most certainly begin to alter very drastically, its focus shifting noticeably away from material towards spiritual standards. Altogether, an almost dramatic easing of tension would be experienced practically all over the world, and a relaxed, happy, near-holiday atmosphere 'come over' millions of people.

No one, except those 'in the know' would be able to account for such beneficial and remarkable changes in the basic structure of human nature as a whole over the course of only a few generations. Perhaps they would not learn the real reason for a long while, until it reached them quite naturally in their own lives.

The Avatar would not have hit them historically, but crept very silently, like the proverbial 'thief in the night', out of their very hearts, as the most intimate friend of everyone.

All this, of course, assumes the best that might happen to us, but is scarcely an assured future. Whoever holds the Keys of Heaven, Man firmly holds those of Earth, and shows no signs of letting go. An alternate outcome to the alteration of human nature by Avatar or otherwise, might indeed be a sort of spiritual 'Noah's Ark' scheme amounting to the withdrawal from incarnation of Souls more valuable in other states of existence, and allowing the remainder living on Earth to blow themselves into whatever Hell they wanted, providing some means was found to confine this disaster to those who intentionally bring it upon themselves.

That is something only the 'Lords of Cosmos' could work out, and doubtless it is among the Plans on the Divine Drawing Board. In the meantime, Initiates of the Holy Mysteries of Light must simply proceed with their routine duties in whatever Way they are employed, keeping various channels of Consciousness clear, forming up Cosmoi around their Nil-Nucleus contacts, and attending to whatever administrative or other work they have been allotted as their individual share of the Plan for Perfection. There is nothing else to be done. Not a single Soul must be compelled or coerced in the slightest way towards the Mysteries. They must come to the Portals entirely of their own Inner volition or not at all, and however many or few obtain admission, each has to pass those Portals by themselves, one at a time. It is the only Way In.

The Scope of Magic Today

Magic is very much of our time. What else is likely to liberate us one by one from the confusions that confine our consciousness amid all the muddles, fears, frustrations, and futilities that attract our attention almost exclusively earthwards? What is the use of mankind exporting its commercial travellers to the Moon, Mars, Venus, or any other point of Outer Space, when we are incapable of making intelligent contact with our own Inner Space actualities? Mathematics and mechanics may serve on our Outer Journey, but what, except Magic, will lead us Inwardly to the most Ancient Civilizations of Cosmos existent therein? What will teach us how to interpret the signals we receive from thence correctly and sensibly in terms of our ordinary familiar Outer-world?

Oh yes, there is plenty of scope for Magic today, with all the force of its past Traditions and the highest hopes of its future promise. It may be a specialized field of action, but there are many different kinds of specialists needed. If every available Initiate and Circles of Companions throughout the entire Mysteries of Light got on steadily and quietly with their particular specializations in their own spheres of immediate action, we should all be infinitely better off, and on much sounder spiritual lines than most people are wavering along at present.

Should anyone sincerely feel the rightful place of their Soul to be with the Children of the Holy Mysteries of Light, and is uncertain of proper procedure towards their Point of Entry, there are several matters to bear in mind. The first is this. Whoever sits supinely awaiting some wonderful Angel or Great Master to lead him Lightward, will wait until he learns more sense. He will not receive any spectacular revelations, or Calls from On High, or any indications of a supernatural summons. The initial impetus must come from Within him, of his own True Will. Other substitutes should be suspect. During his whole development as an Initiated Soul, he will have to rely more and more for his guidance on the Inner Voice that speaks to him in Spirit, rather than anything he reads or is told by other Souls. Although this Voice utters Truth, he may not always hear it properly, or have understood what it meant. Therefore, when mistakes are made, let him blame his faulty judgement, or badly formed opinions of what he received Rightly from the Light Within. Even the worst mistake is always less serious than a deliberate refusal to learn from it.

Let none expect to encounter amazing 'Temples of White Magic' full of mysterious robed Brethren and Priestesses doing all sorts of conjuring tricks with Consciousness specially for the edification of open mouthed Neophytes. No Temple on Earth can possibly be greater than the Temple of Truth which exists in each living Soul. At their very best, Earth-established Temples can only be lesser simulacra of their Inner realities. Whosoever cannot find his Way through the Portals of the Temple in himself will never enter Truth otherwise. All that actually happens when Initiates of Light consort physically in Earth-Temples, is that they open up their own individual Temples to each other, so that together they work in an expanded Inner Temple large enough for them all. Since trained associates use the same Base-Pattern, it will admit everyone operating its particular Symbology.

It is a relatively simple matter to become increasingly selective in more specialized Circles, by setting Symbol-locks on chosen Portals. Thus, the entire entry-system can be closely guarded from Within. Hidden Keys are not *revealed*, they have to be *found* by Souls with enough initiative to seek them. Clues may be offered in profusion, and a traditional place to conceal some vital piece of information is often the last one suspected—on the seeker's own back, so that a *double* reflection is necessary for its discovery. This allegory is well worth investigating.

There is only one way to become an authentic Initiate of the Holy Mysteries of Light. Of one's own Will in one's own Cosmos. The Soul of every Initiate must become as a Sun set in its own System, empowered by the Nil-Nucleus of Eternal Energy at the Secret Spiritual Centre. Naturally the Cosmos of each individual Soul links with those of others to form the Galaxies of Inner Space. That is the Law of Light which must be accepted by all who are willing to live in it.

How do we 'live into' this Spiritual state? Analogously to the same way we 'lived into' the Material state we now occupy. By the Sperm and Egg method, converted into terms of Conscious Energies. As we should all realize, even if we do not remember the process with our ordinary minds, we 'came to light' in this world as a single individual sperm out of millions, gaining contact with a single egg, the gestation and hatching of which provided us with physical bodies to live on Earth with, and reproduce other living entities at Will. The second, and Spiritual Birth our Souls must undergo in order to achieve fulfilment in an entity in Spiritual Spheres, calls for a similar individual effort.

None need fear exclusion from their 'Inner Egg' by others pushing them aside from it, because there are sufficient 'Eggs' for all in the Womb of the Great Mother, BUT, all must find their own, and enter it themselves. That is the inexorable Law of Life on all levels, and we cannot come to any sort of Light, Inner or

Outer, without it. Certainly we may rely on external help from sympathetic Souls in any Sphere of Existence, but they can do no more than offer us means of helping ourselves. The Ultimate Law of Life is I.AM.

This 'coming to Inner Light' is no rat-race, where success is only gained from the failures of others. There is no competition for selection, or any opportunity for buying the best places. Nor is there any point in trying to interfere with, or 'make capital' out of other Souls, since this only prevents personal progress. As Souls, we belong to the same spiritual categories, and deliberate injuries inflicted on others do indeed result in injurious repercussions. The more we evolve, the less easy is it to hurt others without getting hurt ourselves.

The Bomb shows the principle of this well enough, and even the most evilly disposed entities hesitate to destroy those or that which ensures their existence, however much they hope to pervert everyone and everything for their own purposes. In human circumstances, any child whose birth took the life of its mother would die itself of starvation and neglect unless others cared for it. In the Mysteries, the Child of Light seeks 'innocence and harmlessness' so that, harming none, the secondary 'Birth of Spirit' is experienced in the most natural way as a direct outcome of the closest intimate contact possible between what might be called the 'Soul-sperm', and its 'Spiritual Egg' through which an Emancipated Entity becomes itself into Inner Life. It will continue its conscious evolution, as in Earth-life, according to its inherent individual Pattern. In material language this would amount to the genes and chromosomes, but in other parlance we might call it the relationships between the cortices of consciousness, or primal points of typified energy. The Holy Mysteries should and do provide their Initiates with facilities for setting these vital arrangements in themselves AS THEY WILL, within the limits of their extent in LIGHT.

Suppose we were able to pre-set the patterns of our physical genes as we liked. Within reason, we might literally be any sort of person we wanted. Pattern the genes properly, and, accidents apart, the entity is assured of its abilities and potentialities. This, actually, is a very major aim in the Magical Mysteries.

Once Initiates learn how to lay out power-patterns of consciousness in Cosmic relationships between cortices of energy on deep enough life-levels, they can 'sow at seed-depth', and, when this pattern is projected into the Matrix of Manifestation, they may indeed BE WHAT THEY WILL. This alone is sufficient reason for all the ritualization necessary to make those patterns 'come true' in the best possible way. That is why the standard Mystery Patterns such as the Tree, Solar Cross, Rose Cross, etc., have been evolved. We become them—if we WILL. Once we realize this, all the Rites and practices connected with them take on an absolutely new and deeper meaning, an infinitely greater value, and we can appreciate the point of whatever sacrifices we make to continue their Tradition, the greatest possible sacrifice being that of self.

The sacrifice of self

Self-sacrifice is a shockingly misunderstood terms as a rule. Many still think of it in the masochistic sense of tolerating whatever torture may be inflicted by God or Man for the benefit of everybody else except the idiotic entity permitting such a vicious misuse of itself. Others see it as a kind of rather pointless self-denial of even the mildest experience that might conceivably be enjoyed for its own sake.

Actions resulting from masochistic motives with incentives of spiritual greed, such as the usual : 'The-more-I-suffer-on-Earth-the-better-I'll-be-in-Heaven' theme, have nothing to do with real Self-sacrifice at all. We may sacrifice our wealth, health, and even our physical lives, but those deprivations are not sacrifices of Self, but only of its attributes. We can beggar ourselves to our last cent, and ruin our health into the bargain, yet not have sacrificed or given up one iota of the Selves we were during more comfortable times. The expression 'Self-sacrifice' means just what it says—to offer the Self without reservations to the True Will of the Entity behind each individual Which is their own 'Divine Spark' or Immortal Identity. Nothing less, because there can be Nothing more. That is ALL there is to it. Humanity offering itself to Divinity on the altar of its activities. Unity of Will between Heaven and Earth. That is real Self sacrifice as indicated and understood in the Holy Mysteries of Light.

Far from being self-suppression, it is Self-assertion on the highest possible level. In old style terms, we might say that the sacrifice was of the Lower Self to the Higher Self. A shifting of the Will-focus from an Earth-presented personality to the direction of the Immortal Identity behind the same being living through a Light-line extending from one to the other. This is Self-sacrifice. It emphatically does NOT mean foolish and irresponsible behaviour involving unwilling sacrifices from everybody else. Before any Soul considers making sacrificial adjustments to itself, let it realize its position and capabilities to the full. The noblest form of sacrifice always comes from strength—never from weakness. We have no right to offer what is not ours, and what is truly ours except our Souls? That, and that alone, is the Self to be sacrificed in the Rites of the Holy Mysteries.

At the dawn of our history on earth, we found ourselves in a world full of fears and hostilities against which we had to fight by Magic and faith while our slowly developing consciousness learned to cope with external adversities. Where do we stand today after all our evolution? Having overcome most of our dangers and threats from the Outworld, we have done no more than transfer them into other states and conditions which are even more dangerous still because they menace the very foundations of our beings as human Souls. We have turned the old terrifying earthquakes into new horrifying explosions. We have brought all the prehistoric monsters back to life as war-machines. We have liberated slaves from physical bondage and shackled them much more effectively otherwise. Instead of an occasional 'Divine King' voluntary victim, we massacre millions of unwilling ones. We feed bodies and starve souls, heal flesh and hurt spirits. There is not a single old fear or cruelty that cannot be found today in much more modern and improved forms. The more technical progress we make, the more we throw ourselves back into mental and social jungles with every primitive survival-pattern projected into Inner terms.

In the dawning World of our Inner Dimensions, Man stands naked and bewildered again at the beginning of our Inner Ages, frightened and confused at the conditions we have created ourselves, and which nothing but our own efforts will alter. It looks more of a Leaden, than a Golden Dawn ahead of us in the New Age of Mankind, during which we are supposed to evolve into semi-spiritualized beings, capable of conscious living in more than one state of Dimensions.

Man still a Spiritual Savage

Just as we had to use a type of Magic in early Earth-times which has brought us to the present in a variety of ways, so must we still use Magic at this beginning of our Heavenly history, in the hope that it will take us to the ending of the tale in Eternal Light. We may think we have reached a peak point as human people, and along very limited lines we have indeed accomplished a good deal. In comparison to older and other Soul-civilizations, accustomed to existence in finer states of consciousness than ours, Man is still a spiritual savage, untrained, unreliable, and 'un-housebroken' to living in better conditions. Individually, human Souls do indeed evolve until they are fit for acceptance elsewhere than in earthly incarnation. We can only hope this takes place at a sufficient 'leak-rate', to prevent the remainder reaching 'critical mass' and exploding into the nastiest mess Mankind has made of itself yet. At least we may rely on the Inner Guards of the Mystery Portals keeping those open as wide, and for as long as they dare, short of disaster.

Let us not deny our ancient Magical Tradition, but continue its Cosmating Circle with recognition of what we have received through it in the past, and confidence in what we believe we will accomplish by it in the future. Its Principles are perpetual, we have only to line its practices with living as we go along it Lightwardly. The Rites already exist, waiting to be re-written in as many ways as may be required for different types of Ritualists. And again, and again, and again, just as often as we advance enough to understand spiritual speech in a different Divine dialect.

For Mankind to outgrow Magic is unthinkable. It is a permanent part of our basic being. Take Magic out of our lives, and what are we? Little enough to satisfy Souls aspiring much higher than mere socialized security at the cost of their individual fulfilment as spiritual entities by the Right of their own Light. State-control is a poor substitute for Soul at even the best market price, and in a world where our natural freedoms are disappearing every day, we would be wise to remember the spiritual Mystery Systems that kept Inner faith with Light during even the darkest ages behind us.

Circles turn in their own tracks. Who can be certain that the

Mysteries may not have to 'go underground' again in this world, and perhaps in other states as well, so as to maintain contact with the Light of Inner Freedom, for the sake of every Soul Willing to reach It and capable of containing it Rightly? To those who control the States and Organizations throughout this world, what does any individual Soul amount to? An employable unit to be used and disposed of by death. A component to be processed according to requirement, serviced as necessary, and eliminated in an economical manner. Centuries ago, these living beings were called plainly slaves, and they realized quite well who they belonged to. Their one hope was to 'buy themselves out'. Nowadays, their descendants must not be called slaves any longer, nor must they realize their owners, or perhaps that they are owned by anyone at all. They are supposed to be credit-worthy members of the most classified 'classless society' this Earth has ever raised on its surface, and their only hope of ful-filling themselves apart from 'opting out' into ignominious exile, is to sequester sufficient funds to purchase independence from compulsory circles of consciousness. Failing either course, what have they? Who cares? Certainly not their State or other owners, who know well enough that only discontented and determined animals are likely to give any serious trouble.

Bread and circuses served to quieten humanity in the past, and their modern equivalents are doing even better. Self-deter-mining Souls setting up their Spiritual standards in order to assert their Inner Identity and Cosmate with each other AS THEY WILL, are utterly unwanted by Earth-established authorities, and are therefore carefully discouraged. Those intrepid individualists who pass beyond a certain danger point may be bought off, bumped off, or somehow circumvented if they are likely to inter-fere with the intentions of the 'mass-manipulators'. However, providing a Soul who has awakened despite all Darkness around it, is circumspect and self-sufficient with its Inner workings, it will probably meet with no very serious opposition on its Way out of the Outer ways, so long as it goes quietly with a minimum of disturbance in its Earthly vicinity.

Secrecy and caution is an extremely practical procedure for those Souls arousing themselves from apathy and indifference towards attainment of Autonomy by the awakening of True Will in themselves. The more private they are with this vital process, the better for their chances of success. *Verb. sap.*

In the Holy Mysteries of Light, all individual Souls are of paramount importance as such, each being regarded as a free and responsible agent of Divine Energy, bound to their chosen Patterns of Perfection by nothing but their True Wills together. Not only is individualization encouraged, but until a Soul becomes sufficiently individualized to assert its Inner Identity in an independent Light, (or be 'born again') it cannot properly enter the 'Kingdom of Heaven', or 'come into its own' as THAT IT WILLED. This is the real meaning of Magic.

The practice of Magic in the twentieth century and probably more so in the twenty first, is especially for those human Souls who are 'coming of age' sufficiently to seek their own Spiritual heritage of independence in the Kingdom of Light which no 'Darkness covering the face of the Earth' can ever extinguish. Souls Willing to work and fight if necessary for true Inner Freedom in Spheres of Spirit where they may BE WHAT THEY WILL, because they WILL WHAT IS BEST TO BE. For the sacrifice of a self which was no more than a slave of physical circumstances, caught up in a net of confusions and uncertainties, Souls emerge into a state of Spiritual Selfhood in which they direct their own destiny by the Light of Divinity declaring Itself through them with the Creative Word of Will. Is this not more than a fair exchange of Identity?

Let Nothing less be the clear aim of modern Magi, even if its achievement might be millenniums away. The Patterns set by our predecessors in their Rites of rhyme and mime, are emerging as act and fact in our time. Now it is our responsibility to continue the Magical Circles of Consciousness they commenced, and lay out the Inner Design for the future we hope to inherit ourselves by rebirth in bodily or better conditions of living.

We have come a long way since our ancestors struck stones to evoke Light-spirits. Now we have a short breathing space in which to discover how to touch Souls so as to evoke the Spark Within them which will kindle the Flame of Truth from whence the Force that must Form our entire Future will come forth in Freedom. The most marvellous Magical Operation of all! We are at the final fork of the brief two Ways ahead that lead to the

Edge of Nothing, and we must choose between them. The outcome depends upon our Inner perception and Wisdom. Either we move blindly, make our strike, and missing the mark altogether plunge into Darkness, or proceed calmly and clearly into Perfect Light. Which Path will be ours? Who will initiate the first fatal step? Who comes to PEACE PROFOUND?

INDEX

Apart from being an alphabetical reference, this Index has been compiled as a subject indicator giving a comprehensive coverage of the whole work. It will therefore be found especially useful for selecting study-items from the text.